THE SWELL

C E de GZELL

For Alexander, Lachlan, and Isabella

The Swell is a gritty contemporary women's novel set in a fictional hospital, The Bennelong, and includes graphic descriptions of medical procedures and traumatic events. It also includes sexual activity and suicide. Readers who may be sensitive to these elements should consider this before beginning to read.

Medical Hierarchy

Intern

Resident Medical Officer (RMO, or Resident)

Senior Resident Medical Officer (SRMO)

Registrar (includes both unaccredited, junior, and advanced trainees)

Fellow

Consultant

Prologue

2014

Jackhammers. Lulu struggled out of the foggy depths of a deep sleep after a troubled night. God knows why she chose that ringtone. She rolled an arm loose of the doona, stabbing blindly until the incessant noise stopped. She'd probably only hit the snooze button, so unless she got her shit together, the jackhammers would start again in five minutes.

She rolled onto her back. Her closed eyes were just visible and a mess of knotty dark hair framed her head on the pillow. Lulu heard Grace moving about as she became aware of her surroundings and the last vestiges of sleep slipped away. Once she'd gone, Lulu threw the doona back and blinked at the dirty white ceiling. Fuck, she was tired. Every part of her body felt heavy and dull. Her brain was like porridge. The stodgy, clumpy kind they served in the caff. Not like her mum's.

Standing up made her head spin and she paused briefly before grabbing her toiletry bag and heading into the hall, head down, hoping not to run into anyone. She made it to the bathrooms at the end of the corridor and slowly pushed the door open, eyes grazing across the stalls, and let out a sigh of relief. She was alone.

She barricaded herself in a stall, wiped the seat clean, and sat down. Things had happened in here. But a reprieve for now, at least. At the sink, she looked at her reflection in the mirror. Deep purple-grey smudges under her hazel eyes, waxy pale skin, and a harrowed, vacant expression. Oh, and a huge zit on her forehead! Awesome, another reason for ridicule.

An audible sigh of defeat escaped her lips as she went to work. First, her hair. Detangling spray and comb. Five minutes to work through the knots, anxiety simmering all the while. Still pouffy. Lulu turned on the tap and dunked her head in the sink. Once wet, she slicked it into a bun atop her head, a trail of water snaking down her back as she secured it with pins and the school green scrunchy. She grabbed some paper towel and dabbed her face dry.

Should I squeeze it, she wondered. She brushed her teeth, tossing up the varying barbs likely to be thrown her way if she squeezed it, or left the pussy cream pie where it was. Would a band aid help? She could say she'd scratched herself, or maybe blame the dorm cat? Fuck it. Just squeeze the fucker!

A satisfying squirt. She cleaned the mirror and pressed some paper to the bloody crater. Shoulders slumped, she opened the bathroom door again, slowly, tentatively, pulse rising. Head out, innards clenched. Corridor clear. Release. Shuffle to the relative safety of her room, head down. Another reprieve.

She looked at her phone. Shit. Five minutes until the end of breakfast. Not that she'd eat that slop. But she wanted to grab a piece of fruit. She needed to eat at least three things a day. She'd learnt that the hard way.

No time to reminisce. Uniform on. Jumper. Both loose. She no longer had a school bag. One day she'd found it chopped into little pieces and scattered around the room. Her stuff had been missing too, of course. Not the first time. One book wet in the sink, one she dug out from beneath the banana peels and slime of the bin, her fingers slick with gore. Another in the cleaner's closet under the stairs.

That's when she'd started plotting, inventorying its contents. Bleach, ladder, cleaning spray, broom, mop, wipes, even duct tape. Her pulse had quickened as she'd snapped a quick pic on her phone. Later, when Grace was asleep, she zoomed in on the picture, looking at each item. Thinking. There was even a length of rope. The cupboard wasn't even locked.

Now that it was tonight, she was weirdly excited. And scared shitless. It was a double-edged sword: fear/excited, fear, excited, fear… Would she be brave enough to go through with it? She thought so. Lulu bundled her things into a Coles bag. Hand on the doorknob, deep breath, and turn.

Head down, at pace down the corridor. She thumped into the wall as someone shoulder-charged her. No point looking up to see who it was. It didn't matter. Keep moving. Downstairs, voices, noise, Lulu became engulfed in the melee. The house mistress was there. She slowed down slightly and caught her eye, smiling briefly, before continuing. There was a furrowing of the mistress's brow, a wringing of her hands. She knew. Lulu slipped out the door and raced down to the cafeteria before the mistress could stop her. As she trotted quickly down the stairs, she missed the outstretched foot going in the opposite direction and careened down the last few steps. She landed with a thump and a scrape. Raucous laughter behind her.

Pretty girls, blonde ponytails swinging, dark green ribbons tied neatly. Socks pulled up, shoes shined. Laughing eyes, attractive smiles, neat teeth. That's what everyone else saw. Lulu saw only tormentors. Evil petty bitches. Her Coles bag had ripped in the fall, and her stuff had spewed on the ground. Her dress was dirty, her chin and palms bleeding. A tear leaked from her eye. She sniffed and wiped her nose on her sleeve to a chorus of more laughter and snide remarks. A passing sixth former stopped to help her gather her things.

'Are you OK?' she asked.

Lulu nodded, head down, not making eye contact. Not trusting herself to speak.

By the time she made it to the caff, it was predictably closed. But she went around the back and knocked on the staff entrance. The cook opened the door and let Lulu in, taking in her dishevelled appearance. She pointed to a stool, and Lulu was relieved she asked nothing of her. Just found some antiseptic and band-aids, and even some cotton balls at the back of a cupboard. When Lulu had finished cleaning herself up and tossed the balls in the bin, she asked if she could grab some fruit, explaining she'd missed breakfast. The cook let her help herself, so she grabbed some fruit and rice cakes. That way, she could avoid the caff at lunch. Find a quiet spot to hide away. As she was leaving, the cook thrust a Mars Bar and a fresh plastic bag at her. Lulu looked up into her eyes and saw recognition. Another soul battered and bruised by bullies.

Now to get through the day. Lulu picked seats toward the back of class when she could. Her tormentors couldn't pull her hair or throw spitballs, but they could whisper loud enough for her to hear, and send missives laced with hate. She tried to block it out and concentrate, but it was corrosive.

As soon as the bell rang for morning tea, she slipped out and ducked straight into the library, finding a corner to inhabit. No one followed. Her guts unclenched and she ate one rice cake and a mandarin. The library was silent. Some of the girls, her friends once, thought it was creepy, but Lulu found it comforting. The silence amongst the books, stories waiting to be read, endless possibilities. Maybe if she had done things better, her story could have been different. Like those choose-your-own-adventure books when she was a kid. If you didn't like the ending, you went back to one of the choices you'd made earlier and did something different.

Next class, double maths. Her favourite teacher. Where all the trouble started. Praise at the wrong time, in front of the wrong ears. Coming first in tests. In this class, she would endure the front row. Mrs Henson would expect it. She would have to concentrate, knowing she would be called upon. But her brain was so muddled.

Sitting behind her was Kathy, the evil cunt who started all of this. Lulu's shoulders slumped and that clenching in her guts became like a vice. Kathy wore a sinister smile. Every time Mrs Henson was facing the board, Kathy kicked her chair. The first time there were quiet sniggers, but Mrs Henson turned around. After that, only silence with every kick. Kathy did it with little noise, and it didn't hurt, but it was unnerving. The anticipation, the teeth jarring, the shudder through her back and pelvis.

Lulu fantasised about stabbing Kathy. Kick-stab, the knife sinking into flesh, warm blood coming up over her hands, a look of surprise on Kathy's pretty face. Kick-stab.

Shit, Mrs Henson had called on her. She hadn't been paying attention. Her answer was incorrect and Mrs Henson's brow creased. Concentrate. Kick, kick, kick.

By lunch, Lulu's nerves were fried. She was also feeling dizzy again. Library, hide, eat, risk a cat nap. Just double art to go. None of the core tormentors were in this class. People ignored her, and that was fine. Peace.

They were doing clay sculptures now and Lulu enjoyed the feel of moulding the clay. Rubbing and rolling it between her fingers. Smoothing, softening, creating. She got lost in the rhythm of her hands and the music in her ears. For once, not on guard. The bell. Shattering her peace. Packing up utensils, back turned. A blow to the guts. Winded. Someone had 'accidentally' dropped a jar of glaze onto her piece. A fist-sized dent. Ruined. The one thing that had given her any joy in this last year. Her teacher came over. Fussing. Trying to 'fix' it. It was trash. Like her. She tossed it into the bin amidst protests from her teacher, turned her back, and left.

Next few hours were tricky. She had to navigate free time in the dorm before dinner. Bag dumped in her room, quick dash to her spot, out of bounds in the attic storeroom. Sitting on the dormer window ledge. A month ago, when Lulu had found this spot, she'd salvaged a couple of old cushions and brought them up here. It was cold, but relatively comfortable. And she could look out, unseen. Invisible.

Lulu had brought a notepad, pen, and luckily there was enough Wi-Fi for YouTube. She started with the letter. That was hard. Then YouTube. When she'd watched the video five times and practiced with a school ribbon until she had the hand movements committed to memory, she stopped and looked out the window. Girls on the oval practicing hockey. She still had nightmares, in her rare sleeping moments, about those sticks. Lulu shuddered and turned back to her phone. Pics of her family. Tears. Regret.

Movement out the window. Girls heading down to dinner. Attendance would be checked, unlike breakfast. She had to go. She wiped her arm across her wet face. Back to her room. Grace was there. Lulu put her things away but kept the letter she'd written. Tucked it into her bra with her back to Grace. They left for dinner together. No talking, no touching.

Lulu got the smallest amount of food she could and sat on the house mistress's table. Pushing food around the plate. Small mouthfuls of vegetables, a flavourless paste, claggy and bland. During study hall, she pretended to work and sneaked bites of the Mars Bar, savouring the caramel. At lights out, the countdown started.

Lulu waited until two o'clock. Everyone would be asleep. The background adrenaline simmering under the surface was keeping her awake. Time.

Slow, quiet movements. Out of bed. Leave the letter under the doona. Open the door. Slight squeak, quick look back at Grace, a surge of adrenaline. No movement. Pulse slowing slightly. In the corridor, pull but not shut the door. Sneak down the hall. Cleaner's cupboard. Ladder first. Heavy and awkward. Carry it to the bathroom. Knock it into ankles twice. Ouch, fuck.

Door closed. Set it up in the shower stall. Second pass to cupboard for rope. Lift it out from the back. Careful not to knock over the bottles. Heavier than expected. Quicker back to bathroom this time. Close door. On the floor in the shower, hands and fingers twisting, turning, looping. Trying not to remember the past horrors here… Pull tight.

Up the ladder, secure the rope over the steel frame. Drop noose down. Noise in the corridor. Thunder of blood in Lulu's ears. Crouching down, out of sight. Holding breath.

Bathroom door opening. Footsteps into the toilets. Sound of peeing, flushing, footsteps out, door shutting. Long exhalation. Need to hurry now.

Check length and adjust. Now it's time. Chicken out time? No, can't, keep going. Time.

Head in, prickly and rough. Push off ladder, being careful not to knock it over. Drop in weight. So tight, can't breathe. Fuck! Lungs burning. Scratching, clawing, legs kicking wildly. Warm urine trickling down. Can't breathe. Need air. Blood pounding, sweat prickling. Hot. Can't breathe! No! No. No… No… N—

Chapter 1

Poppy tried to keep her face neutral as the corners of her mouth kept threatening mutiny, twitching ever so slightly upward toward a smile. She almost had to pinch herself to be sure this was real. Finally, the life she'd wanted for so long was a reality. A life that almost didn't happen. Dang it, there was that pesky smile again.

'You don't see that every day,' Will said, brushing his unruly shag of hair off his forehead and grinning at her like a loon, effectively bringing Poppy out of her internal reverie and back to the noisy, pulsing beast that was The Bennelong ED, and the patient in front of them with the unexpected problem of a sewing machine needle impaled through her finger.

'It doesn't really hurt,' Mary said, holding it up as they both bent forwards, captivated.

'OK, let's get a closer look,' Will said crouching down in front of her and gently cradling her hand. Poppy watched him eagerly, memorising the way he stretched out each of the fingers, leaving the impaled index finger until last and checking the blood supply and nerve function of each.

Unable to help herself, she asked 'how did it happen?' a thrill of excitement only barely contained.

'It all happened so quickly, I guess. I wasn't paying enough attention. I should have unplugged the machine when I was changing the needles over. I guess I'll never make that mistake again!' she finished, laughing.

Poppy still couldn't believe Mary was sitting here, laughing, completely unfazed. She was itching to take a photo so she could show Gemma and

Lucas later. After finishing his examination, Will stood up and his eyes locked with Poppy's.

'What do we do now?' she asked him, expectantly.

'I'm not sure,' he said after a beat, raking his hand again through his unruly blonde curls.

Poppy had only met Will Charles this morning, being assigned to shadow him today before starting her first shift as a newly minted medical intern on Monday. She had a brief internal cringe thinking back to their awkward meeting. A nurse had pointed her towards the central raised section with counters and computer terminals where the doctors and nurses did their notes and congregated. Will was reasonably tall with blonde shaggy hair, marginally tamed around his ears, and a sprouting of freckles across his nose and cheeks. He was laughing with the guy next to him when she approached.

Poppy waited until he noticed her standing slightly behind him, then said tentatively, 'Hi, are you William? I'm Poppy, one of the new interns… I'm supposed to shadow you today?' *Please be William and not Charles!* She struggled with names, especially when someone had two Christian names. Which one came first?

'Hi, call me Will,' he said, shaking her hand enthusiastically. 'Welcome to the *flight deck*. This is Sebastian.'

They exchanged a *hi* and Sebastian reached over to shake her hand.

'Sebastian is one of the senior Registrars. He's South African, but we don't hold it against him that he supports the Spring Boks.'

They both laughed, and Poppy just smiled awkwardly.

'So, Poppy, where are you from and where'd you go to medical school?' asked Will with a big smile on his face. Poppy couldn't help returning his smile; he was just that open.

'Well, I grew up in Orange, was a boarder in Sydney for high school, and did medicine in Newcastle. So, I guess a bit all over. How about you?'

'I'm from BrisVegas, you know, Brisbane?'

'Sure.'

'But after doing a science degree at the University of Queensland, I came to Sydney to do medicine at the University of Sydney. The Bennelong was my clinical school, so I was keen to stay here as an intern.'

'Has it been a good year?'

'Yeah, it's been really great.'

'Let's go chat with Sebastian,' Will said, pulling Poppy back to the present again. *Focus*, she chastised herself.

Poppy followed like a puppy, still buoyed by the excitement of such an interesting case.

'Seb,' Will said on approach. 'Got a corker for you.'

'I'm listening,' Sebastian replied, looking up from the computer terminal he was typing at. *Jeez, he's hot!* His brown skin was so even and blemish-free, but the lines around his eyes aged him. Poppy guessed he was probably in his late thirties as she noticed the platinum wedding band on his left hand. *Dang.*

'We've got a lady who has a sewing machine needle impaled through her index finger. Blood supply and nerve function is intact and she's in minimal pain. But I don't know… should we just clean it and pull it out?' he asked, and Poppy noticed how he shrugged his shoulders up slightly at the end, showing his uncertainty. She liked that he was so honest, not trying to impress Sebastian, or her.

'Wow, that's a new one,' Seb said to Mary, Will, and Poppy after he'd taken a look for himself. 'OK, won't be long, and we'll get that out for you.'

He pulled Will and Poppy back out into the corridor and said, 'So I agree, the finger looks pretty good. I don't think we need an X-ray. I think you just need to pull it out.'

'But how?' Will asked.

'Well, pliers would be ideal,' Sebastian said, rubbing his freshly shaven square chin.

'Do we have those?' Poppy asked, not sure if it was a dumb question, an instant heat rising up her neck.

'Actually, I'm not sure,' Sebastian said. 'Let's go look in the supply room.'

They rummaged through the surgical instruments and eventually found something resembling pliers.

'Good luck,' Sebastian said and left them to it.

'OK,' said Will, 'do you want to do it, Poppy?'

Poppy locked eyes with him, noticing his completely earnest expression, but couldn't help the reflexive raise of her eyebrows. It was clear he wasn't shirking the responsibility, more that he wanted to give her the opportunity to have a go.

'Sure,' she said, in as confident a tone as she could muster, whilst feeling her legs go mushy at the thought of doing something even Sebastian had never done before.

They got some cleaning supplies and a dressing pack and went back to Mary.

'OK,' Will said to Mary, 'we're going to clean the finger and the needle as best we can and then we're going to pull it out and dress the wound.'

He made it sound so simple, like pulling out a splinter. But for Poppy, it was anything but simple. She was equal parts excited and terrified. What if she pulled it out and they'd made a mistake in their assessment and an artery started pulsing blood? Or what if she nicked a nerve as she pulled it out and Mary ended up with permanent nerve damage and couldn't work anymore? Poppy suddenly felt paralysed with fear, standing there staring at the needle in Mary's finger.

'OK, Poppy,' Will said gently, noticing her frozen state, 'why don't you start by gently cleaning the area, starting at the edge of the needle and working your way out? I'll be right here with you.'

Poppy looked into his eyes and gave him a nervous half-smile and then took a deep, stabilising breath before cleaning the area with chlorhexidine.

'Is that hurting?' she asked Mary, the hint of a tremor in her voice.

'No, it's totally fine,' she replied cheerfully, and Poppy allowed herself to relax slightly and concentrate on what she was doing.

'Great… OK, I'm just going to try pulling it out now?' Poppy said with the upward inflection of a question as she attached the surgical pliers to the needle and clasped firmly. Her hands felt slick with sweat in her gloves, and she was worried she could not grasp it firmly enough to pull it out. She stopped and took another steadying breath, then gripped again, this time more securely. As soon as she felt her grip was solid, she asked Will to hold the finger still for counter traction and pulled back firmly. She was surprised to find the needle slipped out with ease, like a knife sliding through soft butter.

'Nice one, Poppy,' Will said putting pressure on the wound, staunching the blood flow quickly. A tickle of excitement and a small surge of adrenaline coursed through Poppy. She'd just succeeded in her first procedure! *Phew!* She did an internal happy dance. Poppy and Will dressed the finger and Poppy even got to administer a tetanus booster. Another procedure under her belt. She was having a great day!

'Bye, Mary, unplug the machine next time,' Poppy said as she handed Mary her discharge papers.

'I will.' Mary laughed and waved as she headed for the exit.

Poppy and Will ate lunch in a small garden on the side of the hospital. It was popular, but they found a little area to perch on a low wall.

'So, where are you living since you moved down from Newcastle?' Will asked before taking the first bite of his sandwich.

'Oh, I'm really close, just up in Newtown. How about you?'

'Yeah, I'm close too, over in Erskineville. I've been there for the last two years.'

'So apart from liking rugby and being from Queensland, what else do I need to know about you? Do you know what you want to specialise in?'

'Not yet.'

'Oh, thank God it's not just me then,' Poppy said, exhaling the tight ball of anxiety that always formed when she talked about her future career. Just the thought of choosing one thing for the rest of her life sent a shiver up her spine. She couldn't even commit to buying a car!

Will laughed at that. 'Don't worry, lots of us aren't sure yet. My advice is just to soak it all up. These first two years give you a chance to try lots of things. But it's still OK not to be sure at the end of that. Lots of people do a Senior Resident Medical Officer year then to narrow things down a bit more.'

'Oh… I didn't know that.' Poppy stored that titbit away for later.

'Yeah, it's pretty popular, especially Critical Care, which includes ED, ICU and Anaesthetics.'

'Is that what you're thinking about?'

'Yeah, I'll probably do that next year, then I can decide which one I really want to do. So how did you like medicine in Newcastle, did you go to the beach much?'

Poppy laughed lightly. 'A bit, but, growing up in the country, I'm not a massive beach person. But Newcastle was good, the campus is really friendly and the hospital's good. You like the beach, I'm gathering?'

'Yeah. I'm a bit of a surfer, so Newcastle with like five beaches on its doorstep would have been awesome.'

'Do you get much of a chance to surf in Sydney?'

'Every chance I get.'

'Which beach is your favourite?'

'Probably Bronte. It's got more of a consistent swell than Bondi, and it's prettier than Coogee.'

'I like Bronte too. I've been there a few times since we moved. The cafes are nice.'

'Have you ever surfed?'

'Me? No.'

'I'd be happy to take you some time, if you want to learn?'

Poppy laughed again. 'I'm not sure I'd be any good at it.'

'Being good isn't really the point.'

'What do you mean?' Poppy asked, intrigued.

'Well, it's more about how it makes you feel.'

'That's pretty deep,' Poppy said, then immediately regretted it, thinking she might have hurt his feelings. Will had been so open and friendly with her all day, she didn't want to upset him. 'I mean, how does it make you feel?'

'Free and small, all at the same time. And when you catch a wave and you're like really at one with the ocean, it just feels… exhilarating.'

Poppy noticed how Will got a far-away look in his eyes as he said this, clearly picturing himself out in the water. He came back to her as he said, 'Anyway, it's a great way to unwind. And pretty good for your fitness as well.'

'I'll keep it in mind.'

'Do. And I was serious about the offer of a lesson. Anytime.' There was something in Will's expression as he held her gaze that beat longer than usual. She wondered what it meant. He was obviously kind and friendly, but could he be attracted to her? And was she attracted to him?

They brushed the dead grass off their clothes and tossed their rubbish in the bin as they made their way back inside. The outdoor area was shaded and protected from the worst of the heat, but it was still summer in Sydney, and the humidity was energy-zapping. Sweat had plastered Poppy's shirt to her chest and she pulled it away as the air conditioning flowed over her, cooling her moist skin. What would the rest of the shift bring?

Chapter 2

'So, what did you think? Did you enjoy your first shift?' Will asked Poppy as they were grabbing their things from the lockers outside the staff room after evening handover.

'Absolutely. You know so much of medical school is passive – reading, watching, learning. Being active is so much more fun.'

'Totally. And in ED you get to be more active than on the wards, so it's a good place to start – really throw yourself in the deep end… Two bits of advice, though. One: take care of yourself. It's a bit like Vegas in here – no natural light, frenetic pace. So, make sure you keep an eye on the clock and take breaks for the loo and a cup of tea or a meal.'

Aww…he's worried about me. Or am I reading too much into this? Maybe this is the advice he'd give everyone. Stop being so self-obsessed!

'OK, and two?' Poppy kept a neutral expression on her face for fear of giving away her internal dialogue.

'Yeah, number two: always ask for help and advice. No one expects you to know it all. And "loading the boat"', said with finger air quotes, 'shares the responsibility with someone more senior and covers you in case something goes wrong.'

'Thanks, Will. And thanks for today, you've been awesome. What term do you do next?'

'Plastic Surgery. But I've got another day shift here tomorrow.'

Poppy slung her bag over her shoulder, then said, 'Hey, most of the new interns are meeting for drinks and a bit of a party tonight. Do you want to come? You can bring whoever,' she added as an afterthought.

But did she really want him to bring someone else? They'd had such a good time today, he'd been so nice, and she'd been so relaxed in his company, but maybe that was all it was, maybe he was just a friendly guy. And wasn't it OK to just be friends with a guy for once, and not rush to something more?

'OK, sure, what time?'

'It starts from about 7:30. Here's the address,' Poppy said, quickly writing it on a slip of paper she found in her bag. 'And my number's on the bottom, in case you get lost.' Heat rising rapidly as the blush commenced up her neck and into her cheeks. She looked down, embarrassed, but when she looked up again, Will was staring right at her, taking in all of her. Was he checking her out, she wondered? There was a faint fluttering in her chest before she smiled and broke eye contact.

They walked together up to King Street. There was a lot of traffic noise which prevented real conversation. It was still muggy, and Poppy felt her hair sticking at the side of her face. When it was this humid, her naturally wavy honey-blonde hair would frizz unattractively. It was up in a bun, but still, the tendrils that escaped would be forming a coiled circlet. She wondered when they would need to part, and hoped it would be soon so Will wouldn't see her all red and blotchy from the heat.

'I'm down this way,' Will said as they came to Erskineville Road.

'OK, well, see you later,' Poppy said and waved as she continued on, not wanting to linger. *God you're shallow*, she chastised herself. She turned back a few steps later and caught Will staring at her. He gave a sheepish grin and a wave before taking the side street. Poppy smiled to herself. Regardless of whether he found her attractive, and she wasn't yet sure that she found him attractive, she'd had a great day. Her first day as a doctor. She couldn't wait to talk to Gemma and Lucas and tell them all about it. Hopefully they'd also had a good start. Her pace quickened, despite the heat, as she was suddenly excited to get home.

They'd only moved into their new place from Newcastle about four weeks ago and already Poppy was loving it, despite the shock jump in rent. Living in Newtown was like living on the edge of a carnival. King Street was so vibrant. Even late at night there were places open to eat, drink, or browse. Plenty of noise and colour. She'd spent the last few weeks wandering the streets and getting to know the area, including all the tight back lanes and the amazing park and cemetery.

Poppy took a Coke No Sugar from the fridge and sat with one leg tucked under her on one of the couches in the lounge. Gemma and Lucas were on the other one, each with a beer, and soft music was playing in the background. Gemma was lying back with her feet in Lucas's lap whilst he gave her a foot massage. A wave of longing washed over Poppy as she watched their intimacy. I want that, she thought. She couldn't imagine being that comfortable with someone else. All her relationships to date had been short and pretty superficial. She wanted the intimacy, that real connection, but she wasn't sure how to get there.

'Party in the USA' started playing and Poppy exclaimed, 'Oh this is the perfect song for my day!'

'How so?' Lucas asked, one eyebrow raised as he kneaded Gemma's left foot.

'I started off really anxious, worried I'd make a mistake or sound like an idiot or something, but as the day went on, I just started enjoying myself.' She couldn't take the smile off her face. 'What about you two?'

'It was all such a rush!' Gemma proclaimed, suddenly leaning forward and folding her long legs underneath her. 'I got two large IV cannulas in labouring women, only missing once, and delivered a baby. Ooh, and I also assisted with a Caesarean.'

Poppy loved to see her normally studious friend so animated. She was often reserved and sometimes aloof. This innate shyness could be mistaken for arrogance, but Poppy knew better. Gemma had always wanted to do Obstetrics and that was a large part of the decision-making for them ending up at The Bennelong Hospital.

'That's great, Gem. What about you, Luc?' Poppy asked, noticing the flat line to Lucas' mouth and the muscle spasm of his jaw.

'About as shit as I expected.'

His large, puppy dog eyes were narrowed, converting his blonde boy-man look into one of barely contained anger.

'Why, what happened?' Poppy asked.

'The intern was a total prick. He just kept ordering me around, but not actually showing me how to do anything. And the Registrars were in theatre all day, so it was just me and him. Honestly, if it hadn't been for a couple of the nurses taking pity on me, I think I might have taken a swing at him.'

'Really?' Poppy asked, surprised. Lucas had never been violent or seriously angry before. It must have been really awful for him to even suggest it.

'Yeah,' was his one-word response.

Poppy looked over at Gemma whilst Lucas' head was down and raised her eyebrows. Gemma gave a slight shoulder shrug back and a brief shake of her head.

'I'm really sorry, Luc, that totally sucks,' offered Poppy.

'I suspect this entire term is going to suck,' Lucas replied.

'Well, don't jinx it. You never know, Cardiothoracic Surgery might be better than you expect,' said Poppy.

'I'm not sure I have your optimism, Pop.'

It was still hot outside, so Poppy opted for a loose, flowing wrap skirt and a bandana top when she dressed for the party. She wore her hair out, and it fell below her shoulders in gentle beachy waves. She was careful with her make-up and wore some sparkly drop earrings. There were flecks of pale blue in the earrings which matched her eyes nicely. When she admired herself in the mirror, she decided she looked pretty hot. She was lucky to have a relatively flat stomach and OK breasts (not too small or too big), so the outfit flattered her well.

'Ooh, I like that green on you, Gem,' she said as they were heading out, 'it really brings out your eyes.'

'Thanks, Pop.'

'Come on, you two, stop gas-bagging,' Lucas added ushering them out the door. He was clearly not over his day yet. She loved Lucas like a brother, but he could be moody. Once they were at the party she'd be able to mingle and avoid letting his bad mood ruin her night.

The party was being hosted by an intern who, like Will, had also gone to Sydney Uni and had The Bennelong as his clinical school. He had lived in the area for several years with a couple of others in a small workers' cottage on one of the tiny Newtown streets. The trio walked to the party, stopping on the way to grab some chips and booze. The entire three-bed house and yard was probably no bigger than their apartment, but that was Newtown for you.

They plonked their grog in the kitchen, poured themselves a drink, and set about mingling with the others. Music was playing unobtrusively, and a waft of fragrant gardenias permeated from the tiny, paved back courtyard.

Kevita was doing Psychiatry first term, and she was describing a group therapy session she'd been to in the afternoon.

'There were probably five patients, sitting in a circle, with me, the intern I was shadowing, and the Psychiatrist. One of the patients was new to the group and the psychiatrist asked her to tell the rest of the group what had been happening to her. Before she started speaking, I thought maybe she's in with depression? But then she told us how after her baby was born she'd started hearing voices and how initially she'd been able to block them out but they'd become more persistent. They'd been hyper-critical of her parenting and she'd been feeling useless to the point where she didn't feel that she was a good mother and she was having trouble connecting with her baby.'

Poppy found herself leaning in towards Kevita and the story. She wondered what had happened to this young woman and why she was an in-patient in the mental health unit.

'Things got so bad,' Kevita continued, 'that the voices had convinced her that not only was she a terrible mother, but her six-month-old baby was diseased, and she needed to cleanse her to save her. Terrifyingly, the cleansing involved a hot bath with bleach. The baby sustained such extensive burns that she didn't survive,' Kevita finished, her voice dropping to almost a whisper at the end.

'I had to keep swallowing and blinking to stop myself from losing it,' Kevita said.

'Oh my gosh, that's so horrific, the poor woman. Poor family,' Poppy responded.

'I don't know how you could sit through that, Kevita,' Gemma added.

'It wasn't easy. As soon as the patients left the therapy room I started to cry,' Kevita admitted. 'If all of Psychiatry is going to be like that, I'm not sure how I'll get through the term.'

Poppy couldn't fully comprehend the horror of killing your own baby, but she did know loss. It had haunted her for the last five years.

Over Kevita's shoulder she spotted Will arriving with a girl. He looked cute; relaxed in corduroy shorts, a Hawaiian shirt, and Birkenstocks. He smiled when he caught Poppy's eye, and she felt a flutter of excitement. She hadn't realised she'd been waiting for him to arrive. The girl walking over with Will was attractive; taller than Poppy, almost as tall as Will, with a lithe, muscular frame. She had dark straight hair and a relaxed smile, one that suggested she knew just how attractive she was as Poppy clocked heads turning toward her in her peripheral vision. Poppy wondered whether they were dating and a knot of jealousy at the thought surprised her. Just how did she feel about Will?

Poppy turned from the group and made her way over to meet Will, actively letting the distressing story slip from her consciousness like a cloak slipping off her shoulders, down to trail on the floor behind her. She leaned in to kiss him on the cheek. He smelled good. His aftershave had a fresh scent with a hint of citrus but oddly, she could also taste saltiness on his skin. Excitement erupted again in her chest, and heat shot into her nether regions.

'This is Penny…my flatmate,' Will said after they'd kissed hello.

'Hi, Penny, I'm Poppy.'

'Hi,' Penny responded without much interest, scanning over Poppy's head to take in the rest of the group. *Rude.*

'We went to uni together, but Penny's at Prince of Wales.'

This could have been an opportunity for Penny to join the conversation, and Will looked toward her expectantly, but it was clear Penny wasn't even listening and an awkward silence ensued until she stalked off, obviously spotting someone infinitely more interesting in the group outside.

Poppy was relieved to hear that Penny wasn't Will's girlfriend, and she admitted to herself that she was attracted to him after all.

'Will, this is Gemma and Lucas,' Poppy said as they came to join them.

'Are you all friends from uni?' Will asked.

'Yep,' Lucas responded as Gemma surreptitiously checked Will out and Poppy tried to give her the eyebrow tilt as if to say, *cut it out*. 'Poppy said you're from Brisbane?' Luc asked.

'Good old BrisVegas. How about you?'

'Oh, Gem and I are both from Sydney. She's Shire and I'm East.'

'So, is it good to be home then, after Newcastle?'

'Yes, and no. Have to deal with our families more back home.'

Will laughed. 'Can't be that bad, surely?'

'You haven't met Gemma's family,' Lucas said under his breath, bringing his beer bottle to his lips and swallowing before Gemma jabbed him in the ribs with her elbow.

'Hey, you, no casting aspersions,' Gemma said.

'How about you, do you like being in Sydney? You weren't tempted to move home for internship?' Lucas asked Will.

'Actually, I really like Sydney. I miss my family, but I love surfing, so much better access to the beach in Sydney.'

Poppy was happy letting Lucas quiz Will. It enabled her to sneak glances at him. When their eyes connected, Will would smile at her, and Poppy liked the way his eyes softened with little crinkles at the edges. She also liked the way he spoke with Lucas. It was that same relaxed, open, and friendly manner he'd had with her all day. He was clearly a nice guy, and after all the mean guys she'd dated, maybe a nice guy would get her closer to that intimacy she craved.

The music was getting louder, and Poppy's drink kept being refilled. She ate the occasional chips that made their way around, but nothing substantial. An overwhelming sense of love and connection to those around her infused Poppy. These were all her people. They were all on this journey together. How amazing was that? Around ten o'clock, when Gemma and Lucas were leaving, she was sitting on the couch with Will, her hand resting on his thigh, his arm loosely around her shoulders. They'd been talking for some time and Poppy felt the anticipation of a new hook-up prickling just beneath the surface. Gemma leaned in to kiss her goodbye and whispered in her ear, 'Take it slow, Pop, OK?'

'I love you, Gem,' Poppy whispered loudly back. Gemma raised an eyebrow as she looked Poppy in the eye before standing back up and turning to leave as Lucas was pulling her away.

As soon as Gemma had left, Poppy had already forgotten her friend's suggestion to slow down. All she could think about was kissing Will and what it might feel like. He kept staring into her eyes, whenever they weren't talking. *He must be feeling this too.*

'Do you wanna take a shel-fie?' she asked.

'Sure,' he said, leaning further into Poppy's body as she clumsily manoeuvred her phone into a suitable position.

'Yuck, that one's blurry,' she said. 'Let's do another.'

Will's face was touching Poppy's, and his scent was tingling her nose. As soon as she hit the red button to take the photo, he turned his face toward her and gently brushed his lips against hers. They were softer than she expected, like little marshmallows. Poppy's desire rose as their kissing intensified. She pulled Will in closer, lips hungry for more as their tongues began to add to the exploration that is the first kiss. Lost in the moment, their bodies beginning to entangle, it was only the loud, 'get a room' comment that broke the reverie. Poppy giggled, wiping her mouth as she and Will separated, Poppy's leg untangling from his.

'Well, that's embarrassing,' Poppy whispered to Will as people's gazes finally shifted away from them.

'Yeah, a bit like being sprung by the parentals,' Will laughed.

Poppy laughed and lightly slapped his arm.

'Do you want to get out of here?' Will asked, with a hint of uncertainty.

'Absolutely,' Poppy said, rising quickly with a slight swaying, her hand reaching down to his.

They stumbled through Newtown's back streets holding hands. The warmth of Will's hand and the anticipation of what was to come set that flutter off again in Poppy's chest. There was a vague background sensation of nausea, but Poppy ignored it.

Once Will's front door was closed behind them, they were leaning up against it, kissing. Poppy ran her hand down Will's chest and started to unbutton his shirt. His chest was smooth and firm and Poppy enjoyed the sensation of her fingers sliding over his skin. It's silkiness and his surprisingly defined abs were increasing her desire.

Will held her hands and pulled away from her lips.

'Wait, are you shure you want to do this?' Will slurred.

'Absho-lutely,' Poppy slurred back, moving her hands back to fumbling with Will's shirt buttons.

Will stopped her again and said, 'I jusht…don't want to take advantage—'

'You're not!' Poppy exclaimed, leaning forward to kiss Will's neck. Biting his skin in her overexuberance, getting an 'oww' from Will as she did.

Will undid the bottom ties of her bandanna top and lifted it over her head.

'God, you're so beautiful, Poppy,' Will said as he bent his head to kiss her breasts, a small groan of pleasure escaping her mouth. She could feel his cock hardening under his jeans as it brushed against her when he stood back up, and this excited her further. It always turned her on, to know a guy was getting hard because of her. She licked his neck and breathed in his fresh, citrusy scent.

Will stopped for a breath and locked eyes with Poppy. 'When I first saw you today, I couldn't get over how beautiful you were.' Poppy smothered him in kisses in response, desperate to keep going. She appreciated he was saying nice things, but in this moment she wanted to charge ahead and feel him inside her, not talk about her feelings. She still didn't really know what those were. But she did know she wanted him in this moment.

They proceeded to Will's bedroom, Poppy stumbling a little. Soon they were completely naked, and Will had a finger inside her. Poppy was caressing his cock and completely lost in the moment, feeling the sensations as she rocked her hips in time to Will's thrusting. She moaned with enjoyment, and it wasn't long before she came, her body convulsing in a wave of ecstasy. When she finished coming, she bent over his cock and licked up the shaft before placing the tip in her mouth. She enjoyed the slightly salty taste of his skin and the slight shudder from Will at the touch of her tongue.

'Wait,' Will soon stopped her to get on a condom, and Poppy lay back on the bed. She opened her legs to let him enter her, completely unashamed.

They continued in missionary for a while before Poppy felt some friction, her mind losing connection with the experience.

'Let's shift,' she said, rolling Will over and straddling him. His hands went to her breasts and Poppy slowly moved her hips up and down, grinding her pelvis into his, getting her mojo back. *Oh that's nice…* Her excitement rose again and before it could wane, she popped off him and turned around so Will could enter her from behind. He leaned forward licking her neck and had a finger on her clitoris making tiny circles, Poppy moaning in pleasure, 'yes…ooh…yes.' Poppy rapidly came again, and Will followed soon afterwards. They fell off each other into a sweaty mess on the sheets, panting, and catching their breath, Poppy completely satisfied.

Then came the awkwardness of what to say to someone you barely know whom you've just had great sex with…

'Wow,' Will said between puffs as he tried to put his arm around her to cuddle her. Poppy suddenly felt a wave of nausea rising up her chest.

'I'm sorr-ry,' she mumbled, her hand clutching her mouth as she rushed and stumbled to the bathroom. She made it to the loo just in time, vomiting up all the alcohol from earlier.

Will knocked gently on the door, 'are you OK?' he asked.

She couldn't answer, as she needed to vomit again. Luckily, she'd locked the door on her way in so he couldn't enter. Seeing her naked, vomiting, and hugging the toilet bowl was not an image she wanted to give him. She vomited until there was nothing left, then sat against the tiles feeling like a loser – *what a spectacular first impression!*

Eventually, she got up and found some Listerine to gargle. She wrapped a towel around her and braced herself to leave the safety of the bathroom. She opened the door and Will was sitting in the corridor in a pair of trackies, waiting for her. He got up when the door opened.

'Are you OK, Poppy?' he asked kindly as he handed her a glass of water.

She took a tentative sip and said, with her eyes cast down, 'I'm so sorry.'

'Hey, don't worry about it. I'm sorry,' Will said sheepishly.

There was an uncomfortable moment of silence where they were both looking at their feet. *God, he must think I'm a loser. I need to get out of here.*

'Look, I still feel pretty wretched, so I think I'm just going to get an Uber home.'

'Oh, OK,' said Will, and Poppy could hear disappointment in his tone.

He helped her gather her clothes, and she went back into the bathroom to get dressed. As she looked at herself in the mirror, she mouthed silently: *idiot.* She ordered an Uber as she dressed and luckily it was arriving as she emerged from the bathroom, so she didn't need to fill any more awkward silences.

'I'll walk you downstairs,' Will offered.

'No, no, I'm OK, thanks,' said Poppy, and she gave his upper arm a squeeze and bolted out the door.

In the Uber on the way home, Poppy chastised herself. *Stupid, stupid, stupid.* She enjoyed sex, but had a habit of being too open to it when drunk. She liked Will, and she regretted moving too quickly and then embarrassing herself with the vomiting. Why couldn't she have just kissed him and left it at that? Maybe then there could have been a future relationship. Now though, she'd rushed into sex, and her experience told her that a real relationship afterwards was unlikely. In the safety of her own bed, she cried herself to sleep.

Chapter 3

Poppy woke to a pounding headache and her dry, furry tongue sandblasted to the roof of her mouth. She swallowed the acrid taste of last night's vomit and tried to escape the makeshift straitjacket the sheets had become in her restless sleep. When she was finally on her back, she peeled open her eyelids and stared at the ceiling. Heat slipped in under the heavy curtains but at least the room wasn't spinning anymore. Flashes of last night resurfaced and Poppy cringed.

Did she really have sex with Will last night? Lovely, friendly Will? And then vomit in his toilet and run away? Would she never learn? Why did she always rush into drunken sex when what she craved was the connection Gemma and Lucas had? *You know why…*

She shut her eyes again. *Shut up, brain…* Maybe I imagined it all, she thought hopefully for a brief moment. But there was no escaping reality. She'd be known as the Intern who hooked up with a Resident at the first party of the year. A truly fantastic impression to make! Eventually, she had to pull herself from the self-loathing spiral she was on and drag her bones from the bed, her full bladder demanding attention as she wandered, zombie-like, to the bathroom.

'I've made a complete arse of myself,' she said miserably to Gemma after she'd filled her in on the events of last night in between mouthfuls of Vegemite toast.

'I'll grant you, less than ideal way to finish sex. But the sex was good, wasn't it?'

'It was better than good. It was pretty great, actually. At least, that was my impression. But I was pretty drunk, so who knows, right?'

'Hmm.'

Poppy's phone bleeped its text alert, and she looked at it.

'It's from him,' Poppy said as Gemma leant in to read over her shoulder.

> Hi Poppy, just checking in to make sure you're OK. I'm really sorry things ended the way they did, and I hope we can start over. Hope to hear from you, Will.

'What are you going to write?' asked Gemma.

'I don't know. Nothing, maybe?'

Gemma gave her a quizzical look, like Poppy was an animal in an exhibit at the zoo.

'But you liked him, and the sex was sort of great. So, you fucked up at the end, but he's letting it slide. What's the problem?'

'I just didn't want to start like this. First day and I sleep with the first guy who shows me some attention. Then I completely embarrass myself… I'm just too ashamed,' Poppy said miserably.

'Look, I think you're blowing it all out of proportion. I don't think it's as bad as you think. And regardless, Will seems like a nice person. He deserves some response.'

'Argh…' Poppy said and flopped down on the couch, putting the cushion over her face. 'Why is my love life always such a disaster?' she said from under the cushion.

Gemma gently pulled the cushion off Poppy's head so she could look at her and said with a gentle tone, 'Your love life is a disaster because you never really let anyone in. You sleep with the bad boys and the arseholes so that you've got an excuse to keep all those walls up.'

Poppy was stunned by Gemma's brutal honesty and just blinked in response. She was right, but Poppy wasn't about to admit that out loud.

'At some point, Pop, you're going to have to forgive yourself and let yourself love someone.'

Poppy pulled the cushion back over her head. This conversation was way too honest and poked at nerves that were still raw. Now was not the time to open that box that she spent so much time and energy keeping firmly shut.

She agonised over her reply for most of the day, but finally settled on:

> Hi Will. I'm so sorry about last night. Just feel really
> ashamed. Poppy

His reply was swift:

> Don't be. Can happen to anyone. I'd love to catch up later
> in the week and start afresh?

She didn't want to repeat old mistakes of jumping into bed and relationships too quickly. But Gemma was right; Will was a nice guy, he deserved better than what she could give him right now.

Finally, she texted:

> I think I just need some time to settle in here and don't
> want to complicate things just now.

This time there was a pause before:

> OK. Well, I hope to see you around, Will.

Poppy felt a lurch in her stomach. He seemed pissed off in that last text. Could she have just made an even bigger mistake?

Poppy was starting with four evening shifts, 3–11p.m., from Monday. The first two were in subacute, or 'subbies' as she'd learnt from Will, and the next two were in acute. As Monday three o'clock approached, Poppy's stomach flip-flopped as she wondered what the first shift would be like and whether she would know what to do?

At the flight deck she said hello to Seb who was the Registrar on in subbies for the evening.

'Hey, how're you doing?' Seb asked.

'OK, a bit nervous,' Poppy admitted.

'Not to worry, it'll be fine. Just run each case by me or the boss.'

'OK. Who's the boss on?'

'It's Harriet. She's over there. Come on, I'll introduce you.'

Seb walked them over to where Harriet was chatting with a couple of others. She was in bottle-green scrubs and was short and slightly stocky in build. Her hair was dark and frizzy and loose to her shoulders. She looked like she worked out at the gym with obvious upper body tone visible through her scrubs, and defined biceps.

'Excuse me, Harriet. This is one of our new interns, Poppy. She's starting her first shift with us this evening.'

'Hi, welcome,' said Harriet.

'Hi,' replied Poppy, giving a brief wave. *Why did you do that?*

'Well, handover's not for a while, so why don't you start with a patient,' Harriet added.

'OK, thanks, I will.'

And Harriet turned back to her conversation, turning her back on Poppy and her red face.

Poppy felt deflated and dismissed by Harriet's abrupt manner. Some of her confidence ebbed away as she logged in to the computer and clicked on the next waiting patient for subbies. The presenting complaint was 'abdominal pain'. Poppy brought Cassandra, the patient, in from the waiting room and noticed that she walked very slowly, clutching her right lower abdomen. It was obvious she was in a lot of pain.

'You look like you're in a lot of pain, Cassandra, can you tell me what's been happening?' Poppy asked as Cassandra made her way very gingerly up onto the bed and tried to find a somewhat comfortable position.

'I woke up and my tummy was really sore all over, and I thought I might have gastro or something, so I stayed home from work. But the pain just kept getting worse and I didn't have any diarrhoea or anything.'

'Did it stay all over the place or did it move to one place in particular?' Poppy asked, immediately thinking this might be a case of appendicitis, but not wanting to jump to conclusions without the full picture.

'Well, yeah, initially it was all over, then in the last few hours it's been mainly down here,' Cassandra said, pointing to her lower abdomen on the right side.

Yep, still fits with appendicitis.

'Have you noticed a temperature or vomited at all?'

'I've felt a bit warm, but haven't taken my temperature.'

Poppy looked at the observation chart the triage nurse had started and noticed the mild temperature of 37.9°C. When she looked back up at Cassandra, she saw how grey she looked, like a worn-out dishrag.

'And while I was in the waiting room, the pain was so bad that I vomited,' Cassandra added.

'Do you still feel nauseous now?'

'Only mildly. I just feel shaky and just… so much pain. Can you give me something for the pain?'

'Absolutely, as soon as I finish your history and examination, I'll take some bloods and give you some pain relief and anti-nausea medication.'

'OK,' Cassandra said, resignedly.

'What about your bowels – when did you last open them?'

'Yesterday,' she answered flatly.

When Poppy examined Cassandra, there was abdominal guarding, where she tensed every time Poppy tried to palpate her abdomen, and there was intense tenderness in the right iliac fossa. In this spot, there was also rebound tenderness, a classic sign of appendicitis. Poppy put in an IV cannula and took some bloods, then went to find Seb to run it by him so she could give Cassandra some morphine and something for nausea.

Whilst handover started at the acute board, Poppy quickly finished her notes and submitted the blood test requests. When they got to the subbies board, Poppy listened carefully and took notes on the patients she was to take over care of. When they got to Cassandra, Poppy presented:

'Thirty-two-year-old female acute abdominal pain initially diffuse but progressive and subsequent localisation to right iliac fossa with one times vomit and low-grade temp. Have given IV morphine and antiemetic, taken bloods, and would like to order a CT abdo to rule out appendicitis.'

'OK, has Sebastian reviewed the patient?' Harriet questioned.

'Not yet.'

'OK, Seb, could you please review? Poppy, make sure you discuss the bloods and review the CT with Sebastian when they're back.'

'Will do.'

Poppy found Harriet intimidating but felt she'd presented confidently, and not embarrassed herself (yet).

When handover ended, Poppy submitted the CT order.

'Hey, Seb.'

'Yes?'

'Should I call Radiology about the CT to expedite it?'

'No, they'll prioritise it. All ED scans are prioritised.'

'OK.'

She went back to check on Cassandra and found that she was more comfortable after the morphine, but still in pain and curled up on her side. *Well, I guess I just take the next case while I wait for Cassandra's results.*

'Johnny?' Poppy called out in the waiting room.

'Yep,' a young guy replied putting up his hand and using the side of the plastic chair to push himself up to standing. An older guy with slightly greying hair, dressed similarly in work shorts and polo neck T-shirt stood too and put a supportive hand around him to help him hop over to Poppy who could already see his very bruised and swollen foot which he wasn't putting weight onto.

'Would you like me to get a wheelchair?' Poppy asked seeing the creases of pain altering his face with every hop.

'Nah, I'm good.'

'OK, well let's get you to a bed,' Poppy said, opening the sliding doors into the department with her ID badge and leading them to a cubicle.

Once Johnny had climbed onto the bed and sighed loudly, Poppy asked, 'so what have you done to your foot?'

'Dropped a block of cement on it at the building site where I work.'

'That must have hurt.'

'No kidding.'

'And is this your dad?' Poppy asked, gesturing to the older guy who'd accompanied him.

'Nah…my boss.'

'Oh, OK.'

Poppy had already checked the triage note and seen the nurse practitioner had already given him some pain relief and ordered an X-ray, which was still pending.

'How's your pain level since the nurse gave you the Endone?'

'Still pretty bad.'

'If you had to rate it out of ten, with ten being the worst pain you could imagine, and zero being no pain, how would you rate it?'

'Like, an eight?'

'OK, let's take a look,' Poppy said, bending forward to examine Johnny's foot.

It was bad. There was a lot of bruising and swelling over the central part of the foot, and it looked crushed in the middle, exactly like a heavy object had landed on it.

'Can you wiggle your toes for me?'

'Argh…' Johnny cried out as he slightly moved the toes.

'I'm sorry, I know that hurts…what about the big toe, can you move that?'

Johnny grimaced and grabbed the side of the bed as he tried to move the big toe, and groaned as it moved backwards and forwards. He panted loudly at the end, like he'd run two hundred metres, rather than just moved one toe, and Poppy noticed the beads of sweat on his forehead.

'OK, I suspect you've got multiple fractures, but the blood flow doesn't look compromised and you can move the toes, so that's reassuring. Once the X-ray is back, I'll come back. But I'll keep you nil by mouth for now, until we know what the plan is, OK?'

'OK.'

'When was the last time you ate or drank apart from taking the pain relief?'

'About one o'clock.'

'OK, great. I'll be back soon.'

She sat at the computer next to Seb to type up her notes.

'How're you doing?' Seb asked.

Poppy looked up to see Seb typing away, not directly looking at her.

'I've just seen a tradie who dropped a block of cement on his foot.'

Seb stopped typing and focused his attention on her.

'It looks terrible. Crushed centrally. I suspect he has multiple fractures.'

'How's the blood supply to the toes?'

'Capillary refill is ok for now. I was just going to type him up and await the X-ray. He's already had pain relief.'

'OK, sounds like that's all you can do for now. Keep me posted and re-check the toes if the X-ray takes too long.'

'OK, thanks, I will.'

'I reviewed Cassandra as well and agree with you, it's most likely acute appendicitis, but we'll wait for the bloods and CT.'

'Thanks, Seb.'

'Anytime.'

Poppy already liked Seb. He was calm and easy-going, but economical with words. It gave him an air of effortlessness. It didn't hurt that he was so good-looking.

'So, Seb, Will mentioned you like rugby. Do you play?' Poppy asked, hoping to draw him out and learn a bit more about him.

'Oh no, not since school.'

'You look like you spend a bit of time outdoors, though.'

'I surf when I can.'

'Really? I've never tried. Does it take long to learn?'

'Depends on your balance.'

Poppy found his answer mildly cryptic. But she didn't have time to question him further as Cassandra was wheeled past the flight deck on her way back from CT. Her bloods showed normal liver function and electrolytes, but a raised white cell count and neutrophil count consistent with infection. Her inflammatory markers were also elevated. Poppy wasn't particularly confident in evaluating the CT, so she went around to the CT reporting room to look at it with the Radiology Registrar. Her name was Natalie, and she kindly pointed out where the fat stranding around the appendix was suggestive of appendicitis. She also showed Poppy the free fluid in the peritoneum suggestive of a small, localised perforation. Poppy then relayed all this to Seb, who agreed it was time to get a surgical consult.

Poppy dialled the number listed on the phone chart for the on-call Surgical Registrar.

'Yes?' the Registrar answered the phone.

'Hi, my name's Poppy, and I'm one of the ED interns. I was hoping to run a patient by you?' Poppy said, her pulse beginning to race, and her foot jiggling under the desk.

'And?'

The negativity of the Registrar's tone was making her more anxious. She stumbled on her presentation and when she finished and the Registrar hung up, she wasn't sure he was going to come and see Cassandra, he was so abrupt. Poppy stared at the phone in the cradle while the blood pounded in her ears, wondering whether she should ring him back. She internally debated this for a minute, then decided to give it half an hour, and if he hadn't seen her by then, she'd ask Seb what to do.

'Knock knock,' Poppy said before pulling back the curtain for Cassandra's cubicle. Cassandra was curled on her side and she was sweating. She groaned when Poppy came toward her.

'It looks like your pain is worse again.'

'Yep.' Poppy noticed a tear leak from the edge of her eye.

'OK, I'll get you some more morphine. Do you feel sick?'

'Not anymore.'

'OK. Well, the CT does suggest it could be appendicitis, so I've called the Surgical Registrar to come and have a look at you. But I'll get the nurse to get you the morphine now, OK?'

'OK.'

'Jeez, that looks squished,' Seb said over Poppy's shoulder as they reviewed tradie guy's X-rays. 'Better call Ortho.'

'On it,' Poppy replied, reaching over to grab the phone and look up the Orthopaedics Registrar on the on-call list. Everything knotted up inside her and a cold sweat rapidly broke out over her body as she dialled the number and waited for someone to pick up. *I hope he's nicer than the last guy.*

'Hi, is that the Ortho Reg on call?' Poppy asked as soon as they answered the call.

'Yes,' said not too abruptly.

'Hi, I'm Poppy, one of the interns in ED. Can I please talk to you about a patient with extensive crush fractures of the foot?'

'Sure, what's happened?'

Relief coursed through her, and she unclenched her insides as she recounted the story.

'Wow, that sounds pretty bad. Leave it with me. I'll check the scans and be down to see him soon.'

'Thank you!' Poppy finished before putting down the phone with a slight smile forming on the last words. Maybe not all Surgical Registrars were pricks.

Poppy checked her watch and couldn't believe it was already close to 7:30p.m. More than halfway through her first shift. When she lifted her eyes after putting down the phone, she saw Seb talking to one of the nurses in the corner. He raised his chin at her and Poppy stood up and came over to where they were conversing.

'Now's probably a good time for you to go and have a break,' Seb said once he'd finished with the nurse.

'OK.'

'Take half an hour.'

'OK, thanks,' Poppy said brightly and smiled at him. He really was very sweet, Poppy thought. She went up the street to one of the little Thai places and grabbed a takeaway chicken pad Thai and a Coke No Sugar, and ate it quickly in the staff room. She was checking her Instagram after she'd finished eating when Harriet came in.

'Hi,' Poppy said.

'You know, if you've finished, you should get back in there.'

'Oh, OK. I'm sorry. I'll head back now.' Poppy felt the burn of a blush as she hurriedly cleared away her things. Had Harriet taken a dislike to her, she wondered. Or was she this unfriendly to everyone?

She made her way back to the flight deck and noticed a young Asian guy in pale-blue surgical scrubs and gown was typing on one of the computers at the flight deck. Poppy suspected it was the general Surgical Registrar.

'Hi, I'm Poppy. Have you just seen Cassandra?'

'Yes. We'll take her to theatre tonight,' he said. Deadpan.

'Do you need me to do anything else?'

'No.'

No eye contact, no chit-chat. Poppy thought it was comical – he was like a caricature. She had to bite back a giggle at the absurdity and hastily turned and went to say goodbye to Cassandra before updating the board that she was for transfer to the operating theatre.

Poppy's next patient was a woman in her forties who'd cut her hand trying to remove an avocado stone. She was still in her work suit and full make-up, although her mascara had smeared under her eyes, presumably from crying.

'So, I was holding the half avocado in my left hand and was trying to twist the stone out with the knife in my right when the knife slipped and cut me.'

It had cut into the fleshy part of her left hand, below the last two fingers and into her wrist. The triage nurse had already applied a compression bandage, which Poppy delicately removed after she'd put gloves on.

'Can you wiggle your fingers for me?' Poppy asked the patient and watched as she deliberately moved each finger. She thought back to the way Will had examined Mary's finger the other day and tried to emulate him.

'Ouch, it's pretty painful.'

'I think that's a good thing,' Poppy said, trying to sound confident, whilst still compressing the site of the laceration so that the blood didn't start oozing too much. *That means she still has sensation, and the movement means she still has motor innervation, also good. What should I do next?* She continued to inspect the wound whilst thinking, buying herself some time.

'Right, well, your fingers are moving, and you've got sensation, so we will need to clean the wound thoroughly and then stitch you up. Hang tight, I'm just going to get everything ready and grab one of the senior doctors to have a look too.'

'OK... I don't need an operation, do I?'

'No, I don't think so, but I want one of the senior doctors to confirm that.'

'Oh, OK. You've not done this before?'

'Well, I'm an Intern. This is only my first shift.'

'Well, I want someone more senior stitching me up... No offence.'

Poppy blushed and cast her eyes down, 'that's OK, I understand.'

Poppy was looking for Seb but couldn't see him anywhere. She noted Harriet was on the flight deck, so she took a deep breath and approached her.

'Excuse me, Harriet, can I talk to you about a patient?' Poppy asked, trying to be brave despite her hands sweating.

'OK,' Harriet said as she kept typing, not making eye contact with Poppy.

'I've got a lady with a deep laceration to the palm and wrist. There's no obvious tendon or nerve damage to the fingers and good blood supply, but it's pretty deep.'

'OK, I'll finish this and come have a look with you.'

'Thank you,' said Poppy. Poppy then stood there, not knowing whether to wait or go back to the patient.

When Harriet examined the patient's hand and fingers, carefully checking the sensation, movement, and pulses, Poppy watched keenly. She was more thorough than Will had been and she stored Harriet's techniques in her memory bank for the next time.

'OK, it is deep, but I agree there's no significant deep tissue injury, so we can just suture it and the patient can be reviewed in the hand clinic tomorrow. We'll do it together.'

'Thank you,' Poppy said, relief spreading through her.

'No,' interrupted the patient.

'Excuse me?' Harriet replied.

'No, I just want you to do it. She told me she's never done this before.'

'Well, this is a teaching hospital, and Dr Mason is a fully qualified doctor. She has sutured before, but maybe not a complex injury. If she doesn't get opportunities to practice, she will never improve her skills. I will supervise and do it with her, and I assure you the outcome for you will not be any different than if it was just me doing it,' was Harriet's reply before turning her back on the patient and ushering Poppy out of the cubicle, not waiting for the patient to reply.

'Thank you so much for that,' Poppy gushed as they entered the supply room.

'Unfortunately, it is par for the course, and you will need to develop a thick skin to deal with patients. They will be rude, dismissive, and sometimes belligerent, or openly hostile.'

'OK,' Poppy mumbled, not sure if Harriet was insulting her and suggesting she wasn't tough enough, or she was trying to be supportive. She still couldn't get a good read on her.

They moved the patient into one of the procedure rooms once they'd assembled everything they would need, including local anaesthetic, a couple of different suture materials, suture kit, extra disinfectant, gloves and gowns, and a procedure trolley.

It turned out that despite Harriet's abrupt manner, she was an excellent teacher. When they were suturing, Harriet would perform a couple of sutures, then get Poppy to do some. Because Harriet was calm, it made Poppy feel calm and enabled her to focus on what she was doing.

'Yes, just like that,' Harriet instructed as Poppy inserted the curved needle of the suture material whilst using her left hand to hold up the tissue with suture forceps. The skin was tougher than Poppy was expecting, and she had to put some force into the needle to pierce it. But she wasn't rushing, was barely shaking, and she did a neat job. When it was all done, Poppy gave a tetanus booster, bandaged the area, and gave the discharge instructions, including the appointment the next day for the hand clinic.

Poppy was hoping for a thank you from the patient when she gave her the discharge documents and told her she was free to go. But she snatched the envelope from Poppy and pushed past her out of the corridor, muttering over her shoulder, 'I can't believe I've been here for three hours.'

I won't let you take this away from me, she thought as she smiled to herself watching the patient's retreating back. But she was held up at the sliding doors. When the doors wouldn't open, she turned back, glaring at Poppy before saying, 'are you going to let me out?' and stamping her foot.

Poppy swallowed her smile. 'Of course,' she said before moving to the security pad and using her ID to open the doors, allowing the patient to exit.

Another procedure under her belt. The chorus beat of 'Youngblood' pumped in her ears as she pictured herself shadow-boxing away the negative thoughts.

Chapter 4

When Poppy stepped outside the ED after her shift ended, she took a deep breath in, looked up at the night sky, devoid of any stars thanks to the light pollution, and felt a mixture of pride and exhaustion. She'd survived her first shift. Her new life was finally happening. But she did miss the expanse of stars back home, and the sweet, fresh country air. Still, she smiled to herself as she walked up to King Street. Despite it being a Monday and late, there were plenty of places still open. Music pumped out of the pubs as she passed, and Poppy had to edge past several groups of people chatting and taking up space on the sidewalk. The energy of the suburb fit in well with where she was in her life right now. Poppy felt completely alive in her skin. Every nerve ending tingling with anticipation, every muscle awake from use, her brain lively and quick. She hoped these feelings would continue. Poppy quietly entered the apartment, shutting the door softly behind her knowing that Gemma and Lucas would be sleeping, but she was too jazzed for bed. She poured herself a glass of red wine, grabbed some Ben & Jerry's chocolate fudge brownie ice cream, and retreated to her room to watch an old episode of *Veronica Mars* on her iPad. Veronica's sass and kick-arse attitude was just right for her current mood and kept her positive bubble going. When the episode finished, though, she was still too wired to sleep, so she took the end of her wine to the bath and put a Missy Higgins playlist on her Spotify and tried to quiet her mind. A vanilla bean Glasshouse candle flickered on the vanity as 'All for believing' played. Eventually, when she'd turned completely prunie, she'd stilled the whir of the day's events and finally felt relaxed enough to sleep.

Poppy walked into the department the following afternoon and saw Harriet talking with Graham, one of the nurses, near the handover board. Poppy gave Harriet a cheery hello when she saw her, but got the same curt reply as the previous day. She sighed internally and her shoulders slumped. She honestly thought she'd made some ground yesterday over the suturing, but clearly Harriet was a tough nut to crack. Poppy would just have to keep trying. Paul, the Registrar on with her for the shift, however, was the complete opposite. Where Seb was economical with words, Paul was chatty.

'Hi, you must be Poppy. Seb's told me all about you,' he said after introducing himself as Poppy arrived at the flight deck. He was tall and lanky with dark-brown, short hair, and forewent the ED scrubs for dark pants and a white button-down shirt. His pants rode a little high and he had a colourful tourniquet around his shoulders, and rocked on the balls of his feet when he was standing still. He was a bit of a dork really, but in a good way – like a great big Labrador.

'Hi, yes, I'm Poppy… I hope it was all good?' Poppy replied.

'Absolutely,' Paul replied enthusiastically. 'He spoke highly of you.'

'Oh, OK,' Poppy stammered. She didn't think she'd done anything worthy of praise, but was glad it wasn't a negative first impression.

'Well, I am at your service tonight. Let me know how I can help.'

'Thanks,' Poppy said, relaxing slightly.

She had a range of patients this shift from injuries, abdominal or back pain, and what Poppy thought of as the eclectic – the diverse and unusual presentations that seemed to get triaged to subbies. The most memorable eclectic case of this shift was listed as 'foreign body' on the triage note. *Ooh, I wonder if this is like Mary with the sewing needle? It'd be great to get to do another procedure.*

'Hi, I'm Poppy, one of the doctors, you must be Toby,' she introduced herself to the young guy in a sleeveless tank top showing off his bulky biceps, and short shorts, whilst noting there was no obvious foreign body visible. *I wonder where it is?*

'Why don't you hop up on the bed, there, and tell me what's happened?

'OK,' Toby said as he winced and slowly made it onto the bed.

'You look really uncomfortable there.'

'Um-hm,' he replied with his lips pursed tightly together.

Poppy waited, hoping he would volunteer what and where the problem was, but Toby kept his eyes shut and his lips closed.

Eventually, before the silence could become too awkward, she had to probe: 'It says on your triage note that you have a foreign body. Can you tell me what it is and where?'

Toby's eyes flew open and a look of abject fear crossed his face which also reddened, but he still didn't talk to her. *He's a blusher like me. Poor guy, he's obviously really embarrassed about whatever this is.*

A furrow formed between Poppy's eyebrows. Could it be a cockroach in his ear, she wondered. That would certainly be uncomfortable. She approached the bed and rested a hand on Toby's arm, wanting to reassure him that he was safe and hoping this would help him open up.

'Toby,' she said softly. 'I can't help you if I don't know what's happening.'

'I've got something…'

'Yes…'

'Something…stuck in my bum.'

'Ooh,' Poppy said, understanding dawning on her as she removed her hand from Toby's arm.

Of course, Poppy had heard many similar stories during medical school, handed down by other students and teachers, but had never come face to arse with one herself. She masked her shock and continued in what she hoped was a professionally detached manner, her face as neutral as possible.

'Can you tell me what it is?'

'It's…it's…a hairbrush.'

'OK. And how long has it been stuck there?'

'A few…hours.'

'Have you had any abdominal pain, vomiting, temperature?'

'No…but it's really uncomfortable.'

I bet it is!

'I know, Toby. Look, I'm going to have to put a finger in your rectum and see if I can extract it, OK?'

'I guess so,' Toby said, shutting his eyes again and pursing his lips, his face flushing.

She grabbed some KY and gloves and probed his anus to assess how deeply it had travelled. Unfortunately, she could only just touch the end of the handle with her finger and was worried all she'd done was push it in deeper. Toby groaned in pain, further fuelling her fears.

'I'm sorry,' she offered lamely. 'I'll just run this by one of the senior doctors,' and she fled the cubicle.

'Holey-dooley,' Paul exclaimed when they later reviewed the X-ray.

Poppy had been expecting something small, like a pocket hairbrush. She was not expecting the fifteen-centimetre brush the X-ray revealed.

'Yowch,' Poppy said, as some of the other staff came over to see what was happening. Poppy heard the unmistakable clicks of various phone apps as some snapped quick photos before Harriet hustled them away with, 'Come on, back to work.'

The giggles and murmurings continuing as they receded.

'There's no way to retrieve that manually,' Paul explained. 'He'll need a laparotomy to remove it. You'd better get a surgical consult.'

Poppy's heart sank when she saw the on-call sheet and realised that Tim Pan, the grumpy Surgical Registrar from yesterday was on again today. Maybe he'll be nicer today, she thought hopefully.

'Hi Tim, this is Poppy, ED intern, I have a twenty-four-year-old man with a large hairbrush in his rectum that is about nine centimetres from the anal verge. The brush itself is around fifteen centimetres on the X-ray. Can you please review him?'

There was silence on the other end of the phone.

'Tim, did you hear me?'

'Yes.'

'So will you please come and review the patient?'

Again, there was a pause. What is going on, Poppy wondered.

'OK,' he said before hanging up. And just like yesterday, Poppy found herself staring at the phone once she'd placed it back in the cradle. *That guy is so weird.*

When Tim arrived in ED, Poppy followed him into the cubicle and introduced him to Toby.

'Right, Toby, that brush isn't coming out without an operation. If we leave it much longer it could perforate the rectum and cause serious infection, potentially even death. So, we need to make an incision from the bottom of your belly button, down to your pubic area. Then we cut through the muscle layers and open the abdominal cavity. Once we locate the brush in the rectum we will cut through the wall of the rectum to remove the brush, then stitch up each of the layers. The risks include infection, blood loss requiring transfusion, perforation of another organ requiring additional management, hernia, and anaesthetic risks of stroke and heart attack, although all these risks are low… Do you have any questions?'

Poppy watched as Toby lay there in stunned silence. Tim displayed as little empathy for Toby as he did for her. He was that stereotype: overworked, burnt-out surgical trainee striving for success at all costs, but to what end, Poppy wondered. If he hated the work, the patients, and his colleagues, why was he here at all? She certainly didn't want to end up like him.

After Tim had the signed consent form and left the patient cubicle, Poppy stayed behind.

'I know that was pretty overwhelming, Toby. Maybe I can help go through things again for you or answer any questions?' she asked in a soft and soothing voice.

A tear slipped from Toby's eye and he turned his face away from her.

'It's OK to be scared,' she tried to reassure him. 'But these operations often sound scarier than they actually are. We always have to mention all the risks even though they are really low.'

Poppy waited and eventually, Toby turned back to face her.

'I'm not worried about the risks so much as the massive scar on my abdomen and the risk of hernia and not being able to go to the gym. What's everyone going to think?'

Poppy was surprised, she wasn't expecting that that would be what worried him most.

'You don't have to tell anyone why you needed the surgery if you don't want to, Toby. You could just say you needed bowel surgery for an obstruction. It's not a complete lie.'

'Yeah, I guess,' Toby said and turned his face away once more.

'What's that?' Poppy asked after Toby mumbled something else, his face still turned away from her.

Reluctantly he turned partway back and said, still softly so that Poppy had to lean in towards him to catch it. 'And what about my sex life? You know…will I be able to have…anal sex again?'

'Oh, yes,' Poppy said. 'There'll be a period to allow for healing of the rectal wall, but the surgeons will let you know.'

Toby's shoulders relaxed and he nodded at Poppy. She took that as a sign to leave the room and leave him with his thoughts.

'Hey, Lucy, what does this mean?' Poppy asked later, pointing at the code for the next patient in line on the waiting list.

Lucy, one of the young nurses, bent forwards over Poppy's shoulder to get a better look at the computer.

'Oh, that's code for DOA. You need to go around to the ambulance bay and certify the body and sign the forms.'

'Oh,' Poppy said, momentarily lost for words. 'Do I need to do anything on our system?'

'Yep, once you click on the patient and have been out, you come back and discharge them with a one-line note: DOA-certified.'

'OK, thanks,' Poppy replied, trying to keep her voice light. Like this was no big deal.

Like all other medical students, Poppy had seen cadavers before in Anatomy classes, but she had never seen a newly deceased patient. She'd never even seen family members that had died. *OK, this is just part of the job, just another skill to learn and master. It's marginally creepy, but shouldn't be blown out of proportion.*

Poppy cheerily greeted the undertakers.

'Hi, how's it going?' she said as she approached, going for casual nonchalance.

'You might want to wear a mask,' the older of the two quietly suggested.

'OK,' Poppy said. Maybe that's a requirement Lucy forgot to mention, she thought. At the same time she observed the two undertakers – if that was, indeed, what they were called. They moved slowly and silently, in a fluid motion, almost as if they were floating slightly off the ground. So quiet and unobtrusive in their dark suits, white shirts, and demure expressions. They were so perfect for the job, it felt to Poppy like they were actors in a TV show.

After handing Poppy one of the special duck-bill masks, the undertaker also handed her a pair of gloves and quietly informed her it was a 'double-bagger' who'd likely been left for a few weeks.

'OK,' Poppy said, uncertainly. *What's a 'double-bagger'?*

The undertaker brought her over to the rear of the white unlabelled van. He stretchered out the black body bag only fractionally and unzipped a tiny portion of the first bag and then the second, exposing only the head. He then stepped soundlessly back with his head bowed and his hands crossed at his waist. Poppy had been running her mantra through her mind: *check respiration, response to pain, pulse, and pupillary reaction to light.* Given the small opening, she went for response to pain first and reached inside the bag to pinch the skin over the sternum. *No response, check.* Then she felt for a carotid pulse. The skin felt waxy to touch and, oddly, it seemed to slip and move over the deeper tissues. But it wasn't until she opened one pair of eyelids to see maggots crawling where the eye should be that she realised she'd done more than enough.

She gasped audibly, hurriedly signed the proffered form, unable to meet the undertakers' eyes, and scurried back inside, her face blazing. In her anxiety to do all the right things and follow procedure, she'd failed to recognise that this was probably one of those times in life where it was OK not to. She could have trusted the undertakers, looked visually and signed the form. They had tried to warn her. In retrospect, she couldn't even tell if it had been a man or a woman.

When she got back to the flight deck, Paul was there. Poppy must have been ashen, because he put a hand on her shoulder, bent down to look in her downcast eyes and asked,

'Are you OK?'

She couldn't speak. Paul pulled up a chair, gently pushed her onto it and grabbed her a drink of water. He sat next to her and waited until she was ready to talk. The first thing she did was apologise.

'I'm sorry. I must look like an idiot. That was just a bit of a shock.'

'Was it the DOA?' Paul asked.

'Yes.'

'That's OK. Experiencing death for the first time can be very difficult. It's much easier in the abstract.'

'It's not that…' Then it all came rushing out. 'It's just that the undertakers tried to warn me, and they made me put on a duck-bill mask and gloves, and said something about a double-bagger, and a few weeks. And I didn't understand what they meant and then they unzipped both bags, only a tiny amount. I wanted to be thorough. But the skin was all bloated and waxy and moving, and when I opened the eyelids, it was just maggots.'

'Oh, Poppy, what a first time. I'm so sorry. I would've done it for you if I'd known.'

He rested his hand on her shoulder and gave it a squeeze. They stayed like that for a couple of minutes as the other staff buzzed around. Some asking if Poppy was OK, and Paul quietly responding he'd fill them in later.

Poppy wasn't really thinking anything, it was like her mind had transitioned into a void where no thoughts came or went. It was an empty space, like her brain had powered down to standby mode. She stared blankly before the sound of machines, staff, and patients finally penetrated. She took a deep breath, smelling that classic disinfectant smell that is synonymous with all hospitals and blinked a few times before resolving to get back to work.

'I'm OK now,' she reassured Paul as she stood up.

The rest of the shift was a blur – nothing particularly onerous – just a half cast for a broken leg and a young person with the flu. At the end of handover, Paul came up to her at the flight deck and said, 'Right, we're all going up the road for a drink. I think you need it.'

'OK,' Poppy happily agreed. She wasn't ready to go home alone just yet.

Chapter 5

They all trooped to the Marlborough Hotel, known as the Marly to locals. Their group included Paul, Stephanie (the junior Registrar who'd been on the acute side), two of the nurses – Graham and Lucy – and Harriet. Poppy was surprised that Harriet had come. She certainly didn't seem the most sociable of people. Once they'd all gathered their drinks and pulled a few tables together in the courtyard, Paul suggested a toast.

'To Poppy – for surviving a hairbrush up a bum and a double-bagger DOA complete with maggots, all in the one shift.'

Poppy felt herself blushing but also couldn't help laughing. There were some 'oohs' and laughter, and everyone, even Harriet said, 'To Poppy.'

They all took sips of their drinks, and then everyone wanted Poppy to recount the details. For the first time since the DOA, Poppy felt the tension in her shoulders ease a little and enjoyed the retelling.

'When I saw the maggots, I decided not to dirty my steth by checking for respiration. I'd done enough.' Poppy heard their laughter and saw the smiles on their faces and the rest of her inner tension slipped away. There was a bit of jovial banter, and a few crude jokes that non-medicos would not have appreciated, but it all helped ease Poppy's distress. She felt like a true member of the team for the first time. No longer the medical student, someone lesser, but a real doctor. One who had now seen and done things that most other people never would.

Some others shared their horror stories. Even Harriet came and sat next to Poppy at one point, her muscled upper arm leaning into Poppy's and the smell of beer on her breath, and told her a story of one of her worst intern memories.

'I'd been trying to get a catheter into an elderly patient with urinary retention, and he started getting an erection. I didn't know what to do, but I thought I should finish and get it in. But then he orgasmed. I hurriedly pulled out the catheter and raced out of his room.'

'Oh my God, Harriet, that's awful!'

'That's not the worst bit—'

'There's more?' Poppy asked. How could it be worse than that?

Harriet leaned further in toward Poppy, her voice low, in a conspiratorial manner, her frizzy hair tickling the edge of Poppy's face awkwardly.

'When I went and told my Registrar what had happened, he started laughing really loudly right at the nurses' station, drawing everyone's attention. Then he said, "Oh my God, someone actually got a boner looking at you?" and kept laughing.'

Harriet must have seen the look of horror and disbelief on Poppy's face as she sat back and said, 'Don't worry, everything gets easier over time,' and even gave her a brief smile before turning away to talk to Paul and Graham, her thin black Bonds hoodie over her scrub top all that Poppy could see.

Poppy's own experience paled in comparison to Harriet's. At least Paul had been supportive, rather than humiliating her in front of everyone else. Poppy realised how lucky she had been tonight.

'Hi, Mr Marks, I'm Dr Mason, can you tell me what has brought you into ED today?' Poppy asked her first patient of the evening on her next shift. It was her first shift in the acute section and she had the threat of assisting in a trauma hanging over her head. She wasn't sure that she was ready for a trauma or a resuscitation yet. And after her experiences last night, she now realised that absolutely anything could happen.

'I've got pain…in my chest,' he grimaced as he spoke, and Poppy noticed his olive skin had a grey hue to it and a sheen of sweat had formed over his salt and pepper brows.

'Have you ever had this happen before?'

'No…it feels like something's squashing my chest,' he puffed out, between laboured breaths.

'That sounds awful. If ten was the worst pain you could imagine, and zero was no pain, how high would you rate the pain?' Whilst Poppy was asking questions and listening to his answers, she was also letting her eyes rove over his body to pick up any additional clues that might help her diagnose his problem. He was overweight and still dressed in his work suit, his tie loosened and hanging low around his chest. More like a scarf than a tie, and his suit jacket lay crumpled on the chair beside the bed. His right hand was pushed against his left breast, like he was trying to push the pain out of his chest.

'Nine.'

'Does the pain move anywhere, or is it just where you're holding your chest?'

'Mainly here, but I can also feel it in my shoulder and…upper arm on that side,' he said pointing briefly to his left shoulder and arm.

'And you look like it is hard to breathe deeply?'

'Yes.'

'And have you vomited, or had a temperature, or any other symptoms?'

'No.'

Poppy suspected he was having a heart attack and so didn't labour the rest of the history and only did a cursory examination, then jogged out of his cubicle to find Stephanie, the Registrar on with her this evening.

'OK, this is where you find the chest pain and stroke protocols,' Stephanie said as she clicked on a tab on the computer screen. 'Come find me again, once the nurses have done the ECG, and put him on oxygen, that'll help.'

'Thanks, Stephanie.'

'No dramas,' she said, smiling as she turned and went off to see a patient of her own.

The ECG showed classic ST elevation of an acute heart attack. It was a textbook case.

'OK, now you can give him some aspirin and morphine as per the protocol and call whomever is on today for Cardiology.'

'Shouldn't I wait until the blood results are back?'

'No, they'll want to get him to the cath lab for angioplasty or stenting. They won't want to delay.'

'OK, thanks.'

First, Poppy went back to Mr Marks.

'So, Mr Marks, it looks like you are having a heart attack.'

'Really?' he said and Poppy saw the fear that suddenly struck him. 'Am I going to die?'

'No, Mr Marks, it's OK, we're going to give you some morphine for the pain, and also a tablet of aspirin to thin the blood. Then I'm going to call the Cardiology team. They might want to do a procedure to find which artery in the heart is blocked and unblock it.'

'OK. So, I'm not going to die?'

'We are going to take very good care of you, just try to breathe slowly and don't panic… Look, here's Graham with the medications now,' Poppy said as reassuringly as possible as Graham stepped into the cubicle with Mr Mark's medications and a cup of water. 'Once I've spoken with Cardiology, is there someone I can call for you?'

'Yeah, my sister.'

'Is she listed as your next of kin?'

'Yes.'

'OK, I'll do that,' Poppy said before leaving the cubicle again.

Poppy rang Joshua Hunter, the Cardiology Registrar on that evening.

'Hi, are you on for Cardiology tonight?' Poppy asked after introducing herself.

'Yes.'

'Great. OK, I've got a sixty-three-year-old man with acute onset chest pain over the last two hours with associated tachycardia, tachypnoea, and hypertension, and ST elevation in leads II, III, and aVF on his ECG.

'What's his troponin, coags and electrolytes show?'

'Uh…they're not back yet,' Poppy answered, her stomach dropping to the floor.

'Then why are you ringing me now?'

Poppy felt heat rise up her neck, into her face, and prickles of sweat on her scalp.

'I-I thought he might be a candidate for angioplasty and that you'd want the heads up sooner rather than later,' she said as confidently as she could muster, whilst her heart pounded and she wondered if she too might have a heart attack.

'Do you know what the contraindications to angioplasty are?' said with utter disdain.

'Um… No?'

'Well, someone with significant renal failure might not be a suitable candidate for starters. So, without the complete work-up, we might be calling in a lot of staff for no reason.'

'Oh, OK,' Poppy said defeatedly.

'Just text me the ECG and call me as soon as the bloods are back.'

'OK… I will… I'm sorry,' Poppy stammered, but Joshua had already hung up. Poppy felt like someone had slapped her and could almost imagine the stinging pain across her cheeks and the loud ringing in her ears. *Fuck…what an idiot!*

'What the fuck?' Stephanie said after Poppy had filled her in. 'He is such an arse. You can't win with him, and some of the others. They give us a hard time if we ring too soon, but then they give us a hard time if we wait for the results. It's such crap, and all about their egos!' she said heatedly.

I guess that's why Will told me they refer to ED as 'the snake pit'. I'll just have to be more thorough next time.

As Poppy was putting the phone down from calling Mr Mark's sister, she heard Graham taking an incoming trauma call on the 'bat phone'. It was a black phone attached to the wall at the edge of the flight deck with a computer on a shelf next to it and a red light on top that flashed when it was ringing. Patrick (the head of ED, and the consultant on that shift) stood next to him to listen and watch as he typed the summary onto the expected screen. Stephanie and Lucy also gravitated over. After he hung up, Graham gave them the summary: 'Seventeen-year-old male fell from balcony whilst intoxicated. Suspected spinal injury and compound fracture of right leg. Tachycardia en route, conscious throughout.' Poppy had stayed seated but had her eyes glued to Patrick and Graham, her heart rate rising and her brain freaking out. *Will I have to help out? What if I don't know what to do?*

'Graham, get the room ready. Stephanie and Poppy, follow me. Lucy, call the trauma team, then join us in Resus one,' Patrick issued their instructions. *Oh, fuck…*

Poppy followed Patrick and Stephanie and pulled on a disposable gown, gloves, and safety glasses, just as the others had, her hands shaking in the process. She really didn't want to embarrass herself in front of the others, but she had no clue what to do.

'OK, Poppy, have you ever assisted in a resus or trauma before?' Patrick asked.

Did he just read my mind?

'No.'

'That's OK. When they come in and we get the patient on the bed, there will be a lot of noise and movement. Everyone has set jobs and I will be in charge of the room. I want you to put in a large bore IV cannula and take off twenty mills of blood and then Graham will hang a bag of IV fluids to run quickly. You will pass the bloods to Lucy and she'll send them off. She'll be our runner and document as we go. OK?'

'OK,' Poppy said, then went to gather all the equipment she would need in a kidney dish.

What if I can't get the cannula in? What if I stab myself with the needle once I get the bloods off? What if… By the time she had her equipment and turned back around to face the room, Patrick and Stephanie had left, presumably to go and meet the ambulance.

Poppy could feel the sweat in her hands under her gloves and the adrenaline surging, blood pounding in her ears, heart racing, her breaths fast and shallow, and her brain firing rapid thoughts. Instead of these being useful thoughts, she continued to spiral into all the ways she could fuck-up and embarrass herself. She waited at the edge of the large Resus room, the kidney dish shaking in her hands as her eyes kept darting toward the opening, waiting for the ambulance team to arrive. It was a few minutes of silence and nervous energy until Poppy heard them bursting through the trolley bay and security doors, led by Patrick and Stephanie.

As the trolley was wheeled in next to the Resus bed, Poppy heard Lucy at the back say to what she presumed was the boy's parents, 'Why don't you come with me,' as she ushered them out of the room and down the corridor to the quiet room. Poppy briefly observed them as they left – the mum was crying quietly, wringing her hands so much that the tissue held within them looked shredded, and the dad was tight-lipped and clearly tense, shoulders and gait stiff. Both were dressed smartly as if they had just come from some event. The dad put his arm around his wife's shoulders as they disappeared out of her sight.

'All hands for safety log roll,' Patrick said and Poppy hurriedly put her kidney dish of supplies onto the side shelf and rushed to her spot on the side of the bed. She knotted her hands into the side of the plastic sheet under the patient, just as she saw Stephanie do beside her, leaning over the stationary bed to the paramedics' trolley beyond.

'One…two…three,' Patrick said and on three Poppy pulled like Stephanie and the rest of them did, slowly sliding the patient from the trolley onto the middle of the bed, Patrick holding the head stable throughout the transfer. Poppy briefly locked onto the patient's eyes during the transfer and saw a young, tanned, good-looking boy with lines of fear and pain adding years to his age. There was dark-brown dried blood discolouring his blonde hair and etching a course down his face. At least what she could briefly see of his face underneath the stiff, hard collar.

'Oww,' the patient groaned in pain.

'It's OK,' Patrick said quietly to the patient, 'that's the worst of it. Now we're going to run through a quick handover then a trauma assessment. I'll keep telling you what we are doing, OK?'

Poppy thought she heard him murmur an 'OK'.

Should I start trying to get the cannula in, or wait for Patrick to tell me?

Poppy was paralysed with indecision and stood there doing nothing, the sounds around her becoming a sea of noise, no one word distinguishable. She saw one of the paramedic's mouths moving and Patrick's head nodding and occasionally moving too. *They* must *be handing over.* Poppy noticed Stephanie was down looking at his leg. *Should I ask Stephanie?* Then she felt a nudge in her side and looked up to see Graham, who pointed at the kidney dish, flaccidly held in her hand.

'Should I?' Poppy asked.

'Yes,' Graham answered.

Relief passed over Poppy as she finally felt free to move and began the process of placing a tourniquet around the teenager's arm, tightening it, and then started searching for the large vein in the antecubital fossa to insert the cannula into. So focused was she on her immediate task that the noises and movements around her remained blurry and indistinct. *Yes!* Poppy mentally fist-bumped herself as the fourteen-gauge needle slid in with ease and her twenty-millimetre syringe filled easily with dark-plum blood. *The colour of a good South Australian Shiraz, nice and healthy.* She twisted off the syringe, then inserted another and flushed saline to clear the cannula.

'Here,' Graham said at her elbow, as he passed her the giving end of the fluids to connect.

'Thanks,' Poppy said once she'd finished, turned and stood.

There were now more people in the room and hovering at the edge, Poppy noticed as her gaze expanded to take in the whole room once more. But Poppy hadn't finished her task, so she took her kidney dish over to the shelf at the side and attached a needle to the syringe so she could divide the blood into the various blood tubes to be sent to the lab urgently.

'Lucy, do you have stickers?' she asked as she brought the tubes over to be labelled, once she'd discarded her sharps.

'Here,' she replied, handing over the page of identification stickers and a specimen bag.

'OK,' Poppy said, handing back the bag once the tubes were labelled. Lucy turned quickly and jumped back up to flight deck to send the bloods up the vacuum tube directly to the lab.

Poppy turned back to the room and her hearing returned to full volume now that she had completed the task she was assigned. She felt a sense of pride as she looked at the others, but no one was looking at her. *Should I tell Patrick I'm finished?*

She noticed one of the new people in pale-blue scrubs was talking to Patrick at the head of the bed.

'Do you want a central line?' Poppy heard this tall Asian man with black-framed glasses under his safety goggles ask Patrick. *He must be from Anaesthetics.*

Another guy in pale-blue scrubs with a white patient gown over the top was assessing the broken leg, his red curly hair sticking up as he bent down. So, he was either from Orthopaedics or Trauma Surgery. And there was a tiny dark-skinned woman in pants and button-down shirt, observing from the bottom of the bed. *ICU?*

'Poppy, can you do a blood gas?' Patrick asked.

'OK,' Poppy replied, glad to still be a part of the team. She quickly went back to the trolley to grab what she needed, her hands beginning to shake again. Blood gases were not a strength but she wanted to be useful, so didn't tell Patrick she couldn't do it.

'Damn,' she said quietly when no blood filled the syringe.

'Here,' Stephanie said, coming up behind her, 'let's see; if we reposition the needle, we might still salvage this.' She placed her hand over Poppy's and gently repositioned the needle, and suddenly blood filled the syringe. 'There you go,' Stephanie added as Poppy smiled.

'OK, ready for X-ray,' Patrick said, and they all stepped outside the Resus bay and let the Radiographers get to work with the mobile X-ray unit that they wheeled into the Resus room. 'You can go now, Poppy,' Patrick dismissed her.

Poppy felt the sting of rejection, but un-gloved and gowned and headed back to the flight deck. *Was I not being helpful enough? Should I have asked for another task?*

She sighed and then went to check the bloods on the heart attack guy and found these confirmed her suspicions with a characteristic troponin rise. She thought she'd better check to see how he was before she called Joshua back because she didn't want to get belittled again. But when she got to his bed, she found the curtains drawn and someone was in there with him. She pulled back the curtain to find a good-looking guy in dark dress pants, and a white button-down shirt, open at the neck. He was gently tanned with short, mid-brown hair, blue eyes, and a small cleft in his chin. His shirt fitted him snugly, outlining his strong biceps. Poppy realised this must be Joshua Hunter and felt a rush in her chest. Was it attraction or fear? She wasn't sure.

He was bent over the patient, listening to his chest through his stethoscope. When he finished, he looked over his shoulder, noticing Poppy for the first time.

'OK. So, your ECG and blood tests confirm you've had a heart attack. We will get you up to the cardiac catheter lab tonight to identify where the blockage occurred and hopefully unblock it with either a balloon or a small stent like a tiny mesh pipe,' Joshua explained to the patient.

He briefly outlined the procedure and inherent risks and then had the patient sign a consent form.

'OK, it won't be long – we'll get you up there in the next half hour and it should be over within about an hour or so,' Joshua said confidently.

He then wordlessly ushered Poppy out in front of him.

When they got back to the flight deck, he turned on her and, with barely suppressed fury, seethed, 'You were supposed to call me as soon as the bloods were through.'

'I'm sorry, I've been in a trauma and was only just now released. I checked the bloods immediately and was just going to check the patient's condition before I rang you back,' Poppy replied, her legs turning to jelly in the face of his cold fury.

'You should have asked one of the nurses or other doctors to check whilst you were in the trauma. Time is muscle death, and you could have compromised this patient's outcome.'

By now, Poppy was sweating and blushing up to her eyeballs. 'I'm sorry, it's only my first week. I wasn't aware I should do that. I'll make sure I do that next time,' her voice shaking as much as her hands.

'Next time won't help this patient.'

With that, Joshua sat down, picked up the phone and called the cath lab staff to complete the arrangements.

Poppy stood still, rooted to the spot directly behind Joshua. It took a couple of beats for her to gather herself before she finally turned away.

On shaky legs, she found Lucy. 'Hey, you don't need me right now, do you?' she asked with a false smile.

'No, all good. Resus is stable.'

'OK, I might just take a break. I'll be in the tearoom if anyone needs me.'

'Sure, I'll let Steph know.'

'Thanks.'

Licking her wounds in the spartan staff tearoom, Poppy ruminated over her interactions with Joshua and was annoyed with herself on several levels. Partly for feeling like she'd done the wrong thing not once, but twice, but also for finding him so attractive despite him being so rude to her! She ate her soup dinner at the scarred round table in the centre of the room with a deep furrow of her brow and blood pressure that showed no sign of reducing. Her thoughts alternating between single words of *bastard* and *fucking idiot*. She stayed in the tearoom long enough to be sure that Joshua would have left and added *coward* to her list of self-flagellation.

When Poppy came back in, Lucy was at flight deck so she asked about the boy's condition.

'He's stable. We're just waiting for them to take him up to theatre to fix his leg and his spinal injuries.'

'But they don't think he's paralysed?'

'It doesn't sound like it. They told the parents they think he'll walk again, and there's no sign of spinal cord injury at this point.'

What a relief!

'Do you know what happened?'

'I was with the parents when the police came to interview them—'

'The police?' Poppy interrupted, not expecting this detail.

'Yeah. Apparently, he and his mates were getting pissed on their balcony. The parents were out. And it sounds like the friends dared him to jump into the pool from the balcony. They must have seen it in a movie or something. But he missed the pool and landed on the sandstone tiles lining the edge.'

'Oh my God, how stupid.'

'I know, right?'

'I know his parents will be glad right now that he's not going to end up in a wheelchair, but at some point, they're also going to be really angry, don't you think?'

'I think my parents would throttle me,' Lucy said.

After handover, Poppy sought Stephanie out and thanked her for helping with the blood gas.

'No sweat,' Stephanie said. 'They can be tricky. The way I try to do it is to gently feel the pulse with both my index and middle finger, leaving a small space between them, and inserting the needle directly into the space.'

'Thanks, I'll try that next time.'

'Hey, I saw that Registrar giving you a hard time. Are you OK?'

'Oh…yeah… I feel a bit crap about it, but I'll be OK.'

'Hey, why don't we go for one quick drink?'

'Are you sure?' Poppy asked, barely able to hide her eagerness.

'Yeah, come on, I'm always up for a drink.'

When they were grabbing their bags from their lockers, Seb came over and asked, 'Are we going to the Marly?' to Poppy, Lucy, and Graham.

'Hell, yes,' was Lucy's enthusiastic reply.

Poppy laughed and Steph just rolled her eyes.

Seb had been on subbies so Poppy hadn't seen him much of the shift. They didn't stay as long as the previous night, but they spent an hour having a quick drink or two and chatting about the shift. Poppy thought Stephanie was nice. She was probably only a few years older than herself, average height with dark-brown hair, and big brown eyes. Poppy thought she was very attractive. She was from the UK and had worked as an SHO, or Senior House Officer, equivalent to our Senior Resident Medical Officer, before moving to Australia last year. This was her first year as a Registrar. She'd managed to get permanent residency and had joined the Emergency specialty training programme, and was trying to study for her first lot of exams on her days off.

'Look, don't beat yourself up too much,' Stephanie consoled her when they were discussing Joshua Hunter again. 'I've had a few run-ins with him, too, he's a real prick.' Poppy thought she almost sounded like an Aussie, the way she called him a prick.

'But he's so hot,' Poppy said in response.

'I know, right?' Stephanie replied.

They both sighed loudly into their drinks, then Stephanie said, 'Maybe that's why he's so arrogant?'

Seb chimed in with, 'It's not just that he's hunky that makes him arrogant, it's also that he's a complete know-it-all.'

Clearly, Seb had been listening in.

'So, you think he's hot too?' Poppy asked.

'He's scrumptious. But he knows it and that's a turnoff for me,' Seb said.

'So, what's a turn on for you?' Poppy asked.

'My husband. Hot but humble, and more importantly, a supportive partner and father.'

There were simultaneous 'Aww's' from Poppy, Lucy, and Stephanie.

'How many kids do you guys have?' asked Poppy.

'Just one, Brendan, he's four.'

'What about you, Lucy? Do you have kids or a partner?' Poppy asked, trying to complete her circle of knowledge, already knowing Graham's circumstances and Stephanie's (single, no kids).

'No, hopelessly single over here,' she replied.

Lucy was maybe a few years younger than Poppy and was small, cute, and had a brown shaggy bob.

'Me too,' replied Poppy. 'Maybe we should go out sometime?' she suggested, looking between Lucy and Stephanie, who were sitting on either side of her at their round high table on the upper deck.

'I'm in,' said Lucy.

'Me too,' said Stephanie.

'Alright, well, let's look at our rosters and find a good time,' Poppy instigated.

They pulled out their smartphones and put their heads together. When they'd locked in a date, they started chatting about locations and strategies, and laughing over pick-up lines they'd been subjected to. Seb and Graham broke up their girly session by announcing they were leaving, and Poppy went too so she could walk home with Graham who only lived a few streets away from her.

When she got home, she tiptoed through to her bedroom to put down her bag and keys. Sitting on the edge of her bed to remove her shoes, she thought about how she'd already felt welcome by most of the ED staff, and how that had made the transition a little easier. But she missed Gemma and Lucas. Being on evenings meant she hadn't seen them in days. They were her family, and they relied on each other. They'd been a trio since their first year at uni, she and Gemma moving in together six months into the year, and Lucas initially dating Gemma, then living with them soon after.

She longed to know how they were going in their terms so far, and wanted to tell them all about what she was experiencing. Tiptoeing back to the kitchen in her bralette and boxers to get a drink of water, Poppy noticed the note on the kitchen bench. It was from Gemma:

Hi P,

I'm on an overtime shift tomorrow, so we can walk home together. Meet out the front?

(love heart) G

Poppy felt a twinge in her chest. She quickly squiggled a response on the note. It would be so lovely to see and catch up with Gemma. She couldn't wait. She wondered if either she or Lucas had had a run-in with Joshua Hunter? And then she found herself reliving the dressing down he'd given her, but also how his biceps had strained under his shirt when he was bending over the patient. She remembered the fullness of his lips and the spicy scent of his aftershave as he moved past her. *Uggh…*she thought-slapped herself. *Do not get a crush on the haughty guy!*

Knowing she was going to struggle to sleep, she turned her meditation app to a sleep story, turned off her light, and listened to the soothing sound of Eva Green telling her a story about a baby bear. She was asleep before halfway through.

Poppy woke up feeling drained. The night was muggy again, and she had slept fitfully, culminating in a sex dream about Joshua Hunter, leaving her feeling horny and frustrated. She got up and took a long shower and ate breakfast. This would be Gemma's first overtime shift; the gruelling fifteen-hour shift where they worked their standard hours, then stayed on in the evening with a handful of others covering a few wards each until the night shift started. Poppy felt nervous for her. At least Poppy knew she had a few days off after this shift and she, Stephanie, and Lucy were going out the following night. They hadn't quite decided what they were doing yet, but it was likely to be fun and frivolous and a good way to celebrate the end of her first week.

Poppy walked into work that evening, a coffee in hand, and dragging her feet somewhat. She was dog-tired. The ongoing humidity didn't help, and she could feel her hair frizzing at the edges on the ten-minute walk.

'Hi,' she said as brightly to Paul as she could muster, taking the last sip of her coffee before placing it in the bin near the lockers.

'Afternoon,' Paul said, jockeying on his toes, clearly not as affected by the heat as she was. 'I think we're on in acute together tonight.'

'OK, great,' said Poppy as Paul headed in and she shoved her bag into her locker and pinned the key inside her pants pocket.

The first few cases of the evening were relatively straightforward. Another chest pain patient that turned out to be a panic attack rather than something more serious, and an elderly lady with a transient ischaemic attack, or TIA, for which there was a clear protocol and a friendly Neurology Registrar on the phone to accept the admission. After those first two cases, things were quiet, and Poppy took the opportunity to take her break and went to eat in the tearoom. She watched part of a *Veronica Mars* episode on her phone, sipping her Coke No Sugar on the little balcony that overlooked the ambulance bay and the 7-Eleven on the corner. It was still humid with no breeze in sight, and the buzzing of cicadas and local street noise almost overwhelmed her ability to hear her show even with her noise cancelling earphones. After about twenty minutes, she gave up trying, tidied up, and headed back in.

She was walking up to the flight deck when she felt a heightened awareness – her scalp tingled, and her arms shivered as all her hair stood on end. It was also eerily quiet, and no one was at flight deck. A couple of nurses were rushing toward Resus two. Poppy walked quickly over to see what was happening with a tremble of anticipation. She found the room already packed: Patrick, Paul, Graham, and two other nurses, as well as Isabella (a Resident) were all in there working on a heavily pregnant woman. Poppy hung at the fringe, taking in the scene. Her shoulders tensed and a knot formed in her chest. It did not look good. The woman was not moving. Her legs were splayed and there was blood soaked through her clothing turning it a rusty brown colour, running down her legs in tree-like branches, and pooling on the white bed linen. And the metallic smell of blood tainted the air.

Paul noticed her and said, 'Poppy, call O & G. Tell them it's a presumed placental abruption in an estimated twenty-six-week gestation patient.

Unconscious, massive blood loss, hypotensive, foetal distress, need urgent assistance. Then page Anaesthetics with the same.'

'Will do,' Poppy said, feeling her heart rate rising with the surge of adrenaline, but glad to be given a task she knew she could accomplish.

She made the calls as quickly as she could, her hands shaking with every movement and her voice high-pitched. She feared what she might see when she returned to the Resus bay. Patrick had intubated the patient and was hand-bagging with oxygen. Paul had his hand inside the poor woman's vagina and was pulling out large blood clots. Poppy felt nauseated seeing the amount of blood that was sliding from Paul's hands onto the floor, and the metallic smell irritated her nose, which immediately began to run. She turned toward the beeping CTG machine announcing the sluggish trace indicating the baby's heartbeat was too slow. The O & G Registrar who was short with dark, curly hair still in her theatre cap arrived, and the Anaesthetics Registrar was the same tall Asian guy with the attractive black glasses. It was also the same slight ICU Registrar, Sangeetha, from the previous night, not far behind them. All but Sangeetha were in scrubs and had pinched expressions conveying the stress they too felt. Sangeetha was in civvies, like the previous night, but Poppy noticed her slight hands shake as she put on gloves.

Gemma came on the heels of the O & G Registrar and exchanged a worried look with Poppy when she walked into the room. The O & G Registrar looked at the CTG trace whilst Paul and Patrick gave the history. Poppy, still standing on the periphery, listened intently to this. The patient's cervix was not particularly dilated, and the CTG did not show consistent abdominal contractions, but the baby's heartbeat had slowed dangerously. Her membranes were intact, but the blood was pouring out. Her blood pressure was low and her heart rate very elevated. They were already transfusing their third bag of blood. The O & G Registrar then took over from Paul and did an internal exam, confirming Paul's findings. By this point, Andrew, the Anaesthetics Registrar, had put in a central line.

The monitor started alarming and Poppy watched as Patrick put his fingers to the lady's neck trying to feel for a carotid pulse.

'No pulse. Paul, start chest compressions,' Patrick said.

Poppy didn't know what to do: should she remind them she was there, should she step in closer? Paul started chest compressions, and Graham hooked up the defibrillator pads around Paul. Sangeetha called instructions to Andrew of drugs to deliver via the central line from her position near the base of the bed, to the side of the O & G Reg. Poppy was a little awestruck that they all automatically did these things without drama or fuss, and with complete confidence. She was scared shitless, but hopeful that one day she would be confident and brave like them as well.

'We need to get the baby out otherwise they are both going to die,' the O & G Registrar said to Paul and Patrick, her voice firm but tight.

'OK,' Patrick said as the O & G Registrar said, 'prep for an emergency C-section,' and the tension in the room ratcheted up even higher.

Sangeetha moved to the top end of the patient with Andrew, Graham, and Paul, who was still doing compressions, sweat beading on his forehead and the tip of his nose. At the bottom end, Patrick, Gemma, and her Registrar rapidly cleaned their hands and donned sterile gloves and gowns.

'Poppy, Isabella, you two clean the abdomen for them,' Patrick instructed.

Poppy nodded, but wasn't sure what exactly they should do, so she followed Isabella's lead. A gowned nurse passed first Isabella, and then Poppy, a kidney dish filled with what Poppy presumed was chlorhexidine, as well as forceps with sponges attached. Isabella stood on one side and elbowed Poppy toward the other side of the abdomen. Poppy watched as Isabella dunked her sponge in the chlorhexidine, then started from the middle, making increasingly larger circles out toward the edge of the exposed belly.

When she'd finished, she said to Poppy rather brusquely, 'now you do the same.'

Poppy concentrated on her shaking hands holding the kidney dish. She spilled a bit of the chlorhexidine over the edge but retained most of it and heavily soaked the sponge before slopping it onto the patient's distended abdomen roughly in the middle. She copied Isabella's action of small, then larger circles as she went from the centre to the edges and then stood up, lifting her eyes from the belly back to where Isabella had been standing. But she had gone. Now the gowned nurse was in her place holding a green sterile drape ready to place it on the abdomen.

'OK, stand back,' she said to Poppy, who hastily backed away, sloshing more chlorhexidine as she went and slipping slightly. Her face and neck burned with a rising blush, and she felt all eyes were on her, critiquing her performance, but when she looked around, she saw everyone was still busy and preoccupied with their own tasks. No one was looking at her.

Patrick called out, 'Someone page Neonatal Intensive Care and get them here ASAP,' as the O & G Reg prepared to make the first incision and Gemma faced her on the other side of the patient's body, her face white and a picture of abject distress.

'On it,' Graham called out as he raced out of the room.

Paul was still doing compressions, sweat now rolling off his face. Once she had put down the kidney dish, Paul said, 'Poppy, swap in for me.'

'OK,' Poppy said, as an uptick of fear raced through her and her whole body prickled and tingled with anticipation.

She had never felt this way before. Everything felt really slow and super-fast all at once. Poppy grabbed a stool to stand on as she made her way over to Paul so she could reach the chest adequately. She climbed up and felt Paul's presence watching over her shoulder as she positioned the heel of one palm on top of the other hand over the mid-point of the chest. Locking her elbows straight, she used her weight to push down and release over and over again.

It was hard work and as Poppy focused only on what she was doing, the others faded into the surrounding background. She was instantly hot and sweating more, her armpits and groin no longer just moist but wet, and her nose prickled with sweat. She desperately wanted to wipe her forehead, particularly to swipe away the irritating hair that kept being breathed into her mouth, and mop her nose, but all she could do was push down, release, push down, release.

'OK, we've got a shockable rhythm, charge to two hundred,' Poppy heard Sangeetha call out loudly and clearly. She raised her head so she could see Sangeetha, who was now up at the head of the patient, close to Poppy.

'I need to get this baby out first,' the O & G Registrar countered, and Poppy's head swung down to the belly, and the opening that was not quite through the uterus yet. Poppy kept pushing and releasing, but had her head up, watching Gemma who was opposite her. Her head was down, focusing on assisting her Registrar and she saw the scowl between her brows in concentration, and the steadiness of her hands, holding the small retractors.

So Poppy continued her compressions while they opened the uterus and the amniotic fluid burst out like a water balloon as it smashed into the ground. The baby was out within about four minutes and passed off immediately to the Neonatologist. As it swam passed her vision, Poppy saw how small and grey it was. It was not robust like the other babies she'd seen delivered by C-section.

'OK, stand clear,' Sangeetha called as soon as the baby was out, and the cord had been clamped and cut. Poppy stepped off the stool, Paul's proffered hand assisting her, so she didn't slip on the floor, and stood back, watching as Sangeetha kept gazing around to make sure everyone had stopped touching the patient.

'All clear, all clear…delivering shock,' was her next instruction and Poppy heard the electronic sound of the shock being delivered.

Poppy watched as the woman's body arched upward, then slumped back onto the bed, blood still oozing from her abdomen and colouring the green drape between her legs. She felt an almost visceral reaction to this sight, almost like she felt the massive electrical surge in her own body.

'Continue compressions,' Sangeetha called out, and Paul stepped back in. Poppy was glad of the break. It was exhausting. Poppy watched as Sangeetha continued to watch the monitor to see if the rhythm changed. She then turned her head back to the team on the abdomen who were looking for the bleeding source and removing the placenta. As she watched, she saw pads soaked with blood being removed from the gaping belly and being thrown to the ground, over and over. It was harrowing.

'Bag five,' Graham called out, as he hung another bag of blood in the rapid infuser and removed the empty one.

'OK, we need to shock again,' came Sangeetha's call. 'Everybody stop, and stand back. Charge to three hundred.'

Poppy was hoping and praying that this one would work, that this would fix things. The patient's body arched and slumped again, Poppy standing there watching and feeling again that visceral pull.

'One milligram adrenaline, please, Andrew,' Sangeetha called to Andrew.

'Hold compressions.'

Gemma and her Registrar returned to the uterus and the blood which was not stopping.

'OK, I need to perform a hysterectomy,' the O & G Reg called out.

'What do you need?' Patrick asked.

'I'm going to resect above the cervix. Gemma, you take over diathermy. Patrick, can you retract?'

'Sure,' he said, taking up a position beside Gemma as instruments were passed between hands.

Jesus, this is insane! Poppy felt her own blood pressure drop as her head swam and tingles broke out all over her scalp. It was the scariest thing she had ever witnessed. *I wonder if there's a partner, and if he's here yet? Maybe in the quiet room? No one would have had time to fill him in yet into how serious this is, let alone about the emergency hysterectomy.*

'OK, resume compressions please,' Sangeetha directed at Paul. 'We're going to need to shock again, we're still in VF…charge to three hundred.'

Paul went back to CPR, Andrew was hand-bagging with oxygen, and Sangeetha was waiting for the defibrillator to charge. Again, they tried another shock. But again, there was no change. After another ten minutes, the VF had ceased and now the monitor showed asystole. They continued CPR whilst additional drugs were delivered, including atropine, but no output could be recorded. Despite exhausting all medical options, replacing her entire blood volume and more, and performing a hysterectomy in a desperate attempt to stop the bleeding, they had not been successful.

'OK, hold compressions,' Sangeetha said, and watched the monitor as the now flat line spread across the screen. She did not call time of death immediately, but the silence that followed allowed the rest of them to come to the realisation that they had failed, and there was nothing more they could do. One by one they stopped and stepped back from the bed and this devastated body: open, raw and bloody. When all had stopped, Sangeetha quietly called time of death. All the steam of the arrest blown out like a puff of smoke, reducing her to the tiny mouse-like woman she was. At that moment of despair, they all turned, almost as one, with hope toward the baby and the paediatric team whom they had all but forgotten in their battle to save the lady in front of them. Poppy looked to the baby warmer and saw the final stages of the resuscitation they had simultaneously been performing on the baby.

The Neonatologist was hand-bagging with oxygen as the Registrar delivered tiny single finger compressions, and drugs were delivered via the umbilical vein. Andrew went to give help while the rest of the group looked on, Poppy silently crying. The baby was grey, and so tiny. It felt painful to watch the resuscitation to that tiny body. There was no silver lining. The baby was pronounced dead a few minutes later, and Poppy let out a low sob. Paul engulfed her in a hug.

When she pulled herself free, she took in the room. All of them standing dumbstruck, either alone or in the arms of another. Equipment everywhere, and so much blood: the floor was streaked and slippery and they were all covered in it. Poppy didn't know what to do next. How do you move forward from this? How do you even put one foot in front of the other? Poppy looked to Patrick, whose head was bowed and whose gloved hands were clasped in front, as if in prayer. He looked up and their eyes met, the despair in his matching hers.

He took charge of the room again.

'This is a devastating event, and one that I'm sure will scar each of us. But I thank each of you for your effort to save these patients. Each of you did everything you could for this woman and her baby. Thank you all… Now I will inform the next of kin. Graham, you and the nurses please prepare the two bodies for the coroner.' He then stripped out of his gown and gloves and left the Resus bay.

They all numbly took their gowns and gloves off, Poppy throwing hers into the overflowing bin and headed from the room. She wiped her bloody shoes on the blueys that Graham put down, and then felt nausea rise up her chest. She raced outside to vomit. Gemma and Paul joined her quietly and once her stomach was empty, she and Gemma hugged. It was like they were holding each other up after a while. Poppy felt Paul hovering in the periphery and didn't notice when he headed back into ED. When they were ready, Gemma and Poppy wiped away each other's tears and looked at each other. There was nothing to say.

Chapter 6

'Gemma, we've got to get back to the labour ward,' her Registrar said, finding them near the ambulance bay.

'OK, I'm right behind you.'

As her Registrar disappeared back through the ambulance bay doors, Gemma tucked a piece of Poppy's hair back behind her ear and said, 'I'll see you at eleven,' before squeezing her shoulders and turning away.

'Head up, young person,' Poppy called out to her before she disappeared through the glass doors. Gemma turned back, a faint twitch of a smile at the corner of her lips.

It was a comforting phrase they used with each other, originating from an old Jennifer Aniston movie, *The Object of my Affection* they had watched during a 1990s film festival at uni. Poppy hoped it helped Gemma now. How hard it would be for her to go now to another labouring mother and put the last hour to the back of her mind.

Pull it together, Poppy, she told herself. She forced herself to stand up tall, shoulders back, chin raised and once more went into the breach.

The mood at the flight deck was sombre. No one was doing anything quickly. They were all taking time, slowing down, watching the clock tick closer to handover. Poppy had no active patients, so she took the next cab off the rank, her hands still shaking as she used the mouse to capture the patient on the computer. It was an elderly man from a nursing home with a history of mild dementia but acute confusion, agitation, and aggression.

It was time to get back into the present and stop thinking about the last hour.

'Mr Jackson, I'm Dr Mason,' Poppy said as she entered his cubicle, pulling the curtains around to give privacy.

'I need to pick up Cynthia,' Mr Jackson said as he got off the bed, his gown open at the back, his bare, sagging butt cheeks a surprising sight.

'Who's Cynthia?' Poppy asked, holding his gown closed.

'Don't be silly, Joan, you know Cynthia's our daughter. I need to get her from school.'

'Oh,' Poppy said, realising that he must be mistaking her for his wife and he must be back about forty or more years ago in his mind.

'That's OK, Mr Jackson, we've got someone else to pick up Cynthia today. You don't need to worry about that.'

'No,' he said, pushing Poppy out of the way to escape the cubicle, 'I've got to get her, she'll be scared.'

Graham came towards them, 'Need a hand, Poppy?'

'Yeah, thanks.'

'It's OK, why don't we just pop back in here so we can help you,' Graham said, gently steering Mr Jackson back to his bed. 'Why don't I help you get on the bed and tuck you in, while Dr Mason has a quick look at you, OK?'

Mr Jackson grumbled in reply, but didn't resist Graham.

Whilst Graham got him onto the bed and took his obs again, Poppy read the ambulance report. The nursing home had reported that he had become increasingly agitated over the previous twenty-four hours and had developed a temperature. Poppy suspected he had some infective process going on.

'Graham, can you help me while I listen to his chest?'

'Sure, Poppy. OK, Mr Jackson, let's sit you forward now.'

Poppy listened, but his chest was clear and he wasn't short of breath. He also wasn't coughing. While she had his back exposed, she made sure there was no bed sore or visible abscess on his back. *Maybe a urinary tract infection?*

As soon as Graham rested him back on the pillows, he was pushing them away again, 'I need to go,' he said, trying again to get off the bed.

'It's OK,' Poppy said as Graham tried to keep him on the bed, 'we're just trying to help, Mr Jackson, I think you've got an infection.'

'Joan, let me be,' he said to Poppy, pushing her away again, although more gently this time.

'OK, but I'm going to need to take some blood, Mr Jackson, I'm just going to get some equipment, and Graham is going to stay with you,' Poppy said as Graham nodded at her.

On her way back to the bed, she roped in Lucy to help as well. She figured it would need two people to hold him still if she was going to have any chance at getting bloods off and getting a cannula in.

'Mr Jackson, I've got to put a needle in your arm and draw off some bloods now, so we can work out what is wrong with you, OK?'

'No!' Mr Jackson shouted, 'no!'

'It's OK, Mr Jackson, it won't hurt very much,' Poppy tried to reassure him as he became more agitated.

'I don't want to!' he shouted, and Poppy was suddenly self-conscious. Everyone in the department must be able to hear him. *I hope they don't think I'm hurting him.*

'It's OK, Poppy, we will hold him still while you get the bloods.'

Poppy nodded uncertainly. She didn't like the idea of holding him down while he shouted. It felt like they were assaulting him. But equally, she knew he was sick and he needed this done quickly so they could help him. She rationalised it as the best of a bad situation and got herself ready.

Poppy nodded at Lucy and Graham and they held tight as Poppy said, 'OK, sting now, Mr Jackson.'

He tried to move his hand and arm, but Graham was very strong and held him still enough for her to jab the needle in and draw off some blood. After she taped in the cannula, Graham said he'd bandage it in a flipper style with a curved board, like a shin guard, like they do for kids. Hopefully then he'd be less inclined to damage it or pull it out.

'We're going to need a urine sample, too,' Poppy said to Graham.

'Yep, I'll take him,' Graham offered, and Lucy left.

'OK, Mr Jackson, Graham's going to help you to the toilet now.' And she gave Graham a smile of thanks as she left to send off the bloods and order a chest X-ray.

It looked like her guess of urinary tract infection was right with a raised white cell count, and raised protein and leukocytes on urinalysis, and the Geriatrics Registrar accepted the admission without fuss. While Poppy was typing her notes, Mr Jackson came wandering out of his cubicle.

'Joan… Joan, we need to get Cynthia,' he said coming toward her at the flight deck, his sparse white hair standing out on end, his gown swimming on his thin frail frame.

Poppy hopped down. 'It's OK, Mr Jackson, Cynthia is OK. I got her earlier.'

'Oh, did you?' He sounded sceptical.

'Yes, I got her and she's in bed now. So, let's get you back to bed too.' And she took his hand and led him back to his cubicle and helped him get back into bed.

At handover, Poppy wondered if Patrick would say anything more about the incident with the mother and baby. But he didn't. At flight deck afterwards it was clear the night shift staff had already heard – word travelling like wildfire – and were eager to hear more. Poppy stayed silent. She didn't want to relive it, and it was not an anecdote to her yet. It had a profound effect on her, and she needed time to absorb it. She quietly left them to it and, on shaky legs, went to gather her things and wait outside for Gemma.

Paul chased her down as she was exiting. 'We're going up the street. Want to come?'

'No thanks, Paul, not tonight.'

'It's good to be around people after something like this.'

'My flatmate Gemma will finish soon. We'll go home together.'

'Are you sure?'

'Yes. Thanks, though.' And she forced a weak smile.

Paul's face was etched with concern. Poppy knew she must look terrible, but she couldn't dredge up enough energy to care. Paul was hovering, and Poppy hoped he would leave her. She didn't want to talk, she just wanted to go home with Gemma.

'Look, let me give you my mobile and if you change your mind, or you just want to chat, give me a call. OK?'

'OK.'

And he gave her phone a quick call so she could save his number.

'Thanks,' Poppy said and turned away. Finally, he left.

Poppy put her earphones in and leaned against the railing to wait. She put 'Fire' by Peking Duk on, wanting something not too sad just yet. Not yet ready to face her feelings. The strong beat and chorus reverberated through her, but she felt numb. She watched the comings and goings around her, until, ten minutes later, Gemma came jogging out of the entrance. She ran up, and they hugged, hard.

'How'd you go?' Poppy asked, leaning back to look into her friend's face.

'It was hard…hard to put it all in the back and concentrate on the healthy woman in front of me… I wasn't my best self, but she delivered a healthy baby.'

'Come on, let's go home,' Poppy said, putting her arm around Gemma's shoulders.

Poppy pulled the Grey Goose vodka out of the freezer and poured them each a shot when they got in. They sat on one of the sofas and Poppy put some music on softly so as not to wake Lucas.

'Do you want to talk about it?' Poppy asked, one leg tucked under her.

'Yeah, I think I do. How about you?'

'Yeah. You start.'

'I didn't know what we were walking into. All my Registrar said was "we're needed in ED". She didn't warn me what to expect. So, when I walked in and there you all were, and there was blood all over the floor, it was like a punch to the stomach. And then suddenly, you guys are doing CPR, and we're doing the quickest, most barbaric C-section ever. And when we've got to the baby, it's lifeless and grey, and we lift it out, and the blood doesn't stop. Then the shocks and the blood, and that's all I keep seeing.' Gemma was crying, her words delivered in a rush. She took a shot. She looked deflated and Poppy put a hand on her knee.

'I know. When you guys were cutting and I was doing compressions, it was crazy. And it's not like on the practice dummy, it's intense and exhausting and the chest is less springy and kind of more water-logged. And my shoulders started to ache and then I was thinking about the patient's poor partner – one minute you've got a beautiful wife who's going to have a baby soon and the next they're both gone. Ripped away from you for no reason. How do you get past that?'

They sat there, each lost in thought, while Tom Walker was singing 'Leave a light on'. Poppy didn't believe in God, but as she listened to the words, she hoped the partner did. Maybe he could find some comfort in praying that their souls were in heaven. Her thoughts then drifted to her own family and the numbness shifted to hollowness. She didn't want to revisit her own past. Not tonight. But it took real effort to prevent the past from rising up and haunting her. She downed another shot of vodka.

'I've got to go to bed,' Gemma said.

They both stood up and embraced again.

'I love you, Gem.'

'You too, Pop.'

Poppy woke late, feeling dusty. Partly it was the four shots of vodka, but also it was the emotional strain from yesterday. Her first thoughts were of the woman and baby and the blood. She felt raw and hollow. There was an ache in her chest. Not just for them, but also for her own loss, and she found herself crying. Crying for the loss of life in such tragic circumstances. It was so senseless. The crying sent her back to sleep for another hour, and the second time she woke, her eyes were sore and itchy, and when she looked in the mirror, they were puffy. Thankfully, she had a few days off. She didn't think she could cope with another shift right now. ED was a whirlwind of highs, lows, and a feeling of disconnection from the rest of the world. Poppy assumed it was probably a lot like working in a casino, complete with the lack of windows and natural light, but without the occasional ding-ding-ding of the winning pokie machine.

She showered and ate and then walked up to her favourite café, Cuckoo Callay. Jason, the coffee guy she sort of knew (well, at least he knew her name and her regular order) greeted her: 'Poppy, where have you been? Did you go off grid?'

He was early twenties, like Poppy, with dark hair, usually under a newsboy or porkpie hat, and a small goatee. Despite the dark hair, he was quite fair, with a lot of freckles on his face and arms.

'No, just been working evenings.'

'You look tired.'

'Yeah, tough night.'

'You want a large latte?'

'Yes, please, and I think I need one of those white chocolate and raspberry muffins.'

'Sure thing.'

'How have you been? How's the painting going?' Poppy asked him.

'Slowly. I've been doing some extra shifts, so I haven't had as much time as I'd like.'

'When's the exhibition?'

'Countdown now at three weeks, so really got to get cracking.'

'Well, I can't wait to see it.'

'Thanks, Poppy. Alright, latte and muffin coming up. Why don't you take a seat outside and I'll bring it out to you?'

'Thanks, Jason.'

'No problem.'

Poppy took her muffin and coffee into the park. She sat on her favourite bench on the west side, looking down over the sloping grass toward the inner west, shaded by some lovely gum trees. She ate her muffin, savoured her coffee, and patted the occasional dog that came to investigate her. After a peaceful hour, she wandered back through the cemetery on her way home. This little ritual gave her the connection to the real world that she'd missed these last few days in her isolation on evening shifts. Watching normal people going about their usual activities grounded her. Life wasn't all blood, death, and trauma.

Feeling buoyed but not quite back to her relatively optimistic baseline, she headed home and called her mum. They were close and usually spoke on the phone at least once a week.

'Hi, Mum,' she said as her mother answered.

'Hi darling, how is it all going?'

'It's been a bit of a whirlwind, actually. I've been doing evening shifts, so I haven't seen much of Gem and Luc, which is hard.'

'I can imagine. But tell me more about the work. Has it been interesting at least, and have the people been nice?'

'Mostly nice, and yes, lots of interesting cases. ED is pretty crazy, though, the pace, the work. But I've gotten to do lots of procedures, and I even helped in a couple of traumas, so the experience is great,' Poppy said. She felt herself lightening, and that buzz of excitement coming back.

'Well, it sounds like it's as you imagined it would be?'

'Yeah, I guess it is.'

'That's good. You're happy?'

Poppy paused to ask herself that question. Was she happy?

'Yeah, I think I am.' It was a relief to realise that despite the lows of the last few shifts, the highs made up for them and hadn't completely tarnished her (probably) idealistic view of medicine.

Poppy gave her Mum the highlight reel, leaving out most of the gore and certainly not divulging the death of the pregnant woman and her baby. She focused instead on the people and how welcoming they'd been.

'What about you and Dad, anything new your end?' Poppy asked.

'No, same old, same old. Although don't tell Dad this, but I'm worried he's starting to go deaf.'

'Really?'

'Yes, I can be talking to him and he just doesn't respond, even when I prompt him more than once.'

'Maybe he's just concentrating on something else, like the TV?' Poppy suggested.

'Possibly… You're right, it's probably just domestic deafness, as they say.'

'I'm sure it's nothing to worry about.'

'Yes, I'm sure you're right. Well, darling, I must go now. I've got to get to the hairdresser. She gets quite shirty if I'm late.'

'OK, Mum. Love you.'

'I love you too, sweetheart. Bye.'

Poppy smiled as she hung up. The call was a good idea, and on the Poppy meter she was now nearing baseline.

She firmed up her plans with Lucy and Stephanie and then went to the beach for the afternoon. The weather was heavenly and there was nowhere she needed to be. Bronte had become her go-to beach. The surf was a bit rough, but Poppy usually just dipped in at the edges when she wanted to cool down, so that wasn't a major issue for her. The cafes were great, and it was a beautiful beach hamlet. She grabbed her book and earphones and set out.

She chilled on the sand for a couple of hours, enjoying the smell of salty water and occasional coconut oil as the breeze wafted over her. The sound of cars on the headland receded as the squawks of the seagulls swooping down toward the water, or onto some scrap of rubbish on the sand, took over. With daylight savings, it was still light at about 5:30pm when Poppy headed home. She wasn't meeting the girls until 8 o'clock, so she had plenty of time. As she was shaking out her towel, a tall guy with a board loped over and said, tentatively, 'Poppy?'

Poppy looked up and realised it was Will.

'Hi Will,' Poppy said, blushing to the roots of her hair as she did.

'Were you leaving?'

'Yeah, I've been here all afternoon.'

'How was the water?' Will asked, his head briefly turning toward the crystal-clear water ranging from a sea-green to a cyan colour under the shifting light.

'Warm… How's your Plastics term going?' Poppy asked, suddenly self-conscious, wrapping her towel around her waist.

'Pretty good. The Registrar and Fellow are alright, and I've been able to go to theatre a bit and help with some of the simpler cases, so that's been good. And it was quiet this arvo, so I got to nick off early, giving me a chance to get a surf in. How's your week been? Has Seb been looking out for you?'

'It's been pretty full-on, actually. Seb and Paul have been great, though.' *Should I tell him about last night?* Will had been so open and welcoming, and it would be comforting to share it with someone other than Gemma. 'But last night we had a terrible death and let's just say I'm relieved to be having a few days off.'

'I'm sorry to hear that. Do you want to talk about it?'

Poppy searched his face and saw genuine concern, but realised that the beach might not be the best venue and she needed to get ready for tonight.

'Maybe another time.'

'OK. Well, I'm going to get in those waves now. It was good to see you. Hope to see you around.' And with that, he strode down to the water's edge and flopped gently onto his board to paddle out.

Poppy watched him catch a wave, almost mesmerised. He looked so beautiful. His tall, lithe frame strong and balletic. Had she been a fool and missed her chance to see where things might have gone? Maybe she should have told him about last night. Sat down and talked to him and maybe in opening up to him it might have created a new opportunity for them. Why did she always make the wrong decision when opportunities arose?

Chapter 7

'I just love Obstetrics,' Gemma said brightly as they were sitting at home and catching up after Poppy returned from the beach.

'That's great, Gem,' Poppy replied, relieved that they weren't talking about last night.

'What about Gynae, though?'

'Well, I'm only really doing one Gynae clinic at the moment.'

'And unlike me,' Lucas added, 'Gem's had nice Registrars.'

'True, although the midwives can be militant. There's this one who basically orders all the junior doctors around, but is totally sycophantic with the fellows and consultants; it's nauseating.'

'I can't imagine you putting up with that, Gem,' Poppy ventured with a giggle.

'Yeah, she's giving it back two-fold,' Lucas laughed.

'And paying for it… Yesterday, the bitchy one insisted I review a CTG trace every twenty minutes, and it looked completely fine, so I suggested she could keep reviewing it and call me if she had concerns…next thing I know, the consultant is telling me I need to review the CTG every twenty minutes and when I go back down there, she has the biggest smirk on her face. So, I spend the rest of the shift running back every twenty minutes and the CTG remained completely normal.'

'Score one bitchy midwife,' Lucas added.

'Don't worry, I'll get her back somehow,' Gem concluded, a serious furrow forming on her brow.

'We don't doubt it, babe,' Lucas replied.

Poppy would not want to be that midwife. Gemma was fiercely loyal, but once you'd crossed her, there was no coming back.

'What about you, Luc?' Poppy asked tentatively.

'Pretty shit, mate.'

'Why, what's happening?'

'Well, basically, I'm on my own…the Regs and bosses are always either in theatre or clinics, and so it's just me and Steve, the other Resident. The patients are sick and old, and I feel like I've got too many balls in the air all the time, and soon they're going to be falling down on my head.'

Gemma put an arm around his shoulders and said, 'Babe.'

'And when I did call for help today, this arsehole Registrar, Anthony, turns up on the ward and yells at me at the nurses' station, saying how incompetent I am, and how dare I call him from theatre for trivial matters.'

'I'm really sorry, Luc, that sucks.'

Lucas snorted. 'Yeah, Pop, it really does.'

'Well, at least we've got the weekend off,' Gemma said, squeezing Luc's shoulder again.

It sure had been a steep learning curve for each of them.

Lucy, Stephanie, and Poppy were meeting on King Street for dinner and then planned on going to Marble Bar to listen to some music and have a few cocktails. Poppy had dressed in a figure-hugging little black dress – short but not so short that she would flash her butt every time she bent forward or sat down. It suited her, but she always felt she needed something bright to offset the black, so she had on red strappy-heeled sandals, and red and green dangly earrings. Her hair was down, and she had on bright-red lipstick. She felt sexy and confident.

Marble Bar was a beautifully restored Victorian bar with a speakeasy feel. It had a grand curved archway, elaborate plaster ceiling and a beautiful mahogany bar. Jazz was playing in the background, giving the place ambience. They had a quick scout around for a table. Lucy hovered near a group of women who were grabbing their things and standing up to leave. She pounced as soon as their stilettos had brushed past and secured the area before another equally eager group of punters could take it.

'Nice one, Luce,' Poppy proclaimed as she squeezed in.

'No problema,' she replied.

They got comfy and perused the extensive cocktail list. Poppy was tossing up between Autumn in New York with tequila, apple and citrus, and the Lychee rose ensemble with vodka, rose, lychee and citrus. She thought both would suit the weather, but ultimately went for the tequila. Stephanie offered to get the first round and went up to the bar to order.

'Hey, have you heard this band before?' she asked Lucy, pointing to the flyer. The band due to start soon was called Brown Sugar Music.

'No, but when I've been here before, it's mainly been R&B.'

Poppy nodded to herself, thinking that rhythm and blues and soul would fit the surroundings nicely.

When Steph returned with their drinks, Poppy offered a toast. 'To new friends and new beginnings.'

They all clinked glasses and took a sip.

'Ooh, yummy,' said Poppy, very happy with her choice.

They sipped their drinks and chatted, learning more about each other and sharing their various sordid and not-so-sordid relationship histories whilst the band set up. Poppy was just getting a pleasant buzz, but had run out of cocktail, so offered to get the next round. She was waiting at the bar, trying to catch one of the bartenders' eyes, and didn't notice the man sidle up next to her.

'You certainly scrub up well,' he said to her.

'Excuse me?' Poppy said as she turned to face this man, ready to give him hell, and then realised that it was Joshua Hunter.

'Oh, it's you,' she said and blushed. Thank God for the low lighting, she thought.

'Sorry, what I was really trying to say, incredibly indelicately, is that you look gorgeous.'

'Thank you,' Poppy said but felt off balance, and turned back to the bar. This guy who had only just been horrible to her, was now hitting on her?

'It's Poppy, isn't it?' said with only minimal uncertainty. Joshua was clearly incredibly confident in all situations.

'Yes,' said Poppy, not prepared to make this any easier on him.

'That patient of yours is doing well. Big inferior infarct, a couple of stents.'

'Well, I'm glad he's OK,' Poppy said, turning her attention again to the bar in front of her.

'Do you like the band?'

'Yes, they're really cool. And this place is awesome. I haven't been here before.'

'Can I buy you a drink?'

'That's OK, I'm getting a round for my friends.' And Poppy pointed out Steph and Lucy behind her.

'That's OK, I'll buy the round.'

'OK.' Poppy gave the order to the bartender when she finally got his attention, thinking it was the least he could do after being such a prick. Joshua added a few extra drinks for him and his mates and they took the drinks and Josh's mates over to join the girls.

'So how do you all know each other?' Poppy asked, once they were seated and had introduced themselves.

The two boys immediately looked to Josh to answer.

'Well, we all lived together during uni, but Ben's a Med Reg at Prince of Wales, so he's now living in Randwick. And Charlie's an ICU Reg at The Bennelong, so we live just down the road in Camperdown. And you ladies?'

Lucy and Stephanie looked to Poppy. Maybe because she'd brought them over, she thought.

'Lucy and Steph both work in ED. Luce's a nurse and Steph's a Reg.'

'And how are you liking things so far? That is, when jerks like me aren't giving you a hard time?' Josh asked, looking directly into Poppy's eyes. She felt, rather than saw the eye-roll that Steph gave Lucy, but she saw the twitch of a smile at Josh's lips and figured he had better insight than she'd given him credit for.

'You really were a dick.'

Josh laughed suddenly, and she liked the way it sounded, loud and harsh, like the bray of a hoarse.

'You won't let me forget it, will you?'

'Not on your life.'

He smiled, eyes lively as he said, 'Dr Mason, I truly apologise for my appalling behaviour toward you thus far, and I hope that you will find it in your heart to forgive me and allow me the opportunity to make it up to you.'

'Now you're just taking the piss,' Poppy said, but she smiled back at him locking his gaze with hers. *Damn, this man is attractive. And that smell? I could breathe him in all day…*

She had to stop herself from licking her lips when Josh leaned forward to grab a handful of chips that had materialised, and his biceps bulged against his shirt. Her thoughts immediately on what the rest of him would look like naked. Her eyes were roving his body when he turned back toward her, and she knew she was busted. Her face blazed with heat, and she averted her gaze, but not before she'd clocked the twitch in his lips. Was he laughing at her now, or enjoying her watching him, she wondered?

When the band finished at midnight, the group wandered down to the Quay. Not for any particular reason or destination, merely to prolong the time together, chatting and flirting. The night had brought a slight crispness to the late summer air and Poppy felt herself shiver.

'Are you cold?' Josh asked, putting an arm around her and rubbing her arm.

Suddenly Ben started singing.

It transpired that Steph had dared him to sing 'What's new, pussycat?' Not being one to shirk a challenge, he belted out the song at the top of his voice, seemingly unconcerned that singing was clearly not one of his talents. Poppy and Josh started laughing and jogged to catch up. Ben had now hopped up onto a bench seat and was attempting to serenade passers-by. He only knew a few lines of the song and kept repeating them over and over, gyrating his hips suggestively in an Elvis-type way.

'Alright, get down here,' Steph called, tugging him off the chair and pulling his shirt front towards her as she planted a kiss on his mouth. Poppy watched on as they had a decent pash, Ben grabbing Steph's arse, and wondered whether Josh would kiss her tonight. The thought sent a ripple of desire through her body. He'd had an arm around her for a while and they'd been physically close at Marble Bar, and he'd certainly been complimenting her most of the evening, but she was still not sure if he really liked her. And did she like him? She looked over to Charlie and Lucy and noticed they were deep in conversation, politely facing away from Ben and Steph, but not physically close.

'Break it up, you two.' Josh said finally as things were starting to feel awkward.

'Sorry,' Ben said as Steph wiped her lipstick from his face.

'How about we go back to our place?' Josh suggested, looking over to Charlie with his eyebrow raised. Charlie shrugged his shoulders in approval as Steph eagerly said yes on behalf of the girls.

'There's a bus down here we can catch,' suggested Charlie, and they all wandered further down the road.

Their place was quite open-plan with an elevated almost loft-like area where there was a bedroom, study nook, and ensuite. Then, on the main floor, there was a big lounge with balcony and dining area, an open kitchen, with another bedroom and bathroom to the side. They settled themselves in the lounge area and Josh and Charlie organised some drinks and nibbles, and Ben found a good playlist on Spotify.

'How about a game of "I have never"', suggested Ben. Well-lubricated as they were, it took little persuasion to get everyone on board. The classic drinking game where one person says, 'I have never x' and if any of the others have done x, they have to take a swig of their drink. A game that tends to be pretty dirty, and a way of sounding out prospective sexual partners to see how much risqué behaviour they've gotten up to.

'I'll start,' Steph said eagerly. 'I have never cheated on a partner.'

Lucy, Josh, and Ben all drank. Some eyebrows were raised. Next it was Ben's turn.

'I have never driven whilst stoned.'

Ben, Josh and Steph all drank. Then it was Poppy's turn.

'I have never had a threesome.'

Only Ben drank this time and there were a few 'oohs'.

Josh followed with: 'I have never been arrested.'

And again, only Ben drank.

'Whoah. What for?' asked Steph.

'Well, it was all a bit of a mistake, actually, and ultimately, I wasn't charged. But I had just broken up with a girlfriend and I got really drunk and thought it would be a good idea to climb up into her window and beg her to take me back. Unfortunately, she had gone away for the weekend and her parents thought I was a burglar. I landed on her bedroom floor with a bit of a thud and next thing I know there was a dude in his PJs brandishing a baseball bat, and then sirens and police. Anyway, it took a few phone calls and a night drying out in the cells to sort it out. Certainly, a night I'll never forget.'

Everyone started laughing, and Steph reached over and kissed Ben again. When they finished discussing the nitty-gritty of what it was really like to be arrested, it was Charlie's turn.

'I have never been in love.' Josh, Steph, Lucy, and Ben all drank.

'Interesting,' said Josh, noticing that Poppy had not drunk.

And last was Lucy, 'I have never had anal sex.'

Lucy, Steph, Poppy, Ben and Josh all drank, leaving only Charlie the odd man out.

This prompted a discussion on the relative virtues of anal sex. Poppy had tried anal sex a few times and felt it was something she could enjoy if the mood, the timing, and the partner were right, but it wasn't something she would automatically do with everyone. Lucy, on the other hand, felt anal sex was just like ordinary sex, part of the package and generally would be happy to finish off with anal. She felt an orgasm during anal sex was more intense than vaginal or clitoral. The boys and Steph were closer to Poppy's viewpoint and Charlie said he didn't really have any interest or desire in anal, but if a partner really wanted him to, he would try.

By this point, it was now approaching three o'clock and they were all hammered and exhausted. None of them wanted to move, and they settled themselves comfily into the couches or on cushions on the floor. They changed the playlist to something soft and peaceful and continued chatting until they fell asleep.

Poppy woke to light falling on her face and as she blearily opened her eyes, the pain in her head felt like a knife directly piercing from her eyes through her skull. Her tongue was dry, furry, and stuck to her palate and she desperately needed to pee. She dragged herself up to a sitting position and saw that Lucy was lying on the opposite couch, one of her nipples had escaped her dress and her knickers were showing. Charlie was sprawled on some cushions on the floor, snoring, and the others were nowhere to be seen. She looked at her watch, noting the time was just after nine o'clock, and then quietly made her way to the bathroom.

She used the loo then ran warm water over her face until she felt marginally better and then tidied up her make-up. She sniffed her armpits, but she didn't smell too bad, at least on the BO front. Alcohol fumes, who knows? Probably toxic. She skulled some water from the tap and then used her finger with a bit of toothpaste from the tube on the vanity to give her teeth something of a clean. The only thing that probably saved her from vomiting was that solid lining of red curry from the Thai place before they went out. Even still, her head was on fire, and she desperately wanted to be showered and in her own bed right now. When she felt she'd done as much as she could, she quietly vacated the bathroom and went back out to find her things.

Josh had emerged (from the loft, Poppy presumed) and was making coffee from a Nespresso machine dressed in a white T-shirt and grey marle track pants.

'Morning,' he said. 'How are you feeling?'

'Pretty wretched. What time did we go to sleep?'

'I think you passed out around 3:30.'

'How do you look so good?'

'Ah… I had a shower before I went to bed, a huge glass of water with Panadol and Nurofen, and slept in my own bed.'

'Lucky for some.'

'I would have offered to share it with you, but you were too far gone to rouse.'

'I guess I missed out then.'

'Well, there's always next time?' he said, suggestively, raising an eyebrow at her and waiting for her response.

'There's going to be a next time?'

'I hope so,' he said with a playful smile.

Poppy smiled, despite the hideous pain in her head, and said, 'Can I have one of those?' pointing to the coffee machine.

'Of course. What would you like?'

'A flat white please.'

'Do you want something to eat?'

'No, I think just the coffee. Then I'm going to go home to die.'

Josh laughed, and Poppy noticed not just how attractive he was, even on minimal sleep and too much alcohol, but how soft his expression was when he laughed. This laugh wasn't like the brash bray of last night. It seemed more thoughtful somehow. He certainly had surprised her. He was far kinder than her previous interaction had suggested he could be, and she decided she would like to see him again.

Whilst Josh was making the coffee, Lucy woke with a start and rushed inelegantly to the bathroom where they heard her vomiting.

'Oh, poor Lucy,' said Poppy.

Poppy poured her a water and left it on the kitchen bench and Josh pulled out some Panadol and Nurofen. When she re-emerged, they gave her the drink, drugs, and some space to pull herself back together. Charlie snored on, oblivious.

Poppy laughed and said to Josh, 'Is he always like that?'

'I suspect he would sleep through an earthquake,' he said as she laughed.

Steph and Ben emerged from Charlie's room with sheepish looks on their faces. Poppy raised her eyebrows at Steph, who smiled in return. They sat on stools or leaned on the kitchen bench drinking their waters or coffee, mainly in silence. Poppy sensed Steph would probably want to stay and spend more time with Ben, but Lucy still looked green, so she suggested they head off.

'I can give you a lift if you like?' offered Josh.

'Are you sure?' Poppy said.

'Absolutely. Give me two secs.' And he wandered upstairs to grab his keys and wallet.

'How're you doing, Luce?' Poppy asked.

'Pretty bloody awful.'

'Alright, well, let's get you home.'

Josh dropped Lucy home first. She was over in a share house in Enmore. Then he took Poppy home. He parked out the front of her place and turned the engine off.

'I know you probably feel like crap right now, so I'm not going to do anything.' Poppy's shoulders relaxed. 'I really enjoyed spending time with you last night and I'd like to go out, just the two of us. How about a movie sometime tomorrow?'

'OK, I'd like that.'

They swapped numbers and Josh said he'd call in the morning. She smiled at him as she left the car and he waited until she'd got inside the building before driving off. Poppy trudged up the stairs to their flat with a lightness in her chest despite the leadenness of her limbs and skull.

Chapter 8

She found Gemma and Lucas sitting in the lounge drinking coffee and reading the paper, the remains of a big breakfast on the coffee table.

'Jeez, big night? You look rough,' said Lucas.

'Yeah, I feel like the walking dead. I'm going to shower and crash, I'll fill you in later,' Poppy replied as she headed straight for the bathroom.

Several hours of solid sleep later, she emerged craving fatty, greasy food, and took herself up to Cuckoo Callay for a burger and chips and a significant dose of caffeine. Poppy felt much better but still hungover, so she went for her usual ramble through Camperdown Memorial Rest Park and cemetery to walk off the heavy meal and get some air through the cobwebs in her mind. When they had first moved to Newtown after relocating from Newcastle, she had spent a lot of time wandering here and it always helped her mood. There were people busy with kids and dogs in the park, and teenagers smoking in the ramshackle cemetery, it always helped her feel alive. She felt close to normal by her return home, but knew only a quiet night tonight and a good night's sleep would return her to her baseline level of functioning.

Poppy plonked herself on the lounge, and binged the latest Netflix offering for a couple of hours until Gemma and Lucas returned from one of Gemma's niece's birthday parties in the Shire.

'Hi,' Poppy said when they came through the door, pausing the TV.

Gemma came straight over to her and said, 'Right, spill,' as she took a seat beside her on the lounge.

'I'm going to have a shower,' Lucas said in a sour tone before heading to his and Gemma's room.

Poppy raised an eyebrow at Gemma, who waved her off and said, 'You first.'

'OK, well as you know I went out with Stephanie, one of the ED Registrars, and Lucy, one of the nurses,' and she ran her through the events of the night, including her markedly changed feelings towards Joshua and his request for a date for tomorrow. At the end of her blow-by-blow there was a silent pause before Gemma chimed in with, 'But this is the guy who was horrible to you the other night, right?'

'Well, yes, but actually I did the wrong thing, and he's quite charming.'

Gemma seemed nonplussed, and squinted her eyes at Poppy, wrinkling her nose.

'Look, maybe he is alright, but just take things slowly for a bit.'

'He was a complete gentleman last night, and this morning.'

'Well…that's a good start.'

But Poppy saw the frown creasing her friend's brow and suspected Gemma thought she was making a mistake.

'OK, what about you guys? Why's Lucas in a funk?'

Gemma sighed. She was Shire born and bred, with two older brothers, one of whom was in the family electrical business with their father, the other a plumber. Gemma's mum was a childcare educator. Her brothers had five kids between them and there was a lot of familial pressure on Gemma and Lucas to get married and start a family. Every time they went to a family gathering, Gemma's mum would take her aside and ask her when she was getting married and whether she was pushing Lucas to set a date. Meanwhile, her father and brothers would tell Lucas, over beers and a barbie, how good it was to get married and start a family. As Gemma was the first member of the family to go to university, let alone do medicine, there was a lack of understanding of the duration of study and training, as well as the pressure of the job. Gemma would usually come back from these events grumpy and there would often be some friction between her and Lucas. Tonight didn't seem to be any different.

'God, my family just don't get it…they have no clue how tough our lives are right now! We are not in a position to be having a baby. We've only just finished uni, we have no money, and we haven't got our careers even remotely sorted,' Gemma said, her voice raised.

'Yeah, I hear you.'

'I just wish they'd give us a break and let us be.'

'Have you tried telling your mum that?'

'Yes, but it's like she's deaf to it. Every time it's the same discussion and every time I tell her to back off, then we all get snippy and Lucas and I leave early, shitty with each other because we've got to get rid of that tension and frustration somehow.'

'I'm sorry, Gem. I know it's not fun for either of you.'

'The worst thing is, I want to get married and have kids, as you know, but Lucas is just not there yet. And all they achieve by pushing him all the time is him digging his heels in. You know how stubborn he can be once he's made up his mind about something.'

'Yes, I do.' Poppy smiled. 'Did you talk about it at all in the car on the way home?'

'No. Deadly silence and lots of staring out the window.'

'Well, why don't you wait a few days and then bring it up? Wait until he's relaxed and in a good mood and just talk about what you both want without the family pressure?'

'Yeah, I guess…maybe it's worth a try. Thanks, Pop.'

'Anytime, hon,' Poppy said, giving Gemma a hug.

The evening in, sharing a meal, watching a movie, felt like the first time since orientation they'd had a family night. It was homey, companionable, and restorative for Poppy. And she saw the frost between Lucas and Gemma thawing over the hours of togetherness.

The next morning, Sunday, Poppy woke in nervous anticipation of her date with Josh. She didn't know what time things were likely to happen, and she was hopeful it wouldn't be too late, as she was back to work the following day. To distract herself from the waiting, she tidied her room and then went grocery shopping for the week. Gemma and Lucas had already re-stocked most things, so Poppy mainly got fresh fruit and veg and some ingredients for a few meals. They were all relaxed about splitting foodstuffs. They kept a note of what things were running low and whoever was going to the shops re-stocked. A few times a week, they would eat together, or at least leave leftovers, so they felt things were fair.

By the time she got back from the shops, Josh had texted. Poppy felt a brief flush of excitement as she opened the message.

> Hi Poppy. Hope you're feeling better this morning and still keen for a movie. How about a thriller? Dendy Newtown at 2:40pm. Meet you there?

Wow, he sure is confident.

> OK, sounds good. See you there.

She unpacked the shopping, had a bite to eat, and thought about her date. Poppy was definitely attracted to Joshua, but, although she wouldn't say this in front of Gemma, his confidence bordered on arrogance, and she had an inkling that this would rankle over time. For now, though, she wanted to be close to him, breathe in that spicy scent, and feel the heat of his arms around her. Oh, how she hoped he was a good kisser, and that she would soon find out. She felt an injection of heat in her underwear as she thought about it.

Poppy spent some time standing in front of her open wardrobe looking at her clothes and thinking about what to wear. She wanted to look casual, but still hot and desirable. In the end, she went with black skinny jeans and the bandana top she'd worn to the orientation week party. It had a delicate pattern with navy, red, black, and bottle-green geometric shapes on it, and flattered her. It accentuated her small waist and her modest but perky breasts. Her thoughts drifted to Will and that night that was now a distant memory. Was it wrong to be attracted to two guys at once? She still felt like a loser, from what happened with Will, and saw today as an opportunity for a clean slate with a guy she was attracted to and didn't know well.

Red coral drop earrings brought out the red in her top and she paired them with her red strappy-heeled sandals. Natural make-up and a couple of squirts of her favourite perfume behind her ears and around her barely exposed naval, and Poppy was good to go.

The nerves started on her walk up to the cinema. She'd never been stood up before, and didn't honestly think it would happen today, but there was a pang of anxiety – *would he be there, would he like her, would they kiss, should she have sex with him?* Usual first date nerves. She arrived pretty much on time and was relieved to see Josh waiting by the counter. He smiled as he saw her walk up and came over to greet her.

'Hi,' he said.

'Hi yourself,' she said and leaned in to kiss him on the cheek, breathing in that delicious spicy aroma that she now associated with him.

'I've got the tickets,' he said, 'but do you want something to eat or drink?'

'Yeah, sure, and thanks for getting the tickets.'

'No problem.'

They ended up with a choc top each and a soft drink and headed into the cinema. Josh had chosen a psychological thriller, and they chatted while the ads rolled.

'I feel like I know nothing about you,' Poppy said as she took a bite from her choc top.

'Well, what do you want to know?'

She swallowed a shard of chocolate before asking, 'Well, who's in your family, where did you grow up? That sort of thing.'

Josh finished his mouthful, then said, 'Well, my Mum raised me. I'm an only child.'

'What about your dad?' Poppy asked with her mouth full, then said, 'Sorry', for her full mouth.

'They're divorced since I was little. I don't see him much.'

They both ate a few mouthfuls of ice cream, Poppy licking the rim of her cone, before venturing again, 'What about school? I know where you went to uni.'

'Randwick Boys High. And I'm still close to my friends from there.'

'Really? I hardly see my school friends these days. Maybe only once or twice a year kind of thing.'

'Well, we were really close at school, and just kept in touch.'

'That's great.'

'That looks good,' Josh said pointing to the preview that was playing. It was for an art-house movie.

'Really? You'd see that?' Poppy asked.

'Yeah, why, you don't like the look of it?'

'Umm…not really.'

The next preview was for a mainstream movie: *The Long Shot*. Poppy pointed the remains of her cone at the screen and said, 'That's more my style.'

She noticed Josh raise an eyebrow.

Oh no, maybe he thinks my tastes are beneath him? Or maybe he's trying to show off and make himself seem more cultured and high-brow, Poppy wondered.

The movie got underway, and Poppy relaxed into the mood. It was the classic 'who do you trust?' scenario. About halfway through Josh leaned in to whisper in her ear, 'Do you think the best friend is in on it?'

Poppy liked the feel of his breath in her ear and she turned toward him and looked him in the eyes, holding his gaze. She didn't answer his question, but he understood her intentions well enough and leaned back in toward her. He placed one hand at the side of her face and the other at the base of her neck and kissed her. It was soft and gentle, and she responded by moving as close to him as she could. The armrest between them gouged her uncomfortably, but she pushed it to the back of her mind, focusing on the heat that was building between them, and not just where their lips and mouths were mingled. The skin at her neck tingled under his fingertips, sending electric waves up her scalp and ratcheting up her desire. Her kisses grew hungrier and her clitoris throbbed against her underwear. She wanted him badly.

When they stopped for breath, he held her face and looked her in the eyes before sitting back to resume watching the movie. The only difference was this time he had a hand on her thigh.

What, that's it? She watched the side of his face, willing him to face her again and continue the kissing. But he kept his face, and attention, on the movie. *At least his hand is on my thigh, I guess.* It was close enough to her crotch to give that tickle of excitement, hoping he'd just move it a bit further north. Honestly, if he turned to her right at this moment and suggested they go back to his place for sex, she would race him out the door. But he did not, and he didn't make any further moves on her for the rest of the movie.

Slowly, Poppy's desire turned to frustration. and then disappointment; she'd lost all interest in the movie. When it was over, Josh squeezed her thigh as he stood up.

'What did you think?'

'Yeah, it was good,' Poppy said, not overly enthusiastically.

'I liked the twist at the end. I only saw it coming at the last moment.'

'Yeah, me too.' Poppy faked it, having not paid attention.

'Are you working tomorrow?'

'Yeah, back to day shifts.'

'Well, do you want to grab a quick dinner?'

'Sure, that'd be great,' Poppy replied, instantly feeling better again.

Poppy was hoping they could take things to the next level, but Josh proved to be a gentleman again. They had a quick pho, at the bare bones Vietnamese place across the street. She'd not eaten here before, had walked past it several times thinking it looked like a bit of a dive, but was surprised by the depth of flavour in the cheap bowls of pho.

He walked her home, an arm loosely around her shoulders. When they got to her building, he leaned in and pulled her to him, kissing her again. Poppy looped her arms around his neck and pressed her body into his. She ran one of her hands down his back, feeling the tautness of his muscles and briefly resting on his buttocks before he pulled away from her.

'Poppy, I've had a great time, but if we take this further tonight, I won't want to stop and we've both got to work tomorrow.' He held her hand as he continued, 'I want to savour this next bit and really do it the justice it deserves. Are you off on the weekend?'

'No, I'll be on night shifts. I've got Wednesday, Thursday off this week.'

'When's your next weekend off then?'

'I think it's the one after.'

'OK, well, that Saturday, come over, and I'll cook you dinner and we can see where the night takes us?'

'OK,' said Poppy feeling a mixture of disappointment but also slightly special, like he really cared about her. They kissed again briefly, and then he was gone.

'So, how was it?' Gemma asked the moment she stepped through the door of their apartment.

'Good, and frustrating all at the same time,' Poppy replied, flopping on the couch.

'How so?' Lucas asked.

'It was going really well, and we started kissing in the movie…'

'Do I need to put my fingers in my ears?' Lucas interrupted whilst Gemma swatted him with a pillow and Poppy laughed.

'Sadly, no. There wasn't even any over the clothes action, let alone under it.'

Lucas mimed swiping his forehead. 'Phew.'

'Anyway, the kissing was good, but after a few minutes, he just stopped to watch the rest of the movie. And when it ended, we went for a meal and I was hoping we could start where we left off, but he just walked me home.'

'Not even a kiss goodnight?' Gemma asked.

'Well, yeah…and a good one…but he pulled away again and suggested dinner at his place on my next weekend off.'

'Hunh…' Gemma pondered.

'What do you guys think? Maybe he's just not that into me?'

'If he wasn't into you, he wouldn't be suggesting another date… Trust me,' answered Lucas.

'I agree…maybe he's just being honourable and not after a quick shag,' was Gemma's theory.

'Yeah, maybe,' answered Poppy. Their words reassured her, but she was still disappointed. It was weird; every interaction with Josh didn't go the way she expected it to. She constantly felt wrong-footed.

She showered and got ready for bed, but couldn't concentrate on her book or a Netflix show. So, she turned off her light and used her vibrator whilst fantasising about Josh. Conjuring that delicious spicy scent and imagining his warm hand on her thigh inching closer to her clitoris. Her orgasm was strong and left her panting afterward. With that delicious release, she could sleep soundly through the night.

Poppy woke early and had a sit-down breakfast with Lucas and Gemma as the sky rapidly lightened at the balcony doors, before they all walked to work together. Poppy had a spring in her step, and she linked arms with Gemma.

'You're chirpy this morning,' Gemma said, patting her linked arm.

'It's just so nice to be on day shifts like the rest of the world!'

She was looking forward to the end of the day when they could walk home together and even eat dinner together. They usually spent so much time together and Poppy felt adrift without them.

Chapter 9

'Hi, Will, what are you doing here?' Poppy asked, blushing mildly when Will came up to her at the flight deck. She couldn't help the smile that formed immediately when she saw him, her mind briefly wandering to his taut body in board shorts down at the beach. Of course, this just made her blush deepen, so she dropped her chin and looked at her feet, hoping Will wouldn't notice. *Stop behaving like a teenager!*

'We've come to see the patient with cellulitis in bed four.'

'Oh sure, did Renal call you?'

'Yeah.'

'OK, let me come with you.'

And she followed Will and his Registrar to the patient's bedside.

'Hi, Mr Patterson,' Poppy said when they entered his cubicle in acute. His hospital gown was stained with blood and his lined, leathery face was pinched in pain. 'This is the Plastic Surgery team. They're here to have a look at your fistula and the infection, OK?'

'Yeah, alright,' he said, wincing as he slowly raised his painful left arm off the pillow it had been resting on. 'Here, have a look at the wretched thing. I've only had this fistula for six months, and it's already infected. The last one on the right side lasted four years before it crapped out. And I'm due for dialysis today. I hope they don't put a line in my neck again.'

Poppy felt bad for the guy. Regular haemodialysis for chronic renal failure was no picnic, and doing it for years must really wear you down. They hadn't had much exposure to Renal medicine at uni, but she could imagine these patients would be in and out of hospital a lot, just like the chronic lung disease patients.

Whilst Will's Registrar started examining Mr Patterson's arm, Poppy was snatching surreptitious glances at Will. Seeing him at the beach, and how his body moved in the water had reignited the desire she felt. He was busy documenting the proceedings in the patient's file on a mobile workstation and didn't look at her once. When they'd finished and were ready to head off, Will squeezed her shoulder as he said goodbye. Poppy's eager face turned toward him, but her smile quickly faded as his back retreated down the central corridor.

That same drop of disappointment in her gut that she had at the beach returned. *I think I've missed my chance with Will. It's obvious he is no longer interested. He must think I'm too much hard work, and how can I blame him, really? And you know what? Why do I care? I've had a good first date with Josh, and there's chemistry there, so the next date will be even better. We'll be able to explore each other, and I'm pretty keen to feel those biceps for a start!*

An injection of heat shot into Poppy's pants and she smiled as she turned her mind back to work.

Poppy found the day shifts very different from the evenings. There were a lot more people around, not just on the floor in ED but also teams from the wards coming down to consult or admit patients. Things were noisier and busier with less camaraderie amongst the ED staff, just because they were too busy liaising with other people. In the end, she really only saw three patients that first day shift. She spent most of the day liaising with different teams on the ward and ordering and reviewing multiple tests.

While she was waiting outside for Gemma and Lucas at the end of her shift, she checked her phone for messages and was disappointed that Josh hadn't texted. *Should I text him? Would that be too pushy? Maybe I should just wait for him to text me.* She bit the edge of her lip whilst she oscillated between thinking she was big enough and brave enough to just text him if that was what she wanted to do, and worrying about the 'dating rules'.

A group text from Steph to her and Lucy became a diversion.

Steph: Hi, ladies. I checked the roster, and we are all off
on Wednesday and Thursday. Do you want to catch up?

Poppy immediately texted back.

Absolutely! I was worried I'd be all alone while the rest of the world worked. (crying face emoji) What did you have in mind?

Steph: Let's do something fun. Fancy Luna Park?

Poppy: (Ha ha emoji) I'm game. How about you, Luce?

Lucy: I'm out. Going to the Blue Mountains to visit the parentals.

Poppy: Bummer.

Steph: Rain check. How about Wed?

Poppy; Cool, touch base then.

Poppy hugged Gemma when she and Lucas emerged from the hospital entrance at the end of their shifts.

'How was your day, guys?' she asked them.

'Crap as usual,' Lucas grumped.

'What happened?' Poppy asked, wanting to be supportive.

'I had this sick patient, and I didn't know what to do. His blood pressure was starting to drop and his drain output was slowing. And I didn't know if I should order a scan or if he might need to go back to theatre. I was worried he might be bleeding internally. So I called my Reg and asked him to come and review him. And after he came and saw him, as soon as we were back at the nurses' station, he yelled at me in front of the nurses and everyone for "wasting his time". So, once he'd finished his rant, I asked him what I should have done. "Sort it out yourself" was his response before storming off back to theatre. And the patient's blood pressure kept dropping despite my giving him extra IV fluids, and ultimately, I had to call the medical emergency team.

'The ICU Reg who came was really nice, though. In the end, she took the patient to the ICU, but I asked her if I should have done anything differently and she was really great. She sat down with me and asked me all about what happened prior to the call and pretty much gave me a mini tutorial on how to manage the deteriorating patient.'

'Wow Lucas, I'm so sorry you're having such a crap time,' said Poppy.

'Thanks, Pop. Clearly this term sucks, but just talking to that Reg, I actually felt I learned something. And maybe tomorrow or the next time another patient starts to go off, maybe I won't feel so shit scared and out of my depth.'

Poppy put her arm around his shoulders, giving him a quick squeeze.

'Hey, what was the name of the ICU Reg? Was it Sangeetha?'

'Yeah, I think so. Tiny Sri Lankan woman?'

'Yeah, that's her. I've seen her in ED a couple of times. She's really softly spoken, but she knows her stuff.'

'Yeah, and that horrible night that mother and baby died, she wasn't timid,' said Gemma.

'No, you're right, Gem, she was definitely calling the shots.'

'I like her,' said Gemma.

'Me too,' said Poppy and Lucas at the same time, and they all smiled at each other.

When it was time for bed, Poppy still hadn't had a text or call from Josh. She sat with her phone in her hand, thinking again about whether she should text him. And, if so, what she should write. In the end, she decided to be brave and so she went with:

> Hi Josh, hope you had a good day. Thinking about that
> kiss a lot, not sure I can wait two weeks…

I hope it sounds flirty and not desperate! For the next half hour, she constantly checked her phone to see if he'd messaged back and she hadn't heard it, but he didn't. *What does that mean? Is he ghosting me? Or maybe he's just busy or at the gym or something. I'm sure he'll text later.* And so, despite that kernel of anxiety, she turned off her light and went to sleep.

But the first thing she did when she woke the next morning was to check her phone. *Ughh…* He still had not texted back. What did that mean? Poppy wondered.

'What do you think?' Poppy asked Gemma.

'Too soon to tell... just give it some more time.'

'How much more time?'

'Well... it would be weird if he hasn't replied by tonight, I think.'

Poppy headed into subbies without her usual optimistic attitude.

'Oww,' Poppy said, looking up too late as Paul almost bowled her over. 'Oops, sorry,' said Poppy, finally looking up.

'No harm done. How are you?'

'I'm good thanks, you?'

'Yep, all good. I think we're on team subbies together today.'

'Excellent,' said Poppy.

'And you've all got teaching this arvo.'

'Yeah, I'd forgotten that.'

'It's good. I think Harriet's giving the session today.'

'Oh, OK,' Poppy replied, suddenly feeling less enthusiastic.

'Anyway, grab me if you need anything.'

'Thanks, Paul.'

'OK, Mrs Brown, what's brought you in today?' Poppy asked after she led the patient and her husband into the cubicle. She noticed that they were both young, maybe late twenties, so not much older than her. Mrs Brown was dressed in colourful Lululemon workout wear and trainers and her husband was in jeans and a polo shirt. He was holding her hand the whole way from the waiting room and he placed his other on the small of her back to lead her into the room. Poppy thought he seemed attentive, rather than controlling.

When Mrs Brown started to answer her, Poppy noticed how bright her blue eyes were, but how her lids and the area below her eyes were puffy and red, like she'd been crying for a long time.

'I've been cramping and bleeding overnight. Maybe for the last three or four hours. I'm nine weeks pregnant.'

'Oh, OK,' Poppy said, immediately expecting she was miscarrying and feeling sad for her. Out of the corner of her eye, whilst she looked down at the observation chart in the triage note, she saw Mr Brown squeeze and pat his wife's hand. She thought he said, 'It's going to be OK,' as he leaned to whisper in her ear. When she looked up again, Mrs Brown was crying silently.

Poppy felt heartache for her. For them both, really. It must be so awful to feel that excitement of early pregnancy only to experience early pregnancy loss. It's not as wholly horrendous as the loss of mother and child the other night, but still, that little potential child, one you haven't even come to fully picture, has vanished in the blink of an eye.

Heartbreaking. It was a reminder of how many ways life can throw tragedy and loss in your face. *I guess most people experience some form of loss at some point. A cherished pet, a loving parent, a lover, a sister, a child…*

Poppy knew there was nothing she could physically do for her, but wasn't sure what the procedure was.

'I'm so sorry, Mrs Brown. I'm going to have to ask some questions that might be upsetting for you, OK?' Before waiting for an answer, Poppy continued, 'Has the bleeding been continuous? And how much would you estimate that you've lost?'

Mrs Brown choked on her answer, 'Pretty continuous… I've changed four thick pads. So maybe three or four cups worth?'

'OK. And this is unpleasant…but did you notice any clots or larger more solid components?'

Now her husband sobbed audibly. 'Yes, there were some more solid-looking bits,' she replied with her eyes cast down, looking at the hospital blanket that she was twisting in her hands.

'I'm so sorry, Mrs Brown…have you had a temperature or any illness recently?'

'No.'

'OK, I'm sorry to say that this might be a miscarriage. I'll just go check with my superiors and be back soon.'

Poppy quickly and quietly ducked out of the cubicle and pulled the curtain shut behind her. She wanted to give them privacy to mourn together and felt a sudden welling in her own eyes as she swallowed her own grief back down.

'OK, it's straightforward,' Paul said when she found him at flight deck. 'Take blood for a β-hCG level and give the early pregnancy assessment service a call. Because it's during the day, they'll likely just get you to send her straight over, so do the bloods first.'

'And what'll they do there? Just so I can let her know.'

'They do a pelvic ultrasound to see if there is still a foetus and if there's a heartbeat, and whether the cervix is dilated. Then they'll check the bloods and give support and information about miscarriage.'

'OK, thanks. Does that mean you're happy for me to discharge her once I've done all that?'

'Absolutely.'

'Thanks, Paul.'

When Poppy came back to talk to the couple, she found them huddled, heads touching, and was moved by the poignancy of the scene. She felt she was intruding on what was a very private and painful experience for them. But she took a deep breath and quietly entered the cubicle and shut the curtain.

'So, Mrs Brown, I'm going to first take some blood to check the pregnancy hormone level, β-hCG. Then I'll ring the early pregnancy service and we'll get you over there for an ultrasound, OK?'

'Do you think the baby's gone?' Mr Brown asked.

'I don't know. Possibly.'

'Why has this happened?' he asked again.

'I don't know, I'm sorry… Once the ultrasound has been done, they'll be able to give you more information… Let's get the blood sample now.'

Poppy set up her equipment, but Mr Brown continued to ask the same two questions in different ways. Poppy continued to answer as consistently as possible, but she was starting to sweat and feel out of her depth. His grief was palpable and Mrs Brown was shrinking on the bed, like she was desiccating into a husk. She was relieved when she could leave them alone again once she'd finished taking the blood. She needed to shrug off the heavy weight of their pain and move on to the next task, otherwise the lid on her own grief might burst off like the cap on a fire hydrant; her own dark history rushing out in a jet of water before soaking everything around her.

Later, she was having a quick cup of tea in the staff room when Paul joined her.

'Hi, Poppy, how's it going?'

'Good, thanks, Paul.'

'Did the lady with miscarriage get off to EPAS?'

'Yeah, she just left,' Poppy said, squeezing out her teabag and adding a splash of milk.

Paul made a cup too, and they sat at the small, round, scarred table in the centre. *This table must have a few tales to tell.*

'So tell me a bit about you, Paul. Where are you from?'

'I'm from the Gong.'

'Wollongong?'

'Yep.'

'So did you go to the beach a lot growing up?'

'A bit. But cycling became more my thing as I got older.'

'So where did you go to uni, then?'

'I moved up here and went to Sydney Uni.'

'And have you always been at The Bennelong?'

'Since internship, pretty much. A few country terms here and there.'

'Wow, so sounds like you really like it here.'

'I guess it feels a bit like home now.'

'That must be nice, to feel like a part of the place. What about ED? How far along are you in training?'

'This is my final year. Just got to pass my final exams and finish out this year.'

'Wow. That must be exciting, coming to the end?'

'Yeah. I'm definitely ready to take the next step. But lots of study and exams to go first.'

'Yeah. I'm just glad to have a break from exams for a while.'

'Fair enough, too…and Seb tells me you did uni in Newcastle?'

'Yep, but I'm from Orange originally. High school border in Sydney. Bit all round the place.'

'And are you living locally?'

'Just up in Newtown, at the station end. How about you?'

'A little bit further – I'm in Marrickville.'

'Do you have flatmates?'

'Just one. He's almost finished ICU, so often with our shifts we hardly see each other. It means there's less distraction for studying.'

'And do you have a partner?'

'No. 'Fraid I'm single at the moment.'

'Hmm.'

'You?'

'Umm. No, I'm single too.'

Poppy took a long sip of her tea, which had now cooled enough not to scald her hard palate.

'OK, so what do you like to do when you're not studying or working?'

'I often cycle back to Wollongong to visit my family.'

'Don't you get scared cycling on the roads?'

'Sometimes. It can be dicey, but it's a great feeling, and sometimes the views are breathtaking.'

'I can imagine it would give you a real high.'

'It can do,' Paul said, holding her gaze.

Lucy burst through the door.

'Paul, we need you back inside.'

'OK. Ciao, Poppy.'

Poppy felt a sense of relief. Paul was really nice, and really supportive, but sometimes he held her gaze that beat too long. It made her uncomfortable. She wasn't romantically interested in him and didn't want to get into an awkward situation with him. She'd been there before.

Chapter 10

At quitting time, as she waited for Gemma and Lucas, it disappointed her that she still hadn't received a text from Josh. *Maybe I've misread the signals. Maybe he didn't like the kiss as much as I did. Maybe he's seeing someone else. Could the two-week wait be more a brush off than an attempt to have adequate time to get to know each other?* As she was thinking this, one of the other interns, who she'd studied with in Newcastle, came walking past.

Her name was Charlotte, and Poppy had never liked her much. She was one of those people who was pretty fake – she'd gush over you if you had something new and then find some way of giving you a backhanded compliment like, 'Oh that top looks so good on you! I couldn't wear it sadly, as my boobs are just too big.' The kind of girl who'll be friendly when your boyfriend was around but then try to steal him behind your back.

'Hi, Poppy!' she exclaimed, with a bright smile that didn't reach her eyes.

'Hi, Charlotte, how are you?'

'Oh, I'm great. I'm doing Respiratory with Dr Anderson and really loving it. She is just such an inspiration. How about you?'

'I'm doing ED.'

'How's it going?'

'Great, thanks. The staff are really nice and I'm learning lots.'

'Oh, that's great. Oh, and here comes Gemma and Lucas.'

They exchanged hellos, but Poppy knew Gemma and Lucas liked Charlotte even less than she did.

'Come on, Pop, let's make a move,' said Gemma, frostily.

'Oh, are you three still living together? Still the third wheel, hey, Poppy?' she said, laughing like a hyena.

'Actually Charlotte, maybe having relationships as strong as family is just something you'll never know, seeing as how everything is up for grabs in your world,' said Gemma.

Poppy was incredulous. She'd never seen Gemma be so cutting. The three of them walked away, leaving Charlotte with her mouth still gaping.

Once they were out of earshot, Poppy asked Gemma, 'So what prompted that?'

'Have you forgotten when Lucas and I were newly dating and I was visiting my folks and you guys went out and she told him I was screwing someone else and then made a pass at him?'

'No, I certainly haven't forgotten. I almost slapped her on the spot when I saw.'

'And what about that time she tried to get you to miss that re-scheduled exam? That woman is pure evil.'

'Well, I definitely agree with you there,' said Poppy.

'And she has halitosis,' Lucas added, making them all laugh.

They spent the rest of the walk home reminiscing about their uni days and putting Charlotte far from their minds. Despite that, Poppy couldn't quite dispel her disappointment over Josh.

Poppy had never been to Luna Park before. The weather was lovely, warm but not too humid, with a slight breeze. She wore her big summer hat, some short bottle-green shorts and a flowy cotton top. The mid-week, late morning train was fairly empty, and Poppy enjoyed reading the paper in a leisurely way and gazing out the window. She felt like she was on holiday whilst the rest of Sydney was at work.

'Let's start with the Ferris Wheel,' Steph said, dragging Poppy by the arm.

Poppy enjoyed the view over the harbour and bridge as they turned round and round. There were a good number of boats on the harbour, sails flying, making the most of the breeze, and Poppy appreciated in the moment what an amazing city Sydney was. She'd enjoyed her five years in

Newcastle, had made fantastic friendships, but Sydney had so much going for it. Yes, it was expensive, but the beauty of the harbour was unrivalled, and the myriad opportunities in terms of work, culture, and entertainment made the downsides of big city living palatable.

'What next?' Poppy asked.

'Sideshow alley? I think I can take those clowns on.'

Their complete lack of skill on the games designed to knock down pins or shoot targets meant no prizes were easily forthcoming, and clearly professional sports were not in either of their futures. However, the randomness of the moving clown heads saw a gimmick prize of overlarge glasses for Steph which complemented her outfit to a T. They used the photobooth to take some joke pics, taking it in turns to wear the snazzy glasses, and laughed their way to the roller coaster. Again, they were gifted a fabulous view of the harbour at the top of the coaster just before it plunged down, sending their hair flying and Poppy's stomach up into her chest.

The afternoon passed by with hot dogs and popcorn, laughs and squeals, and when they felt they'd had enough, they took themselves next door to Ripples for a few drinks and an early dinner.

'So, tell me more about Ben?' Poppy asked when their drinks arrived.

'Well, the sex has been great. He's got good stamina. But I'm just not sure we've got enough in common to move from boinking buddies to coupledom.'

'Well, have you had a date outside the bedroom?'

'Not really,' Steph replied. 'We mainly just meet up and have sex.'

'Well, maybe you could try meeting at a café for a meal and see how it goes? You obviously had enough to talk about that night we all went out to start things off.'

'True. Yeah, maybe that's a good idea.'

'How's the study going?'

'Slowly. But what about you? What's happening with Josh?'

Poppy filled her in on their date and the lack of contact since.

'What do you make of it?' she asked Steph.

'Yeah, that is weird. Maybe he's just busy?'

'That's a pretty crappy excuse, though, not to respond to a text, let alone call after a date.'

'Fair point.'

After dinner, Steph headed off to Ben's for a booty call, so Poppy caught the train home.

'Hi, Mum,' Poppy said the following day when she rang after a swim at the beach.

'Hi, darling. How are you?'

'Good, busy. How are you?'

'I'm fine, darling. Your dad's been driving me nuts, but that's not unusual.'

Poppy laughed. 'What's he done this time?' Knowing very well that her Mum wasn't really upset with him, she just liked to pretend she was.

'Well, I've been trying to get him to come to my book club, thinking it might be something we could do together. But no, all he wants to do is sit on the couch and watch telly.'

'But, Mum, are there any other men at the book club?'

'No.'

'Well, maybe that's why…he thinks he'll be stuck with a bunch of giggly ladies, drinking their chardies and talking about *Fifty Shades of Grey*.'

'Hunh… I hadn't thought of that… But *Fifty Shades*, that's so 2012.'

Poppy laughed.

'What about you, darling? How's work going?'

'I've had some days off, which is good, but I've got four night shifts coming up, which I'm anxious about.'

'You'll be fine, love. Just take one thing at a time. How about Gemma and Lucas? How are they doing?'

'Gemma's having a great time in Obstetrics, but Lucas isn't having much fun. He's not being very well supported, unfortunately.'

'Why don't you all come up for a visit?'

'That's a nice idea, but it's really hard to get time off together… We'll see.'

'OK, darling, well I'd better shuffle along. I've got a tea cake to take out of the oven.'

'Bye, Mum, I love you.'

'I love you too, darling.'

The following day would be the first of four night shifts, and she wasn't sure how to prepare. Should she stay up late tonight and try to sleep in tomorrow? In the end, she decided to go out. She tried to convince Gemma and Lucas, but neither were keen, so she scrolled through her contacts wondering who she might convince.

She met up with a couple of the other interns who were heading out to King Street. They met up at Earl's Juke Joint, settled into a table with pews for seats and caught up on how their various terms were treating them. After a couple of cocktails, they were considering food options when Will and his flatmate, Penny, walked in. Will spotted Poppy and sidled over. She felt her face lighting up as he smiled in greeting.

'Hi, Will, good to see you,' Poppy said. *Damn he looks good!*

'Hi, Poppy. You remember Penny?'

'Sure. Hi, Penny, how are you? Do you guys want to join us?'

'Sounds good.'

'We'll just shift over.'

They squeezed in closer so Will could sit next to her, and Penny could fit opposite.

When Will went to the bar Poppy watched him; his tall frame and ease in talking to the bartender. He had confidence in who he was without the arrogance that Josh displayed. She liked the person he was: kind, thoughtful. He didn't appear to be a game player, which was refreshing. But he had not shown any sign since that first night of wanting to try again with her. So clearly he just wanted to be friends. And that would have to be OK with her. She could always use another good friend like Gemma and Lucas. They were the best people in her life.

'So, have you been surfing much lately?' Poppy asked when he sat back down again.

'Weekends mostly. Occasionally after work, if I'm not too late.'

'And why do you love it so much?'

'It's a much nicer way to exercise than hitting the weights at the gym with a bunch of other sweaty dudes. And it's a great way to clear your mind. It's just really calming. I can't explain it. But you should give it a try, really.'

'I'm more a swim at the shallow end kind of girl.'

'I think you're braver than you think you are. And look, I got Penny into it a few years ago – you tell her how good it is, Pen.'

'He's right. It's like skating on water. The wind is whipping into you and you're on this wave that's crashing, and you're not dying. It's a rush.'

'Now it sounds even scarier!' Poppy said laughing.

'You could do it,' Penny reassured her. *Was she being friendly?* Poppy was surprised.

They chatted about work and nibbled on bar snacks.

'Should we get some more food?' Poppy asked everyone once the bar snacks had dwindled, looking around at their faces.

'We were just going to have a quick bite,' Will said, looking over to Penny.

'Nah, we can stay longer,' Penny said, and Will nodded.

'Great, well let's order some more food then,' Poppy said cheerfully.

Poppy and Will were sitting side by side, their limbs touching, and Poppy was increasingly conscious of this. He was in the middle of an anecdote from work:

'They literally peeled the face down from the hairline!'

'Oh, gross,' Penny said as the others made similar expressions of eager disgust.

'I've never seen anything like it. The muscles and blood vessels were glistening and bright red, it was like a horror show.'

They were all glued to the story, Poppy included. But she also had a moment to enjoy Will's company. It was reminding her of what it was like to shadow him before her first shift. Such a congenial, inclusive person. *Yep, he'd definitely make a great friend.*

Poppy tried to get back out of her head. Will had moved on to talking about another case from his week.

'So, he was already quite doped up when we came to review him in the anaesthetic bay and he said to us, "Doc, it's not going to leave a bad scar, will it? The chicks really dig me, you know?" And my boss was like, "Don't worry, we'll keep it tiny. The chicks will still love you," And honestly it was so funny, my old English boss using the word "chicks" and talking to a bikie like he was his best mate. It made me smile all day.'

Poppy liked how he always found the good in a situation. Others might have made a big deal of this patient's bikie status and become remote and aloof, but not Will.

The others were swapping anecdotes, but Poppy couldn't help admiring Will and smiling. He turned to her, saw her smiling and asked, 'How about you, Poppy? How's ED going?'

'Pretty good. Most of the staff are really nice.'

'Paul and Seb treating you OK?'

'Those two are the best. And Steph and Lucy and Graham. They're such a good group.'

'Yeah, that is one of the nice things about ED. It feels like a team.'

It felt nice to have this shared group with Will, all such nice people. After a couple more drinks, the others were keen to move on to dancing, but Poppy wasn't in the mood. They convinced Penny to join the dance troupe, so Will and Poppy went for a stroll. They headed to the park and sat on Poppy's favourite bench. The night air was still comfortable, not very humid, and just a light, cool breeze. Poppy listened attentively as Will told her about his family back in Queensland, and his nieces and nephews.

'So, at Christmas, I managed to get home, and it was about forty degrees, and the kids were all red and cranky, so I took them outside and turned on the sprinkler and we ran backwards and forwards over the jets for about half an hour. They were squealing like it was the best thing ever.'

'They'd never done the poor man's swim before?'

'No, they've got a pool at their place, so they've never had to resort to it.'

'Well, now you've inducted them into the great Aussie sprinkler run, they'll never look at a hose the same way again.'

'Probably not.'

Poppy could picture Will being the cool uncle who they would climb all over and who would sit on the floor playing games with them. She liked that mental image of him.

On the walk home she asked him, 'So any advice for how to prepare for nights?'

'Nah, it's going to be a shock to the system, no matter what you do.'

'I thought you might say something like that.'

'You'll survive. I have great confidence in you,' he said, and Poppy noticed the intensity of his gaze. It sent her chest into flip-flop mode. *Is there still a chance?*

'Fingers crossed,' she said, as they arrived at her front door. 'Thanks for walking me home, Will.'

'Anytime, Poppy. Tonight was fun.'

'Yeah, it was,' and, without thinking, she leaned in and kissed him goodnight on the cheek, Will placing a hand on her waist as she did. She let her lips linger on his cheek just a fraction of a second. Just long enough to feel the weight of his hand on her waist and the soft bristles on his cheek. They locked eyes as she pulled away and Poppy was unsure of what she saw there – *was it friendship, or could it be more?*

'Well, night Poppy. Good luck for the night shifts.'

'Thanks, Will, see you on the other side?'

'Yeah, that'd be good.'

Chapter 11

Night shifts in ED were on minimal staffing. Only two doctors on each side and a consultant on-call at home with the expectation that they would not be called. Paul was the senior on for her first three nights. The first shift Poppy was on subbies and found it to be similar to her previous experiences. Although being a Friday night, there was a greater proportion of drunk customers.

One of Poppy's first patients of the night was a drunken homeless man who was '*PFO*' (pissed and fell over).

'Fred, you're a bit of a mess, aren't you?' Poppy asked when she wheeled him into a cubicle.

His clothes were threadbare, but he looked to be wearing several layers despite the relatively warm summer night. And the smell! Poppy was trying to keep her nose closed as she spoke to him, to avoid gagging. It was like a rotting, putrid corpse. That was the only way to describe it. He had several bruises and scrapes and a nasty laceration on his forehead involving the eyebrow. Poppy gloved and donned a gown, wanting to keep their contact as limited as possible. She really didn't want his stench to rub off onto her and she had no idea what might lie under all the filth and dirt covering him.

'Alright, I just want to get some of these clothes off, so I can check all your injuries, OK?'

'No! Not my clothes, don't steal my clothes,' he shouted.

'It's OK, Fred, you can have them back, I just want to check you over… See, I'll put all your clothes in this pink bag, and you can have them all back once we're done.'

'Blurp,' Fred burped, and a paint stripper smell blasted Poppy in the face.

Great, just great. Poppy gagged, but managed to hold down her stomach contents.

'Let's try and get this off first,' Poppy said, trying to thread Fred's arm through the sleeve of what Poppy presumed was once a wool cardigan.

'No.' Fred grabbed the end and pulled back toward himself in some absurd tug-of-war, preventing her from getting it off over his hand.

Poppy stood back, gloved hands clasped in front of her as she surveyed Fred. *I'm going to need some help.*

'I'm just going to get one of my colleagues to give me a hand, OK, Fred?'

He burped again in response, but at least this time Poppy was out of the jet stream.

She made her way back down the corridor to flight deck and spied Lucy coming out of the drug and supply room.

'Luce, can you possibly give me a hand with a patient?'

'Sure, just let me hang these fluids up, and I'll be right with you. Which cubbie?'

'Six. Thanks, Luce, you're the best.'

Poppy slowly made her way back to the patient. She was in no rush to be stuck in a confined space with him by herself again. The stench alone was toxic. But she still made it back before Lucy joined her. She sighed internally, but figured she should try again to start undressing him. A sonorous snore greeted her when she pulled back the curtain. His head jerked up at the sound and his eyes peeled open. He was still in the wheelchair and eyeing her warily, like the prey waiting for the predator to strike.

'OK, Fred, let's try getting some of these clothes off again.'

As soon as Poppy bent forward to try to touch his cardigan he raised his elbow, almost clocking her in the face. She abruptly stepped back and stood again. *Jeez, this is going nowhere fast.* Thankfully, Lucy arrived and when the stench and squalor hit her after opening the curtain she recoiled, taking a step back and raising her eyebrows at Poppy. But she entered the cubicle and stood beside her. This time Fred let out a loud fart as he dozed off to sleep again.

'Thanks for the heads up,' Lucy whispered to Poppy.

'Sorry!' Poppy whispered back.

'OK, what's the plan?'

'We need to get his clothes off so I can actually assess all his injuries. He's obviously got a cut on his forehead under that bandage, but I'm worried there could be more under all of that,' Poppy said using a hand to gesture over all of Fred's body. 'And I thought it would be better to get him out of his clothes from the wheelchair rather than the bed, to try to keep that clean for now. He might even need a shower. I don't know, what do you think is the best way to tackle him?'

'Umm...yep, I think we need to get the clothes off and get him into the shower and then see what we're dealing with. Why don't we just wheel him around to the shower and get the kit off there? We can wash him and check him over then put him in a gown and bring him back.'

'OK, let's do it.'

'I think we need Graham to help, though. We need some extra muscle. I'll grab him. Can you get a gown and blanket to bring with us?'

'Sure. I'll tape that bandage securely on his forehead to keep that dry whilst we shower him too.'

Lucy nodded and left to get Graham.

Fred snored peacefully, letting out the occasional burp, until they had him in the shower stall and the water started running.

'Wha's going on?' he bellowed, suddenly awake again.

'We're just going to get you cleaned up,' Graham said. 'First, we're going to get you standing up. On three, we're going to help lift you. One...two...three,' and Graham and Lucy who each had a grip under a shoulder lifted him to stand whilst Poppy wheeled the chair back out of the way and moved the commode chair into place.

'While you're up, we're going to get your clothes off,' Graham said as Lucy quickly dacked him. 'Lift one leg for us, Fred... Now the other.' Lucy whisked the clothes away to the side and Poppy placed them straight into the pink belongings bag, keeping her nose firmly shut and breathing through her mouth. Lucy went back to holding under a shoulder and Graham continued, 'Now we're going to lower you onto this chair on three...one...two...three.'

Once he was sitting on the commode, with his bottom half naked, Lucy and Graham quickly stripped the rest of his clothes off. Poppy was impressed. They had obviously done this before, it was so slick; Fred had no time to complain or fight back.

'OK, now, Fred, you're going to behave whilst they clean you up, aren't you?'

'A'right,' Fred mumbled, clearly subdued, realising he'd lost this fight.

'Sing out if you need any more help,' Graham said, leaving Poppy and Lucy to continue without him. They couldn't really have two nurses doing this on such a skeleton crew. And Poppy didn't want to leave Lucy to do it on her own, so she stayed and helped as much as she could, and assessed his injuries whilst they were cleaning him.

There didn't appear to be any fractures, which was good, mainly just some bruising to his face and right side, and the laceration above the right eyebrow which was currently bandaged. But when she got behind the commode she noticed a deep ulcer on his left heel. It only became evident when a thick layer of dirt and dried blood covering it fell away when the shower hose sprayed that area.

'Umm…that looks bad,' Poppy said.

Lucy bent around Fred's back and looked at what Poppy was now pointing at. 'Yeah, it does.'

When they finally had him as clean as possible and had dried him off and got him into a gown, he didn't fight them when they manoeuvered him back into the wheelchair which Poppy had wiped clean. Poppy wheeled him back to his cubicle and Lucy stayed to clean the shower stall. She passed Graham on the way and recruited him to help her get Fred onto the bed.

'Right,' she said once Fred was under a blanket on the bed and a bluey was under his left heel. The ulcer had started to ooze after the chunk of dried blood had come off. 'I'm going to get what I need to fix the cut on your head, there, Fred and I'll clean up your heel too. I'll be back in a jiff.'

Fred nodded his head, but by the time Poppy returned with her equipment, he was fast asleep, snoring sonorously again. Whilst his breath was still toxic, at least the rest of him smelt better. The shower had obviously taken it out of him as he slept through the entire procedure, even the local anaesthetic injection. When she'd finished suturing, Poppy stood and moved back in front of Fred to check the cosmesis of the eyebrow, to make sure it was still straight. *Yep, that looks great!* A tickle of pride welled up inside her. This was the first time she had sutured someone completely on her own, and it looked fantastic. *I'll leave the dressing off for now so Paul can have a look.*

Poppy disposed of the sharps, then gently pulled the blanket off Fred's left foot so she could clean and review the heel ulcer. She dipped the leftover gauze into the chlorhexidine and then cleaned the heel, removing the last of the scab. Once it was cleaned, it was obvious the ulceration went down to tendon. Is that bone, Poppy wondered when she probed the base of the ulcer. She left it exposed and went to find Paul.

'Hi, Paul. Can you come and look at a patient for me?'

'Sure,' he said standing up from the computer he'd been working at.

'I've got an itinerant man PFO with a forehead laceration that I've sutured for you to review, but he's also got a deep ulcer on his left heel which has tendon and possibly bone exposed at the base.'

'OK. Why did you suture rather than use glue for the laceration?' Paul asked, not unkindly.

'Well, I was going to use glue, but firstly I was worried about the cosmesis of the eyebrow—'

'Fair point—' Paul interrupted.

'But then I also figured he was likely going to need some form of surgical intervention for the heel, so might as well do it properly. Is that OK?'

'Yeah.'

'Nice job on the laceration. That eyebrow looks great. Well done.'

'Thanks,' Poppy said smiling, her right dimple briefly on display.

'And look, there's no right answer in this situation, but I probably would have just glued. He's itinerant, unreliable for follow-up, and probably wouldn't care about cosmesis either.'

'OK… I can cut them out and glue it, if you think that's best?'

'No, leave it. You're right,' Paul said after bending over to review the heel ulcer. 'That's going to need surgery. He'll be in at least a week, if he doesn't abscond, so they can remove the sutures before discharge.'

Poppy sighed with relief. 'I'll call the Surg Reg.'

'Yep.'

'Thanks, Paul.'

'Don't forget a tetanus booster.'

She typed up her notes and checked the on-call roster. There was a Surgical Registrar on-site twenty-four hours, but as she saw the name listed her stomach dropped. It was Tim, again.

Great, not bad enough to spend two hours inhaling toxic fumes, now I have to deal with the grumpiest Registrar around. Poppy turned around, looking for the lollies she'd seen earlier on the central bench. She grabbed a python and a couple of red frogs and ate them first before calling Tim.

OK, you can do this. Don't let his bad attitude get to you. He's going to be a dick. Just accept it, tell him he needs to review the patient and move on with your night.

'Hi, is that Tim?' Poppy said perkily.

'Yes,' said in a deadpan voice.

'Hi, it's Poppy from ED. I've got an itinerant man with a deep heel ulcer which has exposed tendon and bone at the base for you to review.'

'OK,' he said and hung up the phone, not waiting for any further information, including the patient's name.

How's he going to know who to see? Oh well, I guess that's his problem then.

Poppy updated the handover board that Fred was awaiting surgical review and let Lucy know as well, hoping that someone would notice Tim when he came down and steer him in the right direction. *Duty done.* Poppy took another couple of lollies and moved on.

Half an hour later, when Tim showed up, Poppy went over to him.

'Hi, Tim, I'll take you over to see Fred with the heel ulcer.'

Tim nodded but made no effort to address or thank her. Fred was still unconscious, so Tim just looked at the heel and felt his ankle, popliteal and femoral pulses without waking him. He then turned and headed back to the flight deck, without so much as a word to Poppy. *What a pig!* She sighed but followed like a dog and stood next to him at flight deck waiting for some instructions or information. But he studiously ignored her. Poppy could stand it no longer when he stood and turned to leave. She tapped his shoulder, forcing him to turn back to her. 'So what's the plan, Tim?'

'Admit to Vascular Surgery. Keep him nil by mouth. He can go to the ward.'

Short, sharp sentences. As little information as it was possible to convey. Then he continued on his way back to the wards, Poppy presumed.

Poppy huffed and sat down. 'God, he's a pig.'

'Who, Tim?' Paul asked.

Whoops, I said that out loud!

'I shouldn't have said that.'

'It's OK, I won't hold it against you,' Paul said, smiling.

'Is he always like that? So devoid of human emotion?'

'Pretty much.'

'Why?'

'I don't know. Don't really know much about him. He's just…Tim.'

'But some of the others appear OK.'

'He's been here a couple of years and they work the junior Surgical Registrars pretty hard. Long hours, lots of responsibility, and minimal supervision. It can break some people.'

'It shouldn't be that way.'

'I agree. Look, shift work is hard. ED is tough too. Constantly flicking from days to evenings to nights. It messes up your body clock, ruins your relationships, and turns you a bit loopy.'

'Wow, you're really selling it, Paul.' Poppy laughed dryly.

He laughed too, but said, 'Well, you gotta know what you're getting yourself into. If you can see all that ahead of you and not be deterred, then ED might be for you.'

'Maybe they shouldn't put you forward for careers week,' Poppy suggested, a mischievous grin forming and they laughed again.

Somehow they glossed over Tim and what Poppy assumed was his broken spirit.

Maybe next time I see him I could try to chat with him. I'm sure I can ignore his rudeness and make an effort. Maybe he just needs someone to talk to, someone to give a shit. It's the least I can do. Got to give him at least one chance, right?

Poppy was busy and working constantly until about four o'clock, when there was a lull. Whilst she'd nibbled on some chips and lollies, and had a bottle of Coke No Sugar from the vending machine, she hadn't really felt like eating a proper meal. But she was feeling tired, and she had a vague buzzing sensation in her head. It was a bit like being jet-lagged. She wondered if it would continue for the rest of her nights.

Poppy donned her sunnies as she headed out into the bright sunlight when her shift ended. The heat as she emerged from the air conditioning hit her like a wall. Now the buzzy jetlag feeling turned more into the jackhammer of a hangover. She headed home, her legs feeling heavier with each step. At home she ate some toast, had a cup of tea and an apple, before a long soak in the tub. Then she lowered the blinds and sunk into bed.

Chapter 12

'Watch out, Poppy, the crazies will be out in force tonight,' Graham greeted Poppy as she entered flight deck for her third night shift. Poppy was back on Acute after a relatively straightforward shift the previous night.

'Ah, full moon,' replied Poppy, with a sceptical arch of an eyebrow.

'Don't doubt it, honey, it's a real thing. Right, Paul?'

'He's right. We did a little study the year before last looking at presenting complaints and found a statistically significant spike in mental health and drug and alcohol-related presentations on full moon cycles compared with the rest of the lunar cycle.'

Poppy laughed, not sure if they were teasing her.

'No, seriously,' said Paul. He seemed so sincere, Poppy had to assume he was being honest.

'That's weird.'

'Yep, that's the point. People go a little cuckoo when it's a full moon,' Paul said.

'Oh well, forewarned is forearmed, I guess.'

'Yep, we'll tackle the loonies together,' Paul said with a smile.

With that, they headed to the boards for handover. Poppy spent the first couple of hours sorting out a patient handed over to her. But then the bat phone rang, and the night changed irrevocably. Graham took the call and Paul and Poppy gathered close, waiting for his summary.

'Male, twenties, suicide attempt. Pills at scene. CPR en route, five minutes out,' Graham relayed when he hung up.

'OK,' said Paul. 'Let's get the room ready. Annie,' Paul grabbed the passing nurse, 'can you put out the page to ICU and Anaesthetics, then be our scribe?'

'Sure, Paul,' Annie said.

Graham, Poppy, and Paul prepped Resus one and donned gloves, gowns and eye shields.

'OK, Poppy, here's the plan,' Paul said calmly before detailing what they would do when the paramedics arrived. Poppy could see he was already geed-up, bouncing on the balls of his feet more than usual. Poppy felt her adrenaline surging and her heart rate picking up as sweat prickled inside her gloves and in her armpits.

She stood out of the way at the edge of the room as the paramedics wheeled in the gurney. As the bed passed in front of her, Poppy felt time slow down as she glimpsed the man's face and realised it was Tim, the grumpy Surgical Registrar. *What the fuck?* She audibly took in a breath, and Paul locked eyes with her. *This can't be happening.* Poppy was frozen until Paul called out, 'All hands for transfer to bed.' Poppy forced her limbs to move forward while her brain continued to struggle to process this picture. Tim was so still and grey and she couldn't take her eyes off his face.

'Poppy,' Graham prompted.

'Sorry,' she said as she grabbed the slide sheet and waited for Paul's signal to help slide Tim across from the trolley onto the bed.

Sangeetha and Andrew arrived as the paramedic who had been performing chest compressions stopped briefly during transfer and swapped with her partner. Sweat was running down her face and she was flushed from the effort. They all performed their designated tasks, and it was like a well-choreographed scene. Poppy, despite her shock, concentrated on gaining additional IV access whilst Andrew took over the airway. Graham hooked up leads and monitors, and Sangeetha and Paul got as much information as they could from the paramedics.

'What pills or other substances did you see at the scene?' Sangeetha asked the paramedic who wasn't performing CPR.

'He was found by his flatmate in the bathroom. There was an empty bottle of digoxin and one of diazepam near a half-empty bottle of scotch.'

'Any output or spontaneous respiration?'

'No. We immediately commenced CPR once we did an initial assessment. Delivered two rounds of adrenaline. Down time now at about twelve minutes.'

'OK, anything else you can tell us?'

'No, I think that's it.'

'OK, thank you,' said Paul. 'Poppy, can you take over CPR?'

'OK,' Poppy said as she handed the bloods over to Annie.

There was still no recordable rhythm on the monitors, but this was a colleague. They were going to exhaust everything they could think of to try to bring him back. *Come on, Tim. Don't die…don't die…don't die.* Poppy kept repeating this in her head every time her arms pushed down with a compression. She'd lost all sense of time and what was happening around her. There was just a burning desire for Tim to breathe again. Or for this to be some warped nightmare that she was going to wake up from. A trail of sweat ran down her back and into her underwear and she was starting to puff with each compression. *I'm not stopping, Tim. I'll keep going until I collapse if I have to. Just come back!*

Despite multiple rounds of adrenaline and Poppy continuing to perform chest compressions until her shoulders burned and the sweat was causing tiny rivulets down her face, her hair sweat plastered to her forehead, at no stage was there any cardiac output.

'OK, team. Let's stop…' Paul said after twenty-five minutes. 'Time of death one twelve a.m.'

Poppy climbed down off the stool, taking the hand Paul offered. She looked at Tim's pale, frozen face as she got down and still couldn't believe what had just happened. A shiver ran up her spine and over her scalp. *How can this be real? Why did he do this? Why is this job so hard?*

Poppy didn't break down and cry then and there, but if you asked her later how she got through the rest of the shift, or how she got home, she wouldn't be able to tell you. She was frozen at that point in time, staring at Tim's lifeless face. The endotracheal tube keeping his lips parted like the rotating clown heads at Luna Park. It was only when she got home that she broke down. Lying on her bed listening to Lewis Capaldi singing, 'Someone you loved' as she heaved chest-wracking sobs until she could cry no more.

She kept thinking of how they had failed Tim, and how she had failed her sister.

Her little sister, Lucinda (or Lulu), had been quiet and reserved where Poppy was gregarious and popular. Growing up in Orange, a small country town, Lulu had a few very close friends but struggled with the transition to the large boarding school in Sydney. Poppy was in year twelve but the subsequent year she moved to Newcastle for university and was not physically there for Lulu. Poppy still regretted not phoning enough or visiting her that year, and was completely oblivious to Lulu's slide into depression. She was busy shedding the restrictions of boarding school – partying, making friends, living independently, and, occasionally, studying. She hardly called Lulu and hadn't visited her much in that first term.

It was Poppy's Mum who first alerted her to Lulu's decline. Poppy clearly remembered that phone call and hearing her Mum's voice break as she described how thin and withdrawn Lulu had been on their weekend visit.

'Poppy, I don't understand it… I don't know what's happened… I called the house matron and she said she thought there might be some bullying, but Lulu hadn't disclosed anything to her,' her mother said through tears. Just hearing her mother cry on the phone tore something inside Poppy. Your parents were supposed to be strong and protect you, it wasn't supposed to be the other way around.

'Can you go and visit her on the weekend? Maybe she'll open up to you?' her mum implored.

'Absolutely, Mum. I'll go. And I'll call too, try and see if I can dig anything out of her… Don't worry, Mum, I'm sure it'll all work out OK,' Poppy tried to reassure her, whilst her own anxiety started to gain momentum.

'Hey, Lulu,' Poppy said when she managed to get her on the phone the next night. 'I've got good news! I'm coming down to take you out on the weekend.'

'Oh, OK,' Lulu had replied with no matching excitement in her voice. Her negative tone like a slap in the face. She'd been secretly hoping that her mum was exaggerating, or that Lulu would immediately open up to her. But now, she realised, this was going to be tougher than she thought.

'Yeah,' Poppy tried again, making an effort to keep her voice upbeat, 'I was thinking we could stay at Mum and Dad's flat and have pizza and a movie on Friday night, then get our nails done on Saturday. My treat. What do you think?'

'Umm…whatever.'

There was silence and Poppy waited, hoping Lulu might fill it. But it just dragged on. Eventually, Poppy had to fill it with something.

'Are you OK, Lu?' she asked gently.

'Yeah… Look, I've gotta go, Pop. See you on the weekend.' And she hung up before Poppy could say anything more.

Poppy kept trying to call her the rest of the week, without success. Every time she got one of the girls on her dorm floor they told her Lulu wasn't there, no matter what time she called. Poppy wasn't sure if Lulu didn't want to speak to her, or if the girls weren't letting Lulu know about the calls. But Poppy was hopeful that a visit from her big sister that weekend would help Lulu see how much she was loved.

A phone call from her Mum shattered her sleep early Friday morning.

'Mum?' Poppy croaked out, her brain still half asleep.

'Poppy…' Her Mum's voice cracked and paused after only saying her name.

'What's wrong, Mum?' Poppy responded, suddenly sitting up, wide awake. 'What's happened?' she asked again as she heard her mother crying softly, the phone moving further from her mouth. Then her dad was on the phone.

'Poppy, honey. We've got terrible news… I'm not sure how to say this, but Lulu's no longer with us.'

'What? What do you mean?' Poppy asked, tears suddenly erupting in her eyes, her hand shaking as it held the phone.

'Love, Lulu killed herself,' and he choked back his own sob.

Poppy couldn't believe it. 'No,' she cried out.

'I'm sorry, love, but it's true.'

'How? What happened?'

There was a long pause and Poppy could hear her father breathing on the other end of the phone and the faint sound of her mother crying in the background.

'I want to know Dad.'

He sighed heavily again, then said, 'She hung herself in the shower after everyone was asleep.'

The industrial shower heads suspended directly overhead on a steel supporting bar, supplying each of the shower cubicles in turn. That strong steel beam easily took her light weight, and the height was just sufficient after she'd used the stepladder from the cleaner's cupboard to reach the beam. Of course, her father didn't tell her all these details on the phone, but eventually Poppy had pieced together all the information.

Her roommate had woken, and, finding Lulu's bed empty, gone in search of her and made the horrific discovery. Poppy couldn't accept this. She couldn't accept her beautiful, gentle, thoughtful little sister was gone.

'Are you sure you're OK to drive yourself?' Gemma asked as Poppy packed a small overnight bag to put in Gemma and Lucas' car.

'Yep,' Poppy said shortly, still zipping up the bag, her heavy, swollen eyes lowered on the task. Gemma put a hand on her shoulder, forcing Poppy to stop and look at her. When she saw the concern on her friend's face, she let go of the bag and sat on the bed.

'I'll take it slowly. But I need to get down there, Gem. We're going to meet at the school.'

'OK, but do be careful and let me know when you get there.'

'I promise. I'll text you,' Poppy reassured her friend before hugging her tightly and heading to the car.

By the time Poppy met her parents at the entrance to the school, she was tired. She had been careful on the drive and had maintained her focus on the road, but now her brain felt numb and her limbs leaden. Her mother engulfed her in a hug, and Poppy felt her legs shake as she cried into her mother's neck whilst she rubbed her back. Wind whipped her hair off her shoulders and Poppy stepped out of the embrace before the wind bowled them over. Her dad bent down and kissed her cheek, his face dotted with silver stubble, his shirt creased from the drive. Her mother held her hand

and her father put a hand on her back as they slowly walked as one through the entrance and made their way to the principal's office. The wind was whipping at their ankles, like a sheepdog herding sheep into the pen.

When they met with the principal, the house mistress, and the head of boarding, it was like an out-of-body experience for Poppy. She was in the room, but her mind was hovering overhead, hearing their words as muffled and far away. Not penetrating, not lingering or causing a reaction. Like plastic arrows hitting a metal barrier and falling straight to the ground. She was numb. They were offering platitudes of how sorry they were and what a tragedy it was, but her brain had gone into survival mode, not letting in any more sadness. Her body's way of avoiding complete meltdown. At least for now. None of it felt real. If she had been more present in that moment, would she have railed against them, wanting answers for their lack of pastoral care and their failure to protect and support Lulu?

The headmistress told them Lulu had left a letter, but they had given it to the police and it would be a week before they could read it. Eventually, the shrunken, huddled trio were ushered to Lulu's room and given time alone. It was only in Lulu's room, sitting on her bed, amongst her things, that Poppy finally felt her absence. It was like a part of her heart was missing. Their family could never be whole again without Lulu. How could they? And whilst looking at the framed photo of the two of them laughing and smiling, she finally broke. Deep, guttural sobs erupted from within as the tears poured from her eyes. Her mother and father joined her on the bed, and they gripped each other as if hanging on for dear life. They stayed this way, Poppy sandwiched between them, for a long time.

Poppy's dad's eyes dried first, and he sat up, one hand still resting on Poppy's back and one on his wife's hand. He sat, waiting for them to settle. He had always been a patient man. Not a massive talker, but kind and thoughtful. The kind of father who'd pick you up if you'd been out drinking and didn't have a sober lift home, no matter what the time. This was the first time Poppy had ever seen him cry and, later, when she had more perspective, she would realise what an enormous impact this event had had on them all. In the years after Lulu's death, Poppy's dad would himself become more withdrawn, a shadow of his former self. His interactions with Poppy became primarily via his wife, and they would spend little time alone together. Maybe he was afraid to suffer such a profound loss again, and limited his exposure to Poppy in order to somehow protect himself from such unbearable pain. Poppy did not know.

The opposite was probably true of Poppy and her mother. This tragedy drew them closer together, and they felt the need to keep each other updated about what was happening in their lives, no matter how small. A lifeline to each other, not to be severed. Particularly over the next two years, they spoke at least a few times a week. This had dwindled to at least once a week in these last few months as if those first years of grieving had been the biggest hurdle.

With dry eyes, they packed up Lulu's things. By this time, the school day had finished, and some boarders were returning to the house. Poppy wondered if they could talk to Lulu's dorm mate, and as her parents slowly took Lulu's possessions down to their car, Poppy approached the house mistress with her request. She agreed and Poppy waited. She sat on a chair in the lounge area, where she had sat so many times herself as a boarder, and wondered how a person could be in such despair that they could not see any hope for the future. Not a single ray of light to break the desolation. She could not reconcile that concept with her sister, and she hoped her dorm mate could shed some light for her.

Grace arrived with the mistress in tow and Poppy watched this young Chinese girl shrink beside the house mistress as they approached. Almost like a toddler will hide behind her mother's legs when being introduced to a stranger.

'Hi, Grace, I'm Poppy, Lulu's sister,' she said, watching Grace's downturned face occasionally sneak a glance at her through barely visible eyelashes. Poppy could see that Grace's eyes were puffy like hers and a crumpled tissue was held tightly in one hand.

'I was wondering if I could talk to you…about Lulu…maybe we could go to your room?'

Grace nodded her head and then turned, saying over her shoulder, 'It's this way.'

Of course, Poppy had just come from their room and knew where it was, but she didn't say that. She was hopeful that in her own room, Lulu's presence still heavy in the air, Grace might open up.

Poppy sat on Lulu's now stripped-bare bed, and Grace sat on her own, clutching a toy wombat to her chest, her gaze on her lap.

'That's cute…your wombat,' Poppy offered and Grace looked up, a brief frown forming between her brows. *Maybe she thinks I'm being sarcastic.* She remembered how paranoid teenagers could be, and that desire to fit in with the crowd was so essential at fourteen.

'Which part of the country are you from?'

'Outside Goulburn.'

'Ah, hence the wombat. We didn't see many in Orange. Lots of kangaroos, though.'

'Yeah. They're everywhere.'

Silence descended again and Poppy waited, allowing a bit of space before launching in.

'I am so sorry you had to see Lulu like that. I can only imagine how hard it was for you.'

'Thank you… And obviously I'm sorry for you too,' Grace said with that slightly offhand teenage bravado, betraying the anxiety lurking beneath.

'Thank you. I appreciate that, Grace.'

Here Poppy paused, giving Grace time to settle.

'I was just wondering if you knew anything that might help me understand why Lulu did this. And I want you to know, nothing you tell me will go back to the school. You won't get in trouble for anything you tell me, I promise.'

There was silence for a couple of minutes and Poppy was careful not to fill it. She felt confident that, if she waited, Grace would open up. The horror of finding her roommate's body would weigh heavily on her conscience and likely outweigh any fear of punishment or retribution. Poppy was rewarded with a tearful Grace recounting Lulu's systematic persecution in her time at the school.

It had started in those first couple of weeks of school when Lulu likely had inadvertently shown up one of the popular girls who had been at the school since kindergarten. Lulu probably hadn't even been aware of the offence. She had come top of the class in tests in Maths and Science, finishing with marks significantly higher than this other girl who had enjoyed top dog position for many years. This on its own shouldn't have warranted the subsequent relentless attack, but Grace felt that the marks, along with Lulu's shy nature, probably mistaken for arrogance and snobbery, precipitated the onslaught.

Initially, it had started with snide comments behind Lulu's back, just loud enough for her to hear before the ensuant sniggering. But it progressed to frank and deliberate exclusion from all social events, the odd trip and fall along the corridor, hiding of possessions including her clothes at swimming, and social media cyber-bullying. This popular girl, whom Grace wouldn't name, was so forceful with other girls in the year that Lulu became completely ostracised. Even in the boarding house, she did not find a safe haven or reprieve, and Grace herself admitted being distant and failing to offer support. At this point Grace really lost it and Poppy moved to sit beside her, wrapping an arm around her shoulders as the guilt and remorse overcame her.

When her sobs subsided to the occasional shudder, Poppy asked if Lulu had talked to any of the staff about what was happening.

'No, she was worried it would just get worse. They were smart, did nothing overt in front of teachers or staff.'

'But surely the house mistress must have seen her eating alone, losing weight, not engaging with others?'

'I think she tried to talk to her, but Lulu brushed her off.'

Poppy thought about this for a while as she sat with Grace, squeezing her shoulder. If Grace had been older and braver and stood up for Lulu, maybe things would have stopped. Similarly, if Lulu had complained, would that have changed the outcome? And what about Poppy's role in all this? She had been here last year and whilst she thought Lulu hadn't made many friends and was hanging out with her quite a bit; she hadn't picked up how serious the problem was. So many pieces of this broken puzzle that could have made a difference if only they had been better placed.

'I'm really sorry, Grace. But thank you for talking to me, I really appreciate it… Can I give you my number? If you ever want to talk about it, you can call me.'

Grace wiped the tears from her eyes and looked back at Poppy.

'I think my parents are going to make me see a grief counsellor.'

'Well, maybe that's a good thing?'

'I don't know… I don't want the others to give me a hard time about it.'

'Surely, they wouldn't? This has got to affect everyone. I don't think those girls are likely to keep behaving the way they were. They must feel really guilty for their role in all this.'

'Yeah…they were crying today. And then whispering at lunch.'

'Maybe they think they will get in trouble?'

'Maybe…but I doubt they will.'

Poppy sat and thought about this. Part of her wanted to find those little bitches and shake them up, but what would that solve? She recognised that their individual guilt over this, regardless of any school punishments, was probably enough to change their behaviour in the future.

The following few months her mother dealt with her grief by meeting with the school, media and the community, dissecting teenage relationships, bullying, cyber-bullying, and mental health issues in teenagers. She threw her energy into developing policies and raising awareness. Her dad worked and slowly withdrew. And Poppy? Well, after a month or so of wallowing in despair, Gemma and Lucas had pulled her out of her funk and forced her to return to uni before she failed. But if Poppy was completely honest with herself, it likely affected all her future relationships. She kept things fairly superficial with guys. No relationships lasting greater than six months. Her only true, close and honest relationships were with Gemma and Lucas. Their support over that first year after Lulu's death really cemented their bond together, and, without them, Poppy likely would have dropped out of medicine altogether. Gemma ensured she ate, studied, and showed up for exams.

And what about Tim? The medical community and hospital structure had failed him too, as had Poppy. *I should have done something for Tim. I should have tried to talk to him, find out if he was depressed.* She felt guilt over this and its weight was heavy. When there were no more tears to shed, she slept. Restless and full of horrible images of a bloated Lulu dangling from a shower head and Tim as a Luna Park clown, his head continuously rotating.

Chapter 13

Poppy woke to the smell of onion and garlic frying, a splitting headache, and profound thirst. Her limbs were heavy, and it was a few minutes before she could force them off the bed. The room teetered briefly when she first stood up and she had to stop and let the dizziness settle before she continued. She scurried to the bathroom and ran cold water on her face, gulping water from the faucet, and letting it cascade over her chin. Lucas had prepared homely pumpkin soup, and toasted sourdough bread, and had it ready for when she emerged from the bathroom. They fed her up and waited for her to be ready to talk.

'So, you've heard, then?' Poppy asked after she gulped the last of her water and had mopped her soup bowl clean with the last of the bread.

'My Reg told me about Tim,' Lucas replied.

'It is not your fault, Poppy,' Gemma said, putting a hand on hers.

'We failed him, Gem. I saw he was depressed. I even talked to Paul about it two days ago,' Poppy's voice was rising, then breaking at the end.

'It's still not your fault. You didn't even know him,' Gemma persisted.

'But I saw he was distressed. And if we can't help a colleague in distress as doctors, why are we here?' And with that, Poppy sobbed.

Gemma and Lucas moved so Gemma was on one side with her arm around Poppy's shoulders and Lucas on her other side with a hand on her knee. Poppy didn't cry for long. She'd done most of her crying in the morning, and she wiped her tears away angrily.

'I'm OK, guys, thanks.' And she shrugged out of Gemma's embrace, standing to take her bowl back to the kitchen.

'Pop, what happened to Lulu was tragic, and I'm sure Tim was overworked and under too much pressure. But neither of them asked for help and may have even pushed it away. Ultimately, they did this, it wasn't done to them,' Lucas said.

'Maybe, but they didn't choose to have depression.'

Poppy didn't want to continue this conversation. She had had it before and knew Lucas' views. He didn't have a personal experience and could have a detached, clinical view about it. She dropped her bowl noisily in the sink, signalling an end to the discussion, and then went for a bath and some time to herself.

Her mind was like a whirlpool, circling around and around. Lulu-Tim-Lulu-Tim. All she saw when she closed her eyes was Tim, the Luna Park clown, and the image of Lulu hanging from the shower that her brain had created. It was like the lid she kept firmly on her grief had suddenly popped off, and the misery was pouring out. But she really didn't have time to give in to it right now. She needed to steel herself and prepare to go back to work. *Come on, Pop, you've got to stop thinking about it. You can't change things, so getting stuck in your own vortex won't help you or anyone else.* Thank God she was on subbies tonight. Hopefully it would be simple things that didn't require too much thought or personality. She looked at herself in the mirror as she prepared to leave and saw the deep, dark circles under her eyes like bruises. She didn't bother with make-up, she didn't have the energy and didn't care tonight how people saw her. Eventually, it was time to go.

She thought she'd successfully avoided Gemma and Lucas and that they'd gone to bed, but Gemma popped out as she was heading to the door and grabbed her into a proper hug. No words, just a squeezy hug, then release.

'Thanks, Gem.'

'Head up young person,' she said, and Poppy felt the faintest twitch at the corners of her mouth, but her eyes remained weighed down with sadness.

Steph and Seb were starting their nights tonight, and, as soon as she arrived, Seb took her aside and said, 'I know you don't want to be here tonight, so thank you for turning up. You're on subbies so hopefully it won't be too onerous, but take your time and just remember Steph and I are here, OK?'

'Thanks, Seb.' And he gave her a nod and walked away.

She was not at her best that night and she was lucky the others supported her because she made some mistakes that could have been disastrous if the others hadn't picked them up. First, she wrote the wrong dose of morphine for a patient, writing one hundred milligrams instead of ten.

'Hey, Pop, can I just check this dose with you?' Lucy said, before she dispensed a lethal dose of morphine.

'Oh, shit. Gosh, Lucy, thank you so much. I don't know where my head is tonight. Phew, so glad you saw that.'

'Gotcha, babe,' Lucy said, taking the corrected chart back to the drug cupboard.

Fuck, that was bad. Bad Poppy! Must concentrate!

The second was when she prescribed a penicillin antibiotic for a patient with a penicillin allergy. Again, it was the nurse who picked up the error before they gave the patient the drug.

Seriously, what is wrong with you? At least it would have only resulted in a rash, but still, stupid mistake. A mistake I shouldn't be making. Fuck, what are you doing, Poppy?

Her concentration just wasn't there. It was like the entire night, only half of Poppy's brain was in the moment. The other half was lost in a vortex of thoughts of suicide and depression. Eventually, the shift ended. Thank God, was all Poppy could think. *Time to get the fuck out of here! Hide from being a useless doctor, terrible sister, worthless colleague…*

'Come on, we're heading up the street for breakfast,' Steph told her at the lockers as they collected their things.

'I don't think I can face that, Steph. I'm too embarrassed.'

'No. Not taking no for an answer. You need this, Poppy. We all do. When bad things happen, we band together, that's just what we do.'

'OK.' Poppy relented, her shoulders still low as Stephanie draped an arm around them.

They formed a circle around her and corralled her out the door and up to King Street. When they entered the café, she could smell bacon frying and salivated. For the first time since her nights started, Poppy felt hungry. She decided on eggs benedict with bacon, and a strong latte.

'So, Poppy, last night shift today, what's your plan?' Seb asked her.

'What, you mean how do I convert my body back to daylight hours?'

'Yeah. Are you going to stay up all day or nap and then get up?'

'I don't know. What do you guys recommend?'

Steph and Seb both chorused, 'stay up' and laughed with a 'jinx' from Seb that followed.

'I vote the nap first,' said Lucy. 'I can never make it the whole day when I try to stay up.'

'But if you nap, you feel so much worse when you wake up,' Steph responded.

'Umm,' Poppy said, 'I guess I'll try my best to stay up and see how I go.'

'Play video games or something like that. You know, keep yourself busy enough to avoid falling asleep,' Seb suggested.

'I'm not much of a gamer, more of a reader,' Poppy answered.

'If you read, you'll be asleep in an hour,' Steph said.

'Movie?' Poppy asked.

'Schnoozing again,' Lucy said.

'Maybe I'll go for a swim, then.'

'Yeah, that's a good idea. Just don't overdo it and fall asleep after.'

'God, you make this sound really difficult!'

'Hi, Mum,' Poppy said as she called her Mum on the walk home.

'Hi, darling, how are you?'

'I'm OK, but I just finished nights and I've got a few days off, so I thought I might catch the train up to visit?'

'We'd love that, darling. Text me when you know what time the train gets in, and I'll send your dad to collect you.'

'OK, that'd be great. See you soon.'

A slight lightening of the load of her guilt, sadness and embarrassment followed. It'd be good to see Mum, she thought. She could use that uncomplicated warmth of a familial cocoon. A blink back to childhood. A time of no responsibility or accountability. A time before Lulu died…

She packed lightly and headed for the bus to take her to central station where she'd catch the train, leaving a note for Gemma and Lucas.

The trip was pleasant, winding over the mountains and giving Poppy time to read and listen to music. Whenever she felt sleepy, she forced herself to sit upright and look at the other passengers, imagining lives for them to pass the time. There was an elderly lady clutching her handbag who Poppy imagined was a kleptomaniac with her spoils hidden in the bag, heading for a rendezvous with her fence. Then a pregnant woman clutching the hand of a toddler and trying to keep her entertained who Poppy suspected was running away from her partner, packed bags at their feet. A group of late teens Poppy was certain were ditching school, probably on their way to score drugs. And, finally, a wheezing and sneezing bald man in his fifties Poppy suspected of having bird fancier's lung from caring for his collection of parrots and budgies. It was enough to keep her awake and entertained.

Her dad picked her up at the train station and she held him tightly in a hug, feeling a catch in her throat.

'Hi, Dad,' she said when she could trust herself to speak, surreptitiously swiping a tear away from her face.

'Hi, love, how are you? You look thin.'

'I'm OK,' she said, getting into the front passenger seat whilst her dad put her travel suitcase in the boot.

Head up, young person, Dad doesn't need my drama, he looks to be barely holding his shit together.

'Your mother is so excited you're staying,' he said as he started the old black Mercedes sedan that was on its last legs. Poppy knew her parents could afford to upgrade to a newer model, but her dad had had this car since before Lulu died. Maybe he couldn't bear the thought of parting with it and losing that last connection to her.

'What about you, Dad, how are you?' Poppy noticed his shirt was worn around the elbows, almost threadbare.

'Flag still flying, love,' was his weird answer, before he turned up the radio. He clearly didn't want to talk about anything emotional. And that wasn't new; he'd never been someone to share his feelings or deep opinions, at least not with Poppy.

'OK, Dad.'

Her old house was the same as always. The smell of fresh baked bread greeting her as she entered, and her mum wiping her hands on her apron to come and say hello. They embraced without words and Poppy breathed in her familiar scent of Red Door perfume and Estée Lauder face cream. Her mum led her into the kitchen and sat her at the table while she made her a cup of tea, putting a plate of freshly made choc-chip biscuits in front of her. They were still warm and a little gooey in the middle, just the way Poppy liked them.

Her mum had always been a baker, and Poppy found it incredibly comforting. They solved all the major dramas and hurts in her formative years with biscuits, brownies, and ice cream. The baking gene had not been passed on to Poppy, though, as she could barely bake biscuits from a packet, let alone bread, cakes, scones and slices. Lulu was the one who loved baking, and Poppy recalled memories of Lulu and their mum baking together, sometimes elaborate desserts or multilayered cakes that would take all day, leaving Poppy and her dad to fend for themselves. This often meant watching the test cricket in summer.

Now the recollections of Lulu in happier times were too much, and she visibly slumped at the table. Her mum asked, 'What's wrong, honey? What's happened?' And she came and sat next to her.

'Oh, Mum,' Poppy started, the tears forming in her eyes, blurring her vision.

'What is it, darling, is it work?'

'One of the Registrars, Tim, overdosed, and I was there, and we couldn't bring him back.' Poppy's tears became sobs and her mother put an arm around her and rubbed her back.

'And there was this pregnant woman who died and the baby died too, and it's just, it's all a lot, you know? I'm not sure I can do this, Mum, it's just too much.'

'Oh, Poppy, it sounds tough.'

'And Lucas pissed me off the other night, after the suicide. He said Tim brought it on himself, that he wouldn't have accepted help even if it was offered.'

Her mother sat back and eventually Poppy raised her head.

'What?' Poppy asked when she saw her mother's face.

'I know this is going to sound harsh, Poppy, and I don't mean it to, but Lucas was right.'

Poppy felt like the wind had been knocked out of her.

'What? Mum?' Poppy's voice took on the whingeing tone of an adolescent in her surprise.

'Lulu and Tim did this… And that doesn't mean I don't recognise their suffering or depression, but they left us. Now, I wish with all my heart that Lulu didn't, and my beautiful girl was still here with us, but life moves forward, and you have to find some way to reconcile it and live your life. Because I know the last thing Lulu would want would be for you to be suffering. In her damaged mind she would have thought she was a burden and that leaving us would relieve that burden and enable us to be happy.'

'That's so fucked up.'

'Yes…but her brain was screwed up. She'd so want you to be happy, Poppy, and so do I.'

'I know you're probably right, Mum.' Her mum gave her a quick hug and returned to her baking.

Poppy thought back to Lulu's suicide note:

Dear Mum, Dad and Poppy,

I'm sorry this will cause you pain and I'm sorry you won't understand. And, most of all, I'm sorry I'm such a failure. Please don't blame yourselves. There is nothing you could have done to fix me. I can't continue, and I need to go. Know that I love you all and always will.

Love Lulu xx

'Do you think it's time to go back to the Psychologist?' Mum asked while searching her face, breaking Poppy's reverie.

'Maybe, I'll think about it.'

'Good.'

'How are you doing so well, Mum?'

'I just decided it was time. You only get one life and I want some happiness and peace in mine. Counselling helped me to resolve my thoughts and actively try to see the positives in tough situations.'

'Wow, you sound like a guru,' Poppy said with a laugh.

'No, just your Mum.' They embraced again and Poppy felt some of the weight that had descended in the last few days start to lift.

They ate chicken schnitzels and vegetables and watched some TV that night. And the familiarity of being in her old home and spending a quiet night in with her parents went a long way to lessen the negative thoughts in her mind. But by 8:30p.m. she was flagging, and she crashed out by nine o'clock and slept like the dead, barely moving or dreaming throughout the night.

The next day, she spent some time with her mum, including having a mini spa indulgence before they all went out to dinner at Lolli Redini, one of the well-known foodie restaurants. Thursday after lunch she made the train trip back to Sydney feeling significantly better than when she'd left. It was whilst she was on the train that she received a text from Josh.

> Sorry for not being in touch, I've been studying. Hope we are still on for dinner @ my place Sat. How's 7pm?

Poppy was flabbergasted; she had pretty much written Josh off, and with the events of the last couple of days hadn't even thought about him. She sat staring at her phone and the text for some time thinking about Josh and how she felt. Was she attracted to him? Yes. Did she like him? She wasn't sure. Even if he was studying, as he wrote, that didn't really excuse not answering her text until now, which she considered pretty rude. Did she want to go to dinner? To this question she was undecided. Whilst Poppy was not into game-playing when it came to romance, she needed time to think some more before replying and so she returned to her music and book.

Poppy was unpacking when Gemma and Lucas got home from work. She came out to greet them.

'Hi,' she said slightly sheepishly, and gave them each a hug.

'Hi, how are you?' Gemma asked.

'Pretty good.'

'Hey, we were thinking about Thai for dinner. I'm going to duck up the street. What would you like?' Lucas asked.

'Pad see ew pork? Let me see if I've got some cash.'

'No, that's OK.'

'OK.'

Lucas gave her a quick peck on the cheek and squeezed her hand and then went out.

Poppy returned to unpacking, and Gemma sat on the bed to watch.

'He's sorry that he upset you,' said Gemma after he left.

'I know, and it's fine. Mum thinks he's right…and I do need to move forward.'

'So how are you feeling about work tomorrow?'

'Well, it's not like I have a choice, is it?' A note of snarkiness crept into her voice.

Gemma was silent and there was an awkward pause.

After a beat, Poppy said, 'Look I'm sorry I snapped, I'm just a bit anxious about going back. It's so full-on in ED, it's like Vegas but instead of risking your dosh the consequences could be your life. I'm just not sure I can keep going for the entire term.'

'Yeah, it sounds pretty full-on… But, Poppy, you can do it, and you are doing it. You are literally the strongest, bravest person I know.'

'Thanks, Gem, but I don't know about that.' And she sighed, sitting down beside Gemma on the bed.

'You've just got to take one shift at a time… How were your mum and dad, anyway?'

'Good. Mum was great actually; happy, bubbly, positive. Dad was OK, quiet, but OK… Oh, and guess what, on the train I got a text from Josh.'

'Seriously?'

'Yep.'

'What did it say?'

Poppy pulled out her phone to show Gemma the text.

'What are you going to do?' she asked.

'I'm not sure. I mean, I'd kind of moved on in my mind, almost, and then this text. I just don't know. What do you think I should do?'

'I don't know.'

'I kind of think he's hot, but if he's a bit of a selfish bastard, it's not worth starting something.'

'There's that… but take a step back… go back to how you felt at the end of the date. Did you want to see him again?'

'Absolutely.'

'Well, maybe he deserves one second chance, just to be sure?'

'Maybe. I'll think about it… I thought you didn't like him?'

'I've never met the guy, I have no clue…but I don't like the way he treated you on the phone over that chest pain case. But I know you feel maybe you made a mistake with Will, so maybe give Josh a second chance?'

When she was going to bed, she made up her mind on Josh and sent her text, then turned out her light.

OK. See you Sat @ 7. What's your address again?

One last chance.

Chapter 14

'Who are you down here to see?' Poppy asked Will when he tapped her shoulder at the flight deck the next morning.

'A guy with a de-gloving injury to his hand and arm.'

'Oh, yeah, the builder, we just stabilised him in Resus one. Awful worksite injury. He fell from scaffolding. Looks like he has multiple fractures as well as the arm injury. Ortho should be coming down too.'

'It's nasty. We'll get him up to theatre as quick as we can.'

'That'd be good, he's in a lot of pain.'

Poppy could see Will's Registrar on the phone behind him, and Will's face suddenly etched with concern before he said quietly, 'Hey, Seb told me what happened with Tim. Are you doing OK?'

'It hasn't been easy,' Poppy replied honestly, her shoulders immediately slumping and her stomach dropping. A rush of guilt and sorrow swept over her and flashbacks to her dream of Tim and Lulu's bodies re-entered her mind.

'Look, I'm not very busy today and not in theatre. When you get a chance for a break later, call me, OK? We can eat together.'

'OK, if I can,' Poppy said, thinking she probably wouldn't.

'Do,' he said and squeezed her hand and smiled at her. Then he was gone, and the shift continued. *OK, maybe I will. Maybe it'd be nice to sit with Will and have lunch.*

She got a break, but not until about one o'clock. She texted Will, and he found her in the garden where they'd eaten on that first day together. It was a beautiful day; sunny but not humid, with a lovely late summer breeze. It was about twenty-five degrees, heralding the start of an autumnal change.

'So, how's your term going?' Poppy asked Will, once they were seated under the shade of an overhanging tree.

'Really good, actually. This is the first surgical term I've actually liked.'

'That's good. Are you considering doing surgery?'

'I'm still not sure. I've enjoyed this term, but honestly, most surgeons are pretty awful people, right?'

Poppy laughed and said, 'Well, you're not wrong there.'

'What about surfing?'

'Still getting out on the water at least three times a week.'

'Well, that's good.'

'Yeah, I love it. It really calms me.'

'You seem calm to me all the time.'

'Well, I didn't use to be. I had a bit of a rough time toward the end of my first degree and that was when I took up surfing. It helped me put things in perspective.'

'How so?' Poppy asked, wanting to know more but not wanting to sound nosey. Last time they'd talked about surfing he'd just said it was a good way to exercise, so this was new information, and very personal. She didn't want to mess this up.

'When you're out in the ocean, it reminds you how small we humans are, you know? Just one tiny part of this earth. The ocean is so powerful, and we have no control over it. I guess it just reminds me that there's a lot of things I can't control, so I need to let them go and only focus on the things I can control.'

'Wow, that's pretty deep.'

'Yeah, well a Psychologist also helped,' Will said, smiling again, a brief crinkling at the edges of his eyes.

Poppy allowed herself a small laugh and again enjoyed watching Will's face light up when he smiled. He was fair-skinned and the lines from the sun were clear, but added warmth, not years, to his face.

Wow, that was really honest. That's really nice that he trusts me to talk about something so personal. Poppy smiled again.

'How about you?' Will asked 'How are you really liking ED?'

'I really like the people and the mix of cases. But the shift changes are hard. I constantly feel jet-lagged,' Poppy didn't add that she had also noticed in the last couple of weeks that her pants were getting looser. She'd lost some weight, but that wasn't something she wanted to discuss with Will.

'Yeah, I agree, the work is good, but I don't think I could do the shift changes for the rest of my life.'

'Me either, sadly,' Poppy said.

'Night shifts particularly are hell on the body. Keeping your nutrition up will help with the jet-lagged feeling.'

'Yes, Dad,' Poppy replied with an exaggerated roll of her eyes.

After a moment of silence, Will asked, 'So, do you want to talk about Tim?' It burst the superficial happiness bubble that had been building around Poppy. Her shoulders immediately hunched up around her ears, and she felt her innards clench. Poppy thought about it as she played with her food wrapper, buying some time. That feeling of safety and a desire to unburden herself was there, but she knew this could spiral into a long conversation.

'I do, but not here. I'll have to go back in soon,' she finally said.

'Well, do you want to grab dinner after work? Low-key, I promise, then if you feel like talking, we can.'

'OK.'

'OK. Well, that's settled,' Will said, smiling once again.

Lucas came to ED about four o'clock with his entire team. Consultant, Fellow, and Registrar. It was almost like a scene from *Entourage*. Poppy watched as the others spread out in a wave behind the Consultant, paying homage to the man. He was early fifties, average height, slightly overweight, and with what appeared to be dyed dark-brown hair. His hair had that too perfect, with no variation in colour tell-tale sign of a dye job. He wore a pin-stripe suit with a diagonal striped tie of red and navy and the team went to the board looking for the patient they'd come to see.

It was one of Poppy's cases; a man in his seventies who had an ischaemic foot that Poppy had spoken to the Registrar about just before she'd gone to lunch. Lucas caught Poppy's eye and raised his eyebrows with a look that conveyed the message: *Can you believe I have to work with these douche bags?*

Poppy smiled back in a knowing way. She decided she'd wait for them to find her after they'd seen the patient, thinking the arrogance and aftershave fumes might overpower her if she shared the cubicle with them!

They emerged five minutes later with the Consultant talking in a loud drone to ensure he dominated the room, issuing instructions like commands. Poppy almost expected the Registrar and Lucas to salute with a 'yes, sir' with each order. After issuing his demands, he turned on his heel and left with the Fellow, leaving Lucas and the Registrar to sort things out. Lucas ambled over to Poppy while his Registrar answered a page, barking down the phone like Tim had with Poppy.

'Hey, Pop.'

'Hi, Lucas. So that's Team Douche,' she whispered conspiratorially.

He laughed, a rare sight these days. 'Pretty much.'

'So, what's the plan with Mr Peters?'

'Yeah, we'll take him to the ward and put him on the emergency list for theatre. Can you please ensure he's nil by mouth and arrange an urgent CTA?'

'Sure.'

'Thanks, Pop.'

'No prob. How's your day going?'

'Pretty usual: abuse, sick patients, and rounds with Head Douche. You?'

'It's OK. I saw Will. We're going to grab dinner after work, so don't wait for me.'

'OK, that's good. Actually, he asked about you while you were away.'

'What? When?' Poppy couldn't keep the surprise from her voice. Why hadn't Lucas told her this last night?

'Oh, the day before yesterday? He'd heard about Tim, and I ran into him in the theatre changing rooms. He wanted to know how you were taking it?'

'What did you say?'

'Just that you were shocked, and you'd gone to see your parents for a couple of days. Was that OK?' Lucas asked, a worry line forming between his eyebrows.

'Yeah, totally fine,' she said, giving him a reassuring smile.

'Good,' he replied, his shoulders relaxing and the line receding. 'He seems really nice.'

'Yeah, he is nice,' Poppy said, a smile instantly forming on her face.

'Well, better keep moving. My Reg is tapping his foot and doesn't like to be kept waiting. See you at home.'

'Bye.'

Seb was beside Poppy in an instant, rolling over on his chair. 'Is that your flatmate?'

'Lucas? Yeah. He and my friend Gemma are together.'

'He's not enjoying his surgical term, then?'

'No. Not great culture for the junior staff.'

'Yep, the surgical terms here can be brutal. God knows why anyone would want to be a surgeon, they're all such pricks.'

'Yeah, the good ones are few and far between,' Poppy agreed.

'True that.'

Will was waiting for her when she finished her shift, looking at his phone and leaning against the railing. She had a moment to take him in before he looked up and saw her. He looked good. Casual good looks, and that aura of calm as always. He was so different to Josh with his hit-you-in-the-face Brad Pitt looks and air of arrogance. He looked up and smiled, and Poppy instinctively smiled back.

'Hi,' Will said.

'Hi. Where were you thinking of going?'

'Do you feel like dumplings?'

'Always. Lead on.'

They started walking up toward King Street.

'I saw Lucas with his team this afternoon. They are such a bunch of wankers. He's really hating his term.'

'Yeah, it's not a good one. But there are a few out there. Mine's really good. And I did Urology last year, that was not too bad. Ooh, I also hear the Neurosurgeons are good, too.'

'I've got Urology at the end of the year, so that's good to know.'

'I hope Lucas gets a better term next.'

'Yeah, me too. He's been really flat lately. But I think he has a medical rotation next, and he'll definitely end up as a Physician, so I'm sure he'll be happier.'

The sound of their feet on the pavement was like a metronome ticking out the beat, their steps in time with each other.

'By the way, I watched the first episode of *Russian Doll* the other night, that new series you recommended on Netflix?' Will said, breaking into her thoughts on the beat of their feet.

'Oh yeah, what did you think?'

'It's a bit weird, but I like it.'

'Yeah, it is weird. But funny.'

They arrived at the dumpling place and found a table away from anyone else. Not that there were many people there this early, just a couple of other tables were occupied.

'Can I get you anything to drink?' the waitress asked as she placed the laminated menus on the table.

'Coke No Sugar, please,' Poppy asked as she took one of the menus. *Yuck, it's sticky. Ooh, and my elbows are sticking to the table. This place is a bit of a dump, they'd better have good dumplings.*

'One for me, too, please,' Will said.

After the waitress left and Poppy was perusing the menu, Will leaned in toward her and said, 'I know this place is a bit skeevy, but, trust me, the dumplings are really good.'

Poppy looked up and saw the smile on his face. *It's like he can read my thoughts. Maybe I was scowling without realising it.*

'I hope so,' Poppy said, dropping her gaze again to the menu.

The waitress returned with the drinks and two imperfectly clean glasses. *I think I'll just drink from the can,* Poppy thought. The waitress looked at them with her pen poised on her small, lined notebook, clearly wanting their orders.

'Oh, OK…ten pot-stickers please,' Poppy said.

'Yeah, me too, thanks. And can we get some chilli oil?'

'OK,' the waitress said and left the table.

This place really is a dive. Poppy raised an eyebrow without thinking.

'I promise, the food is worth it,' Will said and they both chuckled. He was clearly as uncomfortable about the cleanliness and the service as Poppy was.

'So, do you want to tell me about Tim?' Will asked once they had both had sips of their drinks.

Poppy looked into Will's eyes and knew she could trust him, and he had opened up to her today, so it gave her the confidence to do the same.

'It was really hard. As soon as they wheeled him in and I saw who it was, I was just really shocked. I mean, I'd just talked to Paul about him only a day or so before, and wondered whether he was depressed. And then there he was with a drug overdose.'

Poppy took a breath, but Will didn't fill the silence. He watched her face, and again, Poppy could see his emotions clearly. It was obvious he felt for her.

'I had to do CPR on him. And it went on and on, and all I kept thinking was, "Please come back, please come back."'

This time, when Poppy was silent, Will said, 'That must have been really hard for you.'

Poppy looked into his eyes again, and thought, *I can trust him*.

'It was…and not just because it was Tim… But also because my little sister committed suicide five years ago,' she said, almost whispering at the end. It was the first time she had said this out loud to anyone outside of Gemma and Lucas. And she felt something shift inside her. Maybe a slight lessening of the weight that had hung with her since then?

'Oh, Poppy,' Will said, his face crumpling in obvious sadness, 'I had no idea.'

'How could you?'

'I'm so sorry about your sister.'

'Thank you.'

They looked at each other, barely aware of the waitress who had suddenly materialised at their sides with their dumplings.

'Here,' she said as she slopped them onto the table, one of Poppy's dumplings almost slipping over the rim of her plate onto the table. She came back a moment later with the chilli oil.

'Thanks,' Will said taking it from her hand before she could slop that, too, onto the table. *No wonder everything is so sticky!*

'Give them a few minutes to cool. I've burned the crap out of my mouth so many times.'

'OK, I will.'

Will looked uncomfortable, shifting somewhat in his chair, before saying, 'Do you think your sister was depressed?'

'Her name was Lucinda. Lulu.'

'That's a pretty name.'

'Yeah… She was younger than me. She was fourteen and I'd just gone up to Newcastle for uni, and she was being bullied at boarding school. I hadn't really noticed before I left. You know, probably too involved in exams and boys and my own problems. And once I left, I was too busy enjoying my freedom. I hadn't been back to visit…'

'You know it's not your fault, right?' Will interrupted.

'Yeah, I do on some levels, but… I still have guilt as well.'

'Oh, Poppy.'

'Anyway, by the time my Mum rang and told me she was worried about Lulu, it was really too late. I couldn't get through to her on the phone, and whilst I'd told her I was coming down for a visit that weekend, she didn't wait that long.'

'I'm so sorry, Poppy, that's just so sad for you, for your family, and for Lulu.' He reached across the table to take Poppy's hand. The squeeze he gave it conveyed the depth of his sadness and support. She nodded her head, and surprised herself by not crying.

They ate in silence for a while, Will sneaking glances at Poppy every now and again. She didn't feel the pressure to fill the silence. It had been good to unburden herself, and she was happy just to eat and look into Will's soulful eyes.

'These are good,' Poppy said when she came to her last dumpling.

'Right?'

'Tim just brought back all my memories of Lulu.'

'I can imagine. How do you feel now?'

'A bit better. I went to visit my parents on my days off and that helped… I was pretty anxious about today, particularly being on Acute, but it was OK.'

'That's good. I just want to say again, I'm really sorry about your sister.'

'Thanks, Will,' Poppy said and meant it.

Usually, when people offered their sympathy about Lulu, Poppy felt frustrated, or annoyed. But here, with Will, she felt different. She accepted his apology in the manner it was given and knew that when he said he was sorry to hear about what had happened, he actually meant it.

'Tim was a prick to me multiple times, but no one wants to see a colleague commit suicide,' Will said after a beat. 'The system is bankrupt. There's not enough staff or supervision, particularly for the surgical trainees. Maybe we could discuss it with Melissa and Dr Anderson? See what the hospital can do to prevent this in the future?'

'That's a great idea!' Poppy said, feeling a jolt of excitement. 'I'm sick of being a bystander. It's time to do something!'

I never did anything after Lulu. Maybe now I can do something that helps someone else in the future. And it shouldn't have to be like this, anyway. The system shouldn't fail the staff so badly. Shouldn't have them so overworked and unsupported that they feel they have no other choice than to quit or kill themselves.

Poppy felt energised, her mind already moving to what they might achieve. It was like a firework had exploded that had been patiently waiting since Lulu's death. A chance to make a difference. That's what she needed. Maybe then she could let go of the last vestiges of guilt that still plagued her.

Chapter 15

Paul was on subbies with her the next day. They hadn't seen each other since Tim's suicide, and he came over to her as soon as she arrived.

'Hi, Poppy, how are you?' Paul asked with a sincere look on his face and a sombre tone. Poppy felt confident that, like with Will, she could be honest with Paul. She didn't feel the need to give the pat 'I'm good' answer.

'Not too bad… I was pretty down after Tim's death, but I spent some time at home with my parents and that helped,' Poppy replied.

'I'm glad. If you want to talk about it, I'm here for you.'

'Thanks, Paul, that's very sweet of you… Actually, Will Charles and I are planning to meet with the medical training unit and talk to them about what we can do for staff mental health,' Poppy finished animatedly.

'Oh,' Paul answered, non-committally.

Poppy noticed his lack of enthusiasm, but decided she wouldn't dwell on it. She wanted to focus on this project. It made her feel good to be doing something positive. It stopped her from thinking too deeply about Tim and Lulu. She knew that well of despair that lived inside her had been building in the last few days and this was keeping a lid on it.

Poppy had been introduced to Melissa O'Brien, head of administration for the medical training and administration unit (MTU), and Dr Katrina Anderson, Respiratory Physician and Director of junior medical officer training, on her orientation day before work officially started. Together they had detailed the terms and their training expectations for the next two years. Melissa, who was in her forties with blonde, shoulder-length hair tending to grey, and who'd been wearing a skirt and knit top with sensible shoes, had struck Poppy as warm and approachable. Dr Anderson, on the other hand, was younger, more stylish, and radiated calm confidence, but her smile never reached her eyes and her porcelain skin reminded Poppy of a china doll – beautiful but cold and unyielding.

Dr Anderson had given them a speech about the importance of a varied experience in the early years of training. 'My aim for you all is that you have a balanced two-year programme that gives you adequate exposure to the core medical and surgical terms as well as Emergency Medicine. Some of you may have arrived today with very clear, fixed ideas about which specialty you would like to pursue. In the past, previous training directors have allowed Interns and Residents to rapidly stream into terms that really limit a broad general knowledge base. This has been at the detriment of the junior doctor and a disservice to them and their patients… I know medical school and specialty training is a long process, but, trust me when I say, these two years will build important fundamental building blocks for you to base your future on.' She had placed both hands on the edges of the lectern, leaning towards them, her eyes scanning the audience, clearly wanting them all to absorb this message.

It was not a popular message. A number of the Interns Poppy knew from Newcastle had chosen The Bennelong because of its strong history in surgical training and the knowledge that they had previously allowed Interns to pick predominantly surgical terms from the beginning. This allowed those who wanted to do surgical specialties to jam experience into the first two years, helping them network and get onto training schemes in their third or fourth years post medical school.

But that was not the reason Poppy, Gemma and Lucas had chosen The Bennelong. Gemma had chosen it because it also had one of the biggest maternity units in the state and she wanted to do Obstetrics. Lucas wanted to stay with Gemma and felt he was tough enough to survive the cutthroat mentality it was known for, and Poppy had wanted to stay close to them. She had no idea where or what she wanted to specialise in, so had no strong opinions about where to train. The Bennelong was also great geographically, so Dr Anderson's words resonated well for her. A broad and general overview would give her time to work out what specialty she wanted to spend the rest of her life doing. Even just thinking that sent a shiver up Poppy's spine. She couldn't even commit to purchasing a car and routinely borrowed Gemma and Lucas' or caught public transport.

Gemma had thought Dr Anderson appeared cold. Poppy didn't admit to Gemma, but she was in awe of Dr Anderson's style. She had been in a dark-navy pantsuit, heels, and her deep-chestnut hair was carefully styled in a low chignon. A baby-pink floral scarf, expertly tied, completed her outfit. *Maybe she just appeared cold because she was uncomfortable in front of a big audience.* She decided she wouldn't be as quick as Gemma to judge and would wait to see how things panned out. And now, Poppy guessed, she would find out who was right after she sent the email from herself and Will requesting a meeting.

They were coming to the tail end of summer and the weather had just started to change with less humidity and cooler nights. It heralded the beginning of the twice-annual gastroenteritis peaks and Poppy spent a lot of that shift reviewing patients with vomiting and diarrhoea.

'So, how long have you been vomiting?' she asked a woman in her fifties who was very pale and whose skin was glistening with a slight sheen of sweat. The aroma of old vomit accosted Poppy's nose and she immediately pursed her lips and swallowed, to prevent herself from retching.

'Um…urpph—' Patrice made a choke-swallowing sound before suddenly expelling forceful vomit straight out in front of her.

'Ohh…' Poppy said in surprise as she tried to jump to the side to avoid the vomit hitting her full-on in the face, but was not quick enough.

Oh my god! I think I'm going to be sick.

Poppy retched and then reached out, trying to avoid the vomit puddle next to her, to grab a sick bag. She hurriedly thrust it in Patrice's direction, who whispered a brief thanks before vomiting again. At least this time it almost all went in the bag. Poppy dry-retched again, and she hurriedly backed out of the cubicle and almost slammed into Lucy.

'Oi, Poppy, watch it,' Lucy said before taking in Poppy's vomit-smeared shirt, sour expression, and dripping hair. Not to mention the stench.

'Hey, can you give this patient some IM metoclopramide and hang a bag of fluids? I'm going to shower and change.'

'Sure thing, Pop,' Lucy replied, grimacing at Poppy's predicament.

Some kind soul had left a partly used travel shampoo bottle in the stall and Poppy gratefully washed her hair and scrubbed herself free of any speck of vomit. She tied her foul clothes into an industrial waste bag and shoved them in her locker.

I'll decide later if they're salvageable. I just hope they don't stink out my work bag!

She wound her wet hair up into a bun on the top of her head and set off back to the flight deck in scrubs, her dripping hair already soaking the back of her top.

It proved to be one of those shifts where Poppy's body felt like it was in the ringer. After the vomiting, Poppy had an incident with a catheter bag leaking urine and spraying all over her shoes when she went to review the urine quality. She had no replacement, so had to make do with a quick wipe-down and some disposable surgical booties one of the nurses kindly found her.

'We've decided, from now on we're going to call you, Calamity Jane,' Graham said.

'Calamity Jane,' Lucy sang, laughing.

'Thanks, guys, that's very cute,' Poppy said, but she wasn't laughing. She was feeling frazzled. The pressure of her looming date with Josh tonight was adding to her stress.

I hope tonight goes well. And I definitely don't want to smell like vomit. Maybe I'll have time to have another shower and wash my hair again before I head to his place, to ensure all traces of vomit are definitely out of my hair.

'OK, Patrice, how are you doing?' she asked toward the end of her shift when she went back to check on her after her antiemetic and bag of IV fluids.

'Much better, thank you… Look, I'm really sorry about vomiting on you. I feel terrible,' she said, colouring.

'That's OK, it's not your fault,' Poppy smiled at her. It was disgusting, but in no way was she to blame. Poppy was just unlucky. Although it would make a good story to tell Gemma and Lucas later. *I won't tell Josh, though. What a turn-off that would be if I did.*

'Have you had the hydrolyte drink as well?'

'Yes, I've had two now.'

'Good. Look, I think you can go home, now that you're keeping liquid down. But take it easy at home, OK? Plenty of fluids, nothing solid for the next twenty-four hours, and you need to be symptom-free for forty-eight hours before you can return to work. I'll go do your discharge papers, and I'll get the nurse to come and take out that cannula.'

'Thank you.'

Her last patient of the day was a ten-year-old boy who'd fractured his leg playing soccer. It was a simple green-stick fracture of the tibia and didn't require surgery, just a cast.

'Charlie, and Mum,' Poppy said to the child and his mother once they were in the procedure room, 'I'm just going to put what's called a back-slab cast on. It goes on the back of the leg, with bandaging around the front to allow for more swelling. Then they'll replace it in the fracture clinic with a new, complete one on Monday.'

'OK.'

'So, Charlie, see this soft cotton,' Poppy asked, showing him the sheets of wadding. 'First, I'm going to wrap this all the way from your foot up to your knee, OK?'

'Is it going to hurt?'

'It might hurt a little, but hopefully the pain relief is helping now, and I'm going to try to do it without jolting your leg too much, OK?'

'OK,' he said, but Poppy could see the fear on his face.

'Mum, do you want to bring your chair a bit closer and hold his hand for me?'

She nodded, and dragged her chair closer. 'Can I give him a lollipop?'

'That's a great idea, I'm sure that'll help the pain, too.'

'What flavour, Mum?'

'Grape.'

'Good,' he said with a serious expression. *Maybe only grape has magical healing properties?*

Poppy waited for Charlie to pop the lollipop in his mouth and start sucking, then gently began wrapping the cotton up his leg. Charlie's mouth formed a tight pucker around the lollipop, but he didn't cry or complain. *God bless his mum, what a smart woman.*

'OK. Now, Charlie, I'm going to measure the plaster length and wet it. It goes from these sheets to a muddy mess if you're not careful,' Poppy said, getting the hint of a smile from one corner only of Charlie's mouth. She carefully measured beside Charlie's leg and cut seven layers to match. Then she submerged it into her dish of warm water, carefully ensuring all layers were wet, without rubbing them together too much. She lifted the layers out of the water and quickly moved back to Charlie's side.

'OK, this is the hard bit, Charlie. I'm going to get your mum to help you lift your leg just off the bed so I can put the plaster at the back and smooth it on your leg.'

Charlie's mum stood up and put her voluminous brown handbag, that she'd been clutching on her lap, onto the seat behind her. She moved to her son, Poppy still holding the wet, soggy plaster just off the procedure bed, dripping muddy-coloured plaster water.

'Like this?' she asked Poppy, tentatively.

'Yes, exactly,' Poppy said. 'I'm going to do this as quick as I can, Charlie,' she finished, noticing him grab the sides of the bed firmly when his Mum lifted his leg. Poppy quickly but gently smoothed the plaster to contour to the bottom of Charlie's foot and up the back of his leg and around the edges of his small calf. Rubbing up and down until it was starting to dry.

'OK, Mum, you can lower his leg now.'

Charlie took a deep breath in when his heel finally touched the bed again.

'That's the worst of it, Charlie. Now we just wait a bit longer for it to be dry, then I'll bandage it onto your leg.'

'You've got dust in your hair. Your hair looks grey,' Charlie said and burst out laughing.

Poppy started laughing too. She looked down her body and saw that she had drying plaster on her scrubs as well, and she could feel something tightening on one cheek.

'Do I have plaster on my face as well?' she asked Charlie, turning to face him.

'Yes,' he said, laughing even harder before saying, 'Oww.'

'I'm a mess. Lucky my shift is about to finish, so I can go take a shower. Let's finish this off, so we can both get out of here.'

When Poppy handed his mum his discharge instructions and came to say goodbye to Charlie, his mum took her elbow and said, 'Thank you. You were really good with him.'

'Actually, I wanted to thank you – that lollipop was a godsend.'

'He's my youngest of four boys. I've been through this before. But I think you've had the best manner of all the doctors we've encountered.'

'Thank you. I really appreciate that,' Poppy said. *I think that's the nicest compliment I've had so far.* Charlie's mum squeezed her elbow, then turned to help Charlie up with the crutches. Poppy watched them hobble down the corridor. *Maybe being a doctor isn't all bad.* She checked her watch for the time. *Shit, handover's started,* and she jogged down the corridor to the handover board.

When she removed her clothes from her bag at home she held her nose before first rinsing them in cold water, then dumping them in the laundry tub and dissolving some Napisan. *I'm not sure if this will work, but tonight I don't care. I'll look at them tomorrow after they've soaked.* When she finally risked a breath, she gagged. The smell was still overpowering.

Poppy showered and took considerable effort with her appearance, going for sultry make-up and a form-fitting burgundy dress that amplified her cleavage. She applied perfume behind her ears and décolletage and wore mid heels in black and her hair loose.

'Whoot-whoot,' Gemma wolf-whistled when she emerged from her bedroom. 'You look hot.'

'Thanks,' Poppy said, doing a quick twirl.

'Have you got protection?'

'Yes, Mum,' Poppy said, laughing. 'Don't wait up!' as she walked out the door.

She arrived at Josh's just after 7:15p.m. and he opened the door wearing a white linen shirt open enough to see a hint of brown, smooth skin, and a pale chino pant. He looked relaxed and as Poppy leant in to greet him with a kiss on the cheek, she smelt that now-familiar spicy scent that was proving to be an aphrodisiac for her. They parted and Josh took a step back, really taking Poppy in before letting her into the apartment. His eyes narrowed in a good way, and he said, 'Wow, you look smoking hot.'

Poppy coloured mildly and said thanks a little sheepishly as she came through the door.

'Something smells good,' Poppy said as she noticed the aroma emanating from the kitchen and various pots and pans bubbling on the cooktop.

'Can I get you a wine?' Josh asked as Poppy took a seat at one of the bar stools.

'Sure, what have you got?'

'I've got a French red.'

'Ooh, sounds good. Thanks.'

He poured the wine from a dusty bottle, and she was suitably impressed. This guy sure had style.

They chatted about work and some people they had in common while Josh finished cooking their meal. Poppy enjoyed watching Josh in the kitchen. He had a quiet confidence about him that made it clear this was a meal he'd cooked before. Josh had placed some nibbles of cheese, nuts, and olives in front of her and Poppy was happy munching away and savouring the wine. When Josh was ready, he ushered her to the table and placed a plate of an aromatic Thai chicken dish on a bed of steamed jasmine rice in front of her.

Poppy breathed in the scents of lemongrass, garlic, ginger and coriander and began to salivate. The food was delicious, and Poppy felt a growing warmth inside from the meal and the wine. A heavy French red wasn't the best pairing for a Thai dish, but she didn't care. After they'd finished, they left the dishes on the table and moved to the couch in the lounge room. Poppy sat turned in toward Josh with one leg tucked underneath her. Josh had one arm on the back of the couch behind her shoulders and was leaning in toward her.

'So you said you went to boarding school in Sydney and did medicine in Newcastle, but what else should I know about you?'

'I don't know,' Poppy said, nudging his shoulder in a playful way. 'What else do you want to know?'

'Do you have any siblings?'

'No,' Poppy said. It was her standard answer, and rolled off her tongue easily. Most times it didn't even feel like a lie. But after her long conversation with Will last night, she immediately felt guilty. No way did she trust or know Josh well enough to share details of Lulu and her suicide and the impact it had had on her life.

There was a pause, and they both looked at each other in that hungry way where you know something's about to happen. Thoughts of Lulu receded into their box, and Poppy focused on Josh's lips. That last kiss had been so good, she was excited just thinking about it. Then Josh reached toward her face and tucked a strand of Poppy's hair behind her ear, sending an electric shiver across Poppy's face, and heat spreading into her chest and groin as his fingers grazed her cheek. She gently moistened her lips with her tongue in anticipation as Josh rested his hand behind her head. Then they leaned towards each other, their lips meeting in a kiss that built quickly in intensity. *That's what I remember…*

Josh's hand then moved down over her throat and onto her left breast, where he squeezed gently, and Poppy felt a further injection of heat in her clitoris. *Yes, that's nice. Not too hard.* Poppy touched Josh's face and then ran her hands down over his muscled chest. *His body is so hard. God, he's hot.* She wanted to move things to the next level and so straddled Josh's lap. They slowly undressed each other, kissing and tasting each other's skin over necks and chests. Josh had no difficulty removing Poppy's dress or bra and could do both in two almost fluid motions, displaying a well-practised skill that Poppy didn't let herself dwell on. *Umm, a practised move.*

She was down to her black lace cheekini and heels, gently rocking on his lap as they kissed, feeling his erection grow beneath her, which further increased her wetness. *Oh, he's nice and hard. I like that.* It turned her on to know she was exciting him and that they were finally going to have sex.

Josh picked her up and lay her on the couch, gently kissing each ankle, sending a pleasant shiver up Poppy's body, as he removed her shoes. What's next, she wondered before he returned to kissing her mouth again briefly. Before she knew it, he'd removed her underwear and was placing a finger inside her. Poppy had a moment of slight discomfort at the suddenness of this move, before the ensuant pleasure of his rhythmic finger action. She closed her eyes and gave herself over to the sensations, sliding her hips up and down in time with Josh's finger thrusting, feeling herself coming closer to orgasm. *Oh, he's good… this is so nice… I'm close…* He suddenly stopped and Poppy's eyes flew open, her enjoyment abruptly curtailed, as he removed his finger and sat back, reaching to unfasten his belt. *Oh, but I was almost there…* She was disappointed, but helped him remove his belt and pants, caressing his erection through his underwear before they too were removed, pleased that the bulge she was caressing was not small.

He quickly and efficiently put on the condom which had obviously been in his pocket in preparation for this event, and again Poppy felt disappointed that there was clearly going to be no further foreplay, but she guided him into her, taking a few strokes for her muscles to relax and for her to start enjoying the sex. Josh kissed her lower neck near her clavicle, a spot she had always found arousing. Shivers of excitement tickled between her shoulder blades and up her neck, and she grabbed his buttocks, pushing him deeper inside her on each thrust, moaning softly. *That's good, that's it.*

There was an awkward moment as Josh tried to get one of Poppy's legs to stretch up toward her face, Poppy feeling pain in her hamstrings as they tightened uncomfortably.

'Let's try this instead,' she suggested, changing positions so that she was astride him, her back to his front in a reverse cowboy move. Josh moved her hips up and down, and Poppy felt how deep he was inside her. With her position over the edge of the couch, her hands leaning on his knees, she found her arousal rapidly rising again. *Oh, that's so deep.* She moaned more loudly as she was approaching climax, but Josh grabbed her hips forcefully holding her down onto his lap, and grunted as he came before she could. *Wait…what?* He collapsed onto her back as his breathing slowed down. When he'd recovered, Poppy got off him and stood.

He asked her, or maybe told her, 'You came, right?'

'Uh…almost,' she replied, barely concealing her disappointment.

'Oh god, sorry, I thought you were coming when I let go.'

'That's OK,' Poppy lied, but there was a new awkwardness that hadn't been there previously.

Poppy shrugged and headed to the bathroom with her clothes. When she came back, dressed, Josh also had his clothes on. He'd refilled their wine glasses and changed the music and they slowly returned to chatting and drinking. There was no further intimacy after the sex and after an hour Poppy could see he wasn't going to ask her to stay over, so she made noises about getting an Uber. Josh ordered one for her, effectively putting an end to the date. He kissed her at the door, holding it open but not showing any signs that he was going to walk her down to the lobby, or even the lift.

'Do you want to catch up next weekend,' he said casually, one hand on her hip, the other holding the door.

'I'll have to check my shifts and get back to you,' Poppy said, one of her eyebrows misbehaving by heading toward her hairline.

'OK,' was his casual reply. *Does he not see anything wrong with this?*

Sitting in the Uber on the way home, Poppy had mixed feelings about the night. It had started well but felt almost transactional toward the end. And whilst she remained attracted to Josh, she wasn't sure she knew him any better now than she did on that first night out.

And when I told him I didn't come, why didn't he offer to finish me off? That's pretty crap, surely? What is it with this guy? And not even walking me out?

Chapter 16

On Sunday when Poppy was preparing dinner she was overcome with abdominal cramps. Uh-oh, she thought. Within the hour she was on the toilet. And there she stayed pretty much continuously until about three o'clock when things finally eased off and she crawled into bed exhausted, dehydrated, and hollow. *Great, now I have gastro.*

She slept for a few hours before the second wave started and the toilet was again her place of residence. Luckily, Gemma and Lucas had had enough time to get themselves ready for work before wave number two, but Poppy worried they would also get sick. When her shaking legs could get off the toilet for longer than two minutes, she found some Powerade in the pantry and took a few tentative sips before crawling back into bed.

When she next woke, Lucas had arrived back, but Gemma was on an overtime shift. Poppy walked slowly to the bathroom again, this time to give it a quick clean with bleach and antiseptic to ensure it was clean and then waved hi to Lucas, not wanting to get too close and infect him.

'I've got gastro,' she said from her bedroom door. 'Stay away from me.'

'Oh no. Yeah, it's all over the wards. Do you need anything?'

'I'll manage, I'll just try to keep some distance from you two.'

'OK.'

She sought shelter back in her bed with the remains of her Powerade and her iPad. She watched a couple of Netflix shows, then fell back into a deep sleep.

She could only remember one dream when she awoke on Tuesday, feeling brighter and slightly hungry. It had been about Lulu. Not the nightmare of her body hanging from the shower, but a mixture of memory and fantasy. Initially, they were little girls on the swings, Poppy egging Lulu on to try and catch her as she swung higher. Then came the fantasy of Poppy and Lulu as adults, lying side by side on the sand at the beach, laughing and enjoying themselves. She sometimes had dreams like this, with an imagined present together, and she often woke feeling part sadness, and part happiness. Sad, knowing it had only been a dream and Lulu was still gone, but also surprisingly happy as if the scenario had really happened, and she'd really been with Lulu on the beach, or at a bar, or fighting over the TV remote. Part of Poppy's brain knew it wasn't possible but another part hoped it was some weird cosmic way of them still being connected. That Lulu's essence was communicating with her subliminally. She tried not to dwell on it, for fear she'd only ruin it, and just enjoy that brief subconscious moment of happiness.

Poppy let the hot water of the shower sandblast her face, neck, and shoulders, then made some Vegemite toast and a cup of tea and ate it at the dining table. Lucas and Gemma came and went, not showing any signs of infection yet, which was reassuring.

I wonder if Josh got the bug, too? A pang of guilt twisted inside her like a snake. It would be entirely her fault if he did. *Should I text him and check? Nah…he doesn't deserve it.*

She had today off, but was due back at work tomorrow. Once nine o'clock ticked over, she rang up Melissa to let her know about the gastro and find out about the hospital's return to work policy. The standard forty-eight-hour rule applied, meaning if Poppy remained free of vomiting and diarrhoea today, she would still need to take tomorrow off to avoid passing on the infection to patients and staff. Melissa would allocate one of the Residents on relief to her day shift tomorrow.

'Thanks, Melissa.'

'By the way, we received your email about Tim. I completely agree with your concerns, and I was going to email you later, but this saves me the trouble. You have an evening shift on Friday. Could you come in early and meet with Dr Anderson and myself at one o'clock?'

'Sure, that'd be great!' Poppy exclaimed, excitement fizzing again, and thoughts of Josh pushed to the side.

Despite Poppy's exhaustion, her mind was already jumping forward, envisaging their eventual successful outcome. Once she got off the phone, she texted Will.

> Good news. Meeting scheduled with Dr A & Melissa Fri
> 1pm in Dr A's office in the MTU. Can u come?

While she was waiting for a response, Poppy got out some paper and a pen and started writing some ideas. She also rang her mum and asked her about what she'd achieved with the school after Lulu's death. Her mum gave her the run-down, then promised to email through the policies they'd enacted. One was school-based: a policy about pastoral care and student well-being. But the second, and more meaningful for Poppy, although probably less useful for the current situation, was a policy that her Mum and a group of like-minded parents got passed through the NSW parliament regarding juvenile mental health and anti-bullying at all NSW public schools.

Poppy spent the next few hours reading and taking notes on these policies and then searching NSW safe work practices and realising the hospital system was often in breach of these legal requirements, particularly when doctors and other staff were on overtime shifts. Some of the surgical trainees almost lived at the hospital. By the time Will texted back in the afternoon, Poppy had an outline of the problems the hospital had around unsafe work practices, and also some suggestions around solutions.

> Sorry, Pop, been in theatre all day, just got ur message.
> Good news, yes, I'll make sure I can make it.

> Brill. Just spent a few hrs trolling govt policies &
> brainstorming. Can u come over tomorrow after work to
> go thru? Poppy texted back.

> OK. I'll swing by about 6ish.

Poppy texted him the address and promised she would feed him. She thought it would be safer to wait until she was definitely not infectious before meeting up with Will.

By dinnertime Poppy was up to a light meal, so she made herself a sandwich with a Coke No Sugar, and ate with Gemma whilst Lucas was on an evening shift.

'You know, the gastro outbreak is getting worse? Two wards are now fully quarantined for gastro only, and the MTU is struggling to cover all the staff off sick,' Gemma informed her.

'Jeez, that's bad.'

'Yeah, apparently it's norovirus.'

'Not surprising, if it's spreading so quickly, I guess.'

'Hopefully it'll burn itself out, but, in the meantime, they've got us all gown, glove and masking to review any patients.'

'Annoying, but sensible.'

'Yeah.'

'I wonder if Josh got it?' Poppy said, remembering her earlier concerns in the day.

'You haven't told me yet how the date went.'

'Yeah, I kinda got side-tracked.' And they both giggled.

'So?'

'Well, it started well, good food, good conversation, attraction.'

'But?'

'But…the sex was OK, but not great.' Poppy explained the limited foreplay, lack of orgasm, and then almost abrupt change in behaviour and dismissal.

'Hmm,' Gemma said, frowning. 'So, how do you feel about it all now?'

'I just don't know. It feels like each time I see him I have this mixed experience – partly good, partly crappy. I'm just not sure things can progress.'

'Yeah, fair enough. Has he called or texted since Saturday night?'

'Not yet.'

'But he could have had gastro like you?'

'He could,' Poppy agreed, nodding.

'Maybe you could text him, sound him out, see what his response is like before deciding whether it's worth any more effort?'

'Maybe. But then I think about all my experiences with Will and every one of them has been positive. I feel safe and completely at ease with him. I've trusted him with Lulu, and I also feel like I know a lot about him. Certainly, more than when we first met, and the same isn't true for Josh.'

'But how does Will feel about you? Do you know?'

'I don't know. I know he cares about me, but it could just be as a friend.'

'And how do you feel about him?'

'I still feel embarrassed about how we started, but I also feel we've moved past that, and if he felt the same, I'd want to take things forward.'

'So, if you had the choice between Will and Josh, who would you choose right now?'

'Will,' Poppy answered quickly and honestly.

'Then maybe that's the answer to Josh, regardless?'

'Maybe,' Poppy answered, wondering what to do next about Josh.

Poppy woke the next morning feeling back to normal. As she was eating breakfast, a text came through from Josh.

> Hi, sorry I've been out of touch since Sat. I came down
> with the gastro that's been going around. Hope you didn't
> get it too! Anyway, wanted to reach out and see whether
> you were free on the weekend? Josh

Wow, Poppy thought, that's a turnaround. *Maybe I've been too judgemental.* Her guilt snake coiled again knowing full well that she must have given him gastro, not the other way around, and yet he was the one checking on her. *Am I a bitch for not checking on him?*

> Hi Josh, I got it too (green sick face emoji). Feeling back
> to normal today tho, yay! I've got day shift Thurs, then
> evening shifts Fri/Sat but am off Sun/Mon/Tue. Not
> allowed back to work til tomorrow. What did you have in
> mind?

> I'm also off today and feeling good. Want to come over?

Poppy sat for a moment, thinking about this. Maybe this time she had been too critical of the date on Saturday. *First-time sex was often a bit awkward, right?* It would be seriously poor form to dump him after having sex the once and giving him gastro. That was a guy thing to do. And what else was she going to do today, anyway?

OK, sounds good. When??

Whenever ur ready. Bring swimmers.

OK.

She got dressed in a bikini with a casual summer dress over the top and threw a hat, sunscreen, underwear and towel in a bag and got to Josh's house around ten o'clock. The weather was heating up – summer's last hurrah, and they had predicted highs in the mid-thirties before a possible evening storm. It was already about 29°C.

Josh was wearing boardies and a white T-shirt with thongs. He kissed her on the lips in greeting, slipping a hand to her waist. Poppy was a little surprised, her body instinctively stiffening, but she told her brain to relax, and kissed him back.

'The weather's nice. Do you want to head to the beach for a swim and some lunch, maybe?' Josh suggested when their bodies parted.

'Sure.'

'How about Bronte?'

'Love it, let's go.'

'OK, great. Let me grab my keys. I put a bottle of water in the fridge. Do you want to get it?'

'Sure.'

Poppy went to the fridge to grab the water, then they headed out. The beach wasn't too packed, and they settled themselves on the sand and chatted for a while before heading into the water to cool off. The water was cool and not too rough, enabling them space to flirt, cuddle and kiss in the waves without being buffeted. Poppy wrapped her legs around his waist, and they floated like this for a while, talking and kissing.

'I think I might have given you gastro,' Poppy admitted after a while.

'Really?'

'Well, that shift before I came to your place for dinner, a patient vomited on me.'

'Seriously?'

'Yeah.'

'Yuck, that must have been awful.'

'If was definitely a low light, that's for sure.'

'I don't think I've ever been vomited on before.'

'Well, I guess there's a first for everything… What's the worst thing that a patient has ever done to you?'

'Hmm, let me think… I had a patient take a swing at me once.'

'No way, what happened?'

'It was also an ED shift, and the guy was really pissed, and he'd hit his head falling into the gutter and was combative. Classic head injury.'

'So, what did you do? Did he punch you?'

'No, he was drunk enough that his swing was more like a windmill and really slow, so I had time to duck and weave, and I kicked his leg out from under him as I was ducking the fist, so he landed heavily on his butt.'

'Wow, did that make him angrier? And were you worried you'd get in trouble?'

'He howled like a baby and stopped fighting after that. Let me stitch him up. And, no, I wasn't worried about getting in trouble. No one saw, and even if they did, I was subduing an aggressive patient. I would do it again.'

It must be nice to be that confident, and be a man, Poppy thought.

'Can you show me how you tripped him up?' Poppy teased playfully.

'OK, you stand like this,' Josh said, positioning Poppy in the shallow water. 'And then swing your arm like this at me,' he said, moving Poppy's arm in a slow upward swing.

'OK, go,' Josh instructed once he was facing Poppy again.

Poppy made the swing and as her right arm swung toward Josh's face he ducked and she felt her left leg lift off the sand as Josh had scooped her leg out with his. She splashed back in the water and Josh's face then appeared above her as she laughed and he leaned in to kiss her, embracing her and pulling her back upright in the process.

They came in for lunch and to cool their increasing fervour, towelling dry and heading to one of the cafes for a meal and a cool drink. Poppy ran her foot up and down Josh's shin in what she hoped was a seductive way while he played with her fingers. Their eyes locked on each other, Poppy not wanting to break their gaze. She found herself licking her lips, even before the food arrived, picturing Josh without his shirt on. His eyes looked a little misty to her, and she wondered if he was thinking about her naked as well.

By the time their sandwiches had arrived, Poppy was aroused and ready to go.

'Are you feeling the way I'm feeling?' Josh asked after watching intently as Poppy sipped her Coke No Sugar through the paper straw.

'What way is that?' Poppy answered playfully, her tongue flicking at the end of the straw.

'Oh, Poppy, you tease,' Josh said, smiling. 'I may need to make you pay for that.'

'Tell me what you're going to do to me?' Poppy asked, her sandwich forgotten on her plate, hungry only for Josh now.

'I think I need to taste you.'

'Cheque!' Poppy called out, raising a hand in the air and looking for the nearest serving staff, Josh letting out an unexpected chuckle, deep and throaty.

They made out in the elevator of Josh's building and were stripping off clothes by the time the door swung shut behind them. The sex this time was better. Poppy reached orgasm and they snuggled afterwards, but it was still not as good as that first time with Will. Although maybe the alcohol that night had inflated her recollections, she was no longer so sure.

They spent the afternoon in bed talking and exploring each other's bodies, but around five o'clock Josh told her he'd need to study so she got dressed and headed home. At least this time she left with a smile on her face. Poppy relayed the details to Gemma when she got back.

'That's great, Pop. I'm glad you feel more confident than you did yesterday.'

'I think I was just too quick to judge the situation, and him.'

'It sounds like things were definitely better today.'

'So much better,' Poppy answered, not able to conceal the smile that rapidly spread across her face.

The sound of the doorbell surprised both Gemma and Poppy. Gemma answered the buzzer and mouthed *Will* to Poppy over her shoulder. Poppy had completely forgotten she'd organised for Will to come by to brainstorm their meeting for Friday. She did a head-thunk and raced to the bathroom to tidy herself up while Will made his way upstairs. She greeted him at the door with a kiss on the cheek and a big smile to disguise the fact she'd completely forgotten their plans. *I hope he can't smell the sex on me!* Poppy reintroduced Gemma and Lucas and offered him a drink and then sat down to work.

Poppy showed Will the notes she'd made yesterday, and they spent the next couple of hours formatting their plan of attack for Friday's meeting. Will suggested they get the head of the Resident Medical Officers' Association, Tarryn, to attend and also raised whether they should bring in the Health Services Union (HSU) representative.

'You don't think that will be too aggressive?'

'Yeah, you're probably right. Let's just stick with Tarryn for now. I'll send her an email.'

'OK.'

Will left about nine o'clock after they'd had a celebratory beer and Poppy felt she'd bluffed her way through the evening, sure that he had not guessed she'd forgotten. *Phew.*

Chapter 17

'Hey, Poppy, Paeds is really backed up. Can you head down there and help out? The Paeds Advanced Trainee is there, so run everything by them,' Seb said to her in the afternoon when there was a bit of a lull in subbies.

'Sure, OK,' Poppy replied, some anxiety rising like bubbles heading up to the surface of a freshly poured glass of Coke. She'd only had a short rotation in Paediatrics in medical school and didn't feel confident, although her experience the other day with Charlie and his Mum had been very positive, so maybe this would be ok, too?

Poppy headed down the subbies' corridor to the Paeds ED which connected at the end. She found two nurses, including Graham, and two doctors, all looking harassed. Poppy introduced herself to the doctors, explaining Seb had suggested she give them a hand.

'Thanks, that'd be great. We're getting slammed with gastro and there's still three waiting. If you could pick up the next one and talk to me afterwards, that'd be great? I'm Preetha,' the Advanced Trainee said.

'No problem.'

Poppy clicked on the next waiting case and, sure enough, it was an eighteen-month-old boy with diarrhoea and vomiting. She went to the assigned cubicle to find an exhausted mother cradling her toddler in her arms. The mother was sweating, probably from holding a sick child for hours on end, and her hair was a mess, sticking up at the side, reminding Poppy immediately of Pippi Longstocking's plaits.

'Hi, why don't you tell me what's been happening,' Poppy said crouching beside the mother and child after she had introduced herself.

'He came home from daycare the day before yesterday, vomiting—'

'Sorry to interrupt, but any diarrhoea?'

'No. He vomited for about six hours fairly continuously, then it slowed down, but he's not keeping down fluids. Everything just comes back up.'

'OK, how much fluid or ice blocks has he had in the last twelve hours?'

'I've tried juice, water, hydrolyte, ice blocks, and even soft drink, but he has a sip or a couple of licks and that's it. At most I think he's maybe drunk half a cup altogether.'

'And any vomiting this last twelve hours?'

'Probably two small vomits of a quarter to half a cup size?'

'And I see the nurses have done a weight, how much did he weigh before he got sick?'

'About twelve and a half kilos?'

Whilst they had been talking, Poppy had also been keeping an eye on the little boy and he was very flat. He hadn't really moved, he looked listless and grey. There was a puddle of orange liquid in a kidney dish and a floating paddle pop stick. Clearly an ice block that hadn't been consumed, and a baby's bottle with probably Hydrolyte syrup discarded on the table. His weight in triage was only 10.9 kilograms, so he had lost more than ten percent of his body weight, which was concerning. The observation chart also recorded his length and head circumference which were within the normal range, and his heart rate which was elevated for age.

'Do you mind if I just have a quick look at him in your arms? We don't have to move him just yet, but I just want to look at his skin and mouth.'

'Sure.'

'Hi, Oscar, my name's Poppy. Can you see this bright light on my phone?'

Oscar's head popped off his mother's shoulder as he was interested in the light. Poppy kept moving it only slightly, just enough to keep him interested whilst she gently pinched his skin on his chubby wrist to see if it was loose as she was expecting it might be, another indication of dehydration. *Tick.*

'OK,' Poppy said, turning off the torch. 'Now look what I can do—' she said, opening her mouth really wide. 'Can you do that too?'

Oscar put his head back down on his mother's shoulder, losing interest, and shutting his eyes.

'Sorry,' his mum offered.

'That's OK, I'll just lift his lip up quickly.'

When she did that, Oscar jerked his head up once more. So she again tried to encourage him to open his mouth, but he mewled weakly and burrowed into his mother's chest.

'That's OK, that's it for now. I'm just going to have a chat with one of the senior doctors, but I think we will need to put in a drip and give him some fluids. He's lost weight and he's quite lethargic.'

'OK,' his mother said.

Jeez, she looks tired. There were deep lines under her eyes, and her skin was grey too. Before she left the cubicle, Poppy asked her, 'What about you? Have you been sick as well?'

'No, I'm fine.'

'When was the last time you had something to eat or drink?'

'That's OK, I'm alright.'

'I'll just grab you a juice and a sandwich from the fridge, OK?'

'Thank you.'

Once she'd given over the provisions, she went to update Preetha.

'So, what have you got?' Preetha asked.

'Eighteen-month-old boy with vomiting for forty-eight hours, minimal oral hydration, weight loss of 1.6kg, flat, tachycardic, reduced skin turgor. No luck pushing Hydrolyte. I think he needs IV fluids.'

'OK, let's have a look,' Preetha said, standing up and walking back with Poppy toward the cubicles.

After reviewing the little boy, Preetha agreed and asked Poppy if she'd ever cannulated a toddler.

'Once in med school,' Poppy replied with a high pitch in her voice.

'Do you want to have a go?'

'Sure,' Poppy replied, trying to sound enthusiastic and confident, but internally thinking, *fuck no!*

'OK, well, the nurses put Emla cream on when he was triaged, so he should have a couple of numb patches of skin by now, so let's go. But with kids you only get one attempt, then you pass up the chain. We don't want to over-traumatise them or their parents.'

'I am absolutely OK with that,' said Poppy with a further spike in her anxiety levels in anticipation of the procedure. That now-familiar thumping heart and sweaty palms.

Poppy set up the procedure room and when she was ready, she took a deep breath before bringing in the mum and bub. Poppy was worried that she wouldn't get the cannula in and the toddler would scream or cry, but the poor little tyke hardly moved. And despite him being dehydrated she was able to get the cannula in first go, keeping the mother calm as well.

'I like the way you worked in there. Very gentle and encouraging. Are you doing a Paeds term?'

'Yes, later in the year.'

'Excellent, I think you'll do well.'

'Thank you.' Poppy felt a little thrill at the compliment, the anxiety slipping away.

That's two good Paeds experiences. Could I see myself doing Paediatrics? Maybe. Certainly not a hard no. She felt her face brighten with a smile as she went to sort out the paperwork for the fluids and admission while Graham got the little boy hooked up and Preetha spoke with the consultant.

Later, Poppy headed back to subbies feeling good. She hated to see sick kids, but she'd really enjoyed working with them today. Each one reminded her of Lulu when the two of them were little. She'd been a happy little kid. Poppy wished she could go back to that time and play with young Lulu again, before the pressures of adolescence dulled her spirit and confidence. Like the dream she'd had of them on the swings together. *If only Lulu could have hung on a bit longer, I'm sure she would have gotten past the bullying. She could have had such a great life! It's just so unfair.* Poppy felt herself gulp as she quickly tried to stem the emotion rising suddenly within. *No, Poppy, pull it together, you've still got work to do.* She stopped briefly in the subbies corridor, willing her emotions to calm down and pushing her guilt and sadness back into that little box inside. Once her legs felt strong, she swallowed again, and walked on.

Poppy had a quiet night at home and on Friday headed to her meeting with Melissa and Dr Anderson before her evening shift. She'd arranged to meet Will and the Resident Medical Officers' Association president, Tarryn, before the meeting to go over their notes and strategy.

'Hi, Poppy, I'm Tarryn,' the short girl with the dark pixie cut hair introduced herself when they met at the library. Poppy was struck by her large brown eyes.

'Hi.'

'OK, let's get started,' Tarryn said, enthusiastically, 'Will tells me you two have done quite a bit of brain-storming. I'm really keen for you to fill me in on what you've come up with.'

She had a real energy about her, Poppy thought. In fact, she reminded Poppy of a kelpie – always wagging its tail, happy to see you, but also alert and energetic. She was certainly a good choice for president – the kind of person who, at a party, or any event really, would make a habit of talking to every person in the room. And each of those people would leave feeling they'd been really listened to. After spending even a short time with her, Poppy thought she'd make an excellent politician.

Their plan of attack was that Poppy would start the conversation, outlining her concerns for the junior medical staff, and then Will would take over outlining some of their suggestions. They would keep the legislation and award specifics for rebuttal, which Tarryn would handle. But as the old Yiddish proverb states, *man plans, God laughs*.

Melissa and Dr Anderson welcomed them into the office and after chair rearrangement to accommodate Tarryn, whom they weren't expecting, they all got comfortable.

Dr Anderson started things off: 'I just wanted to thank you for your email. You raise important concerns, and the death of a valued staff member is tragic.'

But before Poppy could jump in with her planned spiel, she continued, 'Melissa and I have discussed the matter, and we have scheduled a meeting with the directors of each of the specialty training programmes next week to formulate a response to this tragedy.'

As soon as she paused here, Will saw his opening: 'Thank you for this "front-foot" approach. We have some ideas we'd like to discuss with you about how to prevent difficult working conditions and ways to foster a more supportive environment for trainees in the future.'

Poppy smiled at him, but her smile quickly turned to a frown as Dr Anderson cut him off before he could add any detail around their ideas.

'I'll stop you there, Will. I appreciate you three are passionate about this, but I think it is premature to start discussing changes before the directors have been updated on the situation and consider their individual programmes.'

'We'd be very happy to provide written documentation of these ideas to you before your meeting so that they can be considered,' Poppy ventured.

'That won't be necessary at present. Any response to this tragedy will come from the Directors of Training and the board of the hospital.' Her hands were folded on the desk in front of her, clasped together, signalling the closure of discussion. There was a pause after the finality of this statement. Poppy watched Dr Anderson's face with her tight smile in place and likened her to a smiling assassin. It looked like Gemma was right on that first day after all, she really was cold.

But they were not done quite yet. After letting the silence pervade for a minute, and as Dr Anderson began to rise out of her chair, Tarryn chose her moment to weigh in.

'Whilst I understand wholeheartedly the need to ensure a consensus and inclusive approach to any potential changes in junior staffing or training, I'd like to remind you of the NSW safe work hours which were not met in Tim's case.'

Dr Anderson lowered herself back down. 'I will be reviewing his rostering as part of our meeting. But as is often the case, he may have swapped originally planned shifts, thus exposing himself to unsafe work hours.'

'I'd be keen to be included in your review.'

'Certainly, we can include the Residents' Association in our statement after we have completed the review.'

'It may also be useful to your committee to have the Residents' Association involved in decision-making and implementation of any changes.'

'I will certainly keep that in mind and put forward your request for involvement when we review the situation.'

'Thank you.'

Tarryn sat back in her chair, folding her hands in her lap, looking sombre. *Was Tarryn on their side, or her own?*

Their meeting was called to a close without a peep from Melissa, who was seated behind Dr Anderson's shoulder, almost hidden, and they were ushered out of the office.

As they filed down the corridor from the MTU, Tarryn turned toward Poppy and Will. Poppy's head was low, and she almost ran into her, looking up at the last moment.

She grabbed Poppy's wrist and said, 'Let's get out of here and go discuss that.' She dropped Poppy's wrist and pointed behind them toward the MTU with a sneer on her face.

They found a quiet spot in a café down the road to debrief and regroup, Poppy briefly looking around to make sure there were no other doctors seated close enough to hear them.

'What a bitch,' Tarryn said, to Poppy's shock. 'Did you notice her body language? Leaning forward over her arms on the desk? Classic narcissist behaviour. She controlled that entire meeting from the minute we walked in the door, not willing to consider any options from us, or allow even one concession. And closed ranks meeting of Directors of Training? Complete waste of time – no accountability, no changes.'

Maybe she is on our side, then.

Poppy felt deflated, like a balloon being pricked with a pin. She had felt disappointed after the meeting, but Tarryn's assessment was far more damning.

'Do you really think it was that bad?' Poppy asked, looking for any glimmer or prospect of hope.

'Yes. I've only been president for just over a year, but every meeting I've had with her has ultimately been negative. She has her own very specific agenda for junior doctor training and is not prepared to negotiate on anything. I didn't tell you this before the meeting as I hoped finally this tragedy would open up discussions, but, sadly, I was wrong.'

'Well, what do we do now?' Poppy asked, feeling flat and anxious that if they didn't achieve anything, all she would have done is singled herself out as a trouble-maker.

'I think we have to wait for their official report, and I suspect they'll drag their feet on providing that. But, in the meantime, I think we should start galvanising the Residents and Registrars. We need to strike while the iron's hot and get them motivated to force change if necessary. I'll email the entire junior staff body and put up flyers for a meeting, maybe next Friday at doctors' drinks? What do you think?'

Poppy looked at Will and they both nodded their agreement.

'I'll just check my roster to make sure I'm not working,' Poppy said, pulling it up on her phone. 'Yep, I can come.'

Tarryn continued. 'OK, and before I head home today, I'll do a follow-up email from our visit summarising our position, Dr Anderson's responses, and a timeline for follow-up.'

'Great idea,' Poppy and Will agreed.

Tarryn then had to rush off, taking her coffee whilst Will and Poppy stayed.

'So, what did you think, Will?' Poppy asked after Tarryn left, hoping he might have a more positive spin on the situation.

'It was disappointing. My previous interactions with Dr Anderson had been positive, so I was expecting she would welcome our suggestions or at least listen to them. But Tarryn's right, she had no intention of involving us. I just wonder how Melissa feels about all this. Did you notice she sat herself behind Dr Anderson?'

'Yes!' Poppy exclaimed.

'It might be worth having an informal chat with her alone.'

'Yeah, that's a good idea. Are you happy to talk to her? She doesn't really know me from Adam.'

'Sure. I'll wait until mid next week and just drop by her office.'

'Excellent, let me know how you go.'

'Will do.'

'Well, I guess I'd better head back for my shift.'

'Are you off on the weekend?'

'Off Sunday to Tuesday.'

'Do you want to have a surfing lesson on Sunday afternoon if the weather's good?'

Poppy smiled at Will, tipping her head to the side.

'I don't know, Will, I think I'd be pretty useless.'

'Well, you've got to start somewhere, and it's a good way to clear your head. Think about it, and I'll call you late morning.'

'OK.'

They walked back to the hospital together in companionable silence, and, despite the negativity of the meeting, Poppy felt buoyed by Will's friendship. Her flash of panic at being labelled a trouble-maker disappeared in his presence. They separated at the entrance, Poppy heading down the left corridor to ED and Will heading straight ahead to the main hospital. He raised a hand to wave goodbye and Poppy smiled in response.

During her shift she had a text from Josh asking if she wanted to grab dinner on Sunday night. Poppy agreed, a smile stretching her lips, and he arranged to meet in Newtown around seven o'clock.

But despite the positive mood during the evening, Poppy went to bed going over the meeting with Dr Anderson and thinking back to Tim and Lulu, and felt her mood sink. Whilst she knew this wasn't the end of the story, she had felt galvanised planning strategies for change, and was really hopeful she could achieve something positive out of this tragedy. Dr Anderson's response was a slap in the face, throwing that momentum off balance. It meant her sleep that night was fitful. Negative thoughts continued to circle: *had she been a terrible sister? Could she have done more for Tim? Had she just fucked up her future career less than a term in? ARGHH…*

Chapter 18

She woke around nine o'clock on Sunday with a sore head and heavy limbs like she had a hangover, even though she only had one drink after her shift. Poppy thought that the shift changes were really starting to take a toll on her body. She hopped on the scales when she got out of bed and was shocked to find she'd lost 3kg. Her weight was normally stable, and she didn't stress too much about what she ate. Her diet was reasonably healthy, with a few fatty and sugary things here and there. *I guess, with the shifts, I've been eating a bit more haphazardly. I'll have to be more diligent about eating three meals a day from now on. No wonder shift workers have a shorter life expectancy, and I guess it explains the hangover-like feeling.*

She started the morning with a large glass of water before her cup of tea and decided on a high-protein breakfast of poached eggs on toast. Will called when she was cleaning up after brekky.

'Hey, how was the shift?'

'OK, nothing to report.'

'So…have you considered the surfing lesson?'

'Alright, I'll give it a go… But I'm most likely going to be crap at it.'

'Don't sell yourself short, Pop. How about I pick you up at two?'

'OK, see you then.'

'Bye.'

Poppy felt a bit trepidatious. She was a good pool swimmer but wasn't a massive beach person. Growing up in the country, she had only recently spent time at the beach and was more a paddler and sunbaker rather than a body surfer. *I'm not sure I can do this…what if I can't even paddle out on the board? And what about sharks?*

She had gotten herself pretty worked up by the time Will came to collect her.

'What's the matter?' Will asked sincerely when he opened the door and took in Poppy's fearful expression.

'I'm a bit scared,' Poppy admitted quietly.

'Oh, Poppy, there's no need to be scared,' Will reassured. 'Today we're just going to get used to the board and maybe have a bit of a paddle. It's going to be a while before I let you loose on your own on a wave, don't worry,' he said, putting a hand on her shoulder at arm's length and making eye contact, forcing Poppy to look into his blue eyes.

Poppy felt reassured and in that moment she felt again that sense of trust. Will was not the kind of person to put her in a dangerous situation. She let out a sigh of relief, smiled at him, and got into his car.

When they got to the beach, Will donned a rash shirt, and Poppy surreptitiously snuck a peek at this body. She remembered again the feel of his lean, toned torso under her fingertips, and blushed at the thought.

'So, what now?' Poppy asked once he'd taken the board off the roof rack.

'Let's have a quick chat about the basics and then let's hit the water.'

They sat on the sand and Will explained where to position yourself on the board and how to spring up from a lying position.

'Mastering the spring from lying to standing on the board is the first, and probably the hardest step. If you don't get your balance just right, and your feet aren't evenly spaced in the centre of the board, it's an almost certain wipeout. So, I'll demonstrate on the sand, and then you can practice before we try doing it in the shallows.'

He was very relaxed, and it helped keep Poppy's anxiety at bay. Squinting into the sun, Will's eyes crinkled more at the edges, and Poppy loved how his mouth formed a natural smile whenever he glanced in her direction. But she had to stop ogling him as he lay on the board.

'So, you spring, using your upper body strength and core and you want to plant your feet at the same time, about shoulder-width apart, with the centre of your mass in the middle of the board and your weight slightly favouring your front foot.'

'And which foot should be my front foot?'

'It's kind of automatic. One will be more comfortable than the other. Have you ever skateboarded or used a scooter?'

'A scooter, when I was a kid.'

'Do you remember which foot you had in front?'

'Maybe my left…but I'm not sure.'

'OK, let's swap, see which feels more natural. Just try it both ways.'

'OK…'

Poppy bit her lower lip in concentration, her brows knitting together. She lay down on the board.

'OK, wiggle back a bit, you're a bit too far forward,' Will said, gently touching her hips. Poppy felt a tremor of electricity as he touched her skin.

'So, aim for your hips to be back here, that way your chest isn't right up at the tip.'

As soon as he said 'tip', Poppy childishly thought of the tip of his penis, and had to shut her eyes and keep her head down to cast out the image and so Will couldn't see her face.

Jeez, I'm not sure I can do this, I keep thinking about Will's body and the night we had sex. How am I going to keep a straight face?

'That's better. OK, when you're ready, pop up.'

Poppy took a deep breath, trying to clear her mind and concentrate on the instructions Will had given her about her feet and her weight. *OK, one…two…three…*

Poppy popped up onto the board.

'OK, you look a bit stiff,' Will said.

Stiff… Oh shut up, brain, stop being a complete idiot. It's just a surfing lesson. It's not sex!

'Here,' Will continued and placed his hands on her shoulders. 'Relax these,' and he put gentle pressure on her shoulders, pushing them down and forcing Poppy to relax her neck. 'And your hips need to be more like this,' he said moving his hands to her hips and shifting her pelvis. *Oh, I like the feel of those hands on my hips… Bloody hell, what is wrong with you? You had sex with Josh only a few days ago, and now you're lusting after Will. Seriously, get a grip!*

'Yep, that looks better. How does it feel with your left foot in front?'

'I don't know, OK I guess.'

'Alright, well, lie back down and try it again with the right foot in front.'

This time, Will kept his hands to himself and as soon as Poppy popped up, it felt more awkward.

'That's definitely worse.'

'OK, so you lead with your left foot. Let's do it one more time with the left, then we'll go try in the water.'

'But just in the shallow bit, right?'

'Of course, I'm not trying to get you killed. And that's also why I brought you to Bondi. It generally has the worst surf, so it's better for your first lesson.'

They went into the water up to chest height.

'Is this a little deep?' Poppy asked, thinking they were going to start closer in to the shore.

'No, you don't want it too shallow, if you fall face first you don't want to smash straight into the sand. Besides, you have a lovely straight nose, I don't want it to end up bent,' he said a smile breaking out on his face.

Was that just him flirting? Poppy held his eyes a little longer, watching his expression and trying to decode whether he was flirting or not. In the end, she couldn't tell.

'OK, lie on the board,' Will said, staying at her side. 'OK, here comes a little wave, I'm going to count you in. On three, I want you to pop up…one…two…three!'

Poppy sprung up, pushing down with the strength in her arms and trying to get her legs under her quickly in the right position. But her weight was too far back, and the tip of the board lifted out of the water. She squealed as she fell backwards into the water. Will grabbed the board and brought it back while Poppy regained her feet and her pride.

'OK, so weight a bit more forward next time.'

'I'll try,' Poppy said lying on the board.

'OK, one…two…three!' Will called out and Poppy sprung up again. She overcorrected, her weight was too far forward, and nose-dived over the tip of the board; the weight of her body following through and driving her into the sand below. But Will had judged it well and it was really her right shoulder that took the brunt of the impact. This time she spluttered as she broke the surface.

'Are you OK?' Will asked, brows knitted with concern.

'Yep,' Poppy said briefly, rolling her right shoulder back and giving it a rub.

'Ready to try again?' Will asked, clearly from the "get back on the horse" school of thought.

'OK.'

The third attempt was better. Her weight was more centred, and whilst she felt awkward and her neck and shoulders were too tense, she managed to stay upright for at least ten seconds. They kept practising for another half hour or so. Poppy was so busy concentrating on her own body that she stopped thinking about Will's. By the end of the lesson, her shoulders and upper arms ached, and she was panting, but she'd managed to stay on most of the waves until the whitewash once she popped up.

When they were towelling off on the sand, Will asked, 'So, what do you think?'

'It was good. Tiring, but yeah, the sun, the breeze, the physicality of it, and of course, your company. I had a good time. Thank you, Will.'

'You're very welcome.'

'You're a really good teacher.' And it was true, he was. He was relaxed and had this way of instilling confidence that made you feel at ease.

'Well, I had a good student,' he said, smiling at her. Then he pulled his rashie over his head and Poppy got an eyeful of his abs and the light hair tracing down from his belly button into his boardies. The water ran down his body in little rivulets and Poppy's eyes were fixated, her mouth open when Will interrupted her thoughts with a clearing of his throat. *Oh fuck, he just busted me salivating over his body! Fuck, how embarrassing!* She dropped her gaze down to her towel and rubbed more vigorously at her legs, bending forward so her red face was out of Will's eyeline.

When Will dropped her back at her building he asked, 'So another lesson soon?'

'OK, yeah. Thank you.'

'Great. I'll be in touch.'

'Bye, Will.'

'Seeya, Poppy,' he said as she shut his car door. He did a U-turn and drove away. She stood watching his car drive down the street and thought again about the nature of her relationship with Will. *Are we just friends?*

Poppy showered before getting ready to meet Josh in Newtown. He'd chosen a Vietnamese restaurant and Poppy was the first to arrive, so she chose a table with a street view where she could gaze at passers-by. She ordered a beer and waited, her irritation rising the longer it became. She texted Gemma:

He's still not here

Have you texted him?

No. I'm just sitting here, stewing.

Deep breaths. I'm sure he'll be there soon.

Poppy was about to text back when Josh appeared at the table, twenty minutes late. She hoped he hadn't seen her texts.

'I'm so sorry I'm late. I was at the library and lost track of time,' he said as he bent to kiss her on the cheek.

'That's OK,' Poppy lied through gritted teeth. His hair was wet from the shower and he smelled strongly of the aftershave Poppy liked so much. That whiff of spice went quite a way to Poppy forgiving his tardiness.

Once they'd ordered, Poppy asked, 'So, how's the study coming along? Your exam's in a month or so?'

'Yeah, five weeks now. It's OK, just the final stretch, trying to really push through. It's exhausting.'

'I can imagine. Are you feeling confident?'

'Reasonably. The failure rate is still pretty high, but I think I'm on track.'

'And your clinical exam is a few months later if you pass the written?'

'Yeah, about three months apart and you don't find out your result on the written for about six weeks, so you just have to assume you've passed and start prepping for the clinical exams.'

'That's brutal.'

'Pretty much. Do you know what you want to do?' Josh asked Poppy.

'Not yet. I don't think it'll be surgical, but beyond that, I don't know.'

'Fair enough.'

'What do you want to specialise in after your exams?'

'Cardiology.'

'When did you come to that decision?'

'I think I knew early in med school I would be a physician. And then during my internship I did a Cardiology term, and it just felt natural, where I fitted, if you know what I mean?'

'Sure. Kismet.'

'Yeah. The lightbulb moment. Maybe it'll be like that for you too.'

'I hope so.'

When they were standing on the street after finishing their meals, Josh said, 'So, I can't really have a late night, but you're welcome to come back to my place for a while if you like?'

Poppy's brows knitted. *What? So, it's just sex and out the door, is that what he's suggesting?* Poppy's blood pressure started to rise.

'Ahh…' *Was everything with this guy transactional? He wants to get his rocks off and then get a solid eight hours sleep before work? I'm just the person that fulfils his physical needs?*

Poppy understood that this was a highly stressful time for him, so close to his exams, but she didn't want to become his 'booty-call' girl.

'Actually, I'm pretty tired too. These shift changes are getting pretty brutal.'

'OK, I understand,' Josh replied. 'Look, the next few weeks are going to be hell. I'm not sure I can be relied upon for anything at the moment.'

What does that mean? Does that mean, I'll call for sex, but I don't want anything beyond that? Or, I'm not going to call you at all, and this is where it ends?

Poppy wasn't sure how to respond. She wanted to be understanding about the stress of his exams and certainly didn't want to come across as needy or petulant.

'I understand,' she replied eventually, although she wasn't sure she really did, and she felt Josh was a bit cold. Although maybe it was just a manifestation of stress, and they were just getting together at the wrong time. Things were just so confusing.

But…there was still this niggle in the back of her mind that this wasn't going anywhere. *Look, there's nothing to be gained from making a scene in the middle of King Street. Just let him go, and have low expectations about the future.*

Whether she'd listen to herself was another thing entirely.

'OK. Bye, Josh,' she said as she leaned in to kiss him on the cheek, then turned and began her walk home, refusing to turn around to see what his reaction was.

Chapter 19

'Where have you been, Poppy?' Jason asked when she reached the front of the queue at Cuckoo Callay for breakfast on Monday. She was excited to have a day off and decided to treat herself to breakfast and large amounts of coffee.

'Work has just been crazy. And I've been doing weird hours.'

'That's no good. You do look tired.'

'Thanks!' Poppy said with a laugh.

'Well, good, but tired,' Jason clarified as he turned to put some coffees on a tray. Poppy noticed a shade of pink sweep up his neck. A fellow blusher, she thought.

'OK.'

'Hey, you're working in Emergency at the moment, aren't you?'

'Yeah,' Poppy answered cautiously.

'We had a bit of an emergency ourselves the other day.'

'Really, what happened?'

'Well, you know that old guy who comes in here with his greyhound?'

'Yeah… I think his name's Stephen.'

'Yeah, maybe. Well, he collapsed, right here at the table.'

'No.'

'Yes. He wasn't choking or anything. He just…keeled over.'

'What'd you do?'

'Well, we obviously called an ambulance…but we were all rushing around not really sure what to do, and the dog was licking his face and then howling when we tried to move it out of the way so we could see if he was breathing.'

'And was he?'

'I think so. Did you see him in ED at all?'

'No…what did you do with the dog?'

'We had to hang onto him for a few hours until the cops could organise someone from the pound to pick him up.'

'The poor dog must have been so sad and scared.'

'Probably… Anyway, I hope he makes it. I'll just take these coffees out.'

'Yeah,' Poppy answered flatly. She had met Stephen and his greyhound, Max, at the park several times and he was always friendly. Max was a supreme runner despite his advanced age and would really tear down the hill after a ball. Poppy wondered if he had a family member who might collect Max from the pound.

She was sitting at an outdoor table when Jason brought over her coffee.

'Hey, don't forget about my exhibition this coming weekend. You're still coming, aren't you?'

'Yes, I'll be there,' Poppy said. When he went back inside she put it in her calendar so that she wouldn't forget. She was hoping Gemma, or maybe Steph, would not be working so she could drag one of them along.

She spent the rest of the day catching up on housework and shopping. Tarryn sent through a couple of emails – one the follow-up to their initial meeting on Friday, with a curt response from Dr Anderson confirming the content but not offering any actual involvement in the process. The second was the confirmation of the meeting with the doctors this Friday. It reminded her to send a message to her friends to encourage them to be there.

She sent a group text to Gemma, Lucas and Steph:

> Hi, don't forget about the special meeting in the RMO lounge this Friday. Pizza and beer provided! Spread the word!

As she hit send a new message from Will arrived with a 'ding'.

> Did you see Tarryn's email? Dr A still not playing ball. Should we go surfing this weekend?

Yes! That'd be great.

She was so excited to have the whole weekend off. It would be really nice to spend some more time with Will. Maybe she'd be able to better work out what they were to each other?

Over the next three days, Poppy tried to drum up support and interest amongst the ED docs to attend the meeting.

'Come on, Seb, it'd be great to have some support from you guys in ED,' Poppy implored when she cornered him at flight deck.

'Look, I understand what you're doing, and honestly, I do hope for some changes for the ward staff. But in ED, we're well supported. The senior Regs support the junior Regs and our specialty training programme is actually pretty good.'

Poppy knew that Paul and Seb were at the end of their training, soon to be Consultants themselves. They wouldn't want to jeopardise their job prospects. She understood, but was still a little disappointed.

'I get it,' she said in response, turning back to her computer, resigned to the fact that probably none of the ED staff would come to the meeting.

'I'm sure you'll get lots of the ward teams coming, though,' Seb tried to reassure her, even placing a hand on her shoulder before heading back down to subbies.

It was hard not to let it get her down because Poppy knew that institutional change could only come if senior staff supported the junior staff, and without kind people like Seb and Paul committing to even attend a first meeting, she feared they would fail before they even got off the ground. She hoped her friends would have more luck convincing senior Registrars on the wards.

She texted Will on her break later to see how he was doing drumming up business.

> How're you going with the Surg Reg's? Will they come
> on Friday?

She watched the three dots appear on her screen and flash on and off for a few minutes before Will's reply finally came through.

Not getting many who will commit. Maybe only a few of
the really junior ones will come.

What, not even Tim's colleagues?

I think they're all too scared to rock the boat more. And
they haven't replaced him yet, so they are even busier at
the mo.

But they are the ones most likely to benefit, if we can get
some changes. Surely, they can see the advantage of being
involved?

You know how powerful fear is. They probably think
we're unlikely to be successful, and on the off chance we
are, they can opt-in then.

*Great. Now we're definitely going to fail. If we can't convince anyone to come to the
first meeting, we'll never convince the hospital they need to make changes.*
When Poppy didn't reply straight away, Will texted again.

They may also have been warned off by the consultants.

Really, you think?

Possible.

Then we're sunk.

Don't give up just yet. Let's see how Friday goes. Maybe
the physician trainees will be more receptive.

I hope so (fingers crossed emoji)

Poppy felt a dark cloud hanging over her for the rest of the day. It was
more evidence to the ongoing hierarchical power of the hospital system.
The most vulnerable group, the junior doctors, were the most exploited and
the least likely to complain for fear of affecting future job offers. It didn't
help that their contracts were often only one to two years long, meaning
they would have to re-interview frequently just to stay at the same place.
Poppy now rested her hopes on Tarryn's likeability and exuberance in

reassuring everyone that if they banded together, they could achieve change. She would have to cross her fingers and wait until Friday.

Home alone on Friday, she watched the clock. Everyone else was at work, but she had to distract herself until she could go in for the meeting. The day yawned in front of her and every minute felt like an hour. She was jittery with anticipation.

Come on, Poppy, you've got to calm down. There's nothing you can do right now, so you may as well find something to keep yourself occupied.

First, she put on one of her favourite movies, *The Hunger Games*. She'd loved the books and watched the movies until she knew all the scenes basically by heart. But even Jennifer Lawrence's version of Katniss was not enough to hold her attention. So, she went down to Victoria Park pool to swim some laps. The crisp water and physical exertion served its purpose of clearing her mind as she focused on the regular breathing every second stroke.

After Lulu's death, she really got into swimming. She'd not been particularly fast in school competitions, but she enjoyed the solitude that it provided. So, whenever she felt her head buzzing, she took herself down to the campus pool and swam laps until the only thoughts in her head related to physical pain and breathlessness. The University of Newcastle pool was indoors, but set in bushland. They had floor-to-ceiling windows that lifted up and out, channelling the breeze in the summer and locking heat in when shut in winter. They'd play the radio through the speakers and Poppy would sometimes sing along in her head to whatever pop song was playing as she caught that burst of sound when her ear broke the surface as her head rotated to breathe.

Victoria Park pool was outdoors, so Poppy wore a rash shirt over her one piece and made sure she covered the rest of her fair skin with suncream. It was another scorcher, and by the time Poppy walked the short distance from where she'd placed her towel, bag, and thongs on the grass, the soles of her feet were burning. She sat beside the diving block at the deep end and let her feet find relief in the water while she put on her cap and goggles. The cold, clear water swirled around her ankles, immediately cooling her down and lowering her heart rate. She slipped beneath the surface, the cold shock always a surprise, and resurfaced to hold onto the edge until she was ready to push off.

Her feet pushed powerfully against the edge of the pool and her body sprung forward, gliding on the water before taking her first stroke. Her mind was clear at the beginning of her lap, as it always was until she found her groove, and then her mind would wander. Today when she found her rhythm, her mind immediately went back to the meeting and her fears of failure. She knew that if there wasn't strong support tonight, it would be unlikely that things would proceed any further and Tim's death would end up being as pointless as most other suicides.

I need this… I need this to work… I feel like this is my chance to change things…not just for Tim, not just for Lulu, but also for myself…

Her rhythm faltered, and she took a break at the shallow end. She took deep breaths in and out and looked around her. The pool was pretty empty, only two others doing laps, and a mother and child playing in the shallow end at the far side of the pool designated for recreational swimming. Poppy looked up to the sky, squinting her eyes and shielding them with her hand. There was not a cloud in sight and the harsh summer sun was punishing.

Why do I care so much about this? She watched the man in Speedos swimming toward her in the next lane. His stroke was neat and effortless with minimal splash. He was clearly a strong swimmer and had a well-defined swimmers' body, his muscles moving and glistening above the water with ease.

He swims effortlessly. Nothing in my life feels effortless, except maybe my relationship with Gemma and Lucas. Everything else feels like a roller coaster – adrenaline highs, and then the twisted knots of anxiety and uncertainty. Maybe success in this will help me feel more stable and secure in my own skin?

Poppy headed to the Residents' lounge at around five o'clock. The weekly drinks and pizza would start at 5:30p.m. and Tarryn had planned the discussion to start at about six o'clock, giving enough time for people to finish up their work for the day, and before the evening shifts got busy. Kevita, one of the interns she met at orientation, was there, so she took a seat on the couch next to her.

'Hi, Kevita, how are you? How's psychiatry going?' she asked.

'It's OK. Better than I thought it would be. How about you?'

'ED is going well, but the shifts are pretty tough.'

'I can imagine. I'm not doing ED until the end of the year. I'm hoping by then I'll have a better idea of what being an intern is really like. Psychiatry doesn't really feel like medicine. There's a lot of sitting around and talking.'

People arrived in dribs and drabs, and when the bar opened at 5:30p.m. Poppy grabbed a beer for herself and Will, who had just arrived, and they sat on one of the window ledges.

'So, how do you think it's going to go?' she asked Will after she took a sip of the cold beer.

'I don't know. I hope we get enough people interested to move things forward, but… well…let's not jinx it.'

'Fair enough.'

The pizza was from Frank's, a local institution on Parramatta Road, and Poppy thought it was the best pizza she'd eaten in a long time. It was the first chance she'd had to come to one of these, and it felt almost like a party. It was great that they put it on every week. When she changed terms, she was going to make it a routine to come as often as she could. She only saw the ED staff down in their vault, walled off from the rest of the hospital, and the crazy shift work meant they were further ostracised. It was nice to be amongst others for a change. The atmosphere lifted her spirit, and she was suddenly hopeful. Maybe things would go better than they expected.

At six o'clock, Tarryn headed to the front of the room.

'Come on,' Will said to Poppy, and they moved to stand near Tarryn.

'Alright, welcome everyone. Thank you for coming. We're meeting tonight to talk about what happened to our colleague who committed suicide, and what we can do to ensure it doesn't happen to anyone else,' Tarryn started.

Murmurs greeted her words.

'And for those who don't know, this is Poppy and Will, who are really driving this issue,' Tarryn continued, gesturing to Poppy and Will to her left side, who gave awkward waves to the group.

'What we really want are safe work practices for the junior staff and more support, both teaching but also for mental health and mentorship…

We met with Dr Anderson last week, but all she offered was a closed-door meeting of the heads of training. That took place this week, but she has not advised us of any outcome yet.'

It was interesting watching Tarryn build the crowd's attention at this point.

'But, to be frank, after being in this position for a while now, I doubt anything will change unless we force it.' As she paused here, Poppy heard more murmurs in the crowd and someone actually called out, 'How?'

'We need to band together. If we all join forces, we can apply more pressure. Especially if we bring in the Health Services Union. We need you all to join this fight. Each of you has the potential here to benefit. We are stronger as a group than as individuals.'

Poppy was inspired by her attitude. She showed none of the anxiety that Poppy felt, and even though Poppy knew she too was invested in this succeeding, she didn't seem to feel the weight of that pressure, like Poppy did.

'How can you guarantee we won't be victimised?' someone asked.

'Are you a member of the HSU?'

'No.'

'Then I recommend you join. I have forms here at the front for anyone who is interested, and I strongly urge you all to join. The higher the number of members from junior staff, the stronger their ability to support and protect us. And I strongly believe that if we can go to the Medical Training Unit with the support of the union and an increase in the number of registrations based on this issue, we will be in a powerful position to negotiate. But without strong union numbers, I think we will have a much harder road and limited, if any, success.'

There was further muttering amongst the crowd and Poppy looked at Will, who shrugged his shoulders.

'Can I ask for a show of hands for those who are already union members?'

Maybe five people in the room of about forty put up their hands.

'Let me give you something to think about. About ten years ago, a few Residents noticed their overtime was being underpaid. They questioned it with Payroll and the administration, but got no resolution. Ultimately, these couple of Residents galvanised the Residents' Association and subsequently the Union. And while it took several months, ultimately an audit was demanded by the ombudsman and numerous instances of underpayment were found and subsequent back-pay enforced. But without those two Residents starting the ball rolling, and refusing to let it slide, joining the union, and continuing their fight despite significant roadblocks put up by this hospital administration, there would never have been the back pay. We can be very powerful as a group, especially with union support.' This time she put her hands on her hips when she finished.

'What about the impact on those Residents' careers?' the same guy asked.

'Well, they are both successful consultants in inner Sydney hospitals, so I don't think there's been any impact on their careers.'

That silenced him, well done, Tarryn.

'What about the media?' someone else asked.

'That's a great question. I think the media could be very useful in this negotiation, but not yet. After we see the hospital's response, or lack of, at that point it is likely the media may be very helpful.'

The murmurings now sounded more positive to Poppy's ears.

'Are there any more questions or concerns?' Tarryn asked.

None were forthcoming.

'Well, I'll be around for the next hour if you have questions or suggestions, and union enrolment forms are at the front. You can also access them online via the Residents' Association website. Poppy and Will are also here to answer questions.'

Tarryn paused before adding, 'Please think about this seriously, we are fighting for ALL of you, and we need your support. Please also talk to your peers who may not be here tonight. You can also email me anytime. Thank you.' With that, Tarryn turned to engage Will and Poppy.

'So, what do you guys reckon? How many will sign up and get on board to help?'

'Less than twenty,' Will offered.

'My guess, five to ten new registrations.'

'Wow, that low?' Poppy asked, shocked by the pessimism. She had been feeling buoyed toward the end of Tarryn's speech, and had seen nods in the crowd.

'Apathy and fear are hard to derail in my experience. How about we meet up again at the end of next week? I'll send around a campus reminder Tuesday and push on Dr Anderson for a report on Wednesday.'

'And I'll swing by Melissa Monday or Tuesday,' said Will.

'OK, well let's stay in touch and find a suitable time,' Tarryn said before touching Poppy's shoulder briefly and heading to the bar. She was quickly joined by a couple of Residents asking questions. Poppy hoped that it was a good sign and showed people were more interested than Tarryn feared.

Will and Poppy ended up together in a corner and somehow talking about travelling.

'Well, you know I love my surfing, so I've been thinking about a surfing holiday in Indonesia. One of my best mates from uni is keen and we've started planning it. I'm hoping we can go toward the end of the year. Seb and his husband might come too.'

'Do you know where exactly you'll go?'

'Well, they do these private chartered cruises, so you kind of go where the best surf is and stay on the boat.'

'You obviously don't get seasick.'

'No, I'm good.'

'I've never been to Indonesia,' Poppy said.

'I've only been on the ubiquitous Bali holiday,' Will confessed, and Poppy laughed and leaned in to knock him on the shoulder, craving some physical contact. She was a little tipsy after two beers and felt her feelings for Will pushing to the surface again. When he laughed, he developed little crinkles at the edges of his eyes and Poppy wanted desperately to touch his face.

'What about you, Pop, any big trips planned?' Will's question pulled her back into the reality of the situation and their friendship status. He hadn't bumped back her shoulder and nothing about their conversation screamed 'flirting'.

'Not really. Gem, Lucas, and I were thinking of going skiing in New Zealand – we've blocked a week off together toward the end of July. But nothing's booked yet.'

'Do you ski or snowboard?'

'Ski. Wait, don't tell me you're a boarder?' Poppy said.

'Well…sorry to disappoint, but yeah, I'm a boarder.'

'Oh, no!' And again Poppy jostled him. 'But boarders have no etiquette. They just stop suddenly in the middle of a run, or fall over right in your path.'

'I'll have you know I am a very considerate boarder!'

'Well, I'll have to see it to believe it!'

'Well, I guess the only solution is that I may have to crash your holiday so you can,' and as he said this, he held Poppy's gaze, something unsaid passing between them. *Maybe there's still hope?*

'Come on,' Will said, putting an arm around her shoulders, giving them a slight squeeze, 'Let's go. I'll walk you home.' *Now that felt more like a friendly squeeze, maybe I was just reading too much into it. The beers must have gone to my head.*

They walked up Missenden Road, huddled together as a crisp breeze funnelled down, a stark contrast to the heat of the morning. The season was definitely turning. As they got closer to Poppy's place, she asked Will what he really thought about their meeting and chances of getting support.

'I just don't know, Pop. Tarryn's pessimism is pretty convincing.'

'Well, even if we get a few more eager people on our side, that might be enough to really get momentum going. I just want to help everyone.'

'I know you do, Pop. You've got such a big heart.'

'I'm doing this for Lulu just as much as for Tim.'

'I know,' he said suddenly closer to her, their arms were almost touching as they walked. Poppy could almost feel the heat from his body.

At Poppy's front door Will looked down at her, searching her face. *Please kiss me…please kiss me.*

But the mention of Lulu and Tim had quashed whatever flirtation had started, and after that lingering eye contact, Will stood upright and said, 'OK, night, Poppy.'

'Night, Will.'

Poppy was surprised a few days later when she received a text from Josh.

> Hi Poppy, I heard you're creating a stir. Very exciting! I'd be keen to meet up and talk about what's happening at the Med Reg level. It might help your cause.

The last time they had seen each other, he'd given the impression he was too busy for anything but study, so Poppy was really surprised that he wanted to get involved in this.

> OK, that'd be great. Can I get back to you on a time?

> Sure. Look forward to it.

> I'll be in touch.

Tarryn texted Will and Poppy during the following week:

> Numbers going up!

> Poppy; Great news (smiley face emoji). Josh, one of the Med Reg's also wants to meet up to discuss examples of under-resourcing/lack support.

> Will: I also got good info out of Melissa.

> Poppy: What'd she say?

> Will: Lip service only. DOTs to encourage trainees to report concerns to them directly and reminder of employee assistance programme. And will ask trainees to report a colleague who is struggling. Will fill in more in person.

'How crap is that?' Tarryn said when they met up for dinner to talk next steps. 'Not only are they not offering any positive steps for change, but they are allowing the same problem of fear and isolation to continue. All this does is further discourage trainees from speaking up for fear of being branded as someone who 'can't cut it' or who has significant mental health issues.'

Poppy could visibly see this news firing Tarryn up, like she was charging into battle, sword held aloft. It had the opposite effect on her. She felt like a tyre with a slow leak- her enthusiasm slowly escaping. She visibly slouched in the booth they were sitting in.

Will noticed and said, 'But hey, Pop, Melissa is on our side. She's fed up. She told me she's been watching for years the junior staff being abused mentally and physically and when Dr Anderson came along, she felt finally there would be change, but whilst she talked the talk of revolutionising the Resident programme, she's done little to support trainees. Dr Anderson silenced her before they met with us, but she's on our side. So, she's going to work for us in the background. She'll feed us information and encourage the junior doctors to join the union whenever someone comes to complain about shifts or term supervision or bullying. She's going to be a great asset, Pop.'

'Will, that's brilliant,' Tarryn said, slamming a hand down on the table, making their drinks jump.

'Yeah, that is good news, but it still doesn't change the fact that with no Director of Training support, this is really going to be an uphill battle,' Poppy said.

'True,' said Tarryn, 'but, as you mentioned, a number of Medical Regs are coming on board, and I think we'll get some of the Surgical Regs through Lucas and Will, and with a growing number of interns and Residents we can take the next step and set up a meeting with the HSU. Poppy, send me your schedule for next week and I'll try to get a meeting when we are all free. And, Poppy, if you can meet with Josh and get some examples from him on paper, that'd be great. Will, you try to do the same from the Surgical trainees and I'll keep working on the interns and Residents.'

Poppy glimpsed Will's face darkening briefly at the mention of Poppy meeting up with Josh. She wondered what it meant. Was there some history between the two of them she didn't know about? *Could he be jealous?*

On her walk down to the hospital, after dinner, she texted Josh.

> Hi. Just had a meeting about the crusade (horseback emoji). Could we meet up in the next few days to discuss? Keen to get some examples. Likely meet with union next week. Thanks, P xo

Josh texted back quickly.

Sure. I'm on study leave so can work around your schedule. Let me know when suits.

How about Sun evening?

Sure. 5pm my place?

OK, see you then.

By the end of the exchange, she'd made it into the department and put her bag in a locker. She headed into flight deck, her head full of frustration with the administration and the powers-that-be continuing the status quo because it suited them when clearly it was detrimental to the junior staff.

'Hey, Pop, how are you?' Steph asked as they almost collided, Steph heading into the locker area as Poppy was heading out.

'I'm good, how about you? Are you coming or going?'

'Coming, subbies. You?'

'Me too!'

'Cool, it'll be good to hang out together. I feel like I haven't seen you in ages. Wait for a sec while I put my bag away?'

'Sure.'

Moments later, Steph was back, tying her hair up into a loose ponytail.

'How's everything with Ben?' Poppy asked.

'Oh, that's over. I did what you suggested and tried a proper date, and it turns out we're only compatible in the bedroom.'

'Oh, I'm sorry,' Poppy said, feeling guilty.

'It's OK. It means I can concentrate on studying again.'

'Well, I guess that's a plus?' Poppy said, inflection rising at the end.

'Yeah, I need to, exams are looming!'

'Hey, are you working Saturday night?'

'No, why?'

'I ducked into Cuckoo Callay this morning for a coffee and Jason, the barista, has his art show this Saturday and I promised I'd go, but I'm not keen to go by myself. Want to join?'

'OK. Anything is better than studying on a Saturday night. Besides, don't they usually give out free alcohol?'

'Yeah, but it's usually shit.'

'I'm not picky.' And they both laughed, Steph draping an arm around Poppy's shoulders.

'If you ladies are free, we should start handover,' Harriet said.

'Sure,' Steph said and she and Poppy hurried over, but Poppy thought she detected the twitch of a smile as Harriet said this.

It ended up being a good evening, busy but not crazy, and it was great to be on with Steph and Lucy, too. Having their little threesome together brought a festive attitude to the work, and they joked and caught up when they were typing up notes at the flight deck.

Poppy even got to reduce a dislocated shoulder, with Steph's supervision. There was also an eighty-something lady from a nursing home with dementia who was one of Steph's patients, but had taken a shine to Poppy and kept wandering out of her cubicle looking for her, mistaking Poppy for her daughter. Poppy spent half of the shift escorting her back whilst holding her gown closed. It was endearing, but nobody wanted to see a wrinkly, naked old lady bottom!

Chapter 20

'Hi,' Poppy greeted Paul at the acute handover board the next evening shift.

He nodded, but didn't respond before starting the handover. She hadn't seen Paul for a few days and he didn't seem his usual, slightly hyper self. He looked tired and his face was an insipid grey colour. After handover, Poppy wanted to talk to him more, but Paul ducked around to Resus to check on a patient. *That was weird. So unlike him.*

About an hour later she sought Paul out to present a case to him.

'Hi again, can I talk to you about a patient?' she asked him.

'Sure. Shoot,' he said, keeping his eyes fixed to his computer terminal.

'OK, so I've just seen a woman in her thirties with a previous kidney transplant who has fever and abdominal pain. I'm worried she might have organ rejection. I've taken bloods and put in a cannula for IV fluids. But I didn't want to give her opioids for the pain until I've seen her renal function.'

'Yep, that's smart. If you're right and she's going into failure then we'll have to reduce the opioid dose.'

'That's what I was thinking, yeah.'

'Sounds like you're on top of it.'

He had barely made eye contact with Poppy throughout the exchange, and before he could rush off again, Poppy put a hand on his shoulder, forcing him to look at her and asked, 'Are you OK, Paul? You don't seem yourself tonight.'

Paul looked down into his lap, removing their eye contact again and Poppy was worried something really serious was going on.

After a pause he said, 'I'm OK, just a family thing.'

'Do you want to talk about it?'

'Maybe later, I need to check on a patient.'

'Oh, OK… Well, I'm here for you.'

It was then that Paul looked at Poppy. There was a beat before he said, 'Thanks, Poppy' and walked away.

When she re-presented the case after the bloodwork was back, Paul still seemed preoccupied, so Poppy took another stab at getting him to open up.

'What's happened, Paul?'

'My mum was just diagnosed with breast cancer,' Paul blurted out.

'Oh, Paul, I'm really sorry to hear that.'

'Yeah, she hasn't had her surgery yet, she just got the biopsy result yesterday.'

'That must be really scary…for all of you.'

'Yeah. My mind keeps jumping to worst-case scenarios.'

'I can imagine… That's the problem when you know too much, though. The biggest likelihood is that it'll be early stage and she'll have treatment and then be cured, though, right?'

'Yeah, you're right. I should be focusing on the likely outcome. Thanks, Poppy.'

'You're welcome.'

'OK, we'd better get back to it.'

'OK.'

Over the rest of the evening Poppy found herself mainly reviewing her cases with Harriet rather than Paul who she couldn't quite catch again; he seemed in perpetual motion. He refused a trip to the pub at the end of the shift and no amount of strong-arm persuasion from the whole team would change his mind. Eventually they gave up and Poppy felt a bit sad that she couldn't fully engage Paul and so she only stayed for one drink and then went home. She arranged for Steph to meet at her place the next night to go to Jason's art exhibition together.

When Steph arrived at seven o'clock on Saturday, she was dressed to the nines with a skimpy black dress, barely leaving anything to the imagination, and five-inch stilettos.

'Wow, you've gone all out,' Poppy remarked, opening the door to let Steph in.

'Thanks, it's my one proper night off from work or study so I want to make the most of it. You never know, I might get lucky!'

Poppy was dressed in skinny jeans and a cowl-neck black top with a row of fake diamantes at the top for subtle bling. She wasn't particularly excited about tonight and hadn't really gone to much effort, but now, standing next to Steph, she felt underdressed.

'I think I need to dress this up a bit,' she said to Steph before returning to her bedroom to swap the jeans for a black kilt mini-skirt and changed to knee-high boots.

'Is this better?' she asked Steph, doing a twirl for her as she emerged from her bedroom.

'Much better. I love that skirt!'

'Yeah, me too.'

The exhibition was at a small local gallery in Enmore, so it was only a short walk. Jason had told Poppy that one of his art school classmates was also exhibiting and the small space was already densely packed when they arrived. They squeezed in, grabbing a complimentary glass of bubbles each and joined the loop around the artworks.

Jason's works were on one side of the gallery with a partition in the middle separating out his friend's work. Poppy's modicum of loyalty to Jason meant they started on his side of the room. His were all paintings and to Poppy's untrained eye they appeared to be a sort of hybrid between graphic novel type illustration and more graffiti style street art. The theme appeared to be Thor, and Poppy felt it a bit too adolescent male fantasy for her. His friend's works were a combination of paintings and mixed media and were more cosmic-themed. There was a lot of swirling colours and twinkling lights in the mixed media. Overall, Poppy felt the whole thing was pretty amateurish, but really what would she know? She had no art training and rarely even went to the Archibald Prize, Australia's most famous portrait competition. She would have no clue what was considered good or even on trend. So, she kept her thoughts to herself.

After a couple of laps around and at least three glasses of bubbles and a few measly crackers and nuts, she and Steph took advantage of one of the low lounges in the corner, happily chatting about work and boys.

'So, what's happening with you and Josh?' Steph asked.

'Ugh… I don't know! It's so frustrating. We had a couple of good dates and then he basically said he had no time for a relationship now because of study.'

'Annoying.'

'Yeah, but now I'm going over to his place tomorrow so he can give me some Med Reg stories for our crusade. And I don't know what to expect.'

'Do you think he'll put the moves on you?'

'I don't know, but I have no—' Poppy was cut off by Jason suddenly appearing in front of them, 'Hi,' he said.

'So, what did you think, Poppy?' Jason asked earnestly.

'Fantastic,' Poppy replied, forcing an overly enthusiastic smile to her face, and putting her right-sided dimple to action.

'Yeah, I liked the homage to graphic novels,' Steph said, sounding fancy to Poppy's ears.

'Thank you,' Jason replied, a smile breaking out on his face and his shoulders relaxing. 'Yeah, people are saying nice things, so that's reassuring, I guess.'

'Absolutely,' Poppy agreed, Steph non-committally taking a sip of her sparkling wine and nodding.

'Jason,' someone said, putting a hand on his shoulder, forcing him to turn away from Poppy and Steph.

'You go, you're the man of the moment,' Poppy reassured him.

As soon as he was out of earshot, Steph asked, 'You were saying something about tomorrow and Josh?'

'Yeah, just that I have no intention of sleeping with him again. I feel like it's only a sex thing with him, he doesn't seem that interested in me as a person.'

'But there's nothing wrong with a sex thing,' Steph said.

'No. But it just doesn't feel quite right, if you know what I mean?'

'Yeah, I guess. So, what about Will then? You're spending a lot of time with him on this crusade thing.'

Poppy couldn't help the smile that broke out on her face.

'Ooh…you like him! Your dimple is twinkling!'

Poppy laughed and gently slapped Steph. 'Yeah, I do like him. But I'm not sure if we are stuck in Friendville.'

'Will's a good guy. Decent. I can see you two together, actually.'

'Really?' Poppy said hopefully.

'Yeah.'

'Well, I guess I'll just have to wait and see.'

'Juggling two boys…you are busy!'

'It's not like that!' Poppy said, slapping her again as she folded at the waist cackling.

'Hey, everyone's leaving, and we thought we might go to a club. Do you want to come?' Jason asked, appearing in front of them again.

'Sure,' Steph responded, sitting up straight again, not even checking in with Poppy.

'OK,' Poppy said, less enthusiastically, trying to catch Steph's attention, but failing.

They headed to a club in the Cross and straight to the dance floor. After dancing for a while and getting sweaty and dizzy, Poppy decided it was time for a break and gestured to Steph toward the courtyard seats, but Steph was in the zone and glued to the dance floor. Jason followed her out, and they found a loveseat under one of the trees. Poppy gulped thirstily from her water bottle and, as she was recapping it, Jason leaned in toward her.

'Oh, Poppy, you are so beautiful, I've had such a crush on you,' Jason said.

And to Poppy's horror he planted his sweaty lips on hers. Poppy pushed him gently on his chest, her back scraping into the tree behind her.

'Jason… I'm flattered, I really am…but I'm sorry, I just don't feel the same way.'

'Oh no, I'm sorry, of course you wouldn't, you're this amazing, gorgeous, smart doctor, why would you be interested in a nobody like me?'

'You're not a nobody,' Poppy reassured, placing a hand on Jason's shoulder as he hid his face in his hands.

For a moment, she was worried he was going to cry. She searched the crowd for a sign of Steph, or Jason's friend, but only saw a throng of bodies.

'I am!' Jason said, suddenly sitting upright again, 'I'm just a loser who makes coffee and makes graphic art that no one will ever buy.'

'I'm sure that's not true,' Poppy tried to reassure him. *Fuck, don't let me get stuck here!*

Poppy spent the next twenty minutes listening to Jason's self-pity and offering soothing, reassuring words at the right intervals. She became increasingly frustrated and desperate to find an exit, when Steph finally emerged from the dance floor with Jason's friend, sweat glistening down her cheeks and neck. Despite the sweat, Poppy still took a beat to recognise how amazing she looked. She was truly glowing.

'Steph, I think we should make a move, I'm pretty beat,' Poppy said hurriedly standing up and making eyes at Steph that she hoped she would interpret as *rescue me*. Luckily Steph picked up the signal, and they made a hasty retreat, leaving Jason and his friend little time to latch on and go with them. Steph and Poppy almost ran out the front door and down the road to the train station, laughing and sucking in air, hands on hips as they waited for the train to Newtown. Poppy silently prayed that Jason and his friend wouldn't catch up to them.

When they were finally on the train and breathing at a normal rate Steph asked, 'So what gives?'

'So I went to get a drink and some air, and Jason plants a sweaty kiss on me!'

'Whoops, that's awkward.'

'You're not wrong. Then I try to let him down gently, you know… "I'm just not that into you"… and he whines on about what a loser he is and how he'll never get a girl nor sell his art.'

'Yikes.'

'I kept looking for you and trying to be sympathetic, but it was getting old fast.'

'I'll bet.'

'I don't think I can ever go back to the Cuckoo Callay!'

'Oh, Poppy, don't worry there's like a million others in Newtown and Erskie, you'll find a new local.'

'But the coffee was so good there, and the food.'

'Well then, you'll just have to face him again. Besides, he'll be the one who's totally embarrassed, he's the one who made the unwanted pass.'

'Yeah…' Poppy wasn't convinced.

Chapter 21

'Morning,' Poppy said, nudging Steph's knee, hanging off the side of the couch.

'Is it?'

'Yeah, it's about ten,' Poppy replied. She hadn't been in a rush to get up, either, but was now craving salty food and caffeine.

Steph, whose hair was looking lank and greasy, blinked open a mascara-smudged eye before shielding them to look up at Poppy.

'Blergh…' she said.

'Come on,' Poppy said, and nudged her knee again. 'The sooner we get caffeine and fatty food, the better we will feel.'

'Umm… I know you're right, but you might have to pull me up, I think my joints are stuck like this,' Steph said, raising an arm toward Poppy.

'On three…one…two…three,' Poppy said and then yanked on Steph's arm, pulling her up to a sitting position.

'Ughh…my head hurts,' Steph said, dropping her head into her hands.

'Here, take this,' Poppy said, handing her a glass of water, 'and I'll grab you some Panadol.'

Once Poppy had managed to get Steph tidied up and into some of her clothes, they walked up to King Street for a late breakfast, avoiding Cuckoo Callay and a potential run-in with Jason. Steph left from there and Poppy took an extra coffee to the park and sat on her usual bench. She was due to meet Josh at his place in the evening and would start her night shifts afterward. After everything that happened last time, Poppy was dreading more nights. She was also kind of dreading seeing Josh as well. So, she sat on the bench, sipped her coffee and tried to quash the rising anxiety.

Tarryn texted her and Will whilst she was at the park.

Hey, I've set up a meet with union rep Thur lunch.

Poppy: Cool. I'm meeting Josh tonight for his examples.

The three dots appeared next to Will's name, and Poppy waited, expecting a quick reply. But she watched as they disappeared, wondering what that meant, before they suddenly reappeared. After being mesmerised by the dots appearing and disappearing for a few minutes, a text finally came through from him:

Good. I've got some stuff from surgical. See you Thurs.

Poppy wondered why Will had obviously typed and retyped this message. *Could he be upset that I'm meeting Josh?* Why did she keep getting the feeling that Will had some kind of issue with Josh?

She caught an Uber to Josh's place and got there just after five. She was nervous as she rang his buzzer. *How are things going to be? Will he want to have sex or will it just be about the crusade? How does he even feel about me? He's never made things clear.*

He was waiting for her at his open door when she exited the lift. She wasn't sure how long she'd be at Josh's, so she'd brought her work bag and had worn jeans and a light knit top in case she'd need to grab food and head straight to work after they'd finished. They kissed on the cheek and Josh told her she looked good.

Once they were comfortable in the lounge, drink in hand, Poppy said, 'OK, are you happy if I record you? We want to collate some examples to present to the HSU rep this week.'

'I guess that'd be fine,' Josh replied. *God, why does he always look so casual and nonchalant? I never know what he's thinking, he's always just so cool... OK, if he can be cool, so can I.*

Poppy found the voice recording app on her phone. She pressed record and asked Josh, 'So what can you tell me about support and work conditions for the Medical Registrars?'

'As you know, we, like Interns and Residents, do fifteen-hour overtime shifts regularly and multiple sets of seven nights. During the evenings and weekends there are two Med Regs on; one to cover the wards, and the other to cover the new admissions from ED in the Medical Admissions Unit. On the night shifts there is only one Registrar. So, the Med Regs manage all the sick patients and new admissions until the day shift starts. And during that time, we are often constantly being paged and responding to code blue and medical emergency team calls, as well as managing complex patients…

'Obviously, there's also an expertise variation; first year Registrars may only be in their third year out of medical school, but there are also more senior Registrars and some Advanced Trainees on these overtime shifts. But support from Consultants or Advanced Trainees at home after hours is variable and in such a big, busy hospital, there have been some bad patient outcomes that could have been avoided if the staffing and level of support had been better.'

'Can you give me some examples?' Poppy asked.

'Only anonymously, but I've got three cases here.' And he handed Poppy some photocopies of patient notes.

'These have been de-identified, both the patient details and the Registrar details, but they display poor patient outcomes and I've circled in red the times of these entries. That's important. All three entries, as you'll see from the dates and times, occurred during the same night shift. It shows you one person can't be in multiple places at once. Now, in retrospect, maybe the ICU Registrar could have helped more, but they too were busy. At what point can we ask for more help?'

'Did the Registrar ask for help that night?'

'They were overwhelmed and inexperienced, but who would they call? And who would come?'

'Were these cases reviewed at a morbidity and mortality meeting or entered as incidents on the incident reporting system?'

'Yes.'

'And were any recommendations made?'

'I don't know, maybe the HSU could request the results? There was certainly no feedback to the Registrar involved.'

Poppy nodded, skim-reading the photocopies in her hands.

'OK, well what about teaching and career support?'

'It's all very exam-focused. There remains a "don't complain or makes waves" philosophy just like in surgical training.'

'What about your Director of Physicians' training?'

'That's Luke Harris, Cardiologist. He's very good, very nice, but he only passed his exams a few years ago and like most DPTs is using the position as a stepping stone to build a Staff Specialist appointment here. So he's busy in his private consulting rooms, and whilst he means well, he's unlikely to institute any genuine change or rock any boats in case it jeopardises his own career path. Same old story.'

'Every area in medicine seems to perpetrate the same problems.'

'Yep. And the perennial classic, "Well in my day", Josh said, putting on a bellowing old man's voice.

Poppy would have laughed if it wasn't so bloody depressing.

'Well, thank you so much for this, I'm sure it'll help. Do you have any other examples?'

'I'm sure I can pull some more together.'

'And I know this is a tough question to ask and insensitive, but do you know of any Physician trainees in the last few years that have committed suicide or had any significant mental health issues?' Poppy felt weird asking this so bluntly, but she knew deep down that a pattern across the hospital of brutal work conditions and secondary mental health issues would put them in a strong bargaining position.

Josh sat back and thought about it for a few minutes.

'Actually, there've been a couple of Regs who've dropped out of training before or after the exams because of the conditions; Alice McKenna and Thomas Chen. I think Alice may have even been hospitalised for depression, but I'm not positive. I don't know what they went on to do. Melissa O'Brien probably will though.'

'Thanks, we'll follow up on that.'

'Oh…and it's not mental health related, but there was a Registrar two years ago that had a car accident on the way home from back-to-back fifteen-hour shifts. Oh, what was her name?'

Poppy gave him a moment to see if he could remember.

'Sorry, it's not coming back to me. But if I remember, I'll text you. Again, Melissa will remember.'

'OK.'

Poppy thought for a moment if there was anything else she should ask.

'What do you think we should do?'

'I think you're already doing it. Getting examples from all the different trainees and getting the HSU in. They'll push some action at the hospital level, and they'll push the various training colleges to review trainee accreditation.' Josh paused here.

'I think you're amazing for starting this. We all think it sucks but we're like sheep; we just keep putting up with the status quo.'

The compliment surprised Poppy. As he said it his eyes locked onto Poppy's and took on that partly glazed look of arousal.

'It's just got to improve for everyone's sake,' Poppy said.

'Don't be so modest. It's brave, powerful and sexy what you're doing,' he said, raising one eyebrow.

Oh, fuck…

And with that Josh leaned in toward Poppy and ran a finger down her left cheek, sending a shiver across her face and down her spine. *Do I want this?* He picked up her notebook and pen and put them on the coffee table, then pressed Stop on the phone recorder. He confidently moved in next to Poppy and, locking eyes with her, kissed her, cradling her face in his hands. *Oh fuck… I do…one more time…*

Despite Poppy's previous protestations about not sleeping with Josh again, she couldn't help melting at the gentleness of his caress. She kissed him back and found herself pulling his polo shirt over his head, wanting to feel his skin under her fingertips. They undressed each other, kissing each other's bodies hungrily. *My god this man is hot. This chest…those abs…* All rational thought had escaped Poppy's brain; she was acting purely on desire. Poppy knelt on the floor and took hold of Josh's cock, licking from base to tip and then slipping it into her mouth and using her hand to rhythmically move up and down the shaft as her mouth and tongue worked the tip and frenulum. *He does have a nice cock…*

'Wait, stop,' Josh said as he got close to orgasm. 'I'm not ready to come yet. It's your turn. Lie down.'

Poppy lay on the couch as Josh lay between her legs. He gently caressed her pubic area then flicked her clitoris with his tongue rapidly before sucking it and licking down to her vagina. *Fuck that feels so good.* This sent shivers of excitement through Poppy's body. She didn't want him to stop.

He repeated this, then inserted one, then two fingers into her vagina whilst still working her clitoris with his tongue. *Oh my God…don't stop…* Poppy rocked her hips to Josh's movements, her arousal growing. 'Ye-s,' she shouted out as waves of pleasure rocked her body. The pleasure was intense and the aftershocks kept coming. When her breathing slowed and thought processes returned, she opened her eyes and saw Josh had become fully erect again and was putting on a condom.

'Are you ready?' Josh asked, not waiting for an answer before he pushed his cock into her. *Ooh… Oh I want this… Oh this is good…* Poppy stopped thinking. She could only feel. Feel the hardness of his cock as he thrust into her, over and over again. Feel his butt cheeks under her fingers as she grabbed them and pushed him into her, deeper and deeper with each thrust. Feel his tongue on her neck and in her mouth, the slightly sweet taste of her own wetness subtly on his mouth and lips. Feel her arousal growing again.

'Let's do it from behind,' Poppy said as she pushed Josh gently in the chest.

'OK,' he said, backing out of her, and letting her flip over on the couch. Josh entered her from behind, and, as he slid inside her, she had to grab onto the edge of the couch.

'Oh, that's so good,' she said as Josh grabbed her hips, pulling her back onto his cock.

'You feel so good tonight,' Josh said as his thrusts became faster.

'Yes…harder,' Poppy responded, her breaths coming faster and shorter. She reached a hand down to her clit and worked in rapid circles as her orgasm was getting closer.

'You like that?'

'So much, don't stop…'

'What about this?' Josh asked as he pushed his thumb into her anus.

'Wow!..Yes… Oh my god…yes! Y-e-s!!'

Fresh waves of rapture engulfed Poppy's body and she felt Josh freeze as he too came and collapsed onto her back.

'Wow, that was awesome,' Poppy said when they were lying together in a sweaty mess on the couch.

'Yeah, it was.'

They lay there for a while, Josh with one arm draped over Poppy's chest. They didn't talk, just let their breathing return to normal. When they had finally recovered, Poppy noticed goose bumps on her arms and felt a shiver as she got cold.

'Are you cold?' Josh asked.

'Yeah, a bit.'

'Let's get dressed, shall we?' Josh asked. Poppy thought it sounded very formal, considering what they'd just been doing together.

They stood up and dressed and Josh got them both Coke No Sugars from the fridge after he washed his hands. It secretly thrilled Poppy that he'd made the effort to buy her favourite drink. Maybe he cared more for her than she realised?

They sat on the couch re-hydrating after their vigorous workout, but soon their tummies started rumbling.

'Was that you?' Josh asked her.

Poppy laughed, 'I think it was, but I'm sure I heard your tummy, too.'

'Should we order some takeaway?'

'Yeah, OK.'

They were eating their Thai takeaway when Charlie walked in.

'Hi, guys, ooh, got any spare for me?' he asked, noticing the food.

'Sure, help yourself,' Josh said, pushing a box of Pad Thai toward Charlie.

Once Charlie had scavenged through the Thai detritus, gathering all residual noodles, spring rolls and sauce into a single, piled bowl, he sat on the couch to join them. Poppy couldn't help the smile that crossed her lips as Josh raised an eyebrow in her direction. They were both obviously thinking about what they had just done where Charlie was sitting.

'You sure you've got enough there, mate?' Josh chided him.

'Yeah, bonza… So what have you two been up to?' he asked, pointing a dripping chopstick at them both and raising an eyebrow.

Oh my god, if he only knew! Heat rushed into her cheeks and she kept her eyes on her bowl.

'Not much, just discussing the crap system we find ourselves working in,' Josh said with a straight face, and Poppy breathed a sigh of relief. *Wow, how does he still maintain such control? It's like the last half hour didn't even happen. Does he not remember having his thumb in my arse as he was thrusting as deep and fast as possible into me just a moment ago? Thank god he washed his hands before we began eating…*

'In what way?'

'You know how it is; too high a workload, not enough supervision or training…'

'So, just the glaring obvious, then,' Charlie said sardonically.

'Do you want a more nuanced and detailed review?'

'I'm sure you could supply one in minute detail, but not especially,' Charlie said, a cheeky grin failing to be suppressed.

'Because your attention span is too limited, perhaps?' Josh countered.

Poppy enjoyed listening to Charlie and Josh banter back and forth. Clearly, they'd been friends for a long time and could easily rib each other without hurting their feelings. But even in this small interaction, it was clear to Poppy that Josh was likely the dominant one in the friendship. Maybe that was true for all relationships in his life. *Maybe he just has to be on top. Has to be in control?*

Before she knew it, the time had raced forward, and she needed to leave to walk to work.

'Sorry, guys, I've got to go to work.'

'Are you on nights?' Charlie asked.

'Sadly, yes.'

Josh kissed her briefly at the door, holding it open for her.

'Thanks for the info,' she said, waiting for him to say something about the sex or suggesting a follow-up.

'Anytime,' was his response. Poppy looked him in the eyes, searching for something more, but Josh didn't say anything else.

'OK, bye,' Poppy said kind of awkwardly, not sure whether she should hug him, or what to expect from Josh as she left.

Walking to the hospital, Poppy had that niggling feeling again that she didn't know where she stood with Josh.

Seriously, what is it with this guy? Was that not just seriously awesome sex? Was I the only one there? I mean, that was one of the all-time highs as far as orgasms go. Right up there with what I remember of my sex with Will. And then nothing? No 'when can I see you again?' It's like he just expects everyone wants to just fuck him whenever he wants to…it's obviously not a relationship…more sex of convenience for him. What he wants, when he wants it.

By the time she got to the front entrance, she'd worked herself up to being annoyed and feeling cheap and dirty. Here she was, heading in to work smelling like sex and, like a teenager, with pash rash on her face. She tried to tidy herself up at her locker, scraping her hair back into a fresh bun, but still felt self-conscious. When she went into the ED floor, she grabbed a long-sleeve scrub coat from the linen rack and tied it on over her clothes, hoping it would mask the smell, but she still blushed to the roots of her hair when Lucy and Seb said hello.

Lucy did a double-take, narrowing her eyes, then pointing at her and saying, 'You just had sex.'

No question, just a statement. Poppy blushed again and mouthed 'shush' at her.

'Later, details,' Lucy said in a whisper as she walked away.

'OK,' Poppy squeaked quietly.

Poppy headed to flight deck and tried to get her head into the mindset she would need to get through the night. She pushed thoughts and questions about Josh out and focused. *OK, head high, you can do this.* Night one on subbies.

Chapter 22

'Hey, Luce, what does SA mean?' Poppy asked around four in the morning. That was what the triage nurse had labelled the next patient's presenting complaint on the computer and the patient had already been placed in the procedure room.

'Sexual assault,' said Lucy.

'Oh, I've not done one of these. What do I need to do?' Poppy asked. She had barely seen Seb all night so far. He had obviously been busy with Jack in acute.

'First off, just wait for the on-call sexual assault service officer to get here. They'll talk to her first, then get you if they need it.'

'Is she physically OK? Does she need any X-rays or anything?'

'No, if someone triaged her straight to the procedure room, then she's stable and has no major injuries and can wait for the SA team. Anything with more serious injuries would go to Resus.'

'So once the SA team thinks she's ready, what do I do?'

'Probably nothing. They usually do all the forensics and examination. They may just get you to sign off on meds or discharge.'

'And what about police?'

'They do that as part of their routine.'

'OK, so I just leave them tagged to me and move on?'

'Pretty much.'

'OK, ta,' Poppy said, still feeling out of her depth.

There was a second assault that night.

'Hi, Emma, you've injured your arm?' Poppy asked an attractive woman in her thirties, with shoulder-length brown hair, tied back in a ponytail who was cradling her right arm tightly to her chest in her left arm. Emma nodded her head in response and Poppy noticed the left side of her face was also really swollen, and her left eye was starting to close involuntarily.

'Emma…how did the injury occur?' Poppy asked tentatively, expecting she might already know the answer.

Emma burst into tears. Poppy shifted from foot to foot.

'It's OK, Emma, you're safe here,' Poppy reassured her whilst searching behind her for a box of tissues. She passed them to Emma and waited for her to speak again.

'My-my husband…but he'll kill me. You can't report it!' Emma begged, her right eye filling rapidly with tears as her left was now completely closed.

'You're safe here, Emma,' Poppy again reassured her, not sure if it was completely true or not. 'Do you have any children at home?'

'No, just Natalie,' she said, pointing at the pre-schooler curled up in her unicorn PJs under a blanket in the chair in the corner, whom Poppy had not noticed before in the darkened cubicle.

'I waited until he had passed out, then I grabbed Natalie and drove in here.'

'OK,' said Poppy. *Fuck, she drove herself with what's likely a broken arm? I wonder how long she had to wait for him to pass out? Wow, she is one seriously brave woman. But what kind of hell does she live in?*

'OK, well, let's get you sorted. I'm going to have a quick look at your arm and face. Did he injure you anywhere else?'

'No. He twisted my arm behind my back and punched me in the face. But nowhere else.'

'OK. I'm really sorry this has happened to you, Emma.'

'Yeah, me too.'

Poppy gently examined her arm, confirming for herself it was likely fractured and feeling across her cheekbone and around her orbit to check for any facial fractures. When she finished, she stepped back from the bed and said to Emma, 'I'll check the X-rays, but I do think your arm is likely broken. Would it be OK with you if I talk to the social worker about what your options are? They may be able to get you into a safe house, if that's what you would like?' Poppy suggested. *Please say yes, please say yes…*

'OK,' Emma replied, non-committally.

When she went to check on the X-rays, she saw Lucy at the flight deck.

'Hey, Luce, the patient I've just seen in two—'

'Yeah, what do you need?' Lucy interrupted before Poppy had a chance to finish.

'Look, she's been assaulted by her husband… She waited until he passed out, but on the off chance he wakes up and finds her not at home, could you let the front of house staff know not to let him in?'

'Sure. I'll let security know as well.'

'Oh, that'd be great. Cheers… And also, I wanted to talk to social work about what safe house options might be available, are they on-call?'

'Actually, the sexual assault worker is still here, maybe ask her?'

'Yeah, good idea.'

'That's her, on the phone over there,' Lucy said pointing to the woman sitting down near the printer and talking animatedly on the phone.

Poppy checked Emma's X-rays while she waited for the sexual assault worker to get off the phone. While Poppy was zooming in on the fracture involving Emma's radius and ulna, Seb sat down beside her.

'That's a nasty spiral fracture. Twisting injury?'

'Yes!' Poppy said, impressed. 'How did you know?'

'That's the classic cause of a spiral fracture. Usually, the arm being twisted behind someone's back.'

'Yes, exactly. That's what happened. Her husband did it… Oh and can you check this skull X-ray with me? I can't see a fracture, but her cheek and eye are pretty swollen.'

'Sure.'

They looked at it together, Seb zooming in over the zygoma and around the orbit.

'Yep, just there,' he said to Poppy, pointing to the faintest of lines through the zygoma. 'You'll need to let Max-Fax know in the morning, but I doubt they'll want to do much, just come and review her and make sure the orbit is stable. There's no blood in the eye?'

'I haven't checked, but I will when I go back.'

'OK, let me know if there is.'

'OK.'

'You'll need to let the police know. There's mandatory reporting on domestic violence now.'

'Thanks, OK. And I was going to talk to the sexual assault worker about safe houses.'

'That's a good idea.'

'Thanks. So, just a back slab on the arm in the meantime, and ortho clinic follow-up?'

Seb just nodded and sat down to type up someone else's notes.

When Poppy was doing the cast, Emma opened up a bit more about her home life.

'He was so charming when we first met… So thoughtful and polite to my family… You know, really respectful. Even after we got married, there weren't any problems. Not until…' She paused, checking over her shoulder to make sure Natalie was still asleep.

'Until Natalie was born,' Emma whispered. 'Then everything changed. He'd fly into a rage over the tiniest things…and he seemed to resent all the attention I gave to Natalie. He started drinking every night and then he had a problem with his supervisor and the drinking became out of control.'

Poppy kept working on the cast, giving Emma space to keep talking.

'After he lost his job, things got worse… He started hitting me,' Emma whispered.

'I'm so sorry,' Poppy said quietly.

'Tonight…was the worst…and it was just so stupid. He tripped over Natalie's toys and fell and hit his knee. You should have heard him howl. It was loud. And I made the mistake of trying to shush him so as not to wake Natalie. And then he stormed into her room, shaking her awake, screaming in her face that she was a 'bad girl, a lazy girl'.

Poppy noticed the tears streaming down Emma's cheeks as she paused and glanced at Emma.

'And I tried to pull him away…pull him out of her room…and that's when…he just went ballistic. He grabbed my arm and twisted it behind me, holding my shoulder still, screaming in my face…and with my arm twisted,

I was looking straight at Natalie. And she was just petrified…Then he punched me, and I blacked out.'

'Was Natalie hurt, physically?' Poppy asked, stopping again and immediately wondering if she needed to check on her as well and whether her sleeping could mask a head injury.

'No, no… I checked when I got her in the car. After I passed out, he stormed out of the room and started drinking again.'

Thank God, Poppy thought, at least he didn't hurt Natalie as well.

Poppy's heart was breaking, but she continued to swallow, blinking back the tears and keeping her gaze down on her hands as they smoothed the wet plaster over Emma's arm. Knowing that if she looked Emma in the eyes now, she'd likely cry, and they had all been trained in medical school to maintain detached professionalism. Her tears and sadness would not help Emma. They might even add to her burden if Emma felt she needed to soothe Poppy.

Please go to the safe house. Please keep Natalie safe. She knew the stats on domestic violence cases like this were bad, but she really wanted to protect that little girl in her unicorn PJs. Pretty soon after she finished the cast and was tidying up, the sexual assault worker arrived and took Emma into the family room to have a more private conversation.

'What about Natalie?' Emma asked Poppy as they were starting to head to the corridor.

'It's OK, we can keep an eye out. If she wakes up, we'll bring her to you,' Poppy said.

'Thanks.'

At six o'clock Poppy was shattered; physically and emotionally exhausted. There was no one waiting, so she ducked out, grabbed a Coke No Sugar and some chips from the vending machine and sat on the veranda of the tearoom. A light drizzle was falling and the squelch of the occasional car tyres driving past was surprisingly soothing. The first glow of sunrise was peeking into the sky, and the 7-Eleven attendant was standing out the front of the store, smoking a cigarette. *I wonder what his night has been like?* Poppy savoured the salt of the chips and the fizz of her drink, closing her eyes and focusing just on these sensations, trying to empty her brain of the rest of her night.

Before handover, she returned to Emma's cubicle.

'Hi, Emma, how are you feeling?' Poppy asked.

'OK.'

Poppy saw that Natalie was still asleep in the corner. 'Gee, she's slept well.'

'Yeah, I think most of the time, she sleeps through our rows.'

'It's amazing how deeply kids sleep.'

'Yeah, I think I barely sleep anymore. It's like I'm always on edge that he's going to strangle me in my sleep or something.'

'Emma, that's terrible. I'm so sorry. No one should have to live in fear.'

'Yeah, I know. I think I will go to the safe house. Last night was the last straw. He's never attacked Natalie before, just me… I don't want him to hurt her. And that look of fear on her face… I'll never forget it.'

Poppy nodded. *I hope she does stay away from him, I really do.*

'Well, I just wanted to let you know that the maxillofacial surgeon will come and see you before you get discharged.'

'OK.'

'How were the police, were they OK?'

'They were nice, actually. I'm going to press charges and they said I won't have to be in court in person. I can give evidence via video link.'

'That's great.'

'Yeah. And the safe house sounds OK. They'll even give us some money and help us find somewhere to start again when I'm ready.'

Again, Poppy took a second not sound too eager, desperate not to add pressure to this fragile woman, 'I really hope it all works out for you.' *Maybe she can do this?* She had sounded forceful when she talked about protecting Natalie. Poppy squeezed her left hand before leaving her, taking one last look over her shoulder at Natalie before pulling the curtain of the cubicle closed. Those unicorn PJs were seared on her brain.

Poppy made a determined effort not to obsess over it as she walked home in the drizzling rain. She turned her face toward its gentle caress, letting it cool her down. It was so light, almost a foam, like the tiny bubbles in a bubble bath. *Ooh, bubble bath…* She picked up her pace, knowing now what she wanted to do when she got home.

Chapter 23

On Wednesday morning after the last of Poppy's four night shifts, she and Lucy went for a big brekkie. Jack and Seb still had another night to go, so didn't come along.

'What'll you have?' the waitress at Cinque, the café next to the Dendy cinema, asked once they'd plonked their tired bodies at a table.

'Um… I think I'll have the French toast please. With a large latte and a side of maple bacon,' Poppy said.

'Oh, that sounds great. I'll do the same,' said Lucy, pushing her hair away from her face and tucking it behind her ears.

'I really like your hair like that,' Poppy said, noticing.

'Thanks.'

'How long have you had it short like that?'

'About a year or so. It used to be really long. Like down to my bum, long.'

'Really?' Poppy said raising her eyebrows in surprise. 'I can't picture you with long hair.'

'It was a pain. It used to get tangled in my sleep…this is much easier.'

'And it really suits you.'

'Thanks.'

Their coffees arrived and Poppy took a welcome sip. She watched as Lucy added three sugars.

'Got enough sugar there, Luce?'

'Just right,' she said taking her own sip.

Poppy giggled. 'Those last two nights weren't bad.' They'd had a few lull periods where they'd been able to hang out at flight deck and snack on lollies.

'Yeah, a bit less crazy than the first two.'

'I liked being able to hang out with you and Seb.'

'And Jack, he's not a bad guy.'

'Yeah, he's nice…do I detect a bit of interest there?'

'Maybe…'

'You should go for it, he is nice. You'd be great together.'

'You think?'

'Yeah. He can't be worse than some of those guys you were telling us about.'

'Well, I'd hope so. He is a doctor after all. He should have some manners.'

'I think you might even bring him out of his shell more, Luce?'

'Yeah, I could… OK, it's decided. I will move in there.'

'Good. Tell me how it goes.'

Their food arrived and Poppy poured the maple syrup over her toast and berry compote. There were crushed pistachios and whipped ricotta with the berries and the meal was glorious. Poppy's plate could have been licked clean, it was so spotless by the time she had finished the last morsel. She sat back in her chair as she placed her knife and fork across the plate and rubbed her belly.

'That was so good,' she said to Lucy, who was already finished.

'Yeah, you chose well.'

'Do you want another coffee? We could go for a walk in the park?'

'OK, sounds good.'

They ordered takeaway coffees and settled the bill when the waitress came back.

When they were wandering in the park, Lucy asked Poppy how she was planning to get through the day.

'I think I'll go for a swim. It's a really nice day, not too hot.'

'That's a good idea.'

'How about you?'

'Oh, I'm going to catch the train up to my parents' place in the mountains and stay for a few days.'

'You obviously get along really well, you visit a lot.'

'Yeah, but it's also to help out. My younger sister has Down Syndrome, so it's a help for Mum for me to be there.'

'I'm sorry, Luce, I didn't know.'

'That's OK. And don't be sorry, I love her, I love spending time with her.'

'That's great.'

'Yeah, she's so sweet and everything is beautiful to her. It really teaches you perspective, and to try to just be happy with life.'

'You're right, we should all try to be happy with what we have and look for the beauty in every day. I know I can get too anxious about things and obsess over them.'

Lucy nodded and they sipped their coffees and kept walking.

'How's the campaign going?' Lucy asked after a quiet lap of the park path.

'OK. We're pulling examples together and Will was catching up with Melissa yesterday, so I need to check in with him to see how it went. And the next step is to meet with the HSU rep.'

'That's good.'

'Well, we'll see, I guess.'

Poppy was changing into swimmers when her phone dinged a message. *I hope that's Will getting back to me.* She pulled the final strap over her shoulder before checking.

Melissa remembered the name of the Reg who had the car accident, and I got more deets around 5 Regs who have left training. Can we meet after work today? I can bring takeaway, Will.

Amazing! 5 Reg's, you say, not 2?

5!

Well done. See u 2nt, my place?

There around 6

(smiley emoji)

Poppy grabbed her towel, goggles and cap and threw them into a bag with her water bottle and banana and headed out. She'd been right about it being a beautiful day and perfect for swimming laps. It wasn't as hot as last time she was down here, and she felt a tingle of happiness as she let her toes then her legs plunge into the crisp clear water. Even the sudden rush in her heartrate as she adjusted to the cold water was a pleasure today. Later she would be dog-tired, but right now, in this moment, she was invigorated. She spat in her goggles and smeared the spit around the lenses, then pulled them over her head before pushing off firmly from the wall and starting her first lap.

When she found her groove, and her heart and breathing were synchronised, she let her mind wander. Of course, it went straight to thoughts of Will. *I can't wait to see him tonight. I wonder if there'll be any flirting? I hope so... I like seeing him smile. And I liked seeing his body again when we were surfing... Mmmm...* Poppy's rhythm faltered as she got distracted by lustful thoughts of Will, so she took a break at the end of the lap. Standing up in the shallow end, she pulled her goggles off her eyes, resting them on her cap. She took some deep breaths in and out and looked around her. It was almost empty once more and the local radio station was playing Taylor Swift's 'We are never ever getting back together', and Poppy found herself singing quietly. There wasn't anyone close to her and she didn't feel embarrassed. It did make her think about Josh, though. *Seriously, why did I have sex with him again? It really has to be the last time. There's just something that isn't quite right there, it's time to really move on. Never again!*

When the song finished and she'd finished chastising herself about Josh, she pulled on her goggles and pushed off from the wall again. She had to kick her legs through the pain of fatigue and took longer to get into a groove this time. When her thoughts began to drift once more, she found herself thinking back to Natalie and her unicorn PJs. *I wonder where she and her mum are now... If they are safe... I hope they are... Why can humans be capable of such violence against each other? And why can't we do more to stop it?*

This depressing rabbit hole eventually led back to Lulu as it always did when something sad occupied Poppy's brain. Poppy's arms were starting to feel like lead as she lifted each one, in turn, out of the water then over her head and back into the water again, and her lungs were burning. Each time her head turned to the side for a quick breath, she had to suck in hard to get any relief. *God, I miss you Lulu… Why did you do it, Lulu… Why didn't you wait for me?*

She pushed herself on, reaching further in front of her with each stroke and pulling that water back as her hand scooped down her side. It was a punishment of sorts. Pushing and punishing her body, because she could. Because she was still alive to feel. Even if it was pain she was feeling right now. It was better than numbness. When her legs could no longer kick, she dragged her body to the shallow end and collapsed against the wall. Her head in her arms, her goggles off, as silent tears slipped down her cheeks with the water, and her ragged breaths slowly eased. The happiness and invigoration she had felt when she first entered the pool had turned to exhaustion and sadness. It was often close to the surface, but that sweet little girl, Natalie, had pulled it back out. She lay with her head on her arms for a while until she began to feel a shiver as the breeze caressed her neck and shoulders. Sleep was calling her, and she wasn't sure she'd be able to hold it at bay. Not today after the physical and mental fatigue.

Poppy opened the door to Will, who had arrived with Vietnamese and a six-pack of beer later that evening.

'Hi,' Poppy said, taking the proffered bag of takeaway.

'Hi, I hope Vietnamese is OK?' Poppy could hear the slight hesitation in Will's voice.

'Absolutely. I hope you got some rice paper rolls?'

'Would it be Vietnamese if I didn't?'

'Good point. I occasionally state the bloody obvious,' Poppy admitted.

While they were eating, Will updated Poppy on his meeting with Melissa.

'So, I started off trying to be casual about it—'

'How?' Poppy interrupted before he could continue.

'I just didn't want to storm in there and blurt out what we wanted, so I took a seat and sort of said how disappointed I was with the meeting with Dr Anderson, and how I thought she just really had no intention of listening to us, and then I asked her what she thought. And I just looked at her, and

I could see her wavering. She looked like she was battling whether to be honest or, you know, toe the party line. So, I just waited, hoping she'd just be honest. And eventually she made her decision.'

'So, what did she say?' Poppy said excitedly, wanting to know more.

'She said, "Will, I like you, you've always seemed like a really honest, caring person, so I'm going to be honest with you in return", and I sat up straighter, eager to hear what she would say next, but not wanting to blow it by looking too desperate. And then she continued, "it pissed me off—"'

'What? She said she was pissed off?' Poppy interrupted.

'Yeah, I was shocked. She's always seemed so proper. Warm, but you know, a bit old fashioned.'

'Yeah, I thought so too, but don't stop, go on. What did she say after that?'

'Well, I was going to clarify and ask her how she was pissed off, but I didn't need to, she kept going before I could get a word in: "I was pissed off, that yet again, when given an opportunity to make a real difference, Dr Anderson rejected the opening afforded her. Despite all the times I've heard her in the last few years talk about changing junior medical officer training for the better, she's made no major impact apart from preventing Interns and Residents from only streaming medical or surgical terms together. I've been here for close to fifteen years, and in the last ten I've seen things deteriorate markedly." Now at this point I interrupted and asked her in what way they'd deteriorated.'

'And what did she say?'

'Well, she said, "the Consultants are more hands-off, possibly as their own skills have declined, lending to more pressure and less supervision on the Registrars and junior doctors, when the workloads have increased. So, the most junior are shouldering the most work without enough training and supervision. And the stress is becoming more and more obvious by outcomes such as with Tim, and others."'

'What others?'

'Well, that's what I asked, and that's when we talked about Alice. She probably shouldn't have told me, but she confirmed Alice was hospitalised for depression and she has a record of the medical certificate to that effect.'

'She showed you the medical certificate?' Poppy asked, aghast.

'No, she didn't, but now we know it exists. It might be helpful.'

'Yeah, OK,' Poppy said, relieved that whilst Melissa was obviously being helpful for their cause, she didn't want to think she'd be cavalier with personal records of such confidential matters. 'What about the Reg who had the car accident?'

'Evelyn Lim. Apparently she was really seriously injured in the accident; she ended up in rehab with a permanent brain injury and the family sued the hospital and the Department of Health.'

'Woah, that's tragic. What was the outcome of the lawsuit? Did she know?'

'She did. She even had printed copies of what made it to the papers, which she showed me. Parents won the lawsuit, undisclosed settlement reached.'

'So, she just had all this stuff ready to go?'

'Looks that way. She pulled a file out of her filing cabinet. Looks like she's been compiling all these things together. Every time there's been some negative outcome from what she has perceived to be a system in crisis.'

'Looks like we've come along at just the right time.'

'Looks that way.'

'OK, so what next? What about these five other Reg's?'

'Yeah, so five medical Regs who've left training. She had their performance reviews and handwritten notes on each in the file too. Of the five that left, three successfully completed Physician training at other hospitals, one changed over to Anaesthetics/ICU training, and another GP training. None of the five failed to complete their training programmes. She kept the performance reviews to ensure no one could denigrate the individuals as their reviews show they hadn't left the training because of poor performance.'

'Wow. Did you tell her we were meeting with the HSU?'

'Yeah, I did, and she's given me copies of most of what we talked about, names redacted.'

'Amazing. Have you told Tarryn yet?'

'No, I wanted to tell you first.'

Poppy felt a surge of pleasure and couldn't help the smile that formed on her face.

They ate their food in silence for a moment, Poppy digesting all the information Will had conveyed.

'OK, what about you? How'd you go with Josh?' Will asked, a sudden crispness to his words.

Poppy felt suddenly guilty and wasn't entirely sure why.

'Pretty good,' Poppy downplayed as she grabbed her typed notes and the copies of the patient records Josh had given her.

'This is good, don't you think?' Poppy asked once they'd gone through everything from Josh and Will's surgical trainees.

'Yeah, it's quite a lot of cases, and they are all pretty similar. Lack of staff numbers and supervision.'

Poppy felt a faint flutter of hope, like a little butterfly flapping against a window. Maybe there was a chance to make a real difference.

Tarryn had booked one of the library meeting rooms for their meeting with the HSU rep. Poppy and Will got there first and Tarryn arrived five minutes later with two people in tow. They got settled in the small room, closing the door and introduced themselves around the table.

'I'm Ryan Farrell, the HSU Rep. I've been with the HSU for the last three years.'

'And I'm Georgina Barry, in-house legal counsel for the HSU.'

'So, this is where things are at,' Tarryn started and then outlined the events around Tim's death and their meetings with Dr Anderson and her responses.

'And since then we've been collecting examples of poor patient outcomes from lack of supervision or lack of staff numbers,' Poppy added.

'And we've got examples of staff leaving, having mental health issues, or car accidents,' Will added.

'That's great,' Ryan responded and they handed over all the information they had collated, including the patient notes provided by Josh, and the performance reviews from Melissa.

'I think you've done a great job and put us in a strong position to reach out to the hospital on your behalf and start negotiating,' Ryan said.

'So, what are the first steps?' Tarryn asked

'Well, we'll request a meeting with Dr Anderson, and we'll request Tim's timesheets to be provided at that meeting. It's likely she'll refuse to supply them, and we will then escalate to an audit of all junior medical staff timesheets and rosters looking for breaches in the Safe Work Act.'

'So, you won't use these examples?' Tarryn asked.

'Not initially, no. This is powerful information, and we'll keep it up our sleeves for bargaining better conditions once we get past the initial steps of investigating working hours,' Georgina said.

'Yes, these examples will weigh strongly on the culture, but first steps first.'

'And will we be present for the meeting with Dr Anderson?' Poppy asked eagerly.

She really wanted to see Ryan and Georgina take her down a few pegs.

'I expect she will stonewall us, but we will get you three to be present, at least before and after, if not in the room.'

'OK,' Poppy said, disappointed.

'What about the media?' Tarryn asked.

'I think they will be very useful. I have a good contact at the *Sydney Morning Herald*, and also Channel 9, so I'll be reaching out to them,' Ryan replied.

'So, what do you think?' Will asked, looking at Tarryn, after Ryan and Georgina had left.

'I think that went well,' Tarryn replied.

'It feels like a positive step to me,' Poppy added, feeling hopeful again. Those butterfly wings were tapping harder on the window.

'Hey, do you want to have another surf lesson tomorrow after work?' Will asked after Tarryn had left.

'Sure,' said Poppy, smiling.

'You're not working tomorrow?'

'No, I'm off until Sunday.'

'OK, well how about I pick you up about five-ish? I can usually get out a bit early on Friday afternoons.'

'OK, sounds good.' Poppy couldn't help the smile on her face from growing, imagining Will again in boardies.

'Alright, I'd better get back to the ward and see what's happening. See you tomorrow.'

'Seeya, Will.'

Chapter 24

Poppy was feeling buoyant after the meeting and decided to head into the city and do some clothes shopping. She walked down to Parramatta Road and caught a bus. Even though it was still in work hours the bus was full and Poppy had to stand, clutching a hand strap above her. *I wonder what all these people are doing in the middle of the day?* Her eyes lingered on a mother and child in front her. The child was probably pre-school age, and reminded her of Natalie. Whilst this was a little boy, he still had that cute and chubby pre-schooler body. He was wearing a Thomas the Tank Engine T-shirt and red shorts, his chubby legs jiggling off the end of the seat, his mother holding his hand tightly in her lap. The next time the bus pulled in to a stop, the mother got up, encouraging the boy to walk in front of her as she struggled to grab the pram out of the storage area near the driver.

'Do you want a hand?' Poppy offered, moving forward herself to help the mother pull it loose from the bars.

'Thank you,' she said, smiling before she turned back to her son, 'Careful on the steps,' she admonished as she followed him off the bus.

Poppy smiled as she took their vacated seats and turned her attention out of the window as they whizzed past Broadway and then on into the heart of the CBD. She got off at the QVB and started browsing the stores there, mainly looking for work clothes, which she was running low on. Now that she'd had a couple of paychecks, she felt flush with money for the first time in her life.

She had fun browsing the shops in the QVB and Westfield. There was no time pressure and no one else's needs to fill. When she was putting her shoes back on after trying on a plain black pencil skirt, her phone dinged a text alert. Poppy pulled it out of her bag. It was from Gemma.

Will you be around for dinner?

Doubt it. I'm in the city, shopping.

Three dots appeared, and Poppy finished tying her shoelaces while she waited for Gemma to respond.

Ooh. I might join you. I def could use some retail therapy. And we could get dinner there. Lucas is on overtime anyway.

Sounds good. I'm at Westfield at mo. Just text me when you're close and we can meet up.

OK. See you soon.

By the time she and Gemma met up, Poppy had already bought a work skirt and pants and several work tops, so she took a back seat while Gemma browsed and purchased.

'Hey, while we're here, we should get outfits for the ball,' Gemma suggested while fingering the rack of clothes in front of her.

'I'm not sure we'll find anything for that here,' Poppy suggested, knowing the theme for the Resident Medical Officers end-of-term ball was End of Summer Blow-Out and the shops were mainly stocking autumn and winter gear now.

'Well, we don't want to spend a fortune anyway, so why don't we go to Paddy's Markets?'

'Great idea,' Poppy agreed.

They decided on wearing Hawaiian shirts over bikinis and sarongs. They figured Lucas could wear a Hawaiian shirt and boardies – no way would he want to spend money on an outfit for something like this. Both had sarongs or sarong skirts at home that they liked, so they only needed the shirts. They bought three Hawaiian shirts of different colours that were all the same style, so they'd look like a group.

'What do you think about these?' Poppy asked, holding up frangipani leis. 'Too much?'

'No, they're great. But no way will Luc wear one. Let's just get two.'

'OK.'

After they paid and added these to their bags, Poppy turned to Gemma and said, 'My feet are getting sore. And I'm hungry. Should we get dinner somewhere close?'

'Sure. Let's go to Din Tai Fung at World Square.'

'Yes! Dumplings!'

They ate tray after tray of Xiao Long Bao and when they were stuffed, they caught the bus home.

'How was your meeting with the HSU today?' Gemma asked when they were comfortable on the bus.

'Good, I think. They seem to have a clear plan of what to do next.'

'Are they going to use all the information you've gathered?'

'Yes. But not at first. Firstly they are just going to be asking to look at Tim's timesheets and escalate to an audit of all junior staff timesheets after that. They think the info we've gathered will be more useful for bargaining for better conditions once we can prove overwork and breaches of the Safe Work Act.'

'Well, that's good right?'

'Yeah. I think we've got a chance now. Initially, I was really down, thinking we would get nowhere but Ryan, that's the HSU Rep, seems really confident. Like he's been here before. So that's reassuring.'

'That's great, Pop. And how was it seeing Will today?'

'Good. It's always nice to see him.'

'And?'

'And…he's going to give me another surfing lesson tomorrow after work.'

'That's good.'

'Yeah, it is,' Poppy replied, unable to keep the smile from her face.

'And nothing more from Josh?'

'No. He hasn't texted since the other night. And given his form to date, I don't expect he will.'

'Are you done with him?'

'Definitely.'

Poppy started thinking again about how things had ended with Josh. The sex had been great, but then when she left it was like it hadn't even happened. She had absolutely no idea what he was thinking except when he was aroused and about to make a move. Otherwise, who knows what was going on in his brain, or how many women were in and out of his bed. But Will, that was a different story. Whilst Poppy didn't know if he wanted to take things beyond the Friendzone, she did know that he genuinely cared about her. A smile flickered at the corner of her lips, thinking about it. If she got another chance with him, she wouldn't stuff it up again!

'I thought you might need this,' Will said, passing over a small, short-sleeved wetsuit. 'I borrowed it from Penny. The water's getting cool.'

'Thanks, Will, that's really thoughtful,' Poppy said gratefully. She was a bit of a wuss when it came to cold water temperatures.

'We're going to Coogee this time.'

'Oh?'

'Surf report mentioned a dangerous rip at Bronte and the swell at Coogee is smaller, but more consistent.'

'OK, that's good. I'm not great in a rip.'

'Don't worry, I would never do that to you,' Will said, turning to face her, concern briefly etching the edges of his eyes. He turned back to face the traffic and said, 'Did you see the email from Ryan?'

'Yeah, meeting's all set with Dr Anderson on Tuesday.' *That was a quick change. I thought he looked at me with feeling, but then the shift…all business.*

When they had parked and got out, Poppy slithered into the wetsuit, Will coming up behind her to zip it up. He rested a hand on her hip as he pulled the zip up with the other, and Poppy enjoyed the warmth he left behind.

'Thanks.'

'No problem,' he said, expertly zipping up his own suit.

They grabbed the boards and headed down to the water, Will stopping on the sand and turning back to Poppy.

'Do you want to quickly practice popping up here on the sand, or do you want to go straight in?'

Poppy looked down to the water's edge and shivered involuntarily.

'Let's do a quick practice here first,' she said, suddenly anxious.

She lay on the board then popped up, but immediately knew her weight wasn't quite right, and her feet weren't in the right position either.

'Sorry—'

'That's OK,' Will said, coming closer to her and repositioning her feet and her hips. 'More like this.'

Poppy turned her face in toward his when his hands were on her hips, their faces at the same height for once as he was bending forwards. Their eyes connected, and suddenly there was nothing but them. All the sounds around them receded and Poppy was staring into Will's blue eyes. They softened and his lips parted, and Poppy thought for a moment that he might lean in and kiss her, but then he stood back, his gaze falling to the sand, his hands leaving her body and the moment was gone. *What's wrong? Did I do something? Or am I completely off base and he only wants friendship?* Poppy lay back down on the board, a blush burning her skin.

'OK, let's try again,' Will said and Poppy took a deep breath and concentrated only on what she was doing.

'Much better,' Will said, examining her stance, but keeping his hands to himself this time.

At the water's edge, Will dropped his board. He was right to bring the wetsuit; it was definitely colder this afternoon, despite the warm sun still bathing them in light. Poppy shivered again taking time getting accustomed to the temperature before again lying down on the board. Her board buffeted in the white wash, but after a steadying breath, she pushed her weight through her arms, engaging her core, and popped up onto the middle of the board. It didn't take her long to feel more confident this time. Her balance was definitely better and she was getting her stance right more consistently.

'OK, that's looking good,' Will said. 'I want to go a bit further out now.'

They were barely more than waist deep, and the waves were breaking roughly a metre or so in front of her so there was a fair amount of bounce and chop as Poppy tried to mount the board from a prone position. It was difficult and the first few times she tried, she tipped forward, nosediving off the board.

'Your weight is too much on your front foot,' Will said, grabbing her board before it sailed into shore after she wiped out once more. She still wasn't used to the shock of cold saltwater thrust up her nose when she crashed and burned.

'You OK?' he asked.

'Yep,' Poppy replied once she'd finished coughing, 'just a bit too much water that time.'

Will held her arm and kept her upright as the waves continued their relentless path to the shore.

'OK, I'm ready.'

'Right, well this time just remember, you're mainly weight in the middle, only fractionally toward the front foot, otherwise you'll wipe out.'

'OK.'

Poppy tried again, and this time her weight was too far back and she tipped backwards off the board, her back crashing into the water, her legs in the air, and a great view of the blue cloudless sky before she was underwater once more. This time, she came up laughing.

'What's so funny?' Will asked, his eyes softening with crinkles, just the way Poppy liked.

'Overcorrected.'

'Yeah…but why's that funny?'

'I don't know,' Poppy said, laughing harder. 'I can't help it.' She'd gotten herself into a real laughing jag. 'OK, sorry, I can be serious,' Poppy said smiling broadly.

'Surfing is supposed to be fun.'

'OK, well you look like you're having a blast,' Poppy said mock-serious, and splashed some water up into Will's face.

'Oi,' Will said laughing and jumping back and throwing water back toward her in the process.

They proceeded to splash water backward and forward until Poppy lunged toward Will, grabbed his shoulders and tried to pull him down into the water. But he was too strong and all she succeeded in doing was falling onto his body. He wrapped his arms around her back and their eyes locked again. They were soft and warm and then a smile twitched at the corner of his lips, and, before Poppy knew it, he had twisted her around and dunked her under the water.

This time he was laughing when she broke the surface, her hair bedraggled over her face. She swiped it off her forehead and back over her scalp, and, despite the shock, couldn't help joining in the laughter. Once their laughs had settled, Will said, 'Are you ready to get back to it?'

'Yes, now that you are having fun, too.'

'OK,' Will said swimming easily to the shore to retrieve Poppy's board, which was lapping lazily at the edge. He had a comfortable stroke, Poppy observed; tight, contained movements delivered by his strong torso, no doubt built on years of surfing and rugby. *Well, even if we can only be friends, at least I get to perve on him when we're in the surf. Somewhat of a consolation prize!*

As the sun was going down, Will said, 'I think we should stop now. You look almost blue.'

Poppy tried to laugh, but her teeth were chattering too much, so she simply nodded her head and waded in. While Poppy was drying herself, Will said, 'You did well today. How did you feel about it?' She hadn't bothered to peek up at him under her hair as she was drying herself, she was too cold and tired.

Poppy was still shivering, but she said, 'OK, I had a few moments of brief thrill, but mostly I think I was just concentrating too hard to really enjoy it.'

'Do you want to grab a bite at the pub?'

'Sure, but I don't have any clothes, just this T-shirt,' Poppy said as she pulled it over her head. She'd gotten in his car with the T-shirt and a towel wrapped around her.

'I've got some clean stuff in the boot you can throw over the top.'

'OK.'

'I promise they're clean,' Will said as he grabbed them out of a gym bag in the boot.

Poppy looked sceptically at him, but they smelt alright and the exercise had worked up a thirst and hunger that only a burger, chips, and a beer could quench. Will's track pants were way too long and bunched around her ankles and the hoodie swam on her, too, but she didn't care. In fact they provided some much-needed warmth, and Poppy found the chattering stopped quickly. They wandered over to the Coogee Bay Hotel and found a table in the bistro.

'Can I get you a drink?' Will offered.

'Yes. Sorry, I don't even have my wallet on me.'

'It's OK, it's my shout. What'll you have?'

'A corona with a slice of lime, please.'

'Sure. Back in a tick.'

Will returned with their beers and some menus.

'Thanks, Will, I'll shout you next time.'

'You're on.'

'So, what's good here?'

'The burgers are pretty good.'

'Sold.'

'OK, I'll go order before that group over there,' Will said, pointing to a double table behind them with two large families.

'Good idea,' Poppy said turning back around.

When he returned again he said, 'You did really well today, you're definitely finding your balance better.'

'Do you think?'

'Yes! What are you up to tomorrow? Do you want to fit in another lesson?'

'Are you sure it's not cramping your own surf time?' Poppy asked, realising that Will hadn't touched his board after they left it on the sand when they first went into the water.

'No, I enjoy spending time with you,' he said and smiled.

But just as friends, right?

Poppy blushed. 'OK, well how about late morning sometime? Maybe I could meet you somewhere so you can have a surf first?'

'OK, I'll text you.'

'OK,' Poppy said, just as their page disc started buzzing and vibrating on the table.

When Poppy took the first bite of her burger, she groaned in pleasure. 'Oh, Will, these are good,' she said between bites.

'I told you,' he said, then reached forward with a napkin and wiped tomato sauce off Poppy's cheek.

'Whoops…thank you.' He smiled at her, and Poppy again found herself wishing he would break through the friend barrier they seemed to have created. *Surely he remembers how good we were that first night? But maybe he thinks I'm too much trouble now after I pushed him away the next day. I was stupid, I didn't know how amazing you were back then!*

Poppy wished she could say that to Will's face, but she didn't dare. At least now she had his friendship, and that was better than nothing at all.

'So, what do you think, Gem? Is this all friendship, or do you think he's interested in more?' Poppy asked Gemma over a nightcap after she'd showered and gotten into her summer PJs. She still couldn't convince herself either way and was desperate for some reassurance from Gemma.

'What's your gut feel?'

'I want there to be more, but I can't tell. Like when he's touching me to adjust my weight or balance on the board, I get a thrill, but that's probably just me. He hasn't kissed me or done anything else overt to suggest he still has feelings for me and wants to escalate things.'

'But he's spending an awful lot of time with you.'

'Yes, that's true,' Poppy said, looking down into her glass and swirling the liquid, thinking.

'So, what are you going to do?'

'I don't know.'

'A good first step might be to stop having sex with Josh,' Gemma said deadpan. Poppy threw a cushion at her.

'What?' Gemma asked fake indignantly after making sure her glass hadn't spilled on the couch.

'I know, OK! That was the last time, I swear!'

Gemma threw the cushion back, Poppy ducking, the cushion flying over her head, laughing at Poppy, who eventually joined in.

Chapter 25

'That's great, Poppy,' Will said, smiling as Poppy glided into the chop near the water's edge the following morning.

Jumping into the water, Poppy hugged Will, 'That was so much fun!' She'd just caught her first mini wave after about ten minutes of wipe-outs, and falls of various descriptions from the board.

'You did great!' Will laughed and smiled with her, swinging her briefly off the ground and they both splashed back into the water, laughing, and looking up at the cloudy sky. It was still a beautiful day with a blue sky, but ridges of white clouds high up in the atmosphere like a regiment of soldiers lined up on parade.

'It felt great…the feel of the water churning under the board…powerful almost,' Poppy said as she stood up and swam over to rescue her board which was floating away.

'Wait till you do a real wave, that's the real rush.'

She swam back to him on her board.

'OK, I want to see you do another good one.'

'Yes, boss.' Poppy saluted and paddled past him, over the small waves. They were back at Coogee again and she could smell sausages and onions frying on the barbeque at the surf life-saving club. She'd walked by the lifeguards cooking up a storm on her way down to the sand earlier. There was a sign at the edge of the barbeque stating all funds were going toward new equipment for the club. Her stomach had rumbled, but she figured she could always buy some food after the lesson. She'd made it onto the sand and put her hand up to shield her eyes as she looked out for Will in the water. He was flying down the face of a wave and Poppy stopped, enjoying watching him and the graceful movements of his body. It almost looked like he was telling the wave where to go, he looked so relaxed and powerful at the same time. As he glided in toward the shoreline, Poppy jogged down and waved her arm in the air to get his attention. He came all the way in and she said, 'You make it look so easy out there,' when they finally met up.

Now it was her turn and she focused on her breathing, blocking out thoughts of food and Will's lithe body and watched the small set of waves coming toward her. They were not even a metre tall, so Poppy wasn't scared, she was just getting her concentration right, running through what she needed to focus on, before picking a wave. She was ready and she turned toward the shore, looking over her shoulder, waiting for the right moment to 'pop up'. *OK, go.* Poppy leaped up onto the board, muscles firing, concentrating on her body position and got her feet under her and her arms out to the sides, helping her balance. Her stomach catapulted up into her chest and then crashed down as she glided down the face of the small wavefront before flattening out and gliding in to shore.

'Woo-hoo!' she exclaimed to Will when she dismounted, 'that was even better.'

'It looked it, too. Well done.' And he high-fived her. *I was kind of hoping for more body contact, but OK, I guess that will have to do.* After a few more good waves, Will called her in, to the shore.

'What's up? I want to keep going.'

'I've got to head off now. I'm meeting some friends.'

'Oh,' Poppy said, disappointed, 'where are you off to?'

'We're driving down to Wollongong for a party.'

She couldn't help being disappointed. *Seriously, you have nothing to be upset about. Will has given up heaps of his time to help you. He is consistently generous, you have no reason to be jealous!* Still, she couldn't help it. She was jealous. She wanted Will all to herself. Maybe he would ask her to the party, and they could get a little tipsy and see where things went.

But Will didn't offer to bring her.

'Thanks for the lesson, Will, I really appreciate it.'

'I love doing it. And you're improving so quickly, it's great.'

'Here you go,' Poppy said, handing over the board, and stretching an arm up to undo the wetsuit.

'Here, let me help,' Will said grabbing the pull string and slowly bringing it down Poppy's back. *Touch me…touch my hip.* But her wish didn't come true.

'Thanks,' Poppy said, starting to pull an arm out.

'Just hang onto it. Penny's not surfing these days, and you'll need it for the next lesson.'

'Are you sure?'

'Yes, absolutely… Anyway, I'd better dash. You OK to get home?'

'Yeah, I've got Gem and Luc's car. Thanks, talk soon.'

'Absolutely, bye,' he said and then loped off, a board under each arm.

After a hot shower, she joined Lucas in front of the TV as Gemma was on an overtime shift.

'So, how are things, Luc, any better?' Poppy asked at one point.

'Marginally,' Lucas replied.

'Elaborate?' Poppy pushed.

Lucas paused the show and turned to face Poppy, who noticed that he had lost weight in these last few weeks, his face more drawn, his eyes ever so slightly sunken. Poppy reached her hand into the bowl of salty, buttery popcorn on Luc's lap, grabbing herself a handful.

'Well, I think I've got a better handle on what to do to get through the day and the jobs…'

'I sense a but in there.'

'Yeah…but…they are such a pack of arseholes.'

'Not a single nice one?'

'No,' said with finality.

'I'm really sorry, Luc… At least you can start counting down now until the end of term.'

'Trust me, I am.'

Sunday arrived too quickly, and Poppy was back in ED on a day shift. It became a week of 'threes'. First the three day shifts, and then she had a run of three oncology patients. She hadn't had a single oncology patient so

far, and then three over two shifts. The first one was an oncology classic –
febrile neutropaenia, meaning fever when the white blood cell counts were
depleted from their chemotherapy, making them susceptible to serious
infection. If not treated quickly with multiple broad-spectrum intravenous
antibiotics, it could be life-threatening, and sometimes still was. Poppy
followed the protocol, started the appropriate antibiotics and admitted
them under Medical Oncology.

'Hi, Tracey, my name's Dr Mason, can you tell me what's brought you
in today?' Poppy asked when she reached the next patient's bed, noticing
she was bending over a sick bag, her face obstructed by strands of greasy
brown hair that was fading to grey at the roots. The smell of vomit hit
Poppy's nostrils and she reflexively swallowed to avoid retching.

Tracey wiped the back of her hand across her face as she sat back, and
Poppy saw she was quite pale and sweaty. Poppy reached into the shelves
at the end of the bed and pulled a tissue out of a box and passed it to Tracey
who gratefully wiped her mouth with the hand not clutching the half-full
sick bag.

'You're obviously feeling pretty sick, how long have you been vomiting
for?'

'Since last night.'

Tracey had lain back on the meagre plastic hospital pillow and looked
exhausted. There were dark smudges under her eyes, and she looked much
older than Poppy originally thought she was based on her hair. She checked
the patient label sticker on the observation chart and saw she was in her
late sixties.

'And have there been any other symptoms?'

'It started with just tummy pain. But then I started vomiting too.'

'And where was the pain?'

'All over.'

'OK. Have you opened your bowels?'

'No, not for the last few days.'

'And it says on the triage note that you have lung cancer, is that right?'

'Yes.'

'What treatments have you had?'

'Originally I had chemo and radiotherapy a year or so ago, but then it spread, and I've been on chemotherapy for the last five months.'

'Do you remember the names of the chemo you are on?'

'It's written down on my sheet,' Tracey said as she reached over into the bag which was on the chair beside the bed. 'Here,' she said passing the sheet to Poppy.

'OK. And it says here you last had a cycle two weeks ago?'

'Yeah, I'm due again next week.'

'And do you usually get vomiting with your chemo?'

'I often feel a bit sick the first few days, but nothing like this. And no tummy pain.'

'OK, and apart from the chemo drugs, are you on any other medications?'

'Just Panadol occasionally, and a blood pressure medication.'

'And you haven't had a temperature? And no one else at home is sick?'

'No, I live by myself, and no, I haven't had a temperature.'

'Is it OK if I look at your tummy?'

'Yes,' Tracey said, lying back on the pillow again.

Well she's not jaundiced, but her abdomen is distended. It looked like the skin of a drum stretched tight around her hips.

'It doesn't hurt where I'm pressing?'

'A bit, but not in any one place particularly.'

'I'm just going to tap on your belly now,' Poppy said, percussing the abdomen from the middle out to the flanks. *That sounded dull.* When she found a dull point, she kept her finger on the spot and asked Tracey to roll onto her side, away from her. Tracey groaned, but managed it.

'I'm just going to keep my finger here for a minute and then tap again.'

When she did, it was now resonant. *OK, shifting dullness, so she has ascites. So maybe not a bowel obstruction then.*

After she finished examining her, Poppy got some equipment and took bloods and put in a cannula.

'I'll ask the nurses to come and hang up a bag of fluids and we'll give you something for the nausea and when the bloods are back, I'll come and talk to you again. Do you have someone in the waiting room, or is there someone I can call to come and sit with you?'

'No, it's just me.'

'OK.'

'Hey, Steph,' Poppy said at flight deck. 'Can I talk to you about a case?'

'Sure, shoot,' she replied, typing away at one of the computer terminals.

'I've just seen a lady in her sixties with known metastatic lung cancer who presented with nausea, vomiting and diffuse abdominal pain, two weeks after her last chemo. But I think she has ascites because her abdomen is distended and there was shifting dullness when I percussed her belly.'

'OK.'

'So, I've taken some bloods and I'll hang some fluids and give her an antiemetic, but what else should I do?'

'Was she confused?'

'She didn't appear to be.'

'It could be hypercalcaemia. Let's order a CT abdomen, and let me know when the bloods are back.'

'OK, thanks.'

Poppy sent off the bloods and put in a CT request and then went to let Tracey know. When she opened Tracey's curtain, she saw that one of the nurses had cleaned her up and put her in a hospital gown and given her a fresh sick bag, which was currently empty. Tracey's eyes were closed and she looked comfortable. *I don't really want to disturb her, but I do need to let her know about the CT...*

Poppy approached the bed and gently touched Tracey's arm. 'I'm sorry to wake you,' Poppy said quietly. 'But I just wanted to let you know that I've also ordered a CT of your abdomen. So, they might come and get you for that soon, OK?'

'OK,' Tracey replied and then turned onto her side slowly and went back to sleep. *The antiemetic has obviously helped. That's good.*

The calcium level was very high and the CT did confirm fluid in her abdomen as well as extensive bony metastases in her spine.

'So this is all from the high calcium?' Poppy asked Steph after they went through all the results together.

'Yes, extensive bony mets and bone lysis leading to increased calcium in the blood.'

'So, how do we treat it?'

'You need to aggressively hydrate her. Once she gets urine output, you add a diuretic – 40mg of frusemide, then give 4mg intravenous zoledronate over forty-five minutes. But for now, increase the IV fluid rate and speak to Med Onc.'

'OK,' Poppy said, hurriedly writing those instructions down before she forgot.

Before Poppy rang the Med Onc Registrar, she took the opportunity to look up hypercalcaemia in cancer and its management. It turned out to be helpful, confirming all that Steph had told her with some additional background, and an explanation for why the different drugs were used. When she spoke with the Medical Oncology Registrar, she presented the case well and had a plan for management. There wasn't a lot extra for the Registrar to suggest.

'Hi, Tracey, how are you feeling?' Poppy asked a few hours later when the zoledronate had finished. She was sitting up in the bed, drinking a cup of tea and eating some biscuits. The colour had returned to her face and her hair was now swept up in a neat ponytail.

'Much better, thank you.'

'Your pain has gone?'

'Yes. And I don't feel sick anymore. I feel like myself again.'

'That's great.'

'I think I'm well enough to go home.'

'Well, actually, the Oncology team would like to keep you in. They might need to drain the fluid in your tummy. And, unfortunately, whilst the medications we've given you now will have dropped your calcium level and that's why you're feeling better, it might not hold it for long. They need to decide if you'll need any other changes to your treatment.'

'Oh… I really hate being in the hospital.'

'I can imagine it's not very enjoyable for you.'

'That's an understatement,' she said and barked a laugh, her face cracking into lines as she did. Poppy couldn't help but smile. *I think I quite like you.*

'Well, there're no beds on the ward at the moment, so you might be with us down here for a bit longer. Is there anything else I can do for you?'

'No, I'm alright, love.'

'OK,' Poppy said, and patted Tracey's leg over the blanket before leaving the bed.

Poppy had a surge of pride, knowing that Tracey was improving because she'd done the right things to make her better. It was a pleasant feeling. She'd also learned something new today. Most of the time in ED you didn't get to see the fruits of your labour, it was more a halfway house. A pit stop on the way to other places.

The following shift delivered the third oncology case and an entirely new oncology challenge for Poppy.

'Hi, Paul,' Poppy said breezily when she rocked up to the flight deck for her subbies shift. It was going to be a scorcher of a day and Poppy was pleased she'd be in air conditioning all day. They were predicting temperatures over 40°C, but a southerly buster was likely to come through in the evening, probably around the time her shift would be finishing.

'Hi, Poppy. Are you good?'

'I am. What about you? How are things with your mum?'

'She's OK, thanks, Poppy.'

'And you?' she asked gently.

'I'm OK too. We've got a plan in place and just moving forward.'

'That's good.'

'Yes. OK, let me know if I can help.'

'Thanks, Paul,' Poppy said, looking after him as his long legs loped off down the subbies corridor. *I hope he's OK, really.*

Poppy clicked onto the first waiting patient and read the triage report. The presenting complaint was listed as 'breast pain'.

'Samira?' Poppy called into the waiting room, roving the faces of the people sitting in the moulded plastic chairs. Her eyes settled on two women sitting with their backs to her. One was in a full burkha, and the other in Western clothes but with a satiny purple hijab. Their heads turned toward Poppy's voice and the lady in Western clothes raised her hand in Poppy's direction as her friend in the burkha slowly pushed herself up to standing.

Once they were close to Poppy she said, 'Please come with me, I'm Dr Mason,' and she led them through the security doors. When they got to an empty cubicle in subbies, the friend in Western clothes took the seat by the bed and the lady in the burkha, whom Poppy assumed was Samira, stayed standing. Poppy could barely make out Samira's eyes through the mesh-like opening but she noticed Samira was standing erectly, her left hand resting on the bed.

'Samira has some breast pain,' her friend said.

'OK. Which breast, Samira?'

She didn't answer Poppy, but her left hand came across her chest and hesitated above her right breast.

'Your right breast. How long has it been sore?'

Again, Samira's friend answered on her behalf. 'It's been a long time. Since before we met probably. She's only been in Australia for about a year.'

'Have you felt a lump or a mass?'

This time the friend had nothing to say, and Poppy kept her eyes on Samira, waiting for some indication that she might answer. Eventually, there was the slightest nod of her head.

'What about discharge or blood from the nipple?'

Samira dropped her head and her shoulders slumped somewhat, but she didn't reply. Poppy looked toward her friend.

'Yeah, I don't know. But I think whatever is happening might be infected now, because there's been a smell. So I told her we had to come in and she needed to let a doctor look at it. I'm really glad you're a lady doctor. There's no way she would have stayed if it had been a man.'

Samira then started speaking in Arabic to her friend who responded also in Arabic. Poppy waited, and again tried to see if she could make eye contact with Samira.

Poppy was acutely aware of her own inadequacies, and she wanted to be non-threatening, but she knew she was going to have to get Samira to undress and that she'd be very reluctant to do so. Eventually, she realised it would be quicker just to get this part over with and have a look at the breast rather than keep trying to tease out information, so she looked at Samira and said, 'Look, I know you're uncomfortable about being here, but it sounds like you've had this pain for quite a while, and I'd like to see if I can help you. But in order to do that, I'm going to need to examine your breast. I promise I'll be as gentle and considerate as possible.'

Her friend spoke with Samira in Arabic for a while and then Samira slowly undressed. Poppy was not expecting what she saw underneath. Samira, who was only in her late thirties, had a fungating breast mass that had destroyed the bulk of her right breast, which was bleeding, and malodorous. She tried to contain her shock as she said, 'Oh, Samira, that looks very painful for you. Would you mind lying on the bed so I can have a closer look and feel in your armpits and neck as well?'

The mass was at least nine centimetres and there were palpable lymph nodes in her axilla and neck. Poppy wondered about metastatic disease and examined her abdomen for an enlarged liver, but wasn't confident she could feel one. Samira certainly didn't have any signs of jaundice, which would suggest advanced liver disease. When she'd finished examining her, Poppy asked, 'Can I help you get into a hospital gown, Samira?' Her burkha had been unbuttoned at the front so Samira could remove her right arm and expose her breast, and she had removed her head covering to reveal luscious long dark hair. Poppy was also struck by her exquisite eyelashes and beautiful almond-shaped eyes.

'I'll help her,' her friend said, standing up from the chair as Poppy passed over a gown.

'I'll get one of our female nurses to come and put a dressing on your breast for you. I think it will make it more comfortable. Would you like any pain relief?'

Her friend conversed with her in Arabic and then responded, 'No she doesn't want any.'

Once the gown was on and Samira had covered her legs under the sheet Poppy had to broach the next tricky part of the consultation.

'Samira, I'm really sorry to tell you this, but I think you might have breast cancer.'

Poppy waited for this to be translated and then Samira nodded her head.

'I'd like to do some blood tests and admit you to hospital. The Oncology team will likely want to do a biopsy of the breast or one of the lymph nodes in your armpit or neck and also do some scans of your entire body. Then they can talk to you about possible treatment options.'

This time when Samira's friend translated, Samira's voice became loud and agitated in reply.

'She doesn't want to come to hospital. She just wants antibiotics for the infection and to go home before her husband knows she's left the house.'

Oh shit, is this a domestic violence issue as well? Poppy looked at Samira's friend, hoping she would provide more information about Samira's home situation, but she just stared back at her insouciantly.

When no more information was forthcoming, Poppy tried again.

'I'm not sure whether antibiotics will help much, Samira. I think the cancer has eroded through the skin. We would definitely give you antibiotics, but without cancer treatment this will get worse.'

After translation, this time Samira was silent.

'Can we start with taking some blood samples?'

Samira nodded.

Once Poppy had taken some bloods, she went off to find one of the female nurses to help. Samira's friend followed her out and stopped Poppy at the flight desk.

'Look, Samira doesn't have things easy at home,' the friend stated.

'What do you mean by that?' Poppy asked wanting to be clear about any violence that might be occurring.

'She's only been here about a year, so I haven't known her long, but she doesn't speak a lot of English, and hasn't had a lot of schooling, if you know what I mean?'

'Sure.'

'Anyways, she lives with her husband and his parents… And look, I don't want to say too much… But she doesn't get out of the house much, you know?'

'I see.'

'I had to really push her to come today. She's worried her husband will be angry at her for coming to the hospital.'

'Why do you think he'd be angry?' Poppy asked.

'They don't trust whities.'

'Oh,' Poppy responded, not sure how to get around that kind of deep-seated distrust. 'But there's no violence that you know of?'

'No. He doesn't hit her or anything. He and her in-laws are just controlling.'

'OK. Thank you. I'm glad there's no physical violence. Do you think you could stay with Samira for a while?'

'Just till I have to pick up my kids. Then I've got to go.'

'Thank you.'

Poppy presented the case to Paul, knowing of course that it would be uncomfortable for him to hear considering his own personal issues regarding his mum's new breast cancer diagnosis.

'I'm really sorry, Paul,' she said when she finished.

'That's OK, Poppy. Look, I don't want to put her through any additional trauma, so I won't see her. I know you've done everything appropriate so far. The question is how extensive do we need to investigate this in ED? Clearly, she has at least a locally advanced breast cancer, if not metastatic disease, and will need tissue biopsy and complete staging but that doesn't need to be done in ED. I'd await the bloods and then speak with Med Onc. I'd do a chest X-ray, but I wouldn't order a CT. They can do staging CT and PET scans from the ward.'

'OK, thanks, Paul. It's pretty sad, isn't it? That must have been growing for the whole time she's been in Australia. It was probably there before she arrived.'

'Yep, she probably never thought she could tell anyone.'

Chapter 26

To: Will; Poppy
From: Tarryn
Subject: Dr A doesn't budge

Guys- Ryan and Georgina had their meeting with Dr A today. They said she was very polite, but as immovable as a brick wall. They requested details of Tim's working hours and the rest of the junior staff. Her response; 'I'm not in a position to provide those at present.' Ryan threatened to take things to the ombudsman and, if necessary, the courts, so, she's got a week to come up with the goods. Proceeding as predicted.

Ryan's got the Channel 9 health reporter lined up for a meeting later in the week as a preliminary with an aim for an on-camera interview after the next meeting with Dr A. He is also reaching out to one of the *Sydney Morning Herald* reporters so we can get print coverage too.

Let's stay in touch with any updates. Will, will you touch base with Melissa again?
Tarryn.

To: Poppy; Tarryn
From: Will
Subject: Dr A's revenge

I caught up with Melissa today. Unfortunately, I've got some bad news. Dr A pulled Melissa into her office and demanded she review the timesheets and rosters looking for any discrepancies, particularly swaps to originally rostered shifts, to see if any of the doctors were doing extra shifts. The doctors who Melissa identified as doing extra shifts regularly were brought into Dr A's office and berated for their 'wilfully dangerous behaviour' and told their actions had put themselves and the hospital at risk and they were suspended from work, without pay, for behaviour contravening the NSW Health employees code of conduct!

Will.

Oh fuck! This is all my fault. If I hadn't started this whole thing, this wouldn't have happened. There were always a few Residents and Registrars who were looking to pick up extra overtime shifts, saving up money for whatever reason, and no one usually policed how many shifts people were doing from a safety perspective. *Now Dr Anderson is using them as scapegoats.*

To: Will; Poppy
From: Tarryn
Subject: Scapegoats protected

Guys- I got Ryan on to it, and the docs on the HSU members list. He intervened and made sure it's now suspension with pay. And they've got a hearing date and HSU will represent each of them.

Tarryn.

At least they're getting paid until this can be resolved.

To: Will; Tarryn
From: Poppy
Subject: Bowling and beers

Hi,

Thank god it's Friday, right? What a week. At least Dr A can't inflict any more damage until next week. Therefore, we are going bowling. We've booked a few lanes at Strike Moore Park and hope you guys can make it. 7 o'clock Saturday.

See you there,
Poppy.

After the email was sent, Will texted her:

How about another surf lesson in the morning?

Sure. What time?

I'll pick you up about 10?

See you then (thumbs up emoji)

Poppy was grateful again for Penny's wetsuit and thought if she was going to continue to surf with Will, she would need to buy her own. As she took her time adjusting to the crisp water, she asked Will for his advice on where to get one and what brand to buy.

'What?' Poppy asked when Will's face had cracked into a cheeky grin halfway through his answer.

'It's not that cold,' he laughed in reply.

'Shut up, it is!' Poppy said, affronted, and splashed water into his face. She had only progressed to knee-deep.

'At this rate, I could have made it out the back. Come on, you can do it, just dunk yourself.'

'Humpff,' Poppy complained and shivered before forcing herself under the cold water. When she broke through the surface she had to take a deep breath in to counteract the cold water.

'That's better. OK, time to go out there and give it a go.'

'Yes, boss,' Poppy saluted while her lips turned blue.

She forced herself to lie on the board and start paddling, goosebumps running up and down her arms and legs. *It's not as cold as you think… It's all in your head…* She tried to use mind control to convince herself she was warm, but her teeth were chattering by the time she made it to the line-up.

Poppy waited for the surfer in front of her to take a wave, then turned around and kept watch over her shoulder, desperate to get moving again before her joints stiffened. *Right, go time!* She paddled and pushed herself upright, but had been too slow and her weight was too far forward and she yelped as she nose-dived off the board which flipped up behind her. Even though the waves were only around a metre tall, there was still enough chop to dunk her and sand went up her nose and she coughed on some salty water when she broke through the surface. Will swam over to her.

'Are you alright?'

Poppy spluttered, 'Yes, I'm fine.'

'What do you think went wrong?'

A shiver went through Poppy's body, 'I was cold and too slow popping up, so I wasn't centred or quite upright enough, and my weight was too far forward.'

'OK. Are you ready to try again?' Will asked, gently wiping Poppy's wet hair off her face and looking into her eyes.

No, not really. But she couldn't say that to Will.

'Sure.' *OK, well, you're just going to have to brave the cold. You got this!*

This time she was angry. Angry that she was so cold on such a clear and beautiful day. Angry that Dr Anderson was such a cold-hearted autocrat. Angry that they had to fight so hard to get anyone to care about doctors' rights. Angry that Tim was dead and, most of all, angry that Lulu had left her. She let out a guttural groan as she pushed her weight through her shoulders, clenched her core muscles and jumped her legs up, quickly getting her balance centred and then gliding down the face of the wave, her anger immediately dissipating as the thrill of some miniscule power over her body and the ocean gripped her.

She made it to Will with a broad smile on her face as the wind whipped the fine tendrils of hair at her temples.

'That looked better.'

'It felt better too.'

'Good. And again?'

'Yep.'

This time she powered out, her arms working hard to carry her over a few waves, to the line-up. Thoughts of the cold water were banished from her mind. She wanted to feel that thrill again. To feel powerful. And she did feel it, over and over again. It didn't matter to her that the waves were small. She just wanted that adrenaline rush. So different from the surge of adrenaline in a trauma at work. This one was all positive, and addictive.

'OK, now that you're really getting the hang of things, I want you to start thinking about movement on the board, so you're not just riding straight down the face of the wave,' Will said as they were nearing the end of the lesson.

'How do you mean?'

'OK, stay here and watch me. I'm going to mount the board, get my balance, then shift my weight more to one foot to turn the board in that direction, a bit like you would skiing.'

Poppy watched on as he demonstrated on several small waves. After he'd demonstrated a few times, she swam back out to the line-up thinking about what Will's body looked like when he was demonstrating. The next wave she caught, once she had her balance, Poppy moved her weight toward the outside of her front foot and the board moved in that direction. But it was too far, and she wiped out. On the following wave, she tried again, and as soon as she started to move to the right, she then shifted her weight back toward the left and then back into the centre and avoided falling off. The waves were short and there wasn't much time to try extending the movements. After she'd had a few more goes, Will waved at her from the shore, and Poppy came in.

'Looks like you're able to shift your weight.'

'Yeah, I can feel the movement now, but the waves are too short.'

'Desperate to take the next step?'

'I don't know about desperate…but there's not enough time to really get a good feel on the movement.'

'Yeah. OK, well next time, I'll look for a slightly bigger swell.'

'OK,' Poppy said, surprising herself that there was no fear or anxiety in response.

Those last few sets of waves, she'd been concentrating so hard on her balance and her feet that she hadn't felt the thrill that had overcome her earlier in the lesson. Maybe on a bigger swell, she could do some movements and still get the thrill? When they were drying off at the end of the lesson, Poppy caught Will watching her as she bent over. She'd been so stuck in her own head the whole lesson, she hadn't paid much attention to Will's body or his attitude toward her, but now she wondered what his lingering look meant. *Is he checking me out?* She immediately sucked in her stomach in response and slowed down her leg drying. Rubbing her towel slowly up each leg again. But when she stood up, he was looking out at the water. *Maybe it's just wishful thinking again. But tonight, I'll keep the contact close and see what happens.*

They ended up having quite a sizeable group at bowling that night and had booked out three lanes. There was Gemma, Lucas, Poppy, Will and Penny, Tarryn and her boyfriend, Brad, and several other Interns and Residents. Strike bowling served alcohol, so they ordered some margarita jugs and some snacks, and there was a lot of mingling in between bowls. It was the most fun Poppy had had since starting work. She spent some time getting to know the other Interns and Residents and Tarryn's boyfriend, Brad. He was quite different from her – where she was gregarious, he was quiet and pensive and seemed to be the only person not really engaging or having fun. He didn't shout when someone scored a strike, nor laugh when someone got a gutter ball. It may have just been shyness and anxiety around new people, but it came across as arrogance. Poppy wondered if he might be a bit like Gemma. People often thought she was arrogant and rude, but really, she was quite shy and uncomfortable around new people.

'Alright, pub time,' Poppy announced once they'd finished their two games and everyone was sufficiently lubricated. The pub had a beer garden and it was still early enough for them to nab a couple of tables side by side, and order some more food. Poppy negotiated the seating, so she and Will were next to each other. She felt their legs rubbing against each other and turned to smile at him. He smiled back, staring into her eyes, and Poppy felt the connection. *Maybe tonight will be the night!*

Their connection was broken when Gemma, a bit drunkenly, bumped into them both, wrapping her arms around them and trying to whisper in that loud way that drunks do, 'You two...you're so cute.'

'Thanks, Gem.'

'I really like you, Will, I think you'd be sooo good for Poppy.'

'Ah, OK,' said Will, awkwardly.

'Yeah, OK, Gem, maybe that's enough,' said Poppy, trying to remove Gemma's arm from around her shoulder.

'No, Pop, you know I love you,' Gemma said, taking her arm off Will and positioning her body between them so she could really get close to Poppy's face, 'but you have really terrible taste in guys, and I mean really terrible.'

'Gee thanks, Gem, tell me how you really feel.'

'Remember that guy? What was his name? Oh, that's right, Marco! Yep, remember he was that backpacker who you basically let move in and mooch off us while he shagged not just you, but like two other women?'

'Yeah, I remember Gem,' Poppy said blushing, and giving Gem the big-eyes symbol of stop!

'And what about that guy, Nate? He basically kept demoralising you for months before you finally let him go.'

'OK, Gem, I'm not sure Will really needs to hear all this.'

'No, but you do, Poppy. You are such an amazing person, and I don't think you realise you need to be more in charge of your love life and stop letting douche bags use you.' Poppy suddenly felt panic rising. Was she going to start talking about Josh? That was the last thing Poppy and Will needed.

'OK, Gem, I will,' Poppy said, thinking it was probably quicker and easier to agree with her in her current state of inebriation rather than to try to stop her.

'Good. And don't let this one go, Pop,' she said, turning back around to look at Will, 'he's a keeper.'

'OK, thanks for the advice, Gem.'

'You're welcome, sweetie,' she said, planting a big smooch on Poppy's cheek that Poppy was positive left a lipstick mark as she staggered off and draped her arms around Lucas, who turned into her embrace and let her rest her head on his shoulder.

'I'm so sorry about that,' Poppy said to Will after Gemma had left. 'Clearly, she's had a bit much. She's not normally like this.'

'It's OK, it's clear she just cares about you.'

'Yeah, but look at them.' Poppy gestured to where Gemma and Lucas were slow dancing in the middle of the dance area, Lucas basically holding Gemma up. 'She doesn't realise how lucky she is. Lucas is an awesome guy and they've been happily together for years. Most of us aren't that lucky.'

'True… But it can happen, Pop.'

'Well, I hope so.'

'Me too.' And Will was staring at her again, his eyes slightly misted over and wistful. Poppy felt a somersault in her belly, thinking maybe Will was hoping it would work out between them? Could she be that lucky?

They were interrupted again soon afterward and then there was mass dancing and events conspired that Will and Poppy didn't have any further alone time. Once everyone was sozzled and the staff were getting antsy, they bussed it back to Newtown.

'Right, you lot – off!' The bus driver said when they got to the stop at Sydney Uni. They'd been singing loudly and leaning over people when the bus turned corners.

'OK,' Will and Lucas said, gesturing and herding the rest of them out of the bus and onto the pavement. It was a long, slow walk from the top of King Street, but it did the job of sobering most of them up. Gemma really struggled, though.

'Luc, I can't do it,' Gemma whined as she stopped in the middle of the path.

'Alright. Get on,' Lucas said, leaning forwards in front of her so she could jump up. The poor guy had to piggy-back her most of the way while Poppy carried her shoes and handbag.

'This has been fun,' Will said to Poppy while they lingered toward the back of the group.

'Yeah, it has, hasn't it?'

'I've really enjoyed spending more time with you lately.'

'Me too,' Poppy said, their hands almost brushing each other's as they walked closely together. *Please make a move, please make a move…*

'Oi, come on, Will,' Penny said at the beginning of a side street where Poppy knew they would be turning off toward their apartment building. The whole group had stopped and Lucas was taking a break from carrying Gemma.

'OK,' Will said, his pace quickening and Poppy rushing to keep up with him. *Shit, nothing will happen now. Not in front of everyone.*

When they caught up, Will turned to Poppy and bent down to give her a hug. His lips brushed her ear as he whispered good night. As he started to stand up, Poppy pulled him back down and kissed his cheek, lingering the contact. She could smell that citrus overtone and taste the hint of salt on his skin from their time at the beach that morning.

'Goodnight,' she said as she let him go, their eyes connecting again. *Was that disappointment? Why is the universe conspiring against us? All I want is just one more opportunity to see where things could go. Is that too much to ask? Well, is it?* Poppy watched as Penny's and Will's backs retreated down the side street and then sighed and trudged on to catch back up with the others.

Chapter 27

'Oh, my head,' Poppy said out loud to herself when she finally blinked open her eyes the next morning. She put a hand up to her forehead and rubbed gently but without relief. Her mouth was dry and her tongue furry, and she wondered whether she had brushed her teeth before going to bed after they got home last night. She looked toward her bedside table slowly, but there was no water glass. *Bugger, I'm going to have to get up.*

She slowly rolled onto her side and pushed herself up to a sitting position. The world spun. *Too fast!* She shut her eyes and waited for the spinning to stop, then took her time standing up and hobbled to the bathroom. The relief of emptying her bladder lifted her spirits somewhat and she proceeded to rinse her mouth and splash cool water on her face before emerging and heading to the kitchen for a drink.

'Morning,' Lucas said from the lounge.

'Not so loud,' Poppy replied putting her hands to her head.

'Sorry,' he whispered back.

She took her glass of water over to the couch. Lucas was in boxers and a T-shirt and staring at the TV, mesmerised.

'Are you hungover too?' Poppy asked, thinking he wouldn't usually be still in his boxers, or so fixated on the TV. He was usually at the gym on weekend mornings, having energy to burn.

'Yes, but not as bad as Gemma.'

'She's still in bed?'

'Yep. She had a bit of a vom after we came home last night. So I think she'll be pretty ratty when she does get up.'

'Umm,' was as much as Poppy could muster in reply.

Poppy and Lucas sat staring at the TV, not even bothering to change channels when Gemma eventually emerged like a bear from hibernation an hour later. She was grumbling and grunting, not capable of dialogue.

'I think we need McDonald's,' Poppy said when Gemma had lain down in Lucas' lap. She raised a thumb's up, and Lucas replied with, 'OK, I'll go.'

He gently lifted Gemma's head off his lap and placed it on a cushion and then went to put some clothes on.

'What do you want?' he asked them both.

'Large Big Mac meal with a coke,' Gemma said.

'Medium quarter pounder meal with an extra cheeseburger for me,' Poppy said.

'OK, see you soon.'

When he left, Poppy said, 'Should we change it to *Buffy*?'

'Yes, please,' Gemma replied, 'I have no idea why we are watching golf.'

'We were too tired to change the channel,' Poppy said as she reached over to where the remote lay on the coffee table. The movement caused a sharp pain in her head like someone had stabbed a hot poker into her brain, but she managed to grab the remote and lie back down without wanting to rip out her eyeballs, so she considered that a success.

When Lucas got back with their food, they couldn't even be bothered to get plates. They ate directly from the bags, Poppy saving her extra cheeseburger for the end. The food tasted amazing. Just the right amount of fat and salt, and when she took the last sip of her Coke, she felt better. Not swim laps at the pool better, but closer to human.

Eventually Gemma had recovered sufficiently to apologise to Poppy for her behaviour in front of Will last night.

'Oh, Pop, I was a real dick last night in front of Will, wasn't I?' she said.

'Yeah, you kind of were.'

'I'm so sorry, Pop. I was totally trashed.'

'I know. Don't worry, I won't hold it against you.'

'Oh god, you don't think it will spook him?'

'Well, if he is, then he isn't the guy I think he is.'

'OK, you're right. He's awesome. You have nothing to worry about.' They hugged each other over Macca's wrappers and bags and then returned to the world of Buffy and Angel.

Will texted around midday.

> Hey, Pop. Had a great time last night. Do you feel like grabbing a coffee this arvo? And maybe a walk?

Poppy wasted no time texting back.

> Luv 2. Starting 2 feel somewhat human. Meet at 2?

> Sure. Let's go to Rolling Penny. See you there.

Poppy almost bounded off the couch and into the shower. She didn't want the coma-inducing comfort of the bath. With the shower head on full pelt, it blew off the last of the cobwebs. She carefully chose her outfit; skinny jeans and a form-fitting short-sleeved knit top. Her still-damp hair she tied up into a loose bun and popped on some colourful dangly earrings. Birkenstocks on her feet and she felt casual, but still attractive. She sprayed her favourite perfume behind her ears and down her cleavage and swiped on some lip gloss and mascara. That anxious flutter was back, knowing that this was the closest thing to a date she'd had with Will. The surf lessons and the hospital stuff were different because there'd been no suggestion or expectation of intimacy. But now things might have changed.

Gemma and Lucas wished her luck, and she made her way up through the back streets of Newtown. Will was there at a table when she arrived and stood to kiss her on the cheek in greeting, resting his left hand on her hip. She felt her skin warm where his hand rested and her cheek tingle where his kiss had landed. They sat and ordered coffees and a slice of watermelon cheesecake to share.

'So, how'd you pull up this morning?' Will asked, after the waitress had left.

'Poorly. Had to get Lucas to do a Maccas run, then felt better. How about you?'

'Yeah, pretty average, if I'm honest.'

A silence filled the space and Poppy looked at Will expectantly. There was a new awkwardness between them that had not been there before. Pauses that had previously been companionable, were now loaded with the things unsaid.

'What about Penny?' Poppy finally asked.

'Oh, she seemed fine.' Again, there was another pause then Will started to say, 'I wanted—'

But the waitress arrived with their coffees and then their cake, which she placed in between them. They each took a sip of coffee after she left again, then Will said, 'please', and gestured at the cake.

Poppy took the first bite and felt the crumbly cheesecake filling slide across her tongue, the watermelon adding an interesting twist on a classic flavour. They ate in silence, taking a bite each in turn.

As Poppy licked the last cake crumbs off her fingertips, Will leaned across the table, reaching for her hand. He held it kind of awkwardly and Poppy noticed the moistness of sweat on his palm.

'Poppy, I had a great time last night, and I've really enjoyed spending time with you these last few weeks.'

'Me too, Will.' Poppy could sense he had more to say, so she was careful not to fill the silence that followed.

'I know you felt embarrassed by what happened after that party, but I really hope you trust me now.'

'I do, Will. And you're right, I was embarrassed and ashamed, and I let that fear get in the way. I'm sorry.'

'There's no need to be sorry, Poppy, not at all. But what I was hoping was…maybe we could…start from scratch?'

'Yes, I'd like that,' Poppy said eagerly, her shoulders relaxing, her smile stretching.

'OK, great, now I can stop panicking,' Will said, wiping his forehead and laughing nervously, breaking the tension.

Will caressed Poppy's hand and the ease that had been between them these last few weeks slowly came back.

The café closed at three o'clock so they wandered down to the park and patted some dogs. Poppy wasn't surprised that Will was relaxed and comfortable around dogs. It fit with everything else she already knew about him. They sat side by side, Poppy leaning into Will's embrace, on Poppy's favourite bench. Poppy rested her right hand on Will's thigh, and he cuddled her with his left.

Poppy's hand suddenly felt bright hot, as if touched by fire. Her whole body was heating up from the inside in anticipation. *I think we are finally going to kiss!* She turned her face toward his and found his eyes. They softened and his lips parted. Their bodies moved closer toward each other, their lips gently touching at first. But the kiss grew in intensity, the sounds around them receding as Poppy's desire grew. She wanted all of Will. Soon her legs were draped across his lap as he cradled her back and their mouths ravaged each other. Poppy felt every nerve ending tingling in anticipation and remembered how much surprising chemistry she had with Will. It was different to Josh, more subtle at first, but then it felt like the connection was deeper and somehow more real. Josh was all surface – glowing but superficial.

A nearby throat-clearing interrupted them, and Poppy and Will broke away from each other, Poppy wiping a hand across her mouth. She giggled and noticed Will's face colour briefly and she thought, *how cute*. She'd never seen Will embarrassed before.

'Maybe I should walk you home now,' Will said, standing up and reaching for her hand, the sky darkening behind him.

'OK,' Poppy said, taking the proffered hand and enjoying the warmth and solidity of this simple act.

They talked little on the walk, but Poppy was relishing this minor intimacy. She was too short to rest her head on Will's shoulder, but she did rest her head against his arm, causing Will to stop walking, lean toward Poppy, lift her chin and kiss her gently on the lips. Time slowed and the sounds of cars and traffic faded and there was only Will's warm, soft lips on hers. Poppy opened her eyes again as Will's lips pulled away and she looked deeply into his. They were warm and full of emotion. She was not alone in this moment.

'Do you want to come in for dinner?' Poppy asked at her apartment building.

'I'd love to.'

Their hands remained entwined as they walked up the stairs to Poppy's apartment. Before she opened her door, Poppy turned toward Will and looked at his eyes again. She watched him gently moisten the corner of his lips before leaning down toward her and kissing her again. Still gentle. Poppy reached her arms up and around Will's neck, bringing her body closer to his. Her skin was tingling, and the kiss deepened. Poppy wanted more physical contact. She wanted him to grab her arse or start feeling her up, and she didn't want this kiss to end. She wanted to open the door, rip his clothes off, and have her way with him.

'Oops,' Lucas said as he opened the door to their interlaced bodies, garbage bag in hand.

'Sorry, man,' Will apologised as he disentangled himself from Poppy.

Lucas was still standing there limply.

'I thought Will could join us for dinner,' Poppy said.

'Excellent, I'll just dump this,' Lucas said, holding up the full bag and sidling past them.

'What was all that about?' Gemma asked once they'd made it over the threshold.

'Lucas just sprung us kissing as he opened the door,' Poppy replied. Will was sheepishly standing behind her, his hands deep in his pockets.

'Funny,' Gemma said, smiling. 'Come in, Will, we won't bite. I'll just add some extra pasta,' she added as she made her way toward the kitchen. 'Luc was just making carbonara.'

'Awesome. You'll love Luc's carbonara, lots of garlic.'

'Cool, thanks.'

Gemma raised an eyebrow at Poppy as she passed her, and Poppy knew acutely that Will was feeling awkward. She'd never seen him this unsure of himself. It was very endearing.

Once the food was ready and Will had defrosted somewhat, Gemma turned to him and said, 'Will, I want to say, I'm really sorry about my foot in mouth disease last night. I was really wasted.'

'That's OK. Honestly, it was nice to see that you care about Poppy so much.' He squeezed Poppy's hand under the table. Poppy smiled up at him, thankful to be in his presence and holding his hand.

'Well, she's pretty awesome.'

'I agree,' he said, smiling at Poppy again.

Now Poppy had that urge to rip his clothes off again and felt her face flush with warmth. *I'm so glad no one can see inside my brain right now. The things I want to do to him, and oh how wet I am just thinking about it!*

'So, how long have you two been together?' Will asked, tearing his eyes away from Poppy's.

Lucas and Gemma looked at each other before Gemma answered, 'Almost five years.'

'Wow, that's impressive.'

Poppy noticed Lucas's shoulders had tensed. Maybe he was expecting the marriage question that usually followed, Poppy wondered.

'Yeah, we're really lucky,' Gemma responded, putting her hand on Lucas's.

'I'd better head home,' Will said after the plates were cleared away.

'You sure?' Poppy asked, slightly surprised. *Please stay!* She was hoping they could at least make out some more.

'Yeah. Thanks for dinner, Lucas. Poppy's right, great carbonara.'

'No trouble,' Lucas replied.

'Bye, guys.'

'Seeya, Will,' Gemma said, and Luc gave a brief wave as Poppy and Will headed out the door.

Why doesn't he want to stay?

Poppy walked him downstairs and they stopped at the vestibule. Will bent down toward her and their lips met once more. Thoughts left her brain as Poppy ran her tongue inside Will's mouth and then sucked on his lips before offering a playful bite. He pulled her in closer, leaving his hand on her butt. Their tongues massaging each other, their breathing fast, and Will's growing desire pressed firmly against her as she hooked a foot around his leg. Poppy ran her tongue up his neck and felt the groan that escaped Will's lips before their mouths were joined once more. Will squeezed her buttocks, driving his erection harder against Poppy's groin. She wanted to take him back upstairs; she could almost picture the moment of unbuttoning his shirt and running her tongue down his chest toward that erection. Will was kissing her neck now, just near her clavicle and she groaned in pleasure. *That's the spot…*

The noise of someone's keys in the door startled them and they pulled away from each other. Both wiping their mouths with the backs of their hands and straightening up their clothes, Will awkwardly pulling at his jeans to disguise his large erection. They avoided eye contact with the woman who came through the door, but Will held onto it before it shut.

'I really should go,' he said.

'Do you have to? We could go back upstairs?'

'No, I should go. I want to do this properly this time. You know, go out on a proper date first.'

'OK,' Poppy said, disappointed. She really wanted to have sex with him. But he was right. They had never been on a date. In fact, Poppy had been on very few traditional dates, she was usually quick to go from kissing to fucking and missed the opportunity.

'Pinch me,' Poppy said to Gemma when she came back in, just to be sure she was awake.

'Alright, spill,' Gemma said after the pinching.

Poppy sat cross-legged on the couch with a cushion in her lap and proceeded to tell her about Will's initial awkwardness, then the discussion around starting again, followed by the walk in the park.

'And then lots of kissing.' Poppy rocked herself slightly in her excitement.

She had this weird déjà vu, thinking back to a similar moment with Lulu on her childhood bed in Orange, telling her all about her first kiss with a boy. The excitement and thrill after all the anticipation, as well as the eager audience. It made Poppy pause briefly to internally accept the pain that never ended after Lulu's death.

'Well, he is certainly a nice guy, Pop. I'm happy for you.'

'Thanks.'

'It's good that you know where you stand now.'

'Yes, it's a relief.'

'But you've clearly got to break things off with Josh,' she finished.

'There's nothing to break off. We've never had a conversation around dating or exclusivity, and there's been absolutely no contact since we last had sex.'

'But you know what he's like; he'll just text or call out of the blue. How will you explain that to Will?'

Poppy thought about this. Gemma was right that Josh could stuff things up for her with Will in the way he just seemed to pop back in at random times, but she also saw no reason to text Josh about Will. Similarly, she would happily explain to Will the brief interlude she'd had with Josh when and if it came up. So, she answered Gemma by saying, 'I'll tell Will all about Josh as soon as the topic of exes comes up.'

'Well, just don't leave it too long.'

'Yes, Mum.'

Chapter 28

Early on Monday, she received a text from Will.

> Had a great time yesterday. I'd really like to take you out
> for a proper date. What are your shifts like this week? Will
> xo

> Evenings Monday to Thursday, off Friday/Sat. Then 2 day
> shifts Sun/Mon.

Poppy watched the three dots on her screen as Will quickly responded.

> How about a proper dinner out Frid night, somewhere
> nice?

> I'd like that.

> OK, I'll book something and let you know (smiley face
> emoji).

> Can't wait. Xo

> (rose emoji)

She had a spring in her step after that and decided to make some risotto before her shift in the afternoon. While she was stirring the risotto on the stove, an email alert came through. Poppy picked up her phone, continuing to stir with her left hand, inhaling the garlicky aroma, and opened her email.

To: Tarryn; Will; Poppy
CC: Georgina
From: Ryan
Subject: Update on plan for meeting with Dr Anderson

Good morning,
I just wanted to let you know that we have secured a second meeting with
Dr Anderson, this Wednesday at 1p.m. If possible, I would like you all to
be present, although I do suspect that Dr Anderson won't let you sit in on
the meeting. But even having you sitting outside, I think, will add good
pressure, a 'show of force', if you will. Please let me know if you can't
make it.
I've also lined up Channel 9, and a reporter will be at the main entrance to
interview us after the meeting. Again, it would be ideal if you could all be
there.

Thank you,
Ryan

As the liquid in her risotto was absorbed into the rice, Poppy added
more broth before typing back a response. She knew it was too risky to take
her eyes completely off the rice as it could burn and stick to the bottom of
the pan all too quickly if you didn't replenish the liquid fast enough.

To: Reply all
From: Poppy
Subject: Re: Update on plan for meeting with Dr Anderson

I have an evening shift on Wednesday, so I will just come in early. Are we
meeting near Dr Anderson's office?
Also, is there an update on the suspended Registrars?

Thanks,
Poppy

Before Poppy had time to blink, her phone pinged with more email alerts and Will and Tarryn quickly added their replies, stating they would be able to make it.

Her focus returned to the stove while she waited for Ryan to email back. She'd been feeling incredibly guilty that the Registrars were the collateral damage in this fight, and her role in it weighed heavily on her. She was really hoping that Ryan would have good news on this front. All the broth had been absorbed and Poppy added her chopped butter and parmesan and stirred these in, off the heat. The smell of the garlic and parmesan wafted up. The weather hadn't completely turned autumnal yet, but it was close. Whilst risotto was more a winter food for her, it was easy to reheat and store in Tupperware, even if it lost some of its flavour and became slightly gluggy on reheating.

Another email ping came through as she was scraping the last of the risotto into Tupperware. Poppy put the pan in the sink to soak, filling it with hot water and a dash of washing-up liquid. She wiped her hands on a tea towel before picking up her phone again. *I hope it's Ryan with an update...*

To: Reply all
From: Ryan
Subject: Re: Update on plan for meeting with Dr Anderson

We've got a date for their hearing – it will be Friday midday. Georgina is busy preparing for the meeting and will represent them at the hearing. Let's meet at the main entrance about fifteen minutes before the meeting.

Ryan.

Poppy continued the email exchange, asking whether they could attend to support the Registrars. But Ryan confirmed it would be a closed meeting. Poppy's shoulders slumped and she placed the phone face down on the bench. Have I done the right thing, she wondered? She bit the lower edge of her lip as her brows knitted. Her phone chimed a text ping which startled Poppy, who bit down harder. *Oww.* She placed a finger to her lip and saw a spot of blood as she pulled it back. Her eyes connected with the paper towel on the bench and she tore off a sheet, dabbing the bloody spot where she'd bitten herself, and picking up her phone once more with her other hand. There was a text from Will:

Not your fault.

Maybe not entirely, but if I hadn't started this, they wouldn't be in this position.

Hopefully Ryan will get them a warning/slap on the wrist and they'll be back to work.

I hope so. (Fingers crossed emoji)

The three little dots appeared and then faded away. Poppy watched the phone for another minute before putting it aside and heading back to the sink to wash up.

'Mr Tait?' Poppy called into the waiting room, her gaze roving the assembled waiting patients looking for who might respond, knowing already she was looking for someone homeless by the NFA (no fixed address) listed on the triage information. She watched as someone toward the far end raised their hand and then two men stood up and turned toward her. They both had greying hair, and were padded thickly with multiple layers of clothing, including long overcoats, threadbare and ripped in places. Each of them was carrying multiple bags, Poppy presuming that this was their possessions. Both had fingerless gloves on their hands, with one of the men, the one who had raised his hand, having a bandage over his index finger. They staggered as they walked toward Poppy, who received a blast of alcohol fumes and BO as they approached her. She coughed discreetly then tried to breathe through her mouth.

'Hi, I'm Dr Mason, would you like to follow me?' she said, turning to open the access doors and leading them through into subbies and a cubicle. With her back to them as they walked, Poppy heard them bickering quietly behind her.

'A woman doctor,' one of them said.

'No, it's a lady doctor.'

'You say tom-ato, I say tom-a-to.'

'Oh, shut up, you fool.'

'You're the fool, don't tell me to shut up.'

A smile twitched at Poppy's lips. This will be fun, she thought. *They're like those two old guys in The Odd Couple. I wonder which one is which?* Poppy had never seen the original series, although her Mum told her about it when she mentioned watching the remake a few years ago. Once she'd ushered them into the cubicle, she asked the gent with the bandage to take a seat on the bed. His friend stood close enough to the bed to stay touching his mate, and close enough that between the two of them, Poppy was already feeling a bit lightheaded from the alcohol fumes. She took a step back toward the corridor, and left the curtain open for now.

'OK, what's happened to you tonight, Mr Tait?'

'Right—' the friend started before the patient interrupted.

'It's my finger, I'll tell the story, thank you.'

'No need to get crotchety.'

'Well, as I was about to say before I was rudely interrupted,' the patient continued, giving his buddy the side-eye in a pointed fashion before continuing, 'my friend here, who has no manners whatsoever—'

'No manners, hey? What do you think this is, the Hilton?'

Side-eye again, and an exaggerated eye roll, before Mr Tait returned his focus to Poppy and his story.

'I was fossicking for my bottle of port in my bags, and couldn't find it.'

'Because you drank it.'

'There was at least half left!'

'In your dreams, buddy.'

Mr Tait turned again to his friend, 'Will you just be quiet and let me finish for once?'

His friend motioned zipping his lips shut.

'Thank you.' And he turned back to face Poppy. 'As I was saying… Blerp…excuse me.'

When Mr Tait burped, the alcohol rushed at Poppy's face and the strength of the vapour combined with the obvious poor dentition almost knocked Poppy over, it was that overwhelming.

'Sorry, where was I?' he turned back to his friend, momentarily losing his train of thought.

'The bottle of port.'

'Yes, the bottle of port… I couldn't find it in my bags, so I said to Jake here, 'What have you done with my port?' And he says—'

'I can tell my bit, thank you… I said, "I don't know what you're talking about, you old fool, you finished that bottle two nights ago."'

Mr Tait's voice bellowed more loudly as he continued, 'So I said, "you're a liar and a thief. I know you've taken it."'

'But show her how you pointed at me when you said it.'

'I did, I pointed at him like this,' Mr Tait said, showing Poppy exactly as he lowered his head and jabbed his finger towards his friend.

'So I said, "You're loony. I don't have your port."'

'Well, I pointed at him again, jabbing my finger like this, and said, "Where is it? You've got it, you thief!"'

By this point, Poppy had decided that Mr Tait's friend Jake seemed more like the Matthew Perry character in *The Odd Couple*, and Mr Tait was clearly the Thomas Lennon character.

'And I told him,' said Jake, the Matthew Perry character, '"don't you point your finger at me."'

'And I said, "I'll point my finger at you if I like."' They were still miming their hand gestures as they recounted their story, and Poppy was finding it all highly entertaining. Maybe she was absorbing all the alcohol fumes through her skin and mucosa and starting to get a bit tipsy herself.

"You get that finger out of my face or I'll bite it off," Jake said, crossing his arms over his chest.

'"You're stealing", I said, pointing at him again.'

"I'm warning you, I will bite it off."

"I'd like to see that, you miserable old bastard."

'"OK", and I bit his finger,' said Jake, with a triumphant smirk, as he rocked back on his heels, clearly proud of himself.

'So here we are,' finished Mr Tait.

'OK, well, why don't I have a look at the damage,' Poppy said, pulling on some gloves and then carefully removing the tape of the bandage, unsure if the finger would be partially severed underneath. When she eased back the bandage slowly, ready to firmly reapply if there was the slightest hint of arterial flow, she took a relieved breath in, unaware she'd been holding it, when she saw that the damage was minimal. There were some deep teeth marks, but no significant bleeding, and the finger was firmly in place. *Phew!* She completed an examination ensuring there was no deep tissue injury while the two men continued their comical banter.

'I'm just going to get some equipment and a tetanus booster and then I'll be back to fix you up.'

'Nothing's going to fix him up,' Jake said, bumping his shoulder roughly into his friend's.

'Shut up you. Haven't you done enough damage for one night?' Mr Tait said, jostling him back. Jake staggered, his weight pushed over to the side precariously and almost ended up on his backside before finally righting himself by grabbing the side of the chair.

'Why don't you have a seat,' Poppy suggested to Jake. She didn't need him to fall over, then she'd be suturing them both.

As she was walking back to flight deck, the two men's voices battling each other behind her, she saw Paul coming from acute.

'Paul, can I run a case by you?'

'Of course. What have you got?'

'A homeless gentleman with a deep bite wound to his index finger. No new nerve or vascular damage. Anyway, I'm thinking just glue, given he's homeless and unlikely to return to get sutures removed. Do you think that's OK?'

'Probably, yes. What kind of bite?'

'What do you mean?'

'Animal?'

'Oh… No. Human.'

'OK, let's have a look,' Paul said, changing direction and heading down toward subbies. 'Which cubicle?'

'Three.'

After Paul had had a look for himself, they returned to flight deck and sat down.

'It's pretty deep and near the joint. The biggest risk will be infection. The mouth is very dirty, and their mouths are probably dirtier than most.'

'I know. One of them belched in my face before and almost knocked me over.' They both chuckled.

'I would wash it out thoroughly with saline, then give him an injection of penicillin and tetanus and glue it. You're right, sutures would be a disaster in him, and it's too deep for Steristrips.'

'OK, thanks, Paul.'

Poppy cleaned the wound, glued and bandaged it, and gave him his injections. By the time she'd finished, Jake was snoring very loudly in the chair.

'Right, Mr Tait, you're all done. You can go now.'

'Do you think I can leave him behind?' he said, pointing toward Jake.

'I think, secretly, you two care about each other.'

Mr Tait scoffed, but turned to his friend and kicked him gently in the side.

'Oi,' he said.

'What?' Jake said, startling awake.

'Time to go. And you owe me a bottle of port.'

'I'll go halves with you.'

'Yeah, alright, you old curmudgeon.'

Poppy watched as they bent to gather all their bags and started lumbering back toward the security doors. She pushed the button to open them, chuckling to herself as their bickering started up again.

Paul seemed a bit more himself that night, more animated, and closer to the slightly hyper puppy that Poppy had first met. During a slow patch in the shift, Poppy asked him how his mum was doing.

'She's doing really well. She's had her surgery, and it's low grade with no lymph node involvement, so now she just needs radiation and hormone therapy.'

'Oh, that's great news, Paul, it must be a relief for you.'

'Yeah, it's an enormous relief. I was really worried about her.'

'Well, I'm glad it's turned out better than you were expecting.'

'Thanks Poppy,' Paul said, 'and what about you? What's happening with the HSU and the hospital?'

'We've got another meeting coming up on Wednesday and the HSU are getting media involved, so we're all hoping we can push Dr Anderson to agree to review the staffing levels and training policies.'

'Well, I hope you're successful.'

'Me too.'

Tuesday's shift was busier in acute. There was one tricky case that took up a lot of Poppy's time. It was a nineteen-year-old boy with a severe headache and nausea.

'I've been feeling bad for the last day or so,' he told her with his eyes shut and the lights in the cubicle off.

'In what way?' Poppy asked.

'Just off. Tired, off my food, a bit achey, and hot. Very hot.'

'Did you take your temperature?'

'No. I'm in the dorms at the uni. I don't have anything like that.'

'OK, and when did the headache start?'

'I don't know. Like earlier today. But it's so bad, and everything hurts, and the light is like lasers in my eyes, you know?'

It was clear to Poppy he had photophobia and that combined with the other symptoms in a young adult in a dorm environment made her concerned about meningococcal disease.

'OK, Nick, I'm going to need to take a look at you. First, I'm just going to lift up your top to see if you have a rash.'

Poppy gently lifted his *The Killers* band T-shirt and shined her phone torch onto his skin. *Damn.* There was a fine reticular rash all over his chest and arms. Some areas were starting to be more confluent and she pushed gently on these and watched to see if they blanched. *Double damn, non-blanching.* Poppy felt a rise of panic, like bile rising up your oesophagus as you're about to vomit.

'OK, next Nick, I want to see if you can put your chin on your chest.'

'Oww, I can't,' Nick said after barely lifting his head from the pillow.

'That's OK. Unfortunately now, I do need you to open your eyes and I want to watch your eye movements.'

As soon as he opened his eyes, the dim lighting caused him to squinch them. When Poppy briefly brought her phone torch up to his face, he recoiled and shut them again.

'I'm sorry about that. When you're ready, I've turned the torch off, but I need to see your eye movements, so I will need you to open them again.'

'OK,' Nick said begrudgingly and opened his eyes slowly.

'Can you keep your head still and follow my finger with your eyes only?'

'It hurts,' he said again, reflexively closing them.

'That's OK. That's enough for now.'

Poppy's hands were shaking as she checked his observation chart that the triage nurse completed. Poppy noticed a path bag with bloods in the chart sleeve and said a silent 'thanks' to Graham who had been in Triage and already taken the bloods including blood cultures. She sent them off immediately, then she went looking for Paul and found him in one of the last cubicles, the curtain pulled around, but his voice audible.

'Sorry, Paul,' she said, poking her head through a crack in the curtains. 'Sorry, can I grab you quickly,' she said.

'OK, sorry, I'll be back in a moment,' he said to the patient and then followed Poppy back to flight deck.

'What's up?'

'I've just seen a nineteen-year-old that I think might have meningococcal.'

'OK, tell me the story,' he said and Poppy recounted her findings.

'Yes, all that fits and therefore we need to rule it out. He's going to need a lumbar puncture. Have you done one before?'

'I've watched them, but not done one myself.'

'OK, well, now's the time. Let's get everything ready and I'll run through the procedure with you, and then we'll do it in the Resus bay.'

'OK,' said Poppy, feeling sweat prickling her armpits and palms. Her hands were now noticeably shaking.

Poppy and Paul donned surgical gowns and gloves, then positioned the patient lying on his side, curled up in the foetal position, to flex the spine. Poppy marked the entry site with Texta, then dressed and cleaned the area and injected local anaesthetic, as Paul had instructed. Then it was time to insert the long spinal needle. Poppy was hot in her surgical gown and could feel the sweat tickling down her back between her shoulder blades, her hands slightly slick inside her gloves. She wished she could wipe her forehead.

'Now feel for that space between the vertebrae again with your left index finger and then slowly insert the needle until you feel the fibrous pressure of the dura. Then push through until the pressure suddenly lessens and you'll have made it to the cerebrospinal fluid space.'

'OK.'

Poppy did as instructed, and was surprised by how fibrous the dura was when she got to it.

'Are you OK there, Nick?' she asked before pushing her weight forward into the bed to break through. Nick grunted, but didn't writhe or cry out. Once she was through, she withdrew the stylus. Poppy expected slow little drops like clear raindrops, but the fluid came out under pressure. She connected the manometer, a plastic tube used to measure the fluid pressure, and confirmed it was very high. Despite that, it still seemed to take forever to collect the fluid into three separate tubes, and Poppy could see it was cloudier than it should be. Once the tubes were full, Poppy removed the needle and bandaged the site.

'OK, Nick, you can roll onto your back again,' Paul said, helping Nick roll over as Poppy labelled the tubes and cleaned up her procedure trolley. They wheeled his bed back around to his cubicle in Acute and asked one of the nurses to repeat his observations.

'Well done, Poppy,' Paul said when they returned to flight deck.

'Thanks, Paul,' Poppy said, feeling relieved that it had gone smoothly.

When Graham came back with the obs, which were still ok, she handed him the drug chart with the antibiotics charted. 'Would you mind hanging the antibiotics?' Poppy asked him.

'No problem.'

'And thanks for taking the bloods in triage, too, that was really helpful.'

'We aim to serve.'

'I'm just going to type up his notes, then I'll go check on him and see if we should call someone for him.'

'I already called his parents from triage. They're a little over an hour away, so they should be here fairly soon.'

'That's brilliant. Thanks, Graham.'

He winked at her and walked off with the chart.

'Poppy,' Graham called out to her from the phone across from her in flight deck half an hour later.

'Yep?' Poppy replied, twisting around from the computer she was using to type up notes on another patient.

'Phone. It's the lab tech.'

'Thanks,' Poppy said, jumping up and quickly taking the phone from Graham. 'Hi, it's Poppy,' she said.

'Hi. I've got the initial biochem on that CSF sample for MRN 201943200.'

'Thanks, yes, 201943200,' Poppy confirmed, looking at the patient list on the screen in front of her to be sure.'

'There's elevated protein, raised white cell count, and low glucose. The rest will be back tomorrow.'

'Thanks. And thanks for staying back late.'

'OK, bye.'

'Bye.'

Those results plus the high pressure meant it was now even more likely this was a case of meningitis. There were multiple viral and bacterial causes of meningitis, but with the rash, Poppy still suspected this would be meningococcal disease. Paul was just heading up to the flight deck in front of her, looking at some blood tubes he was holding, his colourful stethoscope around his neck as always.

'Hey, Paul.'

'Yes?'

'CSF consistent with infection. High protein and white cells, low glucose.'

'Are the bloods back yet?'

Poppy returned to the computer she had logged in and pulled up Nick's file, brushing her hair away from her face.

'Yep.'

Paul stood over her shoulder, leaning down to see the results clearly.

'Mmm, his renal function's off. Let's go check on him.'

'OK,' Poppy said, her heart rate ticking up again. *Please be OK, please be OK…*

Oh shit… He now looked terrible. He was drowsy and his rash was much more confluent. Whole patches were such a deep purply-red that he no longer looked Caucasian, except his face which was still relatively spared of rash.

'Nick?' Paul asked, coming to the edge of the bed and gently squeezing his shoulder, his expression tight.

'Ummm,' Nick responded, barely moving or opening his eyes.

'Let's move him,' Paul said to Poppy who shared his urgency and concern. She released the brake on her side whilst Paul released his, and they quickly wheeled his bed out of the cubicle.

'Graham, grab a few more hands to Resus two please,' Paul said, still polite despite the situation.

'Sure,' Graham replied, as they wheeled past the flight deck and multiple sets of eyes followed their progress.

Once there and the bed was parked, Graham was already back and moving to put an oxygen mask on Nick, who lay limply on the bed like week-old lettuce.

'Poppy, can you please get a bigger cannula in the other arm?' Paul asked and Poppy went straight to the supplies to gather what she needed. Once the second cannula was in, just as Graham had him hooked up to the cardiac monitor, they moved the IV fluid to the new one so Poppy could hand pump the fluid in as quickly as possible. His repeat blood pressure had dropped precipitously. Poppy watched, squeezing the bag in her hands firmly over and over again as Paul took a blood gas from the other arm and Graham collected a second set of bloods.

Once all the blood samples were collected and Poppy's hand was beginning to cramp, she listened as Paul rang the ICU Registrar.

'Nineteen-year-old with presumed meningococcal meningitis, CSF presumptive, has had empiric antibiotics, and is now crashing. Can you come quickly?'

Obviously Poppy couldn't hear the Registrar's reply, but it was brief and then Paul hung up the phone and took the ECG that Graham handed him. He looked at this briefly before heading back to the patient and looking at the monitor. Poppy continued to follow him with her eyes and she saw on the monitor that his BP was still low and now his oxygen saturations were falling and his respiratory rate was increasing.

'He needs a Guedel's and a non-rebreather,' Paul said to Graham.

'On it.'

By the time Paul had the Guedel's in and the non-rebreather attached, the ICU Reg was gliding in behind Poppy's back.

'Central line tray, please,' he said, not wasting any time. It was clear to even Poppy that if they didn't move quickly, Nick could arrest.

Graham expertly pulled a tray from the storage shelves on the side and placed it on a procedure trolley and wheeled it over to Poppy's side of the bed.

Poppy looked down at her hands and realised that her bag was empty.

'I'm out,' she said to the room at large.

Annie, one of the other nurses, quickly jumped to the task and took the bag from her hand as she hooked up a new one.

'Do you want to keep going? I can swap for you.'

'Thanks, please,' Poppy said, grateful for the relief to her hands which were starting to cramp uncomfortably.

As she looked back up to Nick's face she saw that the ICU Reg had almost finished putting in the central line. She'd never seen anyone do one so quickly before. *Wow, this guy is good.* Poppy stood there lamely, watching everyone.

'Poppy, check if that repeat set of bloods is back.'

Poppy didn't bother replying, just moved quickly to the portable computer on wheels at the edge of the Resus room. She refreshed the page and then ran her finger down the screen of biochemistry results.

'Read them out,' Paul said.

'OK,' Poppy said before reading out the abnormal results. His kidney function had gotten worse.

'What do you think?' Paul asked the ICU Reg. 'Heading to haemofiltration?'

'Most likely. We'll see how he goes up in the unit. We'll get an arterial line in up there.' He turned to the monitor again now that the central line was sutured in place. 'I'll give him some noradrenaline down here, but I want to move him quickly.'

'OK.'

While they were delivering the inotropic drugs to increase his blood pressure and putting a pump on the bag of IV fluids, Paul said, 'Can you demarcate the limb rashes, Poppy?'

'Sure,' Poppy replied, searching for the texta she'd used earlier. She found it on the shelf at the side, just where she had left it. At the bed she marked the proximal edge of his arm, chest and leg rashes. When she was on the last arm, she capped the texta and looked at Nick's face again. He was expressionless and barely conscious. *God, he almost looks peaceful, despite the hell his body is in right now. How is that possible?*

All Poppy could think about was how this healthy nineteen-year-old guy could potentially end up losing his arms and legs, but truthfully, he might not even survive long enough for that to be a problem. Paul spoke with the Infectious Diseases consultant and they hung some additional IV antibiotics and the ICU Registrar called the consultant on-call.

When Paul got off the phone, she asked him, 'Could I have done something quicker or better to have avoided this?' Her face was on the brink of crumpling like a paper bag, and her legs felt unreliable.

Paul put a hand on her shoulder, looked her squarely in the eyes, and said, 'No, Poppy. You did everything exactly right. It's just a nasty infection, it can progress so quickly. It is not your fault in any way.'

'It's just so scary.'

'Yep, it's awful, and it's not over for him. The next forty-eight hours will be critical. But the fact that you immediately thought of the correct diagnosis, we got the lumbar puncture quickly and got antibiotics started, I'm hopeful that will help.'

'God, I hope so.'

The ICU Consultant gave the green light, and the team began preparing to move the patient upstairs. Within five minutes he was gone, and Poppy was standing in an empty Resus room with discarded blueys, surgical dressing packs and gauze on the floor, as well as a small spattering of blood from the central line insertion. It was like the desolate wasteland after the chaos of war. And then suddenly a breeze swept in around her ankles and two figures were being ushered in via the ambulance entrance by Graham. Poppy knew this must be the boy's parents, and she turned in what felt like slow motion and locked eyes with the boy's mother, a woman in her early fifties with fear etched deep in the lines on her forehead and a pinched expression on her face. For a split-second Poppy felt a moment of panic as she thought Graham was bringing them to her to talk to, but then Paul jumped down from flight deck and stood in front of Poppy and spoke to them in a slow and gentle way, explaining what had happened and where their son was now. Poppy felt a moment of relief and then felt guilty for it. She had no right to feel relief when they were about to face such fear and panic.

Poppy was still rooted to the spot and watched as the mother grabbed hold of her husband as Paul mentioned he was in ICU and things were critical. He might not survive the night. The mother let out a keening cry and Poppy felt it pull at her insides. The mother's despair tugging on the desolation Poppy felt inside herself, deep in her core in that little box with the lid shut. Poppy forced herself to turn away from them and pushed her legs forward as she walked jelly-like back to flight deck and back to work.

Chapter 29

Poppy met Will, Tarryn, Ryan and Georgina in the foyer of the main entrance before the meeting with Dr Anderson.

'So, we've got our documents all prepared and ready to file with the courts if Dr Anderson plays things as we expect today,' Ryan updated them as they walked toward Dr Anderson's office in the Medical Training Unit.

'Hello, everyone,' Melissa greeted them on arrival. 'Will, Tarryn, Poppy, I'm not sure she was expecting you too, I'll let her know.' They watched as Melissa knocked on Dr Anderson's door, her sensible skirt riding up slightly at the back revealing the bluish hue of varicose veins. She disappeared inside but was back out in a minute.

'Yes, I'm sorry, but she wants the meeting to be with just the HSU reps,' Melissa said, addressing the doctors and offering a sympathetic smile. They nodded and waited. Ryan and Georgina taking the available chairs, Poppy, Will and Tarryn leaning against the wall. It was expected, but still felt punitive to Poppy, like they were naughty children forced to wait outside the principal's office. Poppy watched the clock and roved her gaze over the others and the office, noting the thriving house plant on Melissa's desk and the neat order of her files and in-trays.

Dr Anderson kept them waiting for at least five minutes, her door firmly shut. Poppy suspected it was a power play. Nobody spoke and eventually the door opened, and Dr Anderson came out.

'Hello, come in,' she said briskly, not holding anyone's gaze, and turning abruptly to return to her office. Whilst the meeting was underway Poppy started jiggling her leg unconsciously. *This must be like what it feels like to wait for a verdict in a trial. Waiting to see if things are going to go your way or not.* They didn't have long to wait. The meeting was over within ten minutes. The door opened and Ryan and Georgina bustled out before it was rapidly closed again, without even a glimpse of Dr Anderson.

'OK, let's go,' Ryan said striding in front of the group, expecting them all to follow. Poppy took up the rear and said goodbye to Melissa as they left with an apologetic smile before toeing behind the others. *I wonder how Dr Anderson will treat Melissa for the rest of the day. I really wouldn't want to be in her shoes, that's for sure. I wonder what this silence means. Did it go the way we expected, or are we about to celebrate a win? I guess I'll find out when they interview Ryan for the Channel 9 news.*

As they stepped from the gloom of the foyer into the bright sunlight, Kimmy Lake, the Channel 9 health reporter, was ready with camera and microphone thrust toward them. She had luscious brunette locks, a very short skirt, and bright-red lipstick. The cameraman standing at her side, camera already perched on his shoulder, had the stereotypical paunch expanding his waistline and straining his belt, Poppy noticed. Ryan, Georgina and Tarryn took positions in front, with Poppy and Will hiding in the background. *I hope I'm not too obvious in the back, here, I don't really want to be on the news.*

'Ryan, I'm Kimmy Lake, with the Channel 9 news team. I understand you just had a meeting with The Bennelong administration about the safety of conditions for doctors in training here. As a Health Services Union representative, you represent the doctors, what can you tell us about today's meeting?'

'As you know, Kimmy, today we met with Dr Anderson, the head of the Resident Medical training programme here at The Bennelong Hospital for the second time in the last few weeks. A junior surgical trainee, Dr Tim Pan, committed suicide several weeks ago and the junior medical staff had been requesting consultation around safe working hours, mentorship and support. They were denied involvement and a closed-door meeting of the heads of disciplines determined no changes in training programmes or working conditions were required. We then became involved and requested the details of Tim's working hours and those of all the junior staff. Yet again today, Dr Anderson refused to supply this information.'

'Did she give a reason why she refused to supply it?'

'She stalled for time, but as Tim's working hours have already ostensibly been scrutinised in their closed meeting, this information at least should be readily available.'

'What will be your next steps?'

'As I explained to Dr Anderson today, as they have failed to supply the requested information, we will seek intervention via the courts.'

'Did Tim leave a suicide note?'

What? That's a bit gross, isn't it? The abrupt change in questioning surprised Poppy, but Ryan showed no similar shock and was clearly prepared.

'None that the police have made public. But other junior medical staff report an overworked and poorly supported doctor, and we suspect this contributed to his death. The system here, and at other hospitals, is to work the junior doctors to the bone. They work multiple fifteen-hour shifts a week with limited supervision. When they are under stress or feel out of their depth, they are actively discouraged from seeking help for fear it may jeopardise their career paths. We need an independent review of the hours worked by these doctors to ensure compliance with the Fair Work Act.'

'Tarryn, I understand you are the president of the Resident Medical Officer Association, do you have any comment you would like to make?'

'Junior doctors are working long hours, often with no supervision. This puts patients at risk, but also the doctors themselves. There is a culture of silence brought about by fear. This is not an example of resilience. It is demonstrative of a system that is broken. Tim was not the first junior doctor to commit suicide nor have a motor vehicle accident driving home after an overtime shift. But it is time to speak out for our safety and that of our patients.'

'Thank you both for your time.'

'Thank you, Kimmy,' said Ryan. Tarryn nodded.

The camera man removed his camera from his shoulder and turned the light off.

'Will that be on tonight's news?' Ryan asked after Kimmy and her team had stopped recording.

'Yes. I'd be keen to do a follow-up when you've got more to tell?'

'Absolutely. I'm meeting with a *Herald* journo this afternoon. I'll keep you both in the loop.'

Poppy was amazed at the slickness of Ryan's legalese and the well-choreographed moves. He'd clearly prepared Kimmy and worded-up Tarryn prior to the meeting. She was glad that they had taken over, but did feel a little left out not to be included. When the Channel 9 team had packed up and left, the trio went with Ryan to a nearby coffee shop to debrief and regroup.

'That went exactly as expected,' Ryan said with a tight smile.

Poppy thought he looked pleased with himself. She wasn't so confident there was anything to be pleased about. They hadn't made any progress that she could see, just poked the hornets' nest harder. Her concern must have been obvious because he followed up with, 'Don't worry, team. The news report and the *Herald* tomorrow, as well as the court proceedings, will be very persuasive for Dr Anderson. I think she'll backflip and would offer to handover anything we want to avoid poor publicity and ensure her own job is not threatened.'

Poppy nodded and tried to look agreeable, but she was still sceptical.

'I've got an overtime shift tonight, so I could walk you home?' Will suggested as they made their way back to the hospital.

'OK, that'd be nice,' Poppy replied, feeling instantly less down. 'I might text Gem and Luc and tell them to check out the Channel 9 news tonight.'

'Good idea. Hopefully, I can look too, if I have time.'

When Will met her at the end of their shifts, he came jogging up to her.

'I saw it, did you?' he asked, a huge smile on his face, creasing his temples.

'No, I didn't get a chance. Barely had a break, in fact. How was it?'

'It was really good. The message was clear and it didn't look preachy. It made Dr Anderson look like a villain and the doctors the underdogs.'

'That's good, at least they didn't spin it to make it look like we're all just greedy and money-hungry.'

'Yeah, not at all. I think Dr Anderson's going to really start feeling the heat tomorrow. Her own superiors are going to be raining fire down on her.'

They talked animatedly about this all the way to Poppy's place, but when they stopped to say goodbye, they really stopped and looked at each other. Poppy noticed that Will looked tired. She touched his face as she remarked on this, and he leaned into her hand and reached out to hold her other one. They smiled at each other, then Will leaned down to kiss Poppy. It was gentle at first and then Poppy felt their desires rising and the kiss became deeper, more urgent, and she noticed the growing heat in her body and the firmness of Will's chest against her breasts. They were now leaning against the wall of the building, legs and arms intertwined, mouths locked together. Poppy broke free, pushing back off Will's chest, panting.

'We need to stop,' she said, wiping her lips with the back of her hand, her chin feeling the graze of pash rash.

Will kept one hand loosely on Poppy's waist and said, 'Yeah, let's save it for Friday night.'

'Yeah, we need some sleep.'

'OK.' And he bent down and kissed Poppy gently on the lips and hugged her before letting her go and saying goodnight. Poppy knew it was the right thing, but still felt disappointed. Did she want him to argue, to stay with her? Maybe a little.

Poppy watched him turn and walk away before going inside, pleased that he turned back to wave and smile at her. She had a bath before bed and thoroughly enjoyed pleasuring herself whilst thinking about Will and his smooth, lean surfer's body. Completely forgetting to watch the Channel 9 footage before falling asleep.

When she finally woke, there was a long text from Will on her phone:

> Dr A in the shit... Melissa said she's been fielding calls
> from concerned and occasionally angry senior Consultants
> and hospital board members all day so far...
>
> (shocked face emoji)

Urgent meetings on the way for her with head of Local
Health District and the Sydney branch heads of the
College of Physicians and the College of Surgeons.

(fingers crossed emoji)

This morning's *Sydney Morning Herald* had featured an article with the headline: 'Premier Hospital Hell'. The article went into detail, highlighting Tim's suicide, the concerns of the medical staff over minimum doctor numbers and supervision, and Dr Anderson's refusal to provide an audit of doctor work hours. It also mentioned the car accident of Evelyn Lim and the subsequent lawsuit, settled for an undisclosed amount. The entire article was written to paint the hospital's senior administration and staff as the evil lords and the junior doctors as the impoverished indentured serfs. Tarryn, Will and Poppy were all mentioned by name as the leaders of the crusade, but only Tarryn was quoted with the sound byte from the Channel 9 interview.

Poppy watched the TV footage and read the *Herald* article over breakfast, then returned her mum's missed calls, and Will's additional texts.

'Sounds like you're kicking arse and taking names, my dear,' her mum said by way of greeting.

'Yeah, it's really charging forward now.'

'Good on you, sweetheart. Are you doing OK?'

'Yeah I'm OK, Mum. Work's OK… and I've kind of started seeing someone.'

'Oh that's great, Poppy, give me all the details.' And Poppy filled her in about Will and the surf lessons.

When she'd finished, her mum surprised her by telling her she and Poppy's father had been friends for a few months before they started dating.

'Someone who is a friend first is far more likely to be a good partner than someone who just started as a lover.'

Poppy didn't mention that they had had sex before they became friends. Some information was best not shared with your mother.

Poppy texted Will.

Just finished the smh article, thought it was good. Strong!

Yeah, both that & Ch 9 story very helpful, he replied. Dr A must be shitting herself…

Glad I'm not her today!

Feel sorry for Melissa, tho. Got to get to theatres. Talk later (heart emoji)

Me too. (kiss face emoji)

Poppy had a lazy morning, grabbing coffee and seeing Jason for the first time since that fateful art show.

'Hi, Jason,' Poppy said when she arrived. He looked up from the coffee machine, met her gaze then immediately looked away and down at his hands.

'The usual?'

'Sure, thanks.' He didn't meet her eyes again, but made her coffee efficiently and said goodbye as she left. It was awkward, but like pulling off a band aid, she hoped now they had seen each other they could move on and get back to the easy greetings they'd had previously. She watched some Netflix, had a late lunch, and grabbed a second coffee on her way to work.

As she was putting her stuff in her locker, she saw the notification of a new email and checked it before going in to flight deck.

To: Tarryn; Will; Poppy; Georgina Barry
From: Ryan Farrell
Subject: Update THE BENNELONG v JMOs
Hi all,
I've just received a call from Dr Anderson. She is now happy to provide access to allow an audit of junior staff work hours. I've requested another meeting on Friday after the scheduled disciplinary meeting for the other doctors to discuss next steps. Could we all meet before to finalise what our idea of a win is in this situation? And what we're prepared to negotiate on?
Regards,
Ryan

It would mean no sleep in after her evening shift, but Poppy had started this, and she wanted to be there to shape the next steps.

She went into the shift feeling good and a smile on her face. Things were finally moving forward with Will, the crusade was progressing to a winning position, and she was feeling confident that even if she saw difficult cases, she'd be ok – she'd make a start, ask for help, and ultimately her role here in ED was really to patch the patients up and move them on, either to the wards or back home. Beyond that, she had no control, and learning to accept that did make things less stressful for her. You did your best and then you moved on to the next patient. With that attitude, the shift in subbies was a good one.

Friday morning, Poppy dragged herself out of bed, wading up from the depths of a dream when her alarm went off. She sleepwalked through breakfast and a strong, hot shower woke her up sufficiently to get ready to head in for the meeting.

They met again in one of the library meeting rooms which Tarryn had booked and sat down to discuss what they wanted beyond the audit.

'I'd like to see a formal mentorship and pastoral support programme for the doctors,' Poppy said.

'Yeah, that's good, Poppy. I also think we need an additional Medical Registrar on in the evenings, so there's three in total, and two on overnight shifts,' Tarryn suggested.

'But we don't want everyone just doing more overtime shifts,' Will added.

'No, we need more hiring of staff… I think we need at least five more Medical Registrars hired,' Tarryn concluded.

'The Surgical Registrars haven't been specific about what they want, but they want to be involved in working out solutions for their staffing issues,' Will added. 'To me, they are still afraid of how this will affect them… No one wants to be out on a limb on their own, so it will need to be a collaborative process.'

'OK, thanks everyone,' Ryan said as he and Georgina packed up to go off to the hearings. Ryan had also arranged a follow-up interview with

Channel 9 and the *Sydney Morning Herald* and wanted Tarryn available for comments for both. The others went back to work and Poppy headed home. She had some lunch and then went back to bed for a read and a nap before getting up to prepare for her date with Will.

Ryan had emailed in the afternoon whilst Poppy was resting, and it transpired that Dr Anderson had agreed to set up two committees. One to brainstorm how they could set up a pastoral care and mentorship programme. The second to work out how to improve staff numbers and shift arrangements. He also updated them on the hearing outcomes from today and pleasingly all the doctors had been reinstated and given slaps on the wrist only. Dr Anderson had been clear that from now on there would be better oversight on the administration side to ensure doctors weren't exceeding the safe work recommendations.

Poppy smiled. *What a relief!* There was obviously a lot of work to be done before there was genuine change, but at least now they had a commitment from the hospital. And Poppy, together with Will, Tarryn and the HSU, would hold them to it. The follow up Channel 9 interview would air that night and the *Herald* article would be in tomorrow's paper.

Will had booked Sixpenny, a restaurant in Stanmore, for dinner. Poppy dressed in her little black dress, strappy-heeled sandals, and dangly red earrings. She curled her hair in loose beachy waves and made her make-up sultry with dark kohl on her eyes, and slightly glittery lip gloss. With her favourite perfume and condoms in her bag, she was ready to go when Will arrived at seven o'clock. He was dressed in dark-navy chinos and a white button-down shirt, and his slightly too long, unruly hair was tamed tonight with some product. Poppy liked this look on him. It was more mature and sexier than she had seen him before, and when they kissed hello, Poppy felt the early stirrings of desire.

They Uber'd to the restaurant. It was a tasting menu with matching wines and when Poppy read the menu, her throat went dry. There were ingredients she'd never heard of and things she'd never tasted, including a tartare of kangaroo. *Oh jeez, this could be ugly. What if I spit something out on my plate? He'd think I was a complete moron and the waitstaff would be appalled.* She had to at least pretend she had some sophistication, so she said nothing, sipped her wine, and looked at Will. After a few drinks to warm them up, and the entrée, Will leaned toward her and whispered as he tucked a loose curl over his ear, 'This food is a little beyond my palate.'

'Thank god it's not just me,' Poppy laughed. 'I was starting to freak out.'

'My foot was shaking under the table, I thought I'd made a colossal mistake booking this place when I read the menu.'

They laughed again, and Poppy reached across the table to take Will's hand. She didn't feel like such a dork now. In the end, they were brave together, and they quite enjoyed the dishes, although Poppy was not a fan of the kangaroo tartare.

'So you've got an older brother and an older sister, right?' Poppy asked.

'Yep, and two nieces and one nephew.'

'And which do they belong to?'

'My brother has a son and daughter, and my sister just has an eighteen-month-old daughter, but I think they're trying again now for a second child.'

'I bet you must miss them, living down here.'

'Yeah, I do.'

'Have you thought about moving back to Queensland?'

'Sometimes. Maybe when the time is right.'

When the meal was over, they walked in the general direction of Will's place.

Holding hands while they strolled, Poppy relished the feel of Will's hand in hers. They had just started on the topic of exes.

'Well, I had a girlfriend through the last year of high school and most of my first degree at uni, but there hasn't been anyone serious since then.'

'Why did you break up?' Poppy asked, 'Only if you want to say,' she added as an afterthought, not wanting to seem too pushy.

There was silence as they walked, and Poppy thought she must have offended him, before he finally said, 'It didn't end well.'

'I'm sorry, Will. You really don't have to talk about it.'

They walked on in silence for a time.

'How about you, Poppy, any serious relationships in your past, or did Gemma divulge all the gory details the other night?' he asked with a grin on his face.

'Ha! She sure did. No one special on my end. All scumbags.'

'Well, we might have to change that record, hey?' he asked hopefully, bending down to kiss her cheek chastely.

This should have been an excellent opportunity to break the ice around Josh, but Poppy chickened out, not wanting Will to be disappointed, especially after he was so obviously hurt by his previous girlfriend. She would just have to find a better time to discuss it.

At Will's place, Poppy felt nervous. Having sex now was totally different from the first time when they were drunk and hardly knew each other. Now it mattered more. They liked each other and there was serious potential for a relationship. Somehow, that added to the pressure rather than lessened it.

They went directly to Will's room, and he put on some soft music. Poppy looked around (she'd been too distracted by sex the last time she was there). It was a decent size with a queen futon bed, small desk, and space too for a reading chair. The chair was distressed leather and Poppy could picture Will sitting in the chair, reading. He came over and held her hand. They looked at each other and Poppy felt safe – it was like he was hugging her even though only their hands were touching. He had this way of making her feel at ease just by looking at her. She let her insecurities go and reached up to kiss him.

As they kissed, the passion reignited, and Poppy's animal instincts took over. They undressed each other, Poppy lingering to lick and kiss Will's toned abdomen and Will caressing and mouthing Poppy's breasts. She liked the way he used just the right amount of pressure. Not so firm that it hurt, but enough to make her wet. When they were down to just their underwear, they moved to the bed. Poppy lay down first and Will lay above her, supporting his weight on his elbow. They returned to their thirsty kisses, and Will stroked between her legs, arousing Poppy's clitoris. *Umm that's nice…keep doing just that…*

'Umm, now I want to touch you.' She slid her hand into Will's underwear, stroking his erect penis, enjoying feeling how hard he was. They hastily removed their final layers and Will went down on Poppy. He was good at it, and it did not take long for her to come. Shuddering waves of ecstasy rolled through Poppy's body as she shouted out, 'Yes!'. When the waves eased, she guided him inside her.

The sex was fantastic, their bodies well suited, and they sensed each other's needs well. Poppy had two more orgasms, the last coinciding with Will's, and in her preferred doggy position. When they disentangled themselves, they lay together, catching their breath, with Poppy lying on Will's chest, his arm cradling her.

'Can I say wow this time?' Will teased her.

'Shut up!' Poppy fake-punched him in the arm. 'Not funny.'

'I'm sorry. But seriously, that was outstanding.'

'Yeah, it was,' Poppy replied honestly. Not once during that whole time did she feel slightly off or self-conscious. Unlike how things had been with Josh, where each time things were just a bit off kilter. 'I might want to do it again,' Poppy said playfully.

'I might need a minute. You wore me out!' Will replied.

They slept late and woke, snuggling back into each other.

'So, where were we… OK, what's your favourite movie?' Will asked her.

'Umm. Well, two of my favourites are a bit old, but classic, and I've read both the books.'

'OK, go.'

'So *Shawshank Redemption*, and *Fried Green Tomatoes*.'

'Interesting.'

'I bet you haven't seen either of them.'

'I've seen *Shawshank*. I mean, who hasn't. Seriously one of the best films ever. But I didn't know it was based on a book.'

'Short story actually, by Stephen King, called 'Rita Hayworth and the Shawshank Redemption'.

'A bit wordy.'

'Agreed. What about you?'

'Well, *Shawshank* would be up there. I agree it's a classic. But also, for something more recent, *The Force Awakens*.'

'*Star Wars*, really?'

'Hey don't knock it. And Rey is a seriously bad-ass character.'

They laughed and kissed each other and more sex followed.

Poppy felt closer to Will already, both physically and emotionally, than she had in any previous relationship. And, surprisingly, it didn't scare her. Not even a little bit.

When they finally made it out of bed, they showered and Poppy borrowed some of Will's clothes so they could go get breakfast. The clothes were long on Poppy and roomy, but as he was a slim build, it could have been worse.

'It's such a beautiful day, what do you think about a surf?' Will asked after they had finished their food.

'OK. But I'm going to need to go back to my place first,' Poppy replied.

Once Poppy had changed and thrown some things in a bag for later, they headed to Bondi. They started at the shops so Poppy could purchase a wetsuit of her own so Will would be able to finally return Penny's. The surf was small and Poppy got in a great session. As the swell was low, she could attempt to ride multiple small waves from the crest. Lots of opportunity to keep working on her footwork. Will brought his board and they actually surfed together for the first time. Even sharing a party wave at one point until Poppy looked over to Will, lost her balance, and ditched into the water, spluttering on her way up.

'That was great, Pop, you're really getting the hang of it,' Will said as they were drinking water whilst sitting on their towels and watching the ocean.

'Thanks, Will… But you know, the student is only ever a reflection of the teacher.'

'Aww…shucks,' Will replied, bumping Poppy's shoulder with his.

'I may be starting to get hooked,' Poppy confessed.

'I knew it!'

'It's funny, it's this weird combination of fear, adrenaline, and peace…it's like nothing else I've ever experienced.'

'Yeah, it's addictive, that's for sure.'

They both watched the water for a while, listening to the gentle thwump as the waves broke, and watching the seagulls dip and dive down into the water occasionally under the fluffy white clouds.

'Thanks, Will, for teaching me,' Poppy said, turning back to face him.

'Well, you're not there yet…but you're close.' And he leaned in to kiss Poppy's salty lips.

Will finally dropped Poppy home about nine o'clock. She didn't want to leave his side and delayed the inevitable by prolonging the kissing in Will's car before she finally left. She felt like such a teenager when she sauntered into the flat moments later with Gemma and Lucas sitting up on the couches like two parents waiting for their teenage daughter to come home from her date.

'Good date, then?' Gemma asked when she came to chat in the lounge.

'Oh my god…it was so good,' Poppy answered exuberantly, her smile shining.

'You look happy,' Lucas said when she'd finished filling them in.

'I feel amazing!'

'I'm happy for you, babe,' Gemma added.

'Thanks, hon.'

Poppy floated pleasantly to bed after showering off the last remnants of sand.

Will texted when she was climbing into bed.

> Miss you already (heart emoji)

> Me too. Don't want to be apart from you.

> Me either!

> How about you come to mine Monday for dinner?

> OK. Meet out front at 6?

> Yep.

> OK, you sign off first.

> OK, having best time. Will miss you til Monday.

> Miss you too, but lots to daydream about.

> Kiss face emoji

Kiss face emoji

Goodnight

Goodnight, sweet dreams.

Will finally signed off. Definitely teenage behaviour.

In the morning, she sat down to read the latest *Sydney Morning Herald* article and watch the latest Channel 9 interview.

Dr Anderson was quoted on camera saying, 'Dr Tim Pan's suicide is a tragedy and has highlighted concerns about the workload and support systems in place for our junior doctors. The hospital will be fully cooperative with the audit requested by the HSU, on behalf of the junior staff, and we are also setting up committees to introduce more comprehensive mentoring and support programmes. We are also planning to recruit additional Registrars to improve staff numbers on shifts.'

Kimmy Lake pushed her further, 'Why were you reluctant to make these changes or provide the information to the HSU without a court order, Dr Anderson?'

Poppy watched Dr Anderson's tight lips and stiff posture as she admitted, 'Well, I underestimated the magnitude of the problem, but I want to stress that whilst it will take some time to improve things, we are committed to change.'

Poppy sat back and let out a sigh of astonishment. It amazed Poppy that Dr Anderson had so openly accepted blame and provided such a strong verbal commitment to change. The written article had also provided more details around the additional cases that Josh had provided and mentioned the culture of Residents and Registrars picking up extra shifts without oversight of how many shifts per week they were doing, or whether they were breaching the safe work regulations. It quoted Ryan and Tarryn as being happy with the outcome thus far, but looking to see significant junior doctor representation on the committees and clear timelines for implementing change as well as regular review and improvement once changes had been implemented.

'We will regularly be in contact with our members here at The Bennelong to ensure we don't see the culture sliding backwards and the hospital failing to follow through with their commitments,' Ryan was quoted at the end.

Poppy called her mum on her walk to work, who congratulated her on this ongoing success and she also spoke briefly to Will, who was equally excited with the outcome so far.

'By the way, I cannot stop thinking about you,' Will said. Poppy giggled girlishly then said, 'Me too. I feel like such a teenager.'

'I know what you mean.'

'Anyway, you can't get me all excited now. I've got to work.'

'OK, well, I hope you have a good shift.'

'OK, bye.'

'Bye.'

Chapter 30

'Hey, keep your guard up today, OK?' Steph said at the lockers when she got to work.

'Why?' Poppy asked, an instant knot forming in her chest. *Have I done something wrong? Has a patient made a complaint about me?*

'Look, it's probably nothing,' Steph said, tying her hair up into a loose bun, 'but I just overheard Patrick and Rebecca talking about you in the tearoom.'

'Really, what did they say?' Now she was worried.

'Something about the hospital and how you were making everyone look bad,' she said, closing her locker and pocketing the key.

'Shit. What should I do?' Poppy asked, facing Stephanie, her things forgotten in the locker with the door hanging wide.

'Just keep your head down. And Lucy and I are here, so just grab us if you need anything. Try and stay away from them,' she finished, squeezing Poppy's shoulder before striding off to the department.

'OK,' Poppy said to her retreating back. Now she was shaking. Patrick was the head of department. Despite it being close to the end of term, he could still make her time at The Bennelong painful by influencing other senior doctors. *What am I going to do? How will I cope if he turns everyone against me?*

But the shifts she'd had with Patrick so far had been fine. He'd been distant but not unpleasant, and he'd been good in the traumas. She hadn't yet had any real interactions with Rebecca. Surely they would be professional about this, at least to her face?

At the end of handover, as they were finishing on the acute side and some were going back to flight deck or moving on to the subbies board, Patrick said loud enough that most turned back or stopped in their tracks.

'Poppy…ummm… I've heard you're causing trouble for the hospital… My advice, apply to a different hospital next year.'

Rebecca, who was statuesque with gorgeous, silky red hair and porcelain skin with only a faint dusting of freckles was at his elbow, almost hanging off him like Rizzo off Leo in Grease. Poppy blushed. Her entire face was beetroot and there was a slash of red on her neck. She could even feel the heat in the tips of her ears and she stood rooted to the spot, as did everyone else. Their eyes boring into her like swords. Then Patrick and Rebecca moved forward, Rebecca giving her shoulder the faintest of shoves as she went past. Poppy felt like she'd been punched in the guts, and she was left standing there alone, her mouth hanging open.

After they had moved on, Lucy came up behind her giving her shoulder a quick squeeze and whispered in her ear, 'Hold it together, Pop.'

Poppy didn't know how she got through that shift without bawling her eyes out in the loo. But she knew she couldn't give in to that luxury. She needed to hold her chin up, do her job, and not show any fear. Bullies fed on fear. The blush was bad enough, she wouldn't give them anything more. Steph and Lucy shielded her as much as they could, which helped, but Poppy still had one more interaction with Rebecca toward the end of the day.

It was over a misprint on a medication chart. Poppy had accidentally written metoprolol (a blood pressure medication) 50 micrograms twice daily instead of metoprolol 50 milligrams twice daily. Effectively charting a dose that was way too low. Most of the nurses would have just brought the chart over to Poppy and asked her to rewrite it, but Rebecca clearly wanted to make a scene and humiliate her. She succeeded by loudly at the front of flight deck asking which doctor was looking after bed three (knowing full well it was Poppy).

'I am,' Poppy answered warily.

'I don't know which medical school you went to, Poppy, but I'd expect every intern to know that metoprolol, an incredibly common blood pressure medication, is prescribed in milligrams, NOT micrograms. My nurses all know this, and the government hasn't spent tens of thousands of dollars training them. But maybe they'd all make better doctors than you will.'

Poppy felt like vomiting, but she waited to make sure Rebecca didn't want to add any other insults to her tirade before apologising, 'I'm really sorry, Rebecca, I'll correct it immediately.'

'Which other patients are you looking after? I'll need to check their charts to make sure you haven't made any other mistakes that could kill a patient today.'

But she didn't wait for Poppy to answer, just thrust the chart at her and walked away.

Poppy was shaking as she sat back down to correct the med chart and Steph came over and sat next to her and said, 'Don't worry, only half an hour till handover, then you're out of here.'

'But I'm sure one or both of them will find a way to humiliate me again at handover.'

'Look, when you finish this let's run through your cases in the tearoom just to make sure there's nothing they can pull you up on.'

'OK, thanks, Steph.'

'No problem.' She gave Poppy's knee a squeeze.

Luckily Poppy's cases were pretty straightforward, and handover went smoothly. Rebecca had nothing further to pull her up on and Patrick just made her feel like she was beneath him, his small, rodent-like eyes boring through her when she spoke. When the shift was over Poppy raced out of there as quickly as possible and called Will on the way home, desperate to hear his voice, knowing that he'd say the right things to lessen the panic that had slowly been building all day since that first blow from Patrick in the morning.

'Fuck, that's awful, Poppy, I'm so sorry,' he said. 'I can't believe they would behave like that, it's so unprofessional.'

'Thanks, Will.'

'No, seriously. It's just so uncool.'

'So should I be worried about next year?' Poppy didn't have a clue yet what she wanted to do for a specialty, but she didn't want to get kicked out of one of the best hospitals in Sydney.

'No, not at all. I'm sure that was just Patrick blowing off steam. And besides, you'll be fine. You'll pass all your end of term assessments without an issue.'

Poppy's stomach dropped through her shoes and she stopped walking, in the middle of the footpath.

'Does Patrick do the end of term assessments for the interns in ED?' Her voice breaking at the end of the sentence as panic washed over her.

Will paused, and Poppy's fear grew.

'Look, usually one of the senior Registrars or Fellows will do it, but the head of department will have to sign it off. Do you know which Registrars are on tomorrow?'

'I'm not sure.'

'Well maybe have a chat to Seb or Paul when you see them. I'm sure they'd go in to bat for you.'

'I hope so,' Poppy answered dejectedly.

Despite Will's good intentions, the additional apprehension around Poppy's end of term assessment meant she didn't feel much relieved by the time she got home.

'What do you think, guys?' she asked Gemma and Lucas after filling them in.

Lucas looked down at his feet, not meeting her eyes, and Gemma took a beat before diving in.

'What's the worst that can happen, really? He might give you a shit end of term report, but if all your other reports are fine, it won't matter.'

'So, you think he'll write a mean report?'

'He might.'

'Great. What if I fail my internship and get kicked out and can't find another job?'

'It won't come to that,' Lucas said, finally looking Poppy in the eyes.

'Of course it won't,' said Gemma.

Still, Poppy went to bed with moderate simmering anxiety, like acidic bubbles bouncing around her stomach and up her oesophagus. She lay awake, tossing and turning for a few frustrating hours until her overactive brain finally fizzled out.

Thankfully, neither Rebecca nor Patrick were on the Monday shift. Harriet was in charge and Paul was on with Poppy in subbies. News of Poppy's degradation must have spread.

'I heard about what happened with Patrick and Rebecca,' Paul said at flight deck, leading her quietly toward the back where no one else could hear them. 'That was really unprofessional, but don't let it get to you, OK?'

'I'll try not to. Thanks, Paul.'

He smiled, jogged up and down on his feet once, then turned and walked away.

'Hi, Graham, how are you?' Poppy asked, more cheer in her voice than before.

'I'm OK. I'm sorry about Rebecca, though.'

'Thanks,' Poppy said, raising a slight smile before he continued on his way.

I'm lucky I have nice people around me. If everyone only cared about themselves, this place would be really tough to survive in.

Even Harriet, who was normally abrupt, was overly attentive to Poppy during the shift, and after the end came up to her at the lockers.

'Poppy,' she said.

'Yes?' Poppy asked turning around, suspecting she had forgotten something and Harriet would ask her to come back in to the department.

'I just wanted to say that you've worked hard this term and showed progress.'

'Thank you,' Poppy said, surprised.

'We'll look forward to having you back next year.'

'Thanks,' Poppy said again as Harriet turned and went back to the department just as Paul was arriving at the lockers.

'That's high praise from Harriet, she doesn't normally single people out.'

'Really? Maybe she just felt sorry for me.'

'Maybe in part, but she wouldn't say it if she didn't mean it. Trust me.'

'OK, thanks. What are you up to tonight, Paul?'

'Oh… I'm going out.'

'Yeah? Where are you off to?'

'Just going out to dinner.' *A date! Good on you, Paul.*

Poppy smiled brightly, 'Have a great time! See you.'

'Bye, Poppy. Thank you, you too.'

As she walked toward the main entrance, she began to get excited about seeing Will again. He was coming over for dinner, and Poppy had decided to cook a simple pasta dish – something quick but flavourful with lots of garlic, bacon and butter. They met at the entrance and Poppy felt her heartbeat quicken when she caught Will's eye. He kissed her on the cheek and they briefly embraced, Poppy relishing his scent, before heading off.

'How was today?' Will asked, concern etched on his face.

'Fine. No Patrick or Rebecca, so no issues. Harriet was nice; she said I'd done well this term and she would be happy to see me again next year.'

'Wow, that's good. Maybe that's her way of supporting you without undermining her own boss,' he said, visibly relaxing, his shoulders dropping and his face – which had been tight – began to resemble the carefree Will she knew.

'What about your day?' Poppy asked, keen to move past her issues.

'There were some emails from Ryan – did you see them?'

'No, haven't checked my emails all day,' Poppy replied, so Will filled her in.

A meeting was scheduled in the William Redfern Lecture Theatre the next day to ask for expressions of interest for the two committees to be formed. It was open to all medical staff and attendance was encouraged. Poppy was glad she wasn't on shift tomorrow, so she could easily attend. Ryan emailed that they were starting to receive the audit of the Resident and Registrar timesheets, but it would take weeks to review every doctor over the last twelve months.

'Well, it's starting, that's good,' Poppy said.

'Exactly,' Will agreed.

By the time they got back to Poppy's flat they had caught up on everything. They held hands on the way up and had a brief kiss at the door, but found Gemma and Lucas already home, so they refrained from anything more passionate.

'Hi, guys,' Poppy said as she put her stuff away, and then started prepping the dinner. Lucas fetched Will and himself beers, and Gemma and Poppy went for Coke No Sugars.

After dinner was cleared away, Poppy was keen for some alone time with Will, so they retreated to her room. Poppy noticed Gemma increased the volume of the music as they closed Poppy's door and inwardly thanked her friend. They took their time further exploring each other's bodies and their respective likes and dislikes. They weren't free to really let loose with Gemma and Lucas next door, but they reached a new level of intimacy which was mutually satisfying. There was no rush of sex with a new partner; no short, intense burn, more of a slow smoulder reaching an intense climax – maybe akin to tantric sex. Poppy wouldn't really know, as she'd never had tantric sex, but she felt the delayed gratification whilst they slowly tried different foreplay and sexual positions with lots of communication oddly arousing. It was not something she'd really experienced before, probably reflecting the lack of real trust in her previous relationships.

Afterwards, when they were lying on Poppy's bed, Will decided he'd stay the night. They set an early alarm so that he'd have time to get home and ready for work, but he said he wanted to spend the night cuddled up with Poppy. Further contrast from Josh.

Poppy stirred when Will's alarm went off and she hugged him from behind in a tight bear hold. She kissed his neck gently and he rolled over to kiss her mouth. He whispered goodbye and quietly rolled out of bed and out of the apartment. Poppy turned onto her stomach, her arms tucked up under her pillow and drifted back to sleep. She woke with plenty of time to get up, shower, eat, and get ready to be at the hospital for the midday meeting.

She got a coffee on the way from Jason (marginally less awkward, things were looking up), and was seated in the lecture theatre at twelve o'clock. As Poppy was one of the first to arrive, she took a seat near the edge in the middle of the auditorium. The seats began to fill fairly rapidly, and the meeting got underway by about 12:15p.m. with stragglers still coming in until 12:30p.m. Poppy scoped out the audience and was pleased to see a broad range of ages, sexes and disciplines represented. Lots of junior staff, but at least twenty Consultants as well.

Dr Anderson started the meeting with a statement.

'No doubt you will all have read the papers or seen the TV footage in the last week, or heard rumours on campus, so the first thing I wanted to do today is to set the record straight. One of the surgical trainees committed suicide some weeks ago and this was a tragedy for his family, friends and colleagues, and its impact was felt widely on the campus. As a result, it has highlighted the need for some changes to be made on campus to the way we train and support junior doctors.'

She paused briefly, then proceeded: 'Over the past few years, I have instituted changes to the Intern and Resident training programme to ensure a broader exposure to terms and disciplines in the first two years of training, and to discourage early streamlining into career specialties without solid foundations. However, these changes aren't enough.' She gripped the lectern with both hands and leaned forward for emphasis.

'We need to look deeper, be more innovative, and make broad changes on campus to the way junior doctors are rostered, mentored, and supported from internship right through to them accepting their first Consultant position. To that end I would like to form two new committees. The first to work specifically to structure and implement a pastoral care and mentoring programme, and the second to revise rostering conditions and plan ideal work force numbers to support full capacity shifts with a plan to recruit additional staff. These committees should be broadly represented and will have autonomy to follow through with final plans once approved. Now, before I detail how to become involved, I'm sure there will be questions.'

Poppy was stunned, her mouth agape. Dr Anderson had found a way to make it sound like the whole thing was her idea from the beginning and part of some grand master plan. Rather than a 'mea culpa', it was a 'coup de grâce'. The woman was phenomenal! She was planning to come out of this smelling like roses and delivering a revolution in medical training with a cherry on top and her name branded on everything.

Poppy texted Will and Tarryn:

WTF?!

Their responses were swift:

Will: Stunned

Taryn: Bitch

One of the senior Physicians asked what Dr Anderson meant by revising rostering conditions.

Dr Anderson responded, 'I don't want to overly influence the committees as I do want them to have free rein to be innovative, but a simple solution and a bridging option would be to have three Medical Registrars on in the evening and two overnight.'

Taryn: My fucking idea!

The same Physician followed up with, 'So you're looking to hire additional Registrars?'

'Yes, most likely.'

'And who's going to pay for that?' one of the other Consultants asked.

'Well, the nuts and bolts of any changes will need to be worked out, but I can tell you I've had discussions with the Minister for Health and the heads of the Colleges of Physicians and Surgeons, and we are all looking for collaborative solutions. Everyone is very motivated.'

There were several other questions along similar lines and then Dr Anderson introduced a Psychologist.

'This is Dr Henry van der Merwe, a workplace Psychologist. We will be utilising his expertise both with the committees, particularly the first committee, but also he will be available through the Employee Assistance Programme for sessions for staff privately. This is a fantastic opportunity as Henry has fifteen years' experience working with doctors to manage workplace conflict and staff management, as well as exam preparation. Henry, would you like to say anything?'

Poppy watched as Henry proceeded to the lectern. He was short and overweight with a rather rotund belly. His chinos were a bit crinkled, and his check button-down shirt was coming out of his trousers on one side. It looked like there was a food stain on the left-hand collar. Poppy wondered if his messy, unkempt attire was intentional – a way of relaxing his clients into spilling their guts.

'Thanks, Katrina, yes. Hi, everyone. As Katrina mentioned, I've worked in health coaching and management for a long time and I'm keen to work with you all to find some solutions that will work for everyone going forward.'

'Thanks, Henry. OK, if there are no further questions, I have set the following link up on the clinical staff homepage. It gives you the option to express an interest in joining one or both committees. An email will be sent out at the beginning of next week to all staff with the final make-up of the committees and the chair of each committee who will then contact the rest of the members to set up suitable meeting times. The first progress review will be in two months' time. I look forward to keeping the staff appraised of their progress following that. Thank you for your time.'

With that the meeting ended and people slowly dribbled out of the lecture theatre. Poppy found and linked up with Will and Tarryn and several other junior staff, including Lucas. They deviated off a side corridor to gain some privacy.

'Unbelievable,' Tarryn said, her voice low.

'I know, right? It's like she's reframing this whole situation to make herself the crusading hero,' Poppy said.

'Yep.'

'But do you think we'll get some changes through?' Lucas asked.

'I hope so,' Tarryn said. 'At least we've got HSU support and sounds like she's under pressure to make the bad publicity go away, so hopefully we'll make some headway.'

'And the Psychologist sounds like a positive move,' Poppy said hopefully.

'Let's hope so,' said Tarryn. 'Next step will be the make-up of the committees and how collaborative they are. I'll email Ryan to update him and email the junior staff to encourage people to put their names forward for the committees. OK, I've got to get back to the ward, let's stay in touch.' And with that she was off in her usual bustling way.

'How are you?' Will asked when the others had left, squeezing Poppy's hand and smiling at her.

'Good. Did you get to work OK?'

'Yep. Wish I could have stayed in bed with you, though.'

'Me too.'

'You're off again tomorrow, aren't you?'

'Yep, then day shifts Thursday, Friday and off the weekend.'

'Are you going to the RMO ball on Saturday?'

'Yes, Gemma, Lucas, and I have tickets. Do you?'

'Yes… I was hoping we could, maybe, go together?'

'I'd like that,' and Poppy smiled all the way to her eyes, feeling her right-sided dimple twinkling.

'Great. Do you want to do dinner again on Friday and a surf Saturday morning?'

'Yes, definitely.'

'OK, I need to go. I'll call you later.'

'OK, bye.'

'Bye!'

Will squeezed her hand again and loped off. Poppy enjoyed watching him go and then headed back home.

Chapter 31

Her day off was pretty quiet, but she couldn't stop thinking about Will. Only two more shifts to get through before she could see him again. My god, she really was regressing… Her thoughts were constantly on Will. She just wanted to be near him, touching his body, and she wanted to know everything about him. She couldn't remember feeling like this, really, since maybe her first teenage relationship.

'It's ridiculous, Gem, I can't stop thinking about him,' she confessed.

'You're in love, sweetie.'

Poppy blushed mildly at the thought. Maybe she was finally ready for love? Finally ready to give all of herself and trust someone else. And she felt Will might be the right guy.

These thoughts circled her brain round and round over the next couple of days, to a soundtrack of soppy love ballads like 'Just you and I' by Tom Walker and 'Fresh Eyes' by Andy Grammar. Poppy constantly watched the clock on her shifts, counting down the time until she could talk to or see Will again. Finally, her Friday shift was limping to the finish line. She shot out the doors as quickly as possible, almost running to her rendezvous point, feeling her heart rate rise.

He was waiting for her at the entrance, casually leaning against the railing and watching passers-by. Poppy really liked that about Will; he wasn't always glued to his smartphone. He could stand for five minutes looking around at the world rather than scrolling his Instagram and TikTok accounts. He turned toward her as she approached, like they were connected by some invisible string, and leaned in to kiss her cheek when she reached him, Poppy slipping an arm around his waist and squeezing his side. They strode off smiling at each other, all goofy grins.

They had planned to spend the night at Will's, so Poppy had brought an overnight bag with stuff for a surf and breakfast in the morning. Will cooked a stir fry, and they then watched a movie before another vigorous session in bed. Rising late in the morning, Poppy slowly opened her sleep-crusted eyes and rolled over to lay her head on Will's chest. One arm and a leg draped over his body, his heart beating soothingly below her ear.

Soon Poppy was aroused and wanted to have sex, and Will responded to her obvious interest by fingering her already wet, vagina. Poppy felt warmth flood throughout her body and was rocking her hips and pelvis to Will's movement. *Oh that is so good… Don't stop…* They rapidly progressed from foreplay to sex, Poppy staying on top and rhythmically sliding up and down Will's cock, slightly rotating her hips on the upward thrust to grind her clitoris along the way and increase her pleasure. With her eyes closed, lost in her own sensations, Poppy heard Will starting to groan, and she looked down at his face. A look of concentration was there and Poppy could tell he was trying to hold on. She popped off him, to give him a break.

'Here,' Will said, popping a finger inside her as she lay back down on the bed.

'That's good,' Poppy groaned, as his finger thrusts became harder and deeper. 'Yes… more…' Poppy said, taking short, sharp breaths, her body tightening like a rubber band about to be snapped free. Sudden rapid heat shot through her body as she orgasmed with a guttural groan.

When the judders of ecstasy eased, Poppy wiped a sweat-slicked tendril of hair off her face. Will bent down to kiss her deeply and Poppy reached between them to guide him back into her. They continued in missionary for a while, then in a sideways embrace with Poppy's top leg elevated so Will could manipulate her clitoris. 'That's nice,' Poppy said as her clit grew under his finger, heat spreading again within her. 'Let's do doggy,' she said when she knew she was close again.

'OK,' Will responded, panting, as he came out, holding his cock before pushing back into Poppy once she'd got onto her knees.

'Yes!' Poppy called out as he thrust deep inside her. 'Oh, yes!'

'God this is good,' Will said, 'nothing else feels this good,' as he bent down to kiss her neck briefly before thrusting deeply again.

'I want it in my arse,' Poppy said.

'Are you sure?' Will asked.

'Yes, do it!'

Will came out and tentatively pushed his dick against Poppy's anus. His cock was so wet from her vagina it began to ease in without too much pressure.

'Ummm,' Poppy said, her head down on the pillow, her hips raised high toward the ceiling.

'Good, ummm?' Will checked.

'Yeah, keep going…'

'OK,' he said as his cock burst through the opening.

But as Poppy's enjoyment became clear with increasing groans of 'oh', 'oh' and 'yes', Will's momentum slowly built. Poppy reached down and played with her clitoris and then slipped a finger in her vagina whilst Will continued to thrust gently. Then, suddenly, Poppy experienced the biggest, loudest and best orgasm of her life. Despite knowing Penny was in the next room, Poppy was totally in the moment, screaming 'oh my god' and 'yes, yes, oh…' She could not hold back. Will came soon afterward with a loud groan himself.

Poppy giggled afterwards whilst they lay back collapsed on the bed, slightly embarrassed by her vocal throes.

'Oh my god, that was amazing,' she said.

'It wasn't painful?' Will asked anxiously.

'No. It was honestly the best sex I've ever had.' Poppy leaned over to kiss Will again.

'Did you like it?' Poppy asked him.

'I liked your enjoyment most of all – that was a huge turn-on.'

'But you're not into anal?'

'Not really. But I'd totally do it for you when you wanted to.'

'OK.'

They snuggled and talked for a while before showering and grabbing a quick brekkie and heading to the beach. They worked on Poppy's surfing for an hour or so with Poppy finishing the lesson feeling ready to go out beyond the break and attempt to catch a decent wave. Will told her that the next lesson would be it – time to try on a decent swell.

Poppy put on her black string bikini under the open Hawaiian shirt knotted at the front, and her micro sarong skirt with Havaianas thongs on her feet. She added light make-up and hoop earrings. Gemma had opted for the Hawaiian top done up but knotted at the front to show off her midriff, and a denim skirt with strappy flat sandals. Lucas was in knee-length boardies, and the ubiquitous Hawaiian shirt Gemma had purchased on their shopping trip. Will arrived in boardies too and a slightly different Hawaiian shirt, open to his chest, and thongs as well. His slightly unruly, sun-bleached, wavy hair he left loose and long, and the two stripes of yellow zinc across his nose and cheeks completed his beach look.

'Hi,' Poppy said, reaching up to kiss his lips. 'You look like you're headed to Bronte!'

'That was the point.'

'I know, but you wear it best.'

'Thank you,' he said bending his head down to kiss her again.

When he stood up, her appraised her then said, 'You look very sexy,' as he pulled her hips in towards him and took another kiss, careful not to get zinc on her cheek.

'Alright, you two, that's enough. Time to go,' Gemma said, coming from her bedroom with a small clutch.

'Can I put my lippy in there?' Poppy asked.

'Sure,' Gemma replied and Poppy picked her lipstick up from the kitchen bench and handed it to Gemma.

They caught an Uber to the Rowers at Haberfield and the girls grabbed a couple of the colourful fruity cocktails on offer whilst the boys opted for beers. The place was quickly filling up, so they staked out a counter-height table on the deck with some stools and enjoyed the twilight view over the water. Friends, food and drinks came and went whilst the music was light and unobtrusive.

By nine o'clock the DJ had increased the music volume and people had started dancing inside.

'Let's dance,' Gemma said, grabbing Poppy's hand and tugging her toward the dancefloor. They were very keen, although a little unco-ordinated, dancers. Now that their bellies were full and their heads were floating on cheap cocktails, they eased into their groove with 'Happy' by Pharrell Williams, but before long, and a few more slightly sloshed cocktails later, they were gyrating and sliding up each other's bodies to 'Sexy Back' by Justin Timberlake. Will and Lucas were watching them from the balcony smiling and half laughing at their drunken antics.

Whilst Poppy had focused her attention on Will and Lucas outside, she had not noticed Josh sidle his way over to her. Suddenly a hand slipped around her waist and she turned, shocked to find Josh leaning in to whisper in her ear, 'Looking good, Poppy,' as he pushed his body up against hers. She pushed him away and stepped backwards, stepping on Gemma's toe accidentally.

'Ouch,' Gemma said.

'Sorry,' Poppy replied, turning toward Gemma and trying to move away from Josh.

Josh followed her, again trying to press his body into hers and grab hold of her hips.

She pushed him off again and said, 'Look, stop, Josh, I'm not interested.'

'What do you mean?' Josh asked, a confused look on his face.

'Look, I'm just not. I've moved on.'

'Poppy, this doesn't sound like you talking. What's the matter?'

'Josh, we're just not a good fit. There's no hard feelings, but I'm seeing someone else now.'

As Poppy was now facing Josh and the inside of the venue, she hadn't noticed Will make his way in. He had made it to within spitting distance and had overheard the exchange.

'Is this who you're seeing?' Josh asked, nodding over Poppy's shoulder at Will.

Poppy's stomach dropped to the floor as she turned to find Will standing directly behind her.

'What's going on, Poppy?' Will asked. 'Have you been seeing him as well?' His face distorted with anger as he balled his hands tightly into fists.

'No, no, it's not what you think, Will. I'm not with Josh. It was just a brief thing. It meant nothing,' she stammered out.

'Nice,' Josh said and turned to leave, easily moving to some other young, slightly inebriated woman.

'I can't believe this,' Will said, 'after everything that's happened these last few months, you were with him?' The disgust at the idea of Poppy and Josh together was clearly visible on Will's face. 'That guy is such an arsehole. He's probably been fucking half the intern group by now.' His voice was raised and people were stopping what they were doing to watch the scene before them.

Poppy felt as if she'd been slapped in the face. She stood there motionless, not knowing what to say or do. She'd never seen Will so angry before.

'Look, seriously, Will, I can explain…. It was brief, and before we started seeing each other,' Poppy stammered out. But she didn't think Will heard it. He had a far-off look in his eyes and had started striding away. Poppy was left standing alone on the dance floor, people staring at her.

Gemma put her arms around her and manoeuvred her outside, but Poppy was embarrassed and didn't want to talk.

'I've got to go,' she stammered, shrugging out of Gemma's arms as she made her way to the front entrance, ignoring Josh along the way, hoping Will might still be there waiting for an Uber, but the carpark was empty. Once the front door shut behind her, the music was muffled and Poppy felt alone and devastated. All she wanted was Will. Josh was a brief distraction, but there were never powerful feelings there, on either side. From that very first day shadowing Will in ED, Poppy had been slowly but steadily falling in love with him.

She tried calling him, but it went straight to voicemail. *Shit!* She called again. *Come on, Will, pick up!* But again it went to voicemail.

'Hi Will, it's me. I'm really sorry, I should have told you. Please call me back.' She stood out the front of the Rowers looking at her phone, willing it to ring. Willing him to call back. But after several minutes, she realised he wasn't going to call. She looked out across the car park to the trees illuminated under the street lamps and the darkened sky above. *How did this happen? Why was he so angry? Why didn't he even hear me when I told him it was before we got together? I should have just told him about Josh when I had the chance! I'm such an idiot!*

Chapter 32

Poppy woke surprisingly early. The events of last night hit her afresh as she opened her tired eyes. The crying and tension had exhausted her. But she couldn't stay in bed; she was too fidgety and anxious. She quietly took a banana and slipped out the front door, not wanting to wake Gemma and Lucas. She knew she needed to give Will a little time and space to process things, but with nothing to do and anxiety to burn, she headed to the pool to swim laps. The monotony of the stroke-stroke-breathe allowed her to castigate herself, but as her body tired and her breathing became more laboured, she could only focus on the physical pain and let the mental torture fade.

Stroke – *oh this hurts* – stroke – *my lungs* – breathe – *relief.*
Stroke – *oh this hurts* – stroke – *my lungs* – breathe – *relief.*
Stroke – *oh this hurts* – stroke – *my lungs* – breathe – *relief.*

After she'd swum fifty laps, she was close to vomiting and her legs and arms were like jelly. She could barely pull herself up the stairs to get out. She knew she'd struggle to make it to the changing rooms, so she sat on the side whilst her breathing slowed. More people were arriving, laying out their towels and sunning themselves or dipping into the shallow end before pushing off to swim. A mother and her child were playing in the play area, the toddler in a rashie onesie splashing water with his hands and giggling. The mother was smiling, enjoying the joy of her child and Poppy couldn't take her eyes off them. Such simple entertainment. Poppy couldn't remember feeling joy over something so little. Certainly nothing recently. Everything now was so complex. Even Will was now complex. Things had been so good and straightforward between them but now there was anger and resentment on Will's side and regret and sadness on Poppy's. *Why did it have to turn to shit? Was it too much to ask to be happy for once? To be in love?* Poppy sighed and tore her eyes away from the mother and child. There was no point torturing herself.

When she no longer felt like vomiting, she made her way to the showers. The icy blast of water was pleasant, and she stayed there for a while. Dried and changed, she headed home, trying to decide what to do next. Should she try calling him again? Or just keep waiting for him to calm down? Gemma and Lucas still weren't up, so, after some toast, she headed out again for a coffee. She tried calling Will, but he was obviously still screening her calls.

'Hi Will, it's me. Again, I'm really sorry. I hope we can talk. Please.'

She also sent a text message:

Please, Will, give me a chance to explain.

Poppy felt bereft. Will had been a constant, supportive presence these last few months. And now, with his silence, it was like he'd been cleaved away leaving a void around her… She felt utterly powerless to fix things and she would have to wait impotently now for him to reach out. Worst of all, she could only blame herself, as she should have just told him about Josh as Gemma had suggested. But she knew from her experience after Lulu's death, the *if only's* were a killer, so she just had to accept this significant error of judgement and whatever punishment Will would dole out. She just hung on to hope that his feelings for her would outweigh his anger and disappointment.

Poppy spent the day on high anxiety levels, waiting for her phone to ring or ping with a text notification. She did not let it out of her sight and even took it with her to the bathroom. Gemma and Lucas kindly tried to distract her, and suggested they go to a movie, but Poppy didn't want to risk missing a call from Will. She tried watching TV, reading a book, even going for a walk, but nothing felt right. In the end, at about four o'clock, she walked over to Will's place to see if he was home. The waiting for the confrontation was just killing her.

Heart racing, she pressed his buzzer.

Penny answered, 'Hello?'

'Oh hi, Penny, it's Poppy. Is Will in?'

There was a prolonged pause and Poppy worried Penny wasn't going to even answer her for a moment, then Will came on with, 'I'll come down.'

While she waited for Will to appear, her heart was pounding, blood thumping in her ears, every bit of her body sweating. Then he was there and opening the door. He looked more tired and dishevelled than Poppy had seen him before. His skin looked almost grey and his hair was lank and greasy.

'Hi,' Poppy said, tentatively.

'Hi,' Will replied, making only minimal eye contact. *Shit, he can't even look at me.*

'Look, I know you're furious with me right now, but can we take a walk?' Poppy suggested. *Please say yes, please say yes.*

Again, the interminable pause whilst Will considered this, and finally, 'OK'.

They headed toward Camperdown Memorial Rest Park and what Poppy thought of as her bench. They didn't talk the whole way, but Poppy thought maybe Will's shoulders relaxed just a fraction by the time they sat down. When they were comfortable, Poppy spoke. Not looking at Will, just looking down at the dogs and the park. She didn't really have a plan or know what she was going to say, she just spoke from the heart.

'I know you're angry, Will, and you have every right to be. I should have told you about Josh. I only saw him a couple of times before we started seeing each other.'

'But, Poppy, I've had feelings for you since day one. And we had sex after that first party,' Will said, his voice rising. Poppy noticed he had clenched his fists as well. *Jeez, he's still really angry. I'm not sure anything I say is going to make a difference. I don't know what to do.*

'But then we didn't see each other for a while and you kept your distance, and kept me very much at arm's length, so I didn't think you were interested in anything other than friendship.'

'So you just slept with the first guy to show you some attention? I thought we meant more to each other.'

'We do, Will, we do. But I wasn't sure of anything then. And I've never been good at relationships or emotional honesty.'

'That's an excuse, Poppy, and it's not good enough.'

Poppy paused, then said, 'OK, that's fair. I'm sorry.'

I've totally blown it, haven't I?

They were both quiet then, looking steadfastly at the park and not at each other. How much things can change in a couple of weeks. Last time they were on this bench, they were kissing and desperate to be touching each other. Now it was like they were repelling any contact. It felt to Poppy that their bodies were suddenly getting further and further away from each other. Like the bench was growing, separating them so that now they were more than an arm's length apart.

Poppy resolved to try again. 'Look, Will, I'm sorry. I can't change what I've done. But I can't imagine my future without you. I have loved spending time with you, over the hospital stuff, and learning to surf from you, and getting to know you. I don't want that to stop. I only want to be with you, and I hope you can find it in your heart to forgive me and we can move forward.'

Will sighed a few times and Poppy could see the tension was back in his shoulders. Finally, he spoke again.

'Poppy, I care about you so much… More than you realise and, right now, I'm just angry. I feel a bit betrayed… I'm going to need some time to get through this.'

'OK,' Poppy said, unable to mask her disappointment.

They sat there in silence for a while longer, then Will stood up, looked down at Poppy and said, 'I'm going to go now.'

Poppy looked up at Will, a sneaky tear threatening to roll off the edge of her eye.

'OK … Will you call me?' Poppy asked, scared.

'Yes. But give me a few days, OK?'

'OK.'

And with that, Will turned and left. Poppy sat there for some time; slow, steady tears streaking her face and dripping off her chin. She didn't bother to wipe them away. Eventually, Poppy sniffed, picked herself up and walked home in the dwindling light.

'How'd it go?' Gemma asked when she got back home.

'I'll tell you later,' she said and headed for a bath. She lay there listening to Cold Play's 'Fix you' with a spiced vanilla candle burning, wallowing in self-pity. All she could think was that he was never going to forgive her and how much she'd messed everything up.

Poppy only had four more shifts to go in ED before the term ended. Three evenings at the start of the week, followed by a single day shift on the Saturday. End of term ED drinks were on the Friday night at the Marly, and Poppy was focusing on that to look forward to and get her through this last week.

Feeling flat on Monday morning she lounged around the flat until her shift started, not wanting to be around other people. She did grab a coffee on the way (she wasn't crazy enough to think she'd get through the shift ahead without a caffeine hit), but she went somewhere different where she could just be another nondescript customer in the line and not have to force any chit-chat. She was on Acute this evening with Paul, and, despite it being a Monday, which according to all the ED lifers was the quietest day of the week, ended up being busy. That was perfectly fine by Poppy, who was happy to have the distraction from her own melancholic thoughts, or from any forced socialisation.

She had a few interesting and involved cases as well as a resus to keep her busy. As the weather had been cooling, they were at the beginning of the respiratory illnesses and Poppy had a lady in her late sixties with severe emphysema from long-term smoking, who presented with symptoms of increased shortness of breath and cough above her usual baseline, as well as a low-grade fever.

'OK, Mrs Fenwick, I'm going to get you some medicines to make your breathing better, as well as some antibiotics. While we're getting it all, is there someone I can call for you?'

Poppy saw her struggle to sit up and talk and breathe at the same time. She looked older than her documented age and her hair was as white as snow, her cotton nightgown hanging off her pigeon-like frame.

'My…my…daughter…Elizabeth,' she puffed, despite the oxygen mask.

'OK, is she listed as your next of kin?'

She took a few breaths again before answering, 'Yes.'

'OK, I'll let her know.'

Poppy went back to flight deck and found Paul, looking his usual hyperactive self.

'Hi, Paul, can I talk to you about a patient?'

'Sure, what've you got?'

'I've got a lady in her sixties with infective exacerbation of her baseline emphysema.'

'OK, have you seen the protocol we have?'

'No.'

'OK, I'll show you. It's really straightforward.'

'Great, thanks.'

After she charted the patient's usual puffers and put her on IV antibiotics, regular nebulisers and oxygen, she spoke with the Respiratory Registrar to organise admission, then called the patient's daughter.

'Hi, is that Elizabeth?' Poppy asked when someone answered the phone.

'Yes.'

'Hi, Elizabeth my name is Dr Mason, and I'm ringing you from The Bennelong about your mother, Patricia.'

'Is something wrong?'

'Your mum is OK, but she is sick with a lung infection. She's going to be admitted to hospital and we've started her on some antibiotics as well as nebulisers and oxygen.'

'I keep telling her she's got to stop smoking, but she doesn't listen.'

'Well, it can be very hard to quit when you've smoked for a long time. And, unfortunately, the smoking has damaged the lungs, so these kinds of infections are more likely to keep happening.'

'Yeah, it's not the first time she's been admitted.'

'OK. Would you like to come and see her?'

'I can't come tonight, I've got kids at home. But could you please tell her I'll come tomorrow during the day?'

'Of course.'

'Thank you.'

'You're welcome.'

When Poppy went back to Mrs Fenwick to pass on her daughter's message, she saw she was now on the nebuliser. The white vapour dispersing from the well below the mask. It almost looked like cigarette smoke, which was some kind of weird paradox. Patricia's skin was all wrinkled and her lips were puckered from the habitual smoking; she almost looked like a mummified corpse. Poppy could see how exhausted she was becoming with the breathlessness. It made her feel sad.

Late-stage emphysematous patients, like Mrs Fenwick, moved Poppy the most. That constant struggle to breathe, and the ongoing exhaustion of that breathlessness. Most of them, by that stage, just wanted it to be over. There was no longer any enjoyment in their lives, even at rest. They slept poorly owing to the breathlessness, and generally slept elevated in recliner chairs, watching late-night TV on low volume and dozing on and off for short periods.

When Poppy had sorted Mrs Fenwick out, she moved on to a man in his early sixties with a history of previous heart attack who presented with chest pain. She felt very competent now at managing these cases. The ECG looked pretty convincing for an anterior infarct, and she sent off urgent bloods and prescribed the appropriate medications. Once the bloods were back, she rang the Cardiology Registrar, who unfortunately was Josh. She'd been feeling confident until she heard his voice on the other end of the phone, and then she was all flustered.

'Oh, Josh, hi, it's Poppy,' she stammered out. *Oh, fuck, this is going to be hell. He's totally going to make me pay, isn't he?*

'Hi, what can I do for you?' he said in a supercilious tone.

'Um, I've got a chest pain case to discuss with you if that's OK?' Poppy said as apologetically as she could.

'OK.'

Poppy ran through the details and then waited, expecting some kind of abuse from Josh after the scene at the Residents' ball on the weekend.

'Can you please text me the ECG?'

'OK, I'll do that now.'

'And, Poppy, with such an obvious case, why didn't you ring me when you'd done the initial assessment and seen the ECG? You could have saved an extra half to one hour of muscle death by earlier intervention,' again said in a very superior tone.

'But…' Poppy hesitated, 'at the beginning of the term, you had a go at me for doing just that.'

'Well, now it's the end of term. You need to use your initiative more. Sometimes these protocols just slow things down. If it's an open and shut case, we'd like to know sooner rather than later.'

Poppy was floored. Being abused again and this time for doing exactly what he asked her to do last time. *Fuck him, what a prick!*

'Is this because of Saturday night?' she ventured.

'No, Poppy, this has nothing to do with that. This is about medical acumen. I would have thought you'd have some by now. Right. I'll be in to see the patient as soon as I've seen the ECG,' and with that, he hung up.

Jeez, Will was right, he was an arsehole! I guess Poppy had been distracted by his good looks, and the compliments he'd showered on her, but underneath he only gave a shit about himself.

Thankfully, when he did arrive to see the patient, Poppy was busy in a resus and avoided having to see or talk to him again, which was good. Given her mood had taken a further nosedive, she wouldn't trust herself not to make a scene.

The resus was a lady in her late eighties from a nursing home who was found collapsed in the toilet. CPR was commenced on the scene by staff and then the paramedics, but the patient had not regained consciousness. They continued CPR with Poppy having two goes at compressions, as well as a turn managing the airway over the next thirty minutes whilst they tried their best to resuscitate her. But she never returned to a normal sinus rhythm or spontaneous breathing, and time of death was ultimately called by Paul.

When Poppy was removing her gown and gloves, Paul came over to her and said, 'Well done, Poppy, that was very smooth. First attempt at access and blood gas, and good body position on the compressions.'

'Thanks, Paul.'

'You've done really well here this term, Poppy.'

'Thanks.'

'I hope you'll keep ED in mind for your future.'

'Oh, yeah… I have no idea yet what I want to do, and I've really enjoyed this term. You've all been so welcoming. So, thank you.'

'Anytime, Poppy, anytime.'

That was probably the brightest spark of the shift, despite it occurring around the body of the lady they'd just been trying to resuscitate. She hurried home when the shift was over and quietly slipped into the apartment and, soon after, into bed. There'd been no texts or missed calls from Will, and whilst Poppy knew Will had asked for a few days to think, secretly she wished he would call and tell her all was forgiven. She missed him immensely, and she felt anxious that the longer they didn't talk, the more likely he would be to break things off. As this kind of thinking only increased her sadness, it made Poppy's thoughts turn inevitably to Lulu and the pain in her heart swelled. Would everyone she cared about ultimately leave her?

Chapter 33

Poppy's sleep had been fitful, and she woke close to midday. She hadn't even had any awareness of Gemma and Lucas leaving in the morning because of the depth of her slumber at that point, after hours of tossing and turning, her thoughts swirling the vortex of despair. Despair over losing Lulu and what she might be like if she were still alive. If Lulu had lived through her depression, what kind of career might she have taken? Poppy spent time imagining different jobs for an adult Lulu and whilst it initially made her happy, ultimately her loss was felt more keenly again. Like a limb being amputated giving her phantom pain, that was what it was like to imagine a future or present with Lulu in it – she knew it wasn't real and would only hurt her more, but from time to time she did it anyway.

And what about Will? Had she lost him for good? She ran through various scenarios in her mind. Will forgiving her and them forging ahead. Will initially saying he'd forgive her then changing his mind, and Will not being able to move forward. But she knew there was nothing she could do to force his hand; she just had to wait. And waiting was torture.

When she finally got up, she made herself some porridge, hoping the smell and the bowl of warm goodness, which reminded her of frosty mornings at home growing up in the country, would restore some feelings of comfort and safety. But it failed to do the trick. She still felt jittery and despondent. So next step, she rang her mum.

'Hi, darling,' her mum greeted her on the phone.

'Hi, Mum.'

'What's wrong? You sound flat.'

'Yeah, I've had a rough few days.'

'What's happened, honey?'

Poppy filled her in on the disastrous ball and subsequent interactions with both Josh and Will and her feelings of powerlessness. Poppy's mum listened without interrupting, letting Poppy vent and when she'd finally finished, she said, 'Oh, Poppy. I'm sorry. That sounds rough. But it's like anything else, you'll have to just wait and hope for the best.'

'Yeah, but that's so hard, Mum.'

'I know it is, darling. But be strong. If Will is the right guy for you, and I hope he is, he'll come around.'

'I hope so, Mum.'

'Me too, pumpkin.'

'Thanks.'

'I love you, Poppy.'

'I love you too, Mum.'

During her Tuesday subbies shift she saw an email from Dr Anderson on her break, a flutter of excitement rising inside. It listed the make-up of the two committees and the chairs. Poppy was on the mentoring committee with several Interns, Residents and Registrars, and three Consultants – two Physicians and one Surgeon. There was also the Psychologist, Henry, Melissa, and one of the senior nurses in the hospital. The chair of Poppy's committee was one of the Physicians, a Rheumatologist called Dr Hennessy. She had also emailed introducing herself and requesting the first meeting on Friday at lunchtime, 12:30-1:30p.m. Both committees were reportable to Dr Anderson, and she stated in her email she would try to attend individual meetings from time to time.

Will and Josh were both on the rostering committee as well as Lucas and Tarryn and a few other Residents and medical and surgical Registrars. This committee was larger, with seventeen members compared with only ten in Poppy's committee. She was worried Josh's presence would further infuriate Will, but there was nothing she could do about it. There was an Obstetrician/Gynaecologist chairing the rostering committee and Poppy wondered at this choice. Obstetrics/Gynaecology was like Anaesthetics, Radiology, Intensive Care and ED. These departments were more autonomous than the rest of the hospital. They ran their own rostering schedules and realistically, the greatest change was likely needed in the Physician and Surgical streams. Was it dooming them to fail before they started, Poppy wondered, or was an external mediator needed to help facilitate necessary but unwanted change from the Physicians and Surgeons?

Poppy again heard nothing from Will, and she worried about his ongoing silence. She was starting to think it might be jealousy and Will's hatred for Josh, rather than Poppy's lack of openness ruling his behaviour. Finally, on Wednesday when Poppy woke, there was a text from Will.

> Hi Poppy. I'm sorry I've prolonged the radio silence. It was childish. I think you said you had evening shifts the first few days, but Thursday/Friday off? Do you want to get dinner tomorrow night? Will

Poppy felt her heart lift with possibility. It certainly wasn't a rejection and seemed promising for reconciliation. Poppy felt hopeful for the first time in days. She went about her morning more cheerfully and even hummed along to the radio, occasionally breaking out in slightly off-key singing.

She was back on acute that evening with Seb. Lucy was also on, and Poppy filled her in on what had happened with Will at the ball and the park on Sunday and his text this morning. When she had finished, she asked Lucy what she thought.

'Oh, Pop, what a drama! Look, I think it sounds hopeful that Will wants to catch up over dinner. If he wanted to dump you, he could have just done that by text. He certainly wouldn't need to spend a whole evening with you.'

'You think?'

'Yeah. Most of the guys I date just dump me via text, so yes, I think it's a good sign.'

Seb had overheard most of this interchange (Poppy noticed he had stopped typing whilst they were talking), but in typical Seb fashion, he made no comment.

Gemma was on an overtime shift and she and her Registrar came down to see a lady that Poppy was looking after who had significant vaginal bleeding. After they had reviewed her and the Registrar was typing up notes, Poppy took the opportunity to briefly update Gemma on the text from Will.

'So, what do you think?' Poppy whispered to her friend.

'A good sign, but we can talk more on the way home,' she suggested before she scooted off with her Registrar to perform a Caesarean section.

Poppy approached the bed of Mr Bull and, as had become her custom, took a good look at him as she approached. He was young, maybe early fifties, but he looked ashen and was obviously in a lot of pain, writhing on the bed, unable to still his limbs. A sheen of sweat covered his forehead and soaked through the gown he had on, and he was breathing rapidly. If he wasn't a man, Poppy would have assumed he was in labour, the way he was huffing and puffing.

'Hello, Mr Bull, I'm Dr Mason,' Poppy said as she pulled the curtains around the cubicle.

'You look like you are in pain. Can you tell me what's happening?'

'It just hurts so much, doc,' he said without looking at her, his eyes pursed shut. 'And I'm hot. I feel like I'm on fire.'

Poppy quickly looked at his observation chart and noticed he had a fever in triage up to 38.5 degrees.

'Yes, you've got a fever. Can you tell me where the pain is?'

He pointed to his left flank.

'OK, on that left side. More in the back or the front?'

'The back.'

'Does it move anywhere?'

'It sometimes runs down to my groin.'

'Only some times?'

He nodded his head, but again didn't reply.

'Does it come in waves, or is it there all the time.'

'There's a background pain there all the time, then a wave of the most intense, sharp pain.'

'And how bad is the pain, out of ten with ten the worst pain you can imagine, and zero is no pain.'

'Ten.'

'Always a ten.'

'The waves are a ten. But then it eases to about a six or seven.'

'Have you passed any urine, and does it hurt when you do?'

'Yes, I've peed, but it didn't hurt.'

'Was there any blood in the urine?'

'Not that I could see.'

Umm…pyelonephritis, maybe complicated by a kidney stone.

'Has this ever happened before?'

'No.'

'And you've never had a kidney stone before?'

'No, what's that?' he asked as he gripped his side and curled into a ball, groaning in pain. Poppy watched him and waited for the wave of pain to pass before answering his question.

'Well there shouldn't be any solid parts in the urine, but sometimes a small amount can calcify or another mineral can accumulate and a tiny stone is formed and that can be really difficult to pass down the tube from the kidney to the bladder because the tube is very narrow.'

'Do you think that's what's happening?'

'Maybe, I'm going to need to run some tests. But first I'll get you some more pain relief. And some Panadol for the fever.'

'Thanks, doc.'

'Lucy,' she said as she approached the drug room and Lucy was coming out, a kidney dish and medication chart in hand, her pen tucked behind her ear.

'Yep?'

'When you've given that, could you please give Panadol and morphine to my guy in six, Mr Bull?'

'Sure. Hand it over,' she said offering Poppy her free hand for the additional medication chart.

At flight deck she looked around for Seb. He wasn't there, so she stuck her head into the Resus corridor and saw him coming from Resus one.

'Hey, Seb, do you have a sec to discuss a case?'

'Sure, just let me send these bloods off,' he said as he opened a cannister and put his blood samples in with the request form and then sent them up the vacuum shoot. He turned back to her and Poppy leaned against the counter.

'So, I've just seen this guy in his early fifties and he has left flank pain with radiation to his groin. Peristaltic in nature. Also, a fever to 38.5. No haematuria or dysuria, no background of kidney stones, but he looks really unwell. Do you think it fits with a stone?'

'Let's go see him together.'

They walked back down to his cubicle.

'Thanks, Lucy,' Poppy said when they entered and saw she was delivering the morphine.

'Hi, Mr Bull, I'm Sebastian, one of the senior doctors, I just want to have a look at you, ok?'

'OK,' he said, groaning.

When he rolled over, it was the first time Poppy had seen his eyes properly as he opened them to look at Seb. They were the most crystal-clear blue, and Poppy instantly thought of the blue of a glacier. Possibly the most beautiful eyes Poppy had ever seen.

After Seb had examined him and Poppy had re-taken his observations they left the cubicle and went back to flight deck to discuss him.

'He looks bad, doesn't he?' Poppy asked.

His blood pressure and oxygenation had now dropped when Poppy retook them.

'Yeah, I think we should move him to Resus two. I'd like to do a blood gas and we should give him empiric antibiotics for urinary sepsis. Poppy, can you put in an urgent order for a CTKUB?'

'Sure.'

'Lucy and I can move him into Resus and get the antibiotics started and the blood gas.'

'Thanks, Seb,' she said as she took a seat in front of a computer terminal and began the process of ordering the CT.

Poppy was pushing another five milligrams of morphine slowly via his IV when a porter arrived ten minutes later to take him to CT.

'Poppy, you better go with him, OK?'

'Sure,' Poppy said. *Shit. What if he crashes in CT and it's just me and the Radiology Reg? Fuckity-fuck. Don't crash, don't crash…*

Poppy stood in the console area with the tech while they performed the CT, keeping her eyes peeled on Mr Bull, willing him not to crash. When the contrast images started scrolling up on the screen, the Radiology Reg came out of the reporting room and they looked at the images together.

'There,' she said, pointing on the screen. 'Do you see that?'

'That white dot?' Poppy asked.

'Yep. It's a stone blocking the ureter. And see there,' she said pointing at the kidney. 'There's hydronephrosis, and hydroureter,' she said pointing out the dilated ureter above the stone and the swollen, distended kidney.

'OK, thanks,' Poppy said.

As soon as she and the patient were back in Resus two, Seb was by her side. 'What did you see?'

'The Registrar saw a stone in the left ureter with secondary hydroureter and hydronephrosis.'

'OK. Lucy, can you get a new set of obs, please?'

Poppy looked at Mr Bull's face; he was curled up in agony again, his eyes screwed shut.

'Poppy, let's look at the CT together and look at the bloodwork,' Seb said, walking over to the computer on wheels.

'OK, so the stone is about halfway down the ureter and he's becoming unstable. We'll call Urology, but they may need to put a stent in to keep the ureter open. Why don't you call Urology and I'll call ICU for a review. If he gets much worse he'll need to go to the high dependency unit at least.'

'OK, thanks, Seb.'

Poppy checked the on-call roster at flight deck and dialled the Urology Registrar's number. Seb made his call from the Resus room so he could continue to eyeball the patient.

'Hi, is that the Urology Registrar?' Poppy asked.

'Yes,' a garbled response came after a pause. Was he already asleep, Poppy wondered whilst looking at the clock across from her? It's only 9:30p.m.

'Sorry to disturb you, but I have a fifty-two-year-old man with a renal stone in the left ureter on CT and secondary hydronephrosis and hydroureter whose blood pressure has started to drop and is now tachycardic with a fever of greater than thirty-eight. His renal function is currently in the normal range but we have him in the Resus bay and have delivered empiric antibiotics and IV fluids. We are going to get an ICU review, but would you accept admission?'

'Yes. Can you please ask the ICU Reg to call me after they've reviewed him? He might need to go to theatre if he gets worse.'

'Of course.'

'What's his name?'

'Mr Bull. MRN is 20194462.'

'Thanks.'

When Poppy returned to the Resus bay, the ICU Registrar was already there conferring with Seb. Poppy looked at Mr Bull and saw that he still looked grey, but he looked a bit more comfortable, and his eyes were open again, the blue piercing as his gaze fell on her.

She walked to his bedside.

'How are you feeling, Mr Bull?'

'Still hurts, doc.'

'How bad out of ten at the moment?'

'Like a six.'

'OK, well the ICU Registrar is here and I've spoken with the Urology team. They're both going to be monitoring you really closely overnight to see if things settle and the stone passes.'

'Owwww!' he called out as he turned on his side once more and curled up in the foetal position.

Poppy put a hand on his shoulder and watched the monitor as his heart rate skyrocketed with his pain.

'OK, we'll take him up to HDU,' the ICU Registrar said.

'The Urology Reg asked if you could call him once you'd finished assessing him,' Poppy passed on.

'OK,' he said as he turned and went up to flight deck.

'I'll just give you a bit more morphine,' Seb said to Mr Bull as he drew up the remainder of the vial.

Poppy watched him as he delivered the morphine. She had really enjoyed working with him this term. He was less in your face than Paul, more the silent type. But just like Paul, he'd been very welcoming and supportive. He'd taught her a lot and was always generous with his time. His unflappable nature calming for Poppy. She was going to miss them both.

There was a lull period before handover and Poppy sat chatting with Lucy at flight deck.

'So, I met this guy on the train. And he seemed totally normal, but then when we went out for a meal a couple of days later, he was super weird.'

'In what way?'

'Well, first he was a bit shifty when it came to the bill. I was totally prepared to pay my way, but he tapped his pockets and said he'd left his wallet at home, so I had to pay for us both.'

'Oh, Luce.'

'Well, yeah, I was a bit annoyed, so thought I'd go home after that, but he hit me up for train fare.'

'What did you do?'

'Well, what could I do? I gave him ten bucks and walked home.'

'Oh, Luce, you can pick them.'

'At least he didn't rob me, I suppose.'

'Has that happened before?'

'Yes, about six months ago.'

'Did you meet him on the train too?'

'No, it was a bus actually.'

Poppy couldn't help but laugh as her eyes teared up. Lucy was such a character; she was like Teflon. Nothing stuck to her. The crappy experiences and the shitty guys just seemed to roll off her without breaking the surface. She always seemed to have a cheerful take-it-as-it-comes sort of outlook on life. Poppy didn't think she could be that accepting. Whilst she was generally an optimistic person, she still found that the barbs of life penetrated the surface and left their scars.

'I thought you were going to move in on Jack? What happened there?'

'Non-starter.'

'I'm sorry, Luce, that's a shame.'

Both Seb and Lucy would be at the drinks on Friday, so after handover, Poppy said a quick goodbye knowing she'd see them again. She headed out to the entrance to meet Gemma and waited for a few minutes, wishing she'd brought a jacket with her as it was getting chilly in the evenings. She looked up at the sky but couldn't see any threatening clouds through the trees and the street lamps. At least it didn't look like it would rain on their walk home.

'Gee, I'm buggered,' Gemma said as they were walking up the street.

Poppy turned and assessed her friend's face, noticing the dark smudges below her eyes and the lines around her mouth. 'You do look tired. How's the end of term going?'

'I'm going to miss Obstetrics. It's been so good.'

'So you still want to do it?'

'Absolutely!' she replied animatedly, her face creasing into a smile. 'I wish it didn't have to end so soon.'

'Well, there's always next year.'

'That seems like a long way off right now.'

Poppy knew Gemma was going to make a great Obstetrician. She hoped she, too, would find a career path with that same strong connection.

They snuck into the apartment quietly so as not to wake Lucas, and Gemma headed straight to bed. Poppy had no shifts for the next two days, so she thought she'd have some ice cream and watch a movie on her iPad before going to sleep. She didn't want her head to fall into the vortex of thinking about Will and how tomorrow night's dinner might go, and was hoping if she picked the right movie, it would distract her enough from her own thoughts. Staying away from the rom-coms, she went for a thriller. She chose *Runaway Jury*, and it was a good choice – not so scary that it kept her awake in terror, but gripping enough to take her mind off herself.

Poppy spent Thursday in a state of slowly building anxiety, bubbling away under the surface. She tried her usual distraction technique of swimming laps, but it only quashed the fizzing feeling briefly. By five o'clock, Poppy was very nervous. Thankfully, Gemma got home from work a bit early and spent half an hour calming Poppy down and reassuring her.

'What if that's it, he dumps me and never wants a bar of me again?'

'Pop, it's going to be OK. He wouldn't want to have dinner if he didn't want to make amends,' Gemma said.

Poppy was usually the one who buoyed the others along with her enthusiasm and cheer, so it was a strange turn of events for her to be so rattled. Gemma continued to give similar platitudes until Poppy decided it was time to pull herself together and head out.

'Head up, young person,' Gemma said, and Poppy turned at the door, giving her a nervous half-smile. She headed up to the dumpling place on King Street, where she was meeting Will. He was already at a table when Poppy arrived, and she smiled unsurely and made her way over to him. He stood up as she approached, but didn't lean down to kiss her on the cheek. There was a stiffness to him that made her stomach drop. *I'm fucked… It's over.*

'Hi,' he said.

'Hi, Will,' Poppy replied, sitting down.

'How are you?'

'OK… What about you?' *God, could this be any more awkward?*

'OK.'

Will looked around the room. *He can't even look me in the eyes. It's obvious he's just going to dump me and he's such a nice guy so he's going to buy me a meal while doing it.*

'Have you heard about your rostering committee?' Poppy asked, to try to reignite the conversation.

'Yeah, we've got a meeting tomorrow.'

'Us too.'

'Well, fingers crossed, hey?' Will finished and was then quiet once more, his eyes dropping down to the table and his hands playing with the chopsticks packet.

Poppy wondered if they were going to continue this awkwardly for the entire meal. Thankfully, the waitress came over and they ordered. Once the waitress had left, Poppy offered a nervous smile and waited for Will to say something. *I'm not going to make this easier on him. If he's going to dump me, he's just going to have to say it.* At this point, she hoped, good or bad, that he would just rip off the band aid and get on with it. This prolongation was torture.

'So, I've been thinking a lot the last few days about us, and about you, and I appreciate, Poppy, that you wouldn't intentionally hurt me—'

'I'm so sorry, Will. I would never—'

'I know, I know that… But I guess maybe inadvertently you did hurt me. And for me, this is hard because… Amy, my girlfriend at uni, cheated on me for months before I found out.'

'Oh, Will, I'm sorry,' Poppy said honestly.

'I know. And that's what I've got to accept now because I really care about you Poppy, and I want to give this a real chance and try to move forward.'

'I promise, Will, I'm not Amy, I would never cheat on you.'

'OK,' he said, but his eyes were still on the table.

'You believe me, don't you?'

'I do,' he said not very convincingly.

'I should have told you about Josh. Absolutely. But I was never with Josh, once we started becoming close.'

'But how do you define that, Poppy? I felt close to you from that shadowing day. I wasn't with anyone else after that.'

Poppy didn't know what to say and sat there awkwardly until the food and drinks arrived.

'I know you're hurt, Will. I can see it in your face and your body language…' He looked up at her, finally, and she reached a hand across the table, beside their plates of dumplings to touch his. 'I can't change the past and I'm so sorry that I've hurt you. But… I don't think I've ever felt this way about anyone else before, and I'd do anything to make it right, or get us back to where we were.'

Will kept staring into her eyes and Poppy thought she saw them soften a bit.

'OK. Let's eat.'

They ate, mostly in silence, and when they had finished, Will spoke again. 'I know you didn't mean to hurt me…but I am still hurt, and it might take a bit longer for me to let it go. And I know that's not fair, but I'm trying to be honest about how I feel. I don't want to stuff you around.'

'That's OK, I get it,' Poppy said, her shoulders slumping a fraction.

'So, let's just ease back into things and see how it goes.'

'OK.'

I guess that's all I can ask. Another chance…but it sounds like this is the last one.

They avoided more talk about their relationship and focused on other things. Poppy talked about her last few shifts and the drinks tomorrow night, and Will talked about his upcoming term. He was moving on to Renal Medicine next and had heard that whilst it was busy, most of the Consultants were decent. Poppy was moving to Cardiology and secretly thought it was lucky that Josh would move on, and she wouldn't have to work directly under him.

They didn't linger when they had paid the bill, but Will did walk Poppy home. They had certainly lost their ease around each other, but the stiltedness of the beginning of the evening did lessen somewhat. At Poppy's door Will took her hand and Poppy looked up into his face. He bent down and kissed her on the lips. Their bodies remained separated, but the kiss sent the usual shivers through Poppy. She wanted more, of course, but would have to be content with that for tonight. Will pulled away, kissing her again briefly in the process and squeezing her hand.

'Do you want to go for a surf on Sunday morning?' he asked.

'Yeah, I'd like that.'

'OK, I'll text you… Goodnight, Poppy.'

'Night, Will.'

Poppy watched him turn and walk away, internally crossing her fingers and toes, hoping he would turn back. Before he got to the corner he did half turn his head enough to catch her eye.

'So, how'd it go?' Gemma asked when she opened the door, she and Lucas sitting on the couch in the lounge in their PJs.

'It was pretty awkward, but he said he wants to give things a go. He just wants to ease back into things.'

'Well, it's a start,' Gemma said.

'Yep,' Poppy agreed.

'But it sounds like he still needs some time to thaw,' Gemma added.

'Yeah… Lucas, what do you think about maybe buying him some board wax and giving that to him on Sunday? Do you think it's a bit desperate, or a sweet gesture?'

Lucas thought first and then said, 'Hard to say… I don't think I know him well enough.'

'G?'

'Hunh… I don't think it'll hurt. Maybe marginally desperate, but so what? You just want to offer a sorry gift.'

'Yeah, and not too big, just little.'

'Yeah, I think go for it.'

'Thanks, guys.'

Chapter 34

Poppy spent some time researching surfboard wax before bed and took a trip out to Bondi on Friday morning to buy it before the lunchtime meeting. She dressed in work clothes and headed into the hospital. They were meeting in one of the conference rooms often used for Multidisciplinary Team Meetings, or MDTs. It had a large oval-shaped table in the centre of the room, with videoconferencing and presenting capabilities and a lectern and LED screens at the front. There were chairs around the table, but also beyond them, around the edges of the room. Poppy had trouble finding the right room and entered a little flustered at about 12:40p.m. Thankfully she wasn't the last to arrive, but there were already about six people seated when she entered. Poppy made her way to one of the seats about halfway down the table. When all ten participants had arrived, Dr Hennessy, seated at the head of the table, opened the meeting, introducing herself. She was maybe mid-forties with short blonde hair, greying at the roots, and was wearing a patterned wrap dress that accentuated her ample chest.

'Thank you all for coming and volunteering to be a part of this steering committee. As some of you know, my name is Victoria Hennessy, and I'm a Rheumatologist here. I've worked here for ten years and have previously been the Director of Physicians' Training. I think this is a wonderful initiative, and I am delighted to be a part of it. I'd like to start by going around the room with each of us, introducing ourselves and giving a bit of background to why you're here. Thank you.' Dr Hennessy pointed at Melissa, who was sitting on her right.

'Hi, I'm Melissa O'Brien, and I think I know everyone in the room. I'm head of administration for the Medical Training Unit. I agree this is a wonderful initiative and hope I can help facilitate changes with you.'

Next was the Psychologist, Henry van der Merwe, whom Dr Anderson had introduced last week. Then came a lady in her late fifties.

'I'm Emma Preston, I'm the Director of Nursing. I've worked here for about twenty-five years and have seen the effects of hard shift hours and exams on the junior doctors, and I think we need to do more to support them through this process. I'm happy to help and provide maybe a slightly different perspective looking from the outside in.' Poppy nodded at this, it would be good to have a close outsider's opinion. She would definitely have a different perspective.

'I'm Richard Evans, Colorectal surgeon. I've been at The Bennelong for fifteen years and I believe we need to make changes for everyone's mental health and safety. For too long, we've pushed junior doctors to their limits and Tim's suicide highlights that we can't keep doing the same things year in and year out because it's convenient for the senior staff. We must be willing to accept change.'

'Thank you, Richard,' Dr Hennessy said.

Next in line was one of the Residents, Joanna Barnes, and then came Poppy.

Poppy blushed as she introduced herself.

'Hi, I'm Poppy Mason, I'm an intern. I interacted with Tim in ED on a few occasions and wondered if he was depressed, but I did nothing. I want to help develop programmes to better support the junior doctors, so no other colleague feels alone and without hope.'

'Thank you, Poppy,' Dr Hennessy said, 'but actually we have Poppy to thank for being in this room. She started this entire process after Tim's death and now we have a unique opportunity to work together and really make some changes.'

There were a few murmured thanks to Poppy, and she felt herself blush even further. They then moved on to the rest of the group, including James Peters, a Renal Physician, Kaitlyn O'Connor, another Resident, and Ashwin Chakrabarti, one of the surgical Registrars.

'OK, thank you, everyone. Now I'd like to start by asking, you, Poppy, what your vision for this group is?'

Poppy blushed deep scarlet again.

'I'm sorry for putting you on the spot, Poppy.'

'That's OK.... Um.... Well.... Ideally, I'd like to see two different programmes from this group. One a mentoring programme so that every junior doctor has a mentor throughout their training, and maybe that mentor changes over time, like an intern could have a Resident mentor them the first year, and maybe a Resident has a Registrar, and a Registrar has a Consultant, and they meet up or check in semi-regularly to see how they're going and offer advice and support. And that would build long-term, mutually beneficial, connections throughout their entire career.'

'That's great, Poppy,' Dr Hennessy said. 'Melissa, could you possibly jot some of this on the whiteboard?'

'Yes absolutely.' Melissa headed over to the board and started putting notes under a heading: Mentorship. When she finished, Dr Hennessy asked Poppy, 'And the second project?'

'Well,' Poppy said, not really blushing this time, 'this I thought should be more pastoral care, around avenues for help, counselling, a more structured mental health programme. But I hadn't really thought exactly how that would work in practice.'

'That's OK we can brainstorm that, and I think Henry will definitely be able to help and offer suggestions on how and what practical things we could achieve.'

'Yes, absolutely,' said Henry.

'OK, Melissa, let's call this Pastoral Care and jot down counselling and mental health programme. And before we brainstorm that a bit more with Henry, I just want to ask if anyone had any other specific ideas that wouldn't fit under these two umbrellas?'

There was a pause whilst everyone thought about this, but no one could think of anything new.

'OK, well let's start with Henry and then we can go around the room adding our ideas to the two columns,' Dr Hennessy said. 'I think the goals for today should be to get our ideas up on the board and choose a name for our committee and set up a meeting schedule and then next meeting we can come back with ways to put our ideas into practice. Is everyone happy with that?'

There were lots of murmured 'yes' and nodding heads, and no dissenters.

Henry got up and then moved up and down the room with his back to the board as he spoke. Poppy wondered if this was a tactic he used to engage an audience by moving around and trying to get individual eye contact. Henry suggested some ideas and the rest interjected at times, but once they had some framework for pastoral care, Dr Hennessy again took the reins.

'OK, I think we need a concise name for our committee, the Mentorship and Pastoral Care Committee is too cumbersome. Does anyone have any suggestions?'

Acronyms were thrown around and people were scribbling and rearranging letters on the board, ultimately with a few light-hearted laughs, they decided to call themselves PACMEN: the PAstoral Care and MENtorship Committee. Melissa drew a little Pacman doodle next to the name.

Once they were all in agreement and the time had passed 1:30p.m. Dr Hennessy said, 'Well, we've run out of time for today, but I think it's been a fantastic start, thank you all. I look forward to working with you over the coming months…. We need to have a review in eight weeks, and I'd like to be close to having plans in place for approval by then. I think we can achieve a lot in eight weeks if we are motivated.' There were murmurs of assent.

'Is everyone happy to meet weekly on Friday at this time?' Again, they agreed.

'Melissa, can we have an ongoing booking of this room?'

'Yes, absolutely, I can do that.'

'I'll send around a summary of our ideas this afternoon, and if we can all think about them and come with some expansion of these ideas for the next meeting? Great, thanks, I'll see you next week.'

There were 'thanks' and 'byes' as people got up from their seats and made their way to the door.

'Poppy, can I have a quick word?' Dr Hennessy asked.

'Sure,' Poppy said and walked over to the head of the table.

Once everyone else had left, Dr Hennessy gestured to the seat next to her. Poppy had felt relaxed and safe during the meeting, now she felt slightly on edge.

'I would have liked to meet you before today, Poppy,' Dr Hennessy said. 'I think you've been really brave, starting and following through with this at your level, and I'm really impressed. It shows such courage… I'd really like to get to know you better.'

'Thank you,' Poppy said, a little unsure.

'Medicine is a hard road for anyone, but even more so for women, and I really want to support and foster women in Medicine as well as what we're doing here, but I don't want to be seen as excluding people, so I wonder if you'd be happy to work with me and a group of others on that on the side?'

'Yes, absolutely. I think that's a great idea.'

'Fantastic. And maybe you'll consider me for your mentor?'

'Wow, thank you, that's very generous, Dr Hennessy.'

'Please call me Victoria.'

'OK, thank you.'

'You're welcome. You know Harriet Pearce in ED?'

'Yes, of course.'

'She told me Patrick Feaney has given you a bit of a hard time over this.'

'Well… Kind of,' Poppy said uncomfortably.

'It's OK, this is in confidence.'

'Well, yes, he did.'

'Well, this, unfortunately, is the kind of bullying crap women in medicine have had to put up with for decades and it's time to put a stop to it and stand up and say #TIMESUP!'

'Nice.'

'Yeah, I'm not so old…' And they both laughed.

'OK, well I'll email you separately about this if that's OK? A group of us are going to start a regular dinner night to support each other, debrief, mentor, etc. And I'd like you to come.'

'Thanks, Victoria, I'd love to.'

'Good… OK, well, I'd better get all this down. I'll see you next week.'

'Do you want any help?'

'No, all good, I'll just take some pics on my phone and email it off later. Thanks, Poppy.'

'Thanks, Victoria, bye.'

'Bye.'

Poppy felt elated. It was wonderful to be a part of a group who all seemed committed to achieving something. It was invigorating and gave Poppy a sense that she could achieve anything. With the good juices rolling through her body, she texted Will without hesitation.

> Hi. Had a great first meeting of PACMEN. How'd yours go? Xo

The thinking dots appeared and Poppy waited, wending her way back toward the entrance.

> Just finished. So-so. Not sure we're all on the same page yet. Hopefully will get better. What is PACMEN?

> Our new acronym: PAstoral Care and MENtorship committee.

> Oh… nice one.

> You have time for a quick coffee? You could debrief?

> OK, I'm heading to the entrance.

> See you in 2.

Poppy made it just in front of Will, who had had his meeting in one of the bigger conference rooms toward the MTU. A small knot had formed in her belly whilst she waited. Would it still be awkward and formal, she wondered?

'Hi,' he said, walking up to Poppy quickly. He looked less stiff than at dinner, so that was a good start.

'Hi. So, tell me all about it,' Poppy said. Will recounted the meeting, and there was a stark contrast to the first PACMEN meeting. It seemed Poppy's initial musings on the choice of chair were valid. The Physicians and Surgeons on the committee were already conflicting, and neither side seemed committed to change. The Registrars and Residents had been given little opportunity to have a say as the chair had spent most of the time mediating the bickering Consultants. They hadn't achieved any group aims, or even a committee name.

'Oh, Will, that's so disappointing.'

'Yep, it's pretty crappy. Even Tarryn hardly got a word in.'

'Well, I know Henry, the Psychologist, is supposed to be on both committees. Maybe he'll need to go to yours next to help facilitate.'

'Maybe.'

'Dr Anderson did say he'd done a lot of conflict resolution.'

'Yeah, well, we need that. To achieve anything, the two sides need to find some common ground, or we need to boot non-cooperative people off the committee.'

'Let's hope it doesn't get that far.'

'Fingers crossed. But tell me about yours.'

So, on the way back down the road, sipping their coffees, Poppy filled Will in and felt the flood of caffeine and exhilaration filling her body. Her step was springy, her ponytail was bouncy, and she could feel her dimple was flickering. Poppy noticed Will's face relaxing on the walk back, and hoped she was reading the signs right and he was softening toward her again, his hurt loosening and ebbing away.

Poppy kissed Will's cheek at the entrance and then headed home to lounge for a while.

She changed into something more casual before heading out to drinks with the ED crew that night. They were meeting at the Marly from 6:30p.m. so Poppy had time to catch up with Gemma and Lucas before she left.

'What a waste of time,' was Lucas' assessment of his rostering committee experience.

'Hopefully, the next one will be better,' Poppy tempered his negativity.

'Yeah, babe. And it's great that yours was so productive,' Gemma said, turning toward Poppy.

'I know. And Victoria seems great,' Poppy said.

'I wonder what her women in medicine group will be like?'

'Yeah, I can't wait to find out.'

When Poppy headed out to walk up the road to the Marly, she still had that wonderful happy feeling, like she was floating, and she almost skipped along King Street, getting a few curious looks along the way. Poppy hated to be the first one to arrive at a party, and so arrived fashionably late at around seven o'clock. They had reserved an area upstairs on the veranda and Poppy was pleased to see there was already a group of about seven people when she arrived.

'Hi, everyone,' Poppy said, beaming.

'Hi, Pop,' most replied, Lucy and Steph standing up to give her a hug and Paul grabbing her a stool and offering to get her a drink.

'Hey, did you check your email for your end of term report?' Paul asked before heading to the bar.

'No, I completely forgot. I'll look now,' Poppy said, immediately feeling a tightening in her chest and some rising nausea, her happy glow ebbing away rapidly.

'OK, back in a sec.'

Poppy pulled out her phone and opened her email app. Her hand shook slightly as she clicked on the email from Melissa with the subject title, 'End of term report'. There was an attached PDF file Poppy opened, taking a deep breath and holding it until she read to the end, biting the edge of her lip in concentration. When she finished, she let out a long breath.

'So?' Paul asked when he got back.

'It was actually OK. I was dreading it, thinking Patrick was going to be brutal, but it was unemotional…and fair.'

'Good, I'm glad.'

'Did you have something to do with it?'

'Maybe,' Paul said, smiling.

'Oh my god, thanks, Paul.' Poppy stood up, wrapped her arms around Paul's neck and gave him a big hug. He hugged her back and said into her ear, 'You are most welcome, Poppy. I just hope you come back to us again.'

They parted when Poppy felt a little awkward that the hug might have gone on a bit long, and she thanked him again. She then addressed the group, which now included Seb, Graham, Jack, Katie, and Harriet, as well as Paul, Steph and Lucy.

'Actually, I wanted to thank you all for all the help you've given me this term. It has been such an amazing term and you've all taught me so much… So, here's to you guys,' and Poppy raised her glass.

'To us,' Steph and Lucy said, chuckling. The others joined in on raising their glasses and taking swigs of their drinks.

Interestingly, Harriet spoke up next. She also stood. As she was not tall, it was not as commanding as it could have been.

'Well, thanks to you all for coming. We lifers like Paul, Seb and Graham, like to do this at the end of each term to thank you guys: Poppy, Jack, Katie and Isabella – come in.' Isabella had just arrived.

'Where was I… Yes to thank you for your hard work and putting up with us. ED is a unique place. It's not easy work, it's often crappy hours, so we're all probably a little odd. So, thank you, you've been a great bunch, and we look forward to having you back… Good luck… To the Residents,' she finished, raising her glass.

'The Residents,' the others said, raising their glasses, clinking and drinking.

Poppy smiled beatifically and Steph came and put an arm around her and kissed her cheek. She was fast becoming drunk. And Lucy didn't seem too far behind either. They must have got here early, Poppy thought.

'Thanks, Steph,' Poppy said, giving her arm a squeeze.

'Oh, Pop, we are going to miss you, aren't we, Luce?'

'Yep, we will.'

'I'm going to miss you guys, too. All of you!' She looked at each of their faces in turn. Seb was quiet in the corner, sitting next to Harriet, but he looked rested and benign as always. Paul was across from her, in an animated discussion with Isabella, full of jittery enthusiasm, such a good egg. Graham was chatting to Katie and Jack, and appeared to be giving them fatherly-type advice. Poppy then noticed that 'Clocks' by Coldplay was playing through the speakers. She had no idea why it always made her feel nostalgic, it wasn't even a teenage anthem for her. Maybe it was because her mum loved Coldplay and it was played a lot in her home growing up. Whatever the reason, Poppy felt tingly and a welling in her chest. The camaraderie she had felt here in ED was probably unlikely to be repeated on the wards and she was sad it was ending.

Poppy made a point of spending time talking to each of them over the next few hours. They bought platters of nibbles and chips and drank freely. Poppy did try to curtail her drinks somewhat, as she didn't want to get drunk with a day shift in the morning. However, she was tipsy by the time she left. She walked home again with Graham after lots of slightly teary hugs, kisses, and promises to stay in touch, particularly with Steph and Lucy. Graham hadn't drunk as much and carefully steered Poppy home, making sure she got to the front door safely. Whilst Poppy was confident she was only slightly tipsy, she had trouble walking in her heels and occasionally rolled her ankle, Graham putting a steadying hand under her elbow. 'OK, now don't forget to set your alarm.' Graham said as she opened the door to her building.

'Yes, Dad,' she called over her shoulder, tripping slightly on the front step on her way in.

Graham chuckled and kept walking.

Thankfully, she did remember to put her alarm on before skulling a couple of tall glasses of water and crashing into bed, but it provided a very rude awakening at seven o'clock, as did the pounding headache and rolling nausea.

When she had dragged herself to work after copious caffeine and was putting her stuff away, Graham tapped her shoulder.

'So, you did set your alarm, then?' he asked, looking annoyingly fresh to Poppy.

'Yep.'

'How's the head?'

'Lousy.'

'Figured… Well, see you in there.'

'OK.' Poppy swallowed the last of her coffee and threw the cup in the bin beside the lockers.

At flight deck, Poppy saw Harriet in her usual scrubs leaning against the counter, and nodded her head as a hello. She was thankful that Harriet was the Consultant on today and not Patrick. Poppy felt a real affinity had developed with Harriet, and she was glad her last shift would be with her. Poppy was on subbies and Steph was supposed to be on with her, but she hadn't turned up yet. She flew in through the security doors just as the acute handover was finishing, tying her hair up in a ponytail on the way. Her shoelaces were undone and she had dark circles and a faint spatter of dried mascara under her eyes, and she kind of stank.

'Hi,' Steph said.

'Hi,' Poppy replied. 'Babe, you don't look great.'

'Yeah… Can't talk…feel gross.'

'OK, well try to hold it together.'

Steph gave a thumbs up, but kept her mouth firmly shut.

Poppy really hoped she didn't vomit during handover. When handover finished, Harriet took Steph aside and Poppy didn't see her again for about an hour. Poppy found out later that Harriet had given her a banana bag and an anti-emetic. Graham explained to her it was a fast bag of IV fluids with vitamin B, hence the yellow colour and the name. Steph emerged afterwards, looking more human and behaving more professionally.

Luckily the morning was slow for the first few hours and Poppy and Harriet easily covered all the cases until Steph was up to joining them. But after she was back on deck, the busier things got. There were at least ten sports-related injuries over the next few hours requiring X-rays, casts, boots, or slings, as well as several back pain and abdominal pain presentations.

The shift progressed steadily and that, as well as Steph's hangover, left minimal opportunities for them to spend time hanging out. Harriet also kept a close eye on things. When Steph picked up a patient with a laceration requiring sutures, she asked Poppy to take over. Steph looked at Harriet and Poppy felt awkward. They all made it through, and Poppy got to see Paul at handover as he was coming on for an evening shift. She gave him a hug goodbye and headed to the tearoom with Harriet and Steph.

'Thanks for today, Harriet,' Steph said.

'That's OK, just try not to make it an ongoing thing, alright?'

'Yes… I'm sorry,' Steph said.

'Bye, Poppy,' Harriet said.

'Bye, Harriet, thanks for everything. I've really appreciated all the teaching and support.'

'You're welcome… Good luck next term.'

'Thanks.'

After she left, Poppy asked Steph if she wanted to grab dinner.

'No, I just want to go to bed.'

'OK, fair enough… Well, catch up soon?'

'Definitely… Bye, Poppy.' They hugged and walked out together. Steph turned down Missenden Road toward Parramatta Road and Poppy turned up toward King Street.

She rang Will and chatted to him whilst walking home. She told him all about the drinks last night and her shift during the day.

'Hey, have you heard of a banana bag?'

'Yeah, IV fluids and vitamin B.'

'Yep. Harriet gave Steph one at the beginning of the shift. She was pretty rank! Anyway, luckily my hangover wasn't nearly as bad, and it improved as the day went on. But I think I'll stop for a burger and fries on my way home.'

'Grease is always good.'

'My thoughts exactly!'

'OK, well eat and sleep and I'll pick you up at nine.'

'OK, sleep well.'

'You too, Poppy.'

Poppy sighed as she hung up. She hoped tomorrow things would get back to normal between them. She missed the intimacy and the sex. She ate her greasy food, drank more Coke, and wandered home. *Will tomorrow be better? Will he like the board wax? I hope so. I hope that he forgives me and we can be like we were…*

Chapter 35

Whilst she was hangover free, Poppy woke with a modicum of anxiety, but also a slight tingling of hope that today might be the turning point where she and Will could get back on track. She got her swimmers on and put her wetsuit and towel in a bag and threw some loose clothes over the top. Poppy had wrapped her present for Will last night and she slipped that in the bag. She ate a breakfast bar and a banana and filled a bottle of water and was ready and waiting at the kerb by nine o'clock.

Will arrived on time and he kissed Poppy on the lips when she got in. Poppy took this as an extremely good sign and relaxed a little.

'Ahh, Will, before we drive off, I got you a little something,' she said as she pulled the wrapped surf board wax out of her bag.

'Oh, Poppy, thank you… you didn't have to get me anything.'

'It's only small… It's nothing really.' And she bit the edge of her lip in concentration and anticipation as Will unwrapped the little gift.

'Oh, thanks, Poppy, I was actually running pretty low on wax… Ooh and Sticky Bumps, I like this brand, thanks,' he said, leaning over the centre console to give her a hug.

When he went to pull away, Poppy took a chance and placed a hand on his face, gazing into his eyes, and kissing him deeply. She was pleased to feel his body relax and respond, and they kissed for several minutes. They stopped to get their breath back, and they both chuckled.

'OK, let's grab coffee on the way, but let's get going. The swell at Bronte is supposed to be really good this morning and I want to get you out there before it gets too crowded,' Will said as he pulled out.

Poppy buckled up and relaxed in her seat. Once they had their coffees and were happily sipping away, 'Don't give up on me' by Andy Grammar came on the radio. Poppy slipped a hand onto Will's thigh, transferring her coffee to her left hand. She hoped Will felt similarly moved by the words of the song.

They parked a couple of blocks away, left their clothes in the car and pulled on their wetsuits, walking down with their boards. The day was glorious, cool, but spectacularly sunny, not a cloud in sight, and with very little wind. Poppy watched the waves as they got close to the beach, feeling that bubbly anxiety simmering again. The swell was higher than she'd surfed on so far.

When they made it to the shoreline, Will scoped out the waves and checked for rips and decided on the best spot for them to aim for. They zipped up their suits and Poppy braced for the cold water as they jogged into the surf. Once it was up to her waist she let the board down, lay on top, and paddled out. They went beyond the break and then sat on their boards. Will wanted her to catch a decent wave today, something they had been working up to for over a month.

They were sitting side by side on their boards, waiting for the next set to roll in. Poppy watched her legs dangling below her board and felt a shiver run up her body not entirely due to the cool water, but also because of her fear of sharks.

'Don't you ever get scared of sharks?' she asked Will.

'I used to, but the joy and elation you feel when you catch that perfect wave obliterates the fear and hooks you.'

Poppy wasn't entirely convinced, but despite the slightly queasy feeling in her stomach, she trusted Will, and was determined not to wimp out now. Soon enough, they could see the set forming up and Will told her to get ready before catching the first wave in the set. Poppy lay down on her board, looking over her shoulder, lying in wait, concentrating on the next rise. Before she had time to overthink things, her body took over, and she was paddling fast to get on top of the wave, her heart pounding loudly in her ears. Then Poppy was on the crest and leaping up to stand on the board and time slowed down as she dropped in and glided down the face of the wave all the way to the shore, slipping off at the last moment. Will came bounding into her, splashing up spray around his legs, his board discarded on the beach and grabbed her around the waist, swinging her up in the air.

Poppy was laughing and smiling and when they came to land he asked her, 'So how was your first proper wave?'

'Oh my god, you were right, what a rush!'

Poppy reached her arms up around his neck, pulling him into a kiss, salty and sweet. Their bodies relaxing into the embrace and the perfection of the moment complete, the sun shining down on them.

When they finished kissing, Poppy's board floating in and out with the waves, occasionally bumping into their legs, Will stepped back, looking into Poppy's eyes and said, 'Look, I know we've had a bit of a hiccup in the last few weeks but I really care about you and I think you're amazing.' He swept a strand of her hair behind her ear, gazing steadily at her face. 'I want to be all in from now on and see where this goes, but I need to know that you're all in too.'

Poppy bit her lip and looked into Will's eyes and thought long and hard before answering him. *Can I really do that? Can I bare myself to him, all my fears and insecurities?*

Will saw her hesitate and recoiled like he'd been slapped in the face. He pulled away from her and said, 'OK, I get the message,' as he turned away from her.

Poppy was frozen, all thoughts ceased as he took the first step away from her. Finally, her body thawed enough to respond and a guttural, 'No!' escaped her chapped lips. She flung her body at his and grabbed him in a fierce embrace. With his body turned away from hers she dug her nails into his flesh, repeating over and over again, 'No.' Eventually, she had recovered enough to add, 'Don't go. I want this too.'

Eventually, when her tears had soaked into his hair and onto his shoulder, Will managed to remove her claws and turn to face her. He lifted her chin so that he could look into her eyes, wiped her tears, and said, 'I know you're scared, Poppy. I am too.' And like he was reading her mind: 'While I didn't lose my sister, I have been hurt before, so I know how hard it is to get through that pain and loss. But I think you are worth that risk.'

Poppy gently kissed his soft lips, tasting the salt from the sea, and finally felt something loosen and lift inside her as she said, 'I think you are worth it too.'

The Swell Playlist

'Party in the USA'- Miley Cyrus

'Youngblood'- 5SOS

'All for believing'- Missy Higgins

'Fire'-Peking Duk

'Leave a light on'- Tom Walker

'What's new pussycat'- Tom Jones

'Someone you loved'- Lewis Capaldi

'We are never ever getting back together'- Taylor Swift

'Just you and I'- Tom Walker

'Fresh eyes'- Andy Grammar

'Happy'- Pharrell Williams

'Sexy Back'- Justin Timberlake

'Fix You'- Coldplay

'Clocks'- Coldplay

'Don't give up on me'- Andy Grammar

Acknowledgements

Firstly, I would like to thank you, the reader, for taking a chance on me. I really hope you found *The Swell*, Poppy, and her friends entertaining. This has been a long journey for me, beginning back in 2019. I suffered burnout and turned to writing for therapy. As Poppy began to take shape on the page, I became immersed in her world and where it could go. Writing *The Swell*, slowly helped me work through burnout and continue to take care of my patients and my family. But once I had typed the last word of the first draft in December 2019, my literary journey really began. I knew nothing of the industry and had naïve, fairytale dreams of best seller lists, TV adaptations, and quitting my day job! Needless to say, my expectations have subsequently become much more realistic!

I've learnt a tremendous amount in the last five years and have so many people to thank who have helped me learn and grow on this journey. The first thing I did was a Writing NSW course on editing, and I want to thank Emily Maguire for her thoughtful teaching and her kind words. Despite it being wholly virtual (thanks COVID), it gave me a starting point. From there I did numerous Australian Society of Authors courses, webinars, and even their Pitch perfect and literary speed dating sessions. All of which continued to educate me on the publishing industry and how to keep editing my work. I also entered a number of competitions, some of which provided feedback and I would like to thank the Dorothy Hewett award team 2021 and Craig Cauchi from Queensland Writers Centre Publishable Award 2021. I'd also like to thank Lauren Finger, from Kill Your Darlings, for her feedback and manuscript assessment and all those agents and publishers who read my pages and provided honest feedback. Finally, meeting an amazing group of supportive writers at the Romantic Writers of Australia conference, gave me the confidence to continue on my own.

But my greatest thanks goes to my first readers; Angie Black, Joey Houghton, and my mother, Sylvia Gzell. Their honest feedback and the way they embraced Poppy and cared about her future was a huge support to me. Angie and Joey, particularly, have been my biggest cheerleaders and I wouldn't be able to have endured this long without their support. After much editing, I was lucky that so many friends were keen to read my work and provide more feedback and these include; James Burrell, Nicole Gower, Skye McNeice, Lucinda Morris, Angela Gzell, and Caileen Cacchia. Again, each of you provided new insights and continued to shape the novel and I will likely call on you again, for *Caught in the Undertow*! I'd also like to thank Alec Readfearn for reviewing and providing feedback on my surfing scenes, Dr Paul Bergamin for critiquing my Urology cases for accuracy, and A/Prof James Burrell for correcting the inaccuracies in my meningococcal case. Of course, all mistakes, misinterpretations, and general fuck-ups are my own doing, and I take full responsibility!

Female friendships are really important to me. I've always felt a bit on the outer, never quite fitting in anywhere. I am lucky to finally have a wonderful community of intelligent, brave, and thoughtful women in my life. Special mention goes to the Fit My Day crew, led by the indefatigable, Angie Black, you are my people! My close work colleagues, and my ladies dinner crew (Dr's: Jo Toohey, Yael Barnett, Chelsie O'Connor, Venessa Chin, Julia Crawford, Lucinda Morris, Georgia Harris, Kirsty Hamilton, and Sandy Sampaio), and my oldest and best friends, Skye McNeice, Joey Houghton, and Negar McNamara for always being there for me! I hope my readers also have a community of women to support you. Thank you also to those lovely friends who offered to read for me, but didn't get a chance to, don't worry there will be more opportunities in the future! To anyone I have forgotten to mention, please forgive me.

Dealing with rejection is a big part of the process. Heartfelt thanks especially to my husband, James, and my children, Alexander, Lachlan, and Isabella, who always gave me something positive to hold onto when the negativity of rejection loomed. You are my light in the dark and I love you all. I feel immensely lucky that we share this life journey together.

Finally, to my incredible team who got *The Swell* over the line. First and foremost to Nicky Lovick, my editor. I really landed on my feet with you.

Next, my very talented friend and amazing cover designer, Belinda Mark, who went above and beyond and gave me so many wonderful options to choose from. You are a star in your own right, and I can't wait for us to work on book two's cover. Thank you also to Ian Hooper and the team at Book Reality Experience for putting all the final touches together, your service has been seamless. And to my new friend, author, and mentor, Carrie Clarke for answering all my questions and being a fabulous support for a newbie author.

And lastly, to loved ones no longer with us but forever in our hearts; The Honourable Ian Vitaly Gzell KC, AM, and Mrs Ivana Hayes.

Keep your eyes and ears peeled for book two:

Caught in the Undertow

Poppy is a year older, wiser, and looking forward to taking that step up the training ladder to Resident Medical Officer. She's getting used to her slightly more senior role, including teaching new interns, and the routines on the Respiratory team when a worldwide pandemic hits and life changes irrevocably. The continuous changes, limited support, and unrelenting pressure take its toll on Poppy, threatening to bring her undone, whilst COVID restrictions hamper her love life and that of her flatmates, Gemma and Lucas. What should she do when her consultant goes AWOL, and her Registrar flakes, leaving her stuck working with Joshua Hunter who has done his best to make the last year difficult for her? Will her mind and body stand up to the challenge? And will distance affect her feelings for Will? Join Poppy and her friends in *Caught in the undertow*, coming soon.

About the Author

Dr C E de Gzell is a Radiation Oncologist who specialises in the treatment of patients with brain tumours. She has fourteen peer reviewed medical publications and a PhD in glioblastoma research and is a regular presenter at international and national conferences. A period of burnout in 2019 reignited an old passion for writing and *The Swell* is her debut novel. She lives in Sydney, Australia, with her husband and three children, and a goofy sheepadoodle, Fudge, who keeps escaping. Both her work and family exhaust her but provide endless fodder for the imagination. Connect with her at: www.cedegzellauthor.com, or on Instagram: ce_degzell_author